BY MARGARET MALLORY

(Available in ebook, print, and audiobook)

THE DOUGLAS LEGACY
CAPTURED BY A LAIRD
CLAIMED BY A HIGHLANDER (coming)

THE RETURN OF THE HIGHLANDERS
THE GUARDIAN
THE SINNER
THE WARRIOR
THE CHIEFTAIN

ALL THE KING'S MEN
KNIGHT OF DESIRE
KNIGHT OF PLEASURE
KNIGHT OF PASSION

Captured by a Laird

MARGARET MALLORY

Margaret Mallory ♥

DEDICATION

For my friend Ginny Heim, whose willingness to give me her honest opinion on my manuscripts has saved my readers from many a boring passage.

CHAPTER 1

Scotland
1517

Burning her husband's bed was a mistake. Alison could see that now.

Yet each time she passed the rectangle of charred earth as she paced the castle courtyard, she felt a wave of satisfaction. She had waited to commit her act of rebellion until her daughters were asleep. But that night, after her husband's body was taken to the priory for burial, she ordered the servants to carry the bed out of the keep. She set fire to it herself. The castle household, accustomed to the meek mistress her husband had required her to be, was thoroughly shocked.

"Do ye see them yet?" Alison called up to one of the guards on the wall.

When the guard shook his head, she resumed her pacing. Where were her brothers? They had sent word this morning that they were on their way.

As she passed the scorched patch again, she recalled how the flames shot up into the night sky. She had stood watching the fire until dawn, imagining the ugliness of the past years turning to black ashes like the bed. The memories did not burn away, but she did feel cleaner.

Destroying such an expensive piece of furniture was self-indulgent, but that was not why she counted burning it a mistake. While she could not tolerate having that bed in her home, it would have been wiser to give it away or sell it. And yet she simply could not in good conscience pass it on to someone else. Not when she felt as if the bed itself carried an evil.

Instinctively, she touched the black quartz pendant at her throat that her mother had given her to ward off ill luck. It had been missing since Blackadder broke the chain on their wedding night. After the fire, she found it wedged in a crack in the floor where the bed had been.

"Lady Alison!" a guard shouted down from the wall. "They're here!"

The heavy wooden gates swung open, and her two brothers galloped over the drawbridge followed by scores of Douglas warriors. *Praise God.* As the castle filled with her clansmen, Alison immediately felt safer.

One look at Archie's thunderous expression, however, told her that his meeting with the queen had not gone well. Without a word, her brothers climbed the steps of the keep, crossed the hall where platters of food were being set out on the long trestle tables for the Douglas warriors, and continued up the stairs to the private chambers. They never discussed family business in front of others.

"She is my wife!" Archie said as soon they were behind closed doors. "How dare she think she can dismiss me as if I were one of her servants?"

Alison tapped her foot, trying to be patient, while her brother, the 6th Earl of Angus and chieftain of the Douglas clan, stormed up and down the length of the room. When Archie's back was to her, she exchanged a look with George, her more clever brother, and rolled her eyes. This was all so predictable.

"I warned ye not to be so blatant about your affair with Lady Jane," George said in a mild tone.

"My affairs are none of my wife's concern," Archie snapped.

"A queen is not an ordinary wife," George said as he poured himself and Archie cups of wine from the side table.

Alison found it ironic that the Douglas clan owed the greatest rise in their fortunes to Archie's liaison with the widowed queen. Usually, it was the ladies of the family who were tasked with securing royal favor via the bedchamber.

Archie, always overconfident, had gone too far. While the Council had been willing to tolerate the queen's foolishness in taking the young Douglas chieftain as her lover, they were livid when the pair wed in secret, making Archie the infant king's stepfather. The Council responded by removing the queen as regent. She fled to England amidst accusations that she had tried to abscond with the royal heir.

"How was I to know my wife would return to Scotland?" Archie said, raising his arms. "Besides, I'm a young man. She couldn't expect me to live like a monk while she was gone."

Doubtless, the queen, who was pregnant with Archie's child when she fled, expected her husband to join her. But while the queen paid a lengthy visit on her brother Henry VIII, the Douglas men retreated behind the high walls of Tantallon Castle and waited for the cries of treason to subside.

That was two years ago. And now, Albany, the man who replaced the queen as regent, was on a ship back to France, and the queen was returning. Archie had gone to meet her at Berwick Castle, just across the border.

"Is there no hope of reconciling with her?" Alison ventured to ask.

"I bedded that revolting woman four times in two days—and for naught!" Archie thrust his hand out. "I had her in my palm again, I swear it. But then some villain sent her a message informing her about Jane."

"Must have been the Hamiltons," George said, referring to their greatest rivals.

"Despite that setback, I managed to persuade the queen—through great effort, I might add—that we should enter Edinburgh together as man and wife for all the members of the damned Council to see," Archie said, his blue eyes flashing. "But then she discovered I'd been collecting the rents on her dower lands and flew into a rage."

No wonder the queen was angry. After abandoning her, Archie had lived openly with his lover and their newborn daughter in one of the queen's dower castles—and on the queen's money.

"You're her husband," George said, leaning back in his chair. "Ye had every right to collect her rents. Still do."

Alison did not want to hear about husbands and their rights. She folded her arms and tamped down her impatience while she waited for the right moment to ask.

"Enough talk. We must join the men." Archie threw back his cup of wine. "We'll ride for Edinburgh as soon as they've eaten their fill."

George was already on his feet. She could wait no longer.

"Ye must leave some of our Douglas warriors here to protect this castle," she blurted out. "The Blackadder men are deserting me."

She hoped her brothers would not ask why. She did not want to explain that burning her husband's bed had insulted the Blackadder men and spurred many of them to leave. They disliked having a woman in command of the castle, and she had unwittingly given them the excuse they needed.

"I can't spare any men now," Archie said, slapping his gloves against his hand. "I must gather all my forces in a show of strength to convince my pigheaded wife that she needs my help to regain the Regency."

"The Hamiltons will attempt to do the same," George added.

"But what about me and my daughters?" Alison demanded. "What about the Blackadder lands Grandfather thought were so important that I was forced to wed that man? I was a child of thirteen!"

"For God's sake, Alison, we're in a fight for control of the crown," Archie said. "That will not be decided at Blackadder Castle."

"Please, I need your help." She clutched Archie's arm as he started toward the door. "Ye promised to protect us."

Archie came to an abrupt halt, and the shared memory hung between them like a dead rat.

"Mother did not need to remind me of my duty to my family," he said between clenched teeth. "And neither do you."

Unlike the Douglas men, who lauded Archie's seduction of the queen as a boon for the family, their mother begged him to end the affair. A generation ago, one of her sisters had been the king's mistress. After it was rumored that the king had fallen so in love that he wished to marry her, all three of their mother's sisters died mysteriously.

When Archie wed the queen in secret, knowing full well that every other powerful family in Scotland would oppose the marriage, their mother made one demand of her sons. Archie and George promised her, on their father's grave, that they would protect their four sisters.

"I'll find ye a new husband as soon as these other matters are settled," Archie said. "You'll be safe here until then."

Another husband was not what Alison asked for and was the last thing she wanted. "What I need are warriors—"

"Who would dare attack you?" Archie said. "Now that we are rid of Albany, I am the man most likely to rule Scotland."

Before she could argue, Archie pushed past her and disappeared down the circular stone stairwell.

"Don't fret, Allie," George said, and gave her a kiss on her cheek. "Your most dangerous neighbors were the Hume lairds, and they're both dead."

***

David Hume left his horse and warriors a safe distance outside the city walls and proceeded on foot. If the guards were watching for him, they would not expect him to come alone, or so he hoped. Keeping his hood low over his face and his hand on his dirk, he mingled with the men herding cattle through the Cowgate Port to sell in the city's market.

A month ago, David would have been amused to find himself entering the great city of Edinburgh between two cows. But his humor had been wrung from him. As he walked up West Bow toward the center of the city, the rage that was always with him now swelled until his skin felt too tight.

He paused before entering the High Street and scraped the dung off his boots while he scanned the bustling street for anyone who might attempt to thwart him. Then, keeping watch on the armed men amidst the merchants, well-dressed ladies, beggars, and thieves, he started down the hill in the direction of Holyrood Palace. He spared a glance over his shoulder at Edinburgh Castle, the massive fortress that sat atop the black rock behind him. If he were caught, he would likely grow old in its bleak dungeon. He'd prefer a quick death.

David had walked this very street with his father and uncle. With each step, he tried to imagine how that day might have ended differently. Could he have stopped it? Perhaps, perhaps not. Regardless, he should have tried. From the moment they entered Holyrood Palace, he had sensed the danger. It pricked at the back of his neck and made his hands itch to pull his blade.

The Hume lairds had been guaranteed safe conduct. Relying on that pledge of honor made in the king's name, David did not follow his instincts, did not shout to their men to fight their way out. Instead, he watched his father and uncle relinquish their weapons at the palace door, and he did the same.

Never again.

When he saw the stone arches of St. Giles jutting into the High Street, David's heart beat so hard it hurt. The church was next to the Tolbooth, the prison where the royal guards brought his father and uncle after dragging them from the palace. David's ears rang again with the shouts and jeers of the crowd that echoed off the buildings that day. As he crossed the square, he did not permit himself to look at the Tolbooth for fear that his rage would spill over and give him away.

He turned into one of the narrow, sloping passageways that cut through the tall buildings on either side of the High Street and found a dark doorway with a direct view of the Tolbooth. Only then did he lift his gaze.

Though he had known what to expect, his stomach churned violently at the sight of the two grisly heads on their pikes. His body shook with a poisonous mix of rage and grief as he stared at what was left of his father. They had made a mockery of the man David had admired all his life. His father's sternly handsome features were distorted in a grimace that looked like a gruesome grin, his dark gold hair was matted, and flies ate at his bulging eyes.

David's chest constricted until his breath came in wheezes. He wanted to fight his way into the palace, wielding his sword and ax until he killed every man in sight. But Regent Albany, the man who ordered the execution, was no longer in the palace, or even in Scotland.

In any case, David had too many responsibilities to give in to thoughtless acts that would surely result in his death. He was the new Laird of Wedderburn, and the protection of the entire Hume clan fell to him. When he thought of his younger brothers and how much they needed him, he finally loosened his grip on his dirk, which he'd been holding so tightly that his hand was stiff.

The execution of the two Hume lairds and this humiliating display of their heads made their clan appear weak and vulnerable. That perception put their clan in even greater danger, and so David must change it. This first step toward that end required stealth, not his sword.

He would have his bloody vengeance, but not today.

While he waited for nightfall, he pondered how Regent Albany had managed to prevail over men who were better than him in every way that should matter. The first time Albany captured David's father and uncle, they persuaded their jailor, a Hamilton, to free them and join the queen's side. A furious Albany responded by having their wives taken hostage.

David wondered if Albany understood at the time just how clever that move was, or if he had merely taken the women out of spite. In any event, the trap was set.

By then, Albany was planning to return to France, which was more home to him than Scotland. David's uncle was inclined to wait and seek the women's release from Albany's replacement. But David's father and stepmother had a rare love, and he was tortured by the thought of her suffering in captivity. Because of his weakness for her, he persuaded his brother to accept the regent's invitation and guarantee of their safety.

"Free my wife! Avenge us!" his father had shouted to David as the guards dragged him away.

His father's final words were burned into his soul. While he kept his vigil in the doorway, they spun through his head again and again. He wanted to smash his fist into the wall at the thought of his stepmother living amongst strangers when she learned of her husband's death. Nothing could save the man who held her hostage now. Vengeance was both a debt of honor David owed his father and necessary to restore respect for his clan.

When darkness finally fell on the city, David gave coins to the prostitutes who had gathered nearby and asked them to cause a disturbance. They proved better at keeping their word than the regent. While the women created an impressive commotion, screaming that they had been robbed, David scaled the wall of the Tolbooth.

Gritting his teeth, he jerked his father's head off the pike and placed it gently in the cloth bag slung over his shoulder. He swallowed against the bile that rose in his throat and forced himself to move quickly. As soon as he had collected his uncle's head, he dropped to the ground and left the square at a fast pace. He could still hear the prostitutes shouting when he was halfway to the gate.

A short time later, he reached the tavern outside the city walls where his men waited for him. His half-brothers must have been watching the door, for they ran to greet him as soon as he opened it. Will threw his arms around David's waist, while Robbie, who was four years older, stood by looking embarrassed but relieved. David should admonish Will for his display in front of the men, but he did not have the heart. The lad, who was only ten, had lost his father and missed his mother a great deal.

"I told ye I'd return safe," David said. "I'll not let any harm come to ye, and I will bring your mother home."

Their mother was being held at Dunbar, an impregnable castle protected by a royal garrison. While David did not yet know when or how he would obtain her release, he would do it.

He planned his next moves on the long ride back to Hume territory. In the violent and volatile Border region, you were either feared or preyed upon. David intended to make damned sure he was so feared that no one would ever dare harm his family again.

He would take control of the Hume lands and castles, which had been laid waste and forfeited to the Crown. And then he would take his vengeance on the Blackadders, the scheming liars. While pretending to be allies, the Blackadders had secretly assisted in his stepmother's capture and then urged Albany to execute his father and uncle. It was a damned shame that the Laird of Blackadder Castle was beyond David's reach in a new grave, but his rich lands and widow were ripe for the taking.

And the widow was a Douglas, sister to the Earl of Angus himself. For a man intent on establishing a fearsome reputation, that made her an even greater prize.

CHAPTER 2

Alison ran up the stairs praying that her daughters had not escaped their elderly nursemaid again. Relief swept through her when she burst into their bedchamber and saw them. Both girls had inherited her black hair, dark blue eyes, and slight frame, but the similarity ended there.

Six-year-old Margaret, whose braids and gown were in perfect order, was practicing her stitching. God only knew what her older daughter had been up to. Beatrix's hair was a tangled mess, and the black streaks on her gown looked as if she had crawled across the hearth—which she probably had. Unfortunately, there was no time to change.

"Come quickly," Alison said, holding her hands out to them. "Ye mustn't miss your uncles."

Alison refrained from chastising Beatrix for her filthy gown. Her husband was no longer here to criticize her for being a lax mother, one of her many failings that he had brought to her attention daily. In truth, Beatrix did get into a good deal of mischief. Yet Alison worried far more about her younger daughter. Margaret had a trusting nature and a desire to please.

Alison had been like that once.

"Did Uncle George bring us presents?" Beatrix asked as they started down the stairs.

"Not this time, love."

As they descended, the rumble of men's voices filled the circular stairwell and echoed off its stone walls. Alison paused at the bottom of the stairs to survey the hall, which was filled with Douglas warriors who were making quick work of the heaped platters of food that had taken the servants hours to prepare.

A frisson of unease went up her spine when a man with familiar hard gray eyes caught her gaze as if he had been waiting for her. He elbowed the gray-haired man next to him.

What were Patrick Blackadder and his father, the Laird of Tulliallan, doing here?

She gripped her daughters' hands more tightly as her husband's two kinsmen approached. Though they were only distant cousins, Patrick looked so much like a younger version of her husband that she found it intolerable to be near him.

"Do not stray from my side," she told Beatrix, and gave her a hard look to let her know she meant it.

Perhaps she was being unfair, but she mistrusted both father and son.

"Lady Alison, as exquisite as ever," Patrick said, giving her a thorough perusal that made sweat prickle under her arms.

When he took her hand, she felt as if she were choking. He seemed to take an overly long time pressing his lips to it, but that was probably her imagination. As soon as she could politely do so, she tugged her hand from his grip.

"Your grief over your husband's untimely death must be terrible, dear lady," his father said. After planting a wet kiss on her cheek that made her skin crawl, he shifted his beady gaze to her daughters. "How are my favorite lassies?"

When he reached for a ringlet of Margaret's hair, Alison grabbed his wrist. "Excuse us. My brothers are waiting to see them."

She hurried her daughters past the two Blackadder men and made her way to the high table.

"Lucky lasses, ye have the Douglas good looks," George said, and winked at her daughters as they took their places beside him. "Next time, I'll bring ye silver combs to show off your glossy black hair."

"Why are Patrick Blackadder and his father here?" Alison whispered as she sat on his other side.

"They have a large number of warriors at their command," George said, "and we need all the support we can muster."

"Then take them with ye when ye leave." The sooner they were out of her home the better.

She glanced down the table at Archie, hoping he would notice her daughters, but he was deep in conversation with some of the men.

"I didn't have a chance to ask before," she said, turning back to George. "How do our sisters fare?"

"Sybil is full of piss and vinegar, as always," he said with a grin. "She's breaking hearts left and right at Court, though she makes no effort to please anyone."

Alison smiled. Beatrix took after Sybil, which *mostly* reassured her.

"What of Maggie?" she asked, her thoughts turning to the gentle, kind-hearted sister for whom she had named her younger daughter.

"I hear she's with child again," George said in a quiet voice.

"So soon?" Poor Maggie had not yet recovered from losing the last babe. Her husband should have waited. Men could be such selfish creatures.

Before she could ask about their youngest sister, Archie's voice boomed out over the noise of the hall.

"To your horses!"

Men rose from the tables still guzzling their ale, and some grabbed drumsticks and hunks of bread to take with them.

"God preserve me. Can Archie not give the men time to eat?" she said under breath. She had hoped for more time to persuade him.

With her daughters in tow, Alison crossed the hall to the arched doorway to bid goodbye to the Douglas men.

"Lady Alison," each Douglas warrior said, and dipped his head to her and her daughters as they filed out. Her father and grandfather had required their men to show respect to the females of the family—unlike her husband, who had ridiculed her in front of the household at every opportunity.

Her brothers were the last of the Douglas men to leave. At her signal, her daughters curtsied to them, looking so sweet that they made Alison smile despite her worries. How could Archie look into their faces and not want to move heaven and earth to protect them?

"Don't forget us," Alison said as Archie bent to kiss her cheek.

"Next time we'll speak more about a new husband for ye," he said.

Before she had a chance to tell him she was never marrying again, he swept out the door without sparing a word or a glance for her daughters.

"If anyone troubles ye, send word to us," George said, putting an arm around her shoulders and giving her a squeeze. "But don't fret, Allie, the fight will be in Edinburgh. Nothing will happen here."

***

Two months later...

David had returned to Hume Castle at dawn and crawled into bed after another successful night raid. He felt as if his head had barely hit the pillow when he was awakened by shouts from the courtyard. Judging from the sounds, this was no attack, so he was tempted to roll over and go back to sleep. Instead, he dragged himself out of bed to see what trouble was brewing among his men.

"By the saints," he hissed when he looked out the arrow-slit window.

As he suspected, a fight had broken out among the younger warriors. The older men knew better. What he did not expect to see was his brother Robbie at the center of the trouble, pummeling one of the others as if he meant to kill him.

David pulled on his breeks, grabbed his sword, and headed down the stairs of the tower.

The circle of men who were shouting encouragement went silent and stepped back when they saw David crossing the courtyard. The two combatants, however, were oblivious to his presence. At least, Robbie was. His opponent was on the ground and attempting to protect his face from Robbie's blows.

David grabbed the back of Robbie's tunic and jerked him off his feet. His brother was so blind with fury he nearly made the mistake of taking a swing at David before he realized who was holding him. Once Robbie appeared to have regained a thread of sense, David let his feet rest on the ground, but he did not release him.

At his nod, a couple of the men helped Robbie's opponent to his feet. It was Harold, a mouthy young man three years older and thirty pounds heavier than Robbie.

"Have one of the women see to that cut on your lip," David told him. "I'll speak to ye later about your part in this."

One of the older men should have put a stop to the fight as soon as it started, but they were hesitant to lay hands on Robbie because he was David's brother. That was probably wise.

"Get back to your duties," David told the others, then he turned his brother toward the keep. "Inside. Now."

"But Harold was—"

"Not in front of the men," David ground out between his teeth.

After the doors of the keep closed behind them, Robbie attempted to shrug him off. David gave him a shake before releasing him, then the two of them climbed the stairs and entered David's chamber in silence.

"I won't have ye violate my orders," David said, planting his hands on his hips. "We fight our enemies, not our own men."

"I had no choice," Robbie said, glaring at him. "Harold was making jests about Will."

"What did he say?" David asked, keeping his voice calm. Anger flared in his veins, but unlike Robbie's wild fury, his was cold and controlled. And far more dangerous.

"Harold said we should put Will in a gown and braid his hair," Robbie said. "I couldn't let him say that, even if it's true."

Will's mother had coddled him, and the lad was too soft-hearted for his own good. Still, David would not tolerate anyone ridiculing his brother.

"Just look at him!" Robbie said, pointing out the window.

When David joined Robbie at the window, he saw their younger brother kissing and hugging a pup like a long-lost lover. *Jesu.*

"Ye must do something about him," Robbie said. "He's humiliating."

David rubbed his forehead. Will was so different from him that it was difficult to know what to do. "He's young, and he misses your mother."

"I miss her too," Robbie said in a fierce voice. "'Tis no excuse for behaving like a wee lass."

"Will has a big heart. He'll learn to hide it as he grows older." David hoped for Will's sake that it was true. "He'll be a fine warrior one day, for he's utterly fearless."

"He's fearless because he's blind to everything around him," Robbie said.

David sighed inwardly because what Robbie said was true, and such blindness was dangerous. He wished he could let Will be a child longer, but it was his duty to prepare his brother for manhood. To survive in the Borders, a man must keep his wits about him and his fighting skills sharp. And, above all, he must be respected.

"'Tis my fault. I should have seen this sooner." David had not asked for the responsibility of raising his brothers, but he accepted that it was his. That duty had fallen to him long before his father died, though he could not say how or exactly when it had happened.

"No one dares make jests about Will within your hearing," Robbie said, "but Harold isn't the only one who does it."

"I will handle this—not you," David said, pinning him with a look. "I won't have fighting among my men."

"But—"

"I expect everyone, *without exception*, to follow my orders," David said. "Disobey me again, and I'll not go easy on ye. Understand?"

"Aye," Robbie said, dropping his gaze to the floor. "No more fighting our own men."

"I'm glad that's settled," David said, folding his arms. "Any other orders you're unclear about?"

"Nay, but if I'm saving my fighting skills for our enemies, why won't ye take me on a raid?" Robbie asked. "You were raiding at my age."

God grant him patience. He understood Robbie wanting to go, but raids were dangerous and unpredictable. He would not risk his brother's life raiding, but he was glad to have a different reason to give him.

"The raids have served their purpose," he said.

David had more cattle than he knew what to do with. More importantly, men on both sides of the border feared his name, and no one dared cross Hume territory without his permission.

"'Tis time to take a bigger prize than cattle," David said, staring out the window at the hills beyond his walls.

"Blackadder Castle?" Robbie asked.

David smiled at his brother's quickness. "Aye."

"We'll make the Blackadders pay for the wrongs they've done to us," Robbie said.

"I must make my move before someone else does," David said. "A castle in the care of a young widow is like low-hanging fruit. All the Border lairds have their eyes on it."

From what he'd heard, the widow was meek. She would not hold out long.

"Before they know it," Robbie said, "you'll take Blackadder Castle."

And the widow too. David did not say the words aloud. It was not yet time to share that part of his plan with his brother.

But the widow was the key.

CHAPTER 3

Alison sat alone at the high table, her bowl of stew gone cold, long after she dismissed her children to play. After ten years of marriage, she was finally free. But free to be whom? She did not know who she was anymore.

She could barely remember the arrogant and sometimes thoughtless girl she had been at thirteen when she wed. As the granddaughter of two powerful clan chieftains, she had been raised to think rather much of herself. Yet even with her faults, Alison liked that girl far better than who she had become as Blackadder's wife—a groveling woman with poison in her heart.

Burning his bed had made her feel like that girl again. And she liked that feeling, however fleeting.

When she became Blackadder's third wife, he was forty, twenty-seven years her senior, and she was young enough for him to shape her into the sort of woman he wanted. She had heard him say it often enough to his friends.

Women are like dogs and horses. Best to get them young when they're easy to train.

Blackadder constantly undermined her authority by ridiculing her in front of the household. He overruled decisions she made that were typically in the purview of the mistress of the castle, then criticized her because the household did not run smoothly.

She intended to change all that, but it was not proving easy. The servants were long accustomed to ignoring her requests without suffering any consequence, and the Blackadder warriors were worse. They had followed her order to carry her husband's bed into the courtyard only because they had thought her mad with grief and madness frightened them.

The castle was hers now—or rather her daughters'—and she was determined to take charge of her household.

She took another bite of the tasteless stew and decided there was no better time than the present. Before she lost her courage, she headed downstairs to the kitchens.

"The meals have been lacking." Alison confronted the cook, a thin, hollow-cheeked man with a grizzly beard and a surly expression. "There was no meat again today except for a bit of rabbit in the soup."

"I can't cook what I don't have, m'lady," he said. "I butchered the last of our pigs when your Douglas kin descended upon us, and we have no more."

She suspected that the Blackadder men who deserted the castle had robbed them of their stores. This problem, at least, was easily resolved.

"Then we must replenish our supplies," Alison said, folding her arms. "Until we have more pork, we shall eat beef."

She was proud of herself for standing up to him.

"The Humes have raided our cattle," the cook said. "We've not a one left."

"How could that happen?" she asked. "And why did no one tell me?"

"We've even eaten the hens," he continued, ignoring her questions, "so we've no eggs either."

"Then we'll send one of the kitchen maids to the market in the village to buy more."

"I already did," he said. "She returned empty-handed."

Alison was stunned. "The kitchen maid stole the coins?"

"'Tis no what ye think, m'lady," a young girl who was cleaning pots in the corner spoke up. "The Humes are stopping everyone on the road between here and the village and taking what they have."

"I thought the Hume lairds were dead," Alison said. "My brother told me they were executed for treason."

"Aye, but the son of one of them is the new Laird of Wedderburn," the cook said. "Everyone's talking about him, saying he's worse than his father and uncle put together."

"Worse? That is not possible," she said, her voice falling to a whisper.

There had been terrible rumors, too horrible to believe, about what the Humes had done after the Scottish defeat at the Battle of Flodden. Some claimed they saw the Hume warriors robbing from the bodies of their fellow Scots before leaving the field. The most fantastic rumor was that the king survived the battle and the Humes stole his broken body and hid him away. There were whispers that the king was still alive, albeit senseless. None of the men vying for power wished this particular tale to be true and repeating it was dangerous.

"The new Hume laird braved two hundred royal guards alone," the cook said, "and succeeded in removing his father's and uncle's heads from the Tolbooth in Edinburgh."

"Alone?" She put her hand to her chest. "Surely he would have been caught."

"They say the Devil carried him into the city in a black, swirling mist," the kitchen maid said, her words sending a chill up the back of Alison's neck. "That's why no one saw him until the deed was done."

"They call him the Beast of Wedderburn now," the cook said.

This evil man, this Beast, was blocking the roads to her castle and threatening her household.

"How much food do we have left?" Her throat felt so tight she could hardly get the question out.

"Not much," the cook said, shaking his head.

Alison leaned against the kitchen work table to steady herself as she imagined a huge warrior in black armor, with flames where his eyes should be, stalking toward her out of a swirling black mist.

***

My dearest brothers,

David Hume, the new Laird of Wedderburn, has made clear his intention to take Blackadder Castle. For a fortnight, he has blocked the roads leading to the castle.

Alison heard her enemy's name in the murmurs and whispers of the men in the hall as she sat at the head table writing the message to her brothers. She wondered how it could be that no goods could pass the roads to reach Blackadder Castle, and yet news of Wedderburn's most recent exploits filled her home. Even in the Borders, where violence and thievery were the rule, this David Hume had quickly become infamous.

I am certain he is preparing to lay siege to the castle and starve us out. Our supplies are already dangerously low. We cannot last long.

I beg you, come quickly.

Your loving sister,
A

Alison folded the parchment, dripped the melted wax, and affixed her personal seal. Her grandfather, the earl, was once imprisoned by the king because a loose-lipped scribe shared the content of a sensitive message. Thanks to that lesson, the earl insisted that all his grandchildren learn to write so they could communicate with each other without incurring that risk.

She stood to address the men who had gathered in the hall for the meager noon meal.

"The Laird of Wedderburn and his men cannot cover every mile around us," she said, and held out the sealed parchment. "One of ye must slip past the Humes and deliver this message to my brothers."

The hall went silent. Not one man stepped forward.

Alison swallowed back her panic and pointed to Walter, the large, black-haired warrior who was captain of the guard. When Walter shook his head, she pointed to another.

"Nay," the second man said. "The Beast of Wedderburn would cut me to pieces and feed me to his dogs."

Cowards! She would take a horse and go herself, but she could not leave her daughters.

"Without my brothers' warriors, we are lost," she said, desperation clawing at her stomach. "Is there no one brave enough to try to save us?"

Garrett, a stooped, elderly man who tended the horses, came forward. "I'll go, m'lady."

Alison glared at the other men. Surely the old man's bravery would shame one of them into stepping forward. The silence in the hall deepened.

She brought her gaze back to her lone volunteer. The fate of her daughters, her home, and her lands depended upon this old man sneaking past the claws of the Beast of Wedderburn.

"I'm grateful to ye, Garrett," she said, forcing a smile.

"Don't fret, m'lady, the Beast won't catch me," he said, and winked one filmy eye. "I know all the back routes."

Old Garrett probably had been stealing cattle since he was twelve, like the rest of these Border men, so he might have a chance. She gave him the sealed parchment and squeezed his hand.

"May God bless ye for your courage and guide your path."

***

Alison ignored her growling stomach and tried to concentrate on her needlework as she sat with her daughters by the hearth, but each time the outer door of the hall opened, she looked up.

"I'm tired of stitching." Beatrix slumped her shoulders and gave Alison a pitiful look. "Is it not time to eat yet?"

A rush of guilt swamped her. There was so little food left that she was forced to ration it. Even her daughters had to make do with smaller portions.

"Your uncles will be here soon," she said with more confidence than she felt. "Then all will be well."

"If your Douglas kin were coming, they would be here by now," a deep voice came from behind her.

She turned to see Walter standing over her.

"That devil Hume must have caught the old man," he said.

"'Tis too soon to say that." She refrained from adding that Walter should have volunteered himself. Poor Old Garrett. If Wedderburn had murdered him, it would be her fault.

"'Tis been a full week since he left," Walter said, staring down at her with his hands on his hips, as if there was something she could do about it.

"I know precisely how long it's been." Her nerves were strained after another week with no supplies getting through. She gave her daughters what she hoped was a reassuring smile. Disguising her ever-present fear from them was becoming difficult.

"They're here!" One of the guards burst through the doors and his shouts rang through the hall. "They're here!"

Alison sprang to her feet and clasped her hands together. *Praise God.* Garrett had made it through with her message after all.

"We are saved," she told her daughters. "We shall have a grand feast tonight!"

Her smile faded when she saw that the men were scrambling for their weapons. She grabbed the sleeve of one of them as he ran past her.

"What's happened?" she asked, her heart pounding.

"The Beast of Wedderburn has arrived."

CHAPTER 4

A week after the siege began, Alison went to the top floor of the tower and climbed the metal rungs fixed to the stone wall to reach the roof. When her head cleared the opening, she saw two guards crouching behind the parapet.

"Any sign of the Douglas warriors yet?" she called to them.

Whether Old Garrett delivered her message or not, her brothers were bound to hear of her plight eventually and come. The only question was whether they would arrive before she was forced to surrender.

"You shouldn't be up here," the younger of the two guards said. "'Tis too dangerous. Their arrows can reach this far."

"You're here," she said, and held out her hand for him to help her climb out onto the roof.

Her breath caught as she looked about her. Hundreds of warriors surrounded her castle. Inside the keep, she had been able to pretend the threat was not so grave. But up here she had a clear view of the enemy she faced, and she felt like a doe cornered by dogs.

She had not truly feared for her personal safety until this moment. After all, she was sister-in-law to the queen. Her brother was one of the most powerful men in Scotland. But as she surveyed the armed warriors encircling her home, she understood that a man who would attack her castle in spite of her high connections was not bound by the constraints that would normally protect her.

Her attention was drawn repeatedly to one Hume warrior who sat motionless astride a great black steed. She could not make out his features from this distance. Surely, he could not see her any more clearly than she saw him, yet she felt his gaze piercing her like a shard of ice.

"Is that Wedderburn?" she asked the guard, though she knew in her bones it was.

"Aye, that's the Beast himself."

"Do ye believe we can expect mercy from him?" she asked.

"From Wedderburn?" The guard's expression was grim. "I fear not, m'lady."

"Then we must hold out as long as we can." She thought of her daughters and shuddered.

"I pray that your brothers arrive soon," the guard said.

Alison, too, prayed for deliverance. But she was losing faith that it would come from her brothers.

***

David watched as his archers shot another round of arrows over the walls. How much longer would the damned woman hold out before she gave in to the inevitable? He had hoped to take possession of the castle peaceably, but she did not appear to have the sense to open the gate.

"Shall we set the arrows aflame and burn them out?" one of the younger warriors asked.

"This castle will soon be mine. I don't intend to destroy it," David snapped. "We'll wait them out."

David stared in disbelief as the figure of a woman appeared on top of the roof of the keep, her wine-red gown flapping in the wind like a banner against the gray stone.

"Halt your arrows!" he shouted, raising his hand.

She was making herself a bloody target, standing up there in that gown. No one but the lady of the castle herself would be dressed in such finery. What kind of fool was she to draw attention to herself when arrows were flying?

He had lost all patience with the Lady of Blackadder. It was time to force her hand.

***

"I'm not hungry." Alison waved away the bowl of watery broth, though the smell made her stomach growl. She could not recall when she had last eaten.

She watched the rest of her household hungrily spoon their broth, then lift their bowls to their mouths and tilt their heads back so as not to miss a single drop. Which was worse, to condemn the men to a slow death by starvation or to a quick death by the sword? She could not bear to think of what the women might suffer. And so, each morning, she told herself she would wait one more day for her brothers. But they had not come.

One of the servant's babes began crying again, and that was the last straw. She could not bear it anymore. One more day, one more hour, what did it matter? Her message had not reached her brothers, and the Douglases would not come to save them.

She gripped the table as she stood up and waited for the lightheadedness to pass.

"We shall surrender," she announced to her household. "May God and Laird Wedderburn have mercy on us."

Thump. Thump. Thump.

The walls reverberated with a pounding like thunder. Shouts and screams erupted in the hall. Beatrix and Margaret flung themselves at Alison and clutched at her skirts, wailing.

"What is it?" she shouted, trying to make herself heard over the noise.

"A battering ram," one of the men said before he raced for the door.

After waiting so long to starve them out and force a surrender, why was Wedderburn attacking now?

Thump. Thump. Thump.

The floor vibrated beneath her feet, as if Thor himself were beating his anvil in the castle yard.

What should she do?

If the Humes stormed the castle, there was sure to be a bloodbath. If she gave up peaceably, perhaps some of her household would be spared. She turned to the nursemaid, who was looking about the room wild-eyed, and clasped the woman's hands around her daughters' hands.

"Flora, take the girls to our bedchamber and bar the door," she said. "Open it to no one but me."

She ran out of the keep and stood at the top of the steps. The courtyard was in chaos. Castle defenders were rushing to the gate to help those who were already piled against it, attempting to use their weight to hold it against the ceaseless pounding.

Thump. Thump. Thump.

"Tell him I surrender!" she shouted. "Open the gates!"

Thump. Thump. Thump.

She shouted again, but no one heard her. She ran down the steps. She must make the men heed her. "Surrender! Open the gates!"

The sickening sound of splintering wood reached her ears.

"They're breaking through!" someone shouted. "Run for your lives!"

It was too late. With her heart in her throat, Alison picked up her skirts and ran. She had to reach her daughters before the attackers burst through the gate intent on murder and mayhem. Jostled by her own men, who were also running for the keep, she nearly fell twice, but she managed to make it inside.

The noise in the hall was deafening. The shouts and screams followed her, echoing off the stone walls of the stairwell, as she raced up the stairs to reach her daughters.

"Let me in!" She pounded on the bedchamber door with her fists.

When the door flung open, Beatrix stood in the doorway, with her sister just behind her. Flora sat on a stool in the far corner moaning and rocking herself.

Alison slammed the door behind her and threw the bolt across. When she whirled around, her daughters were staring at her, their eyes wide in their pale faces. She fell to her knees and caught them in her arms.

"There, there." Alison never lied to her daughters, but she lied to them now. "Everything will be all right."

Another glance at Flora, who had been old when she was Alison's nursemaid, told her the poor woman would be no help.

The clank of swords and shouts of men came through the window and filled the bedchamber, sending panic coursing through her veins. The enemy was inside the castle walls now. Alison prayed that the doors to the keep would hold. She buried her face in her daughters' hair, breathing in their familiar scent, and wondered if it would be the last time she held them in her arms.

There was a loud crash, and a roar went up. Suddenly the sounds of fighting were coming from the hall below as well as from the courtyard. She must protect her daughters. But how?

Alison remembered her husband's sword, which she'd placed in the trunk at the foot of the bed for safekeeping, and forced herself to release her daughters. With trembling fingers, she fumbled with the keys tied to her belt until she found the right one.

She heard boots on the stairs as she unlocked the trunk. She tossed aside blankets and gowns to reach the sword.

Click, click. She jumped at the sound of someone lifting the door latch. Her heart pounded in her ears as she lifted the sword from the trunk and struggled to pull it from its scabbard. When she jerked it free, she stumbled backward.

Bang, bang. A fist pounded on the other side of the door. The bolt held, but for how long?

"Stay behind me," she ordered her daughters.

She stood in front of them and faced the door with the sword in her hands.

***

David strode through the battle raging between his men and the castle defenders in the courtyard and headed straight for the keep, intent on his goal.

The castle would fall quickly. The defenders lacked leadership and were in disarray. His only concern was whether the castle had a secret tunnel for escape. During the siege, he had spread his men out through the fields surrounding the fortress to keep watch. But he had concentrated his forces for the attack and most were now inside the castle. If there was a tunnel, he must secure the widow and her daughters before they had a chance to escape. He did not relish the idea of having to chase them down through the fields with dogs.

The defenders had foolishly waited too long to withdraw to the keep, and most were caught in the courtyard when David's men burst through the gate. He barely spared them a glance as he ran up the steps of the keep.

With several of his warriors at his back, he burst through the doors brandishing his sword. He paused inside the entrance to hall. Women and children were screaming, and the few Blackadder warriors who had made it inside were overturning tables in a useless attempt to set up a defense.

"If ye hope for mercy, drop your weapons," David shouted, making his voice heard above the chaos.

He locked gazes with the men who hesitated to obey his order until every weapon clanked to the floor, then he swept his gaze over the women. Their clothing confirmed what he'd known the moment he entered the hall. Blackadder's widow was not in the room.

"Where is she?" he demanded of the closest Blackadder man.

"Who, m'lord?" the man said, shifting his gaze to the side.

"Your mistress!" David picked him up by the front of his tunic and leaned in close. "Tell me *now*."

"In her bedchamber," the man squeaked, pointing to an arched doorway. "'Tis up the stairs."

David caught a sudden whiff of urine and dropped the man to the floor in disgust. The wretch had wet himself.

"Take him to the dungeon," he ordered. The coward had given up his mistress far too easily.

David started up the wheeled stairs to the upper floors with his sword at the ready. He expected to encounter Blackadder warriors, protecting the lady of the castle. But there were none on the stairs and none guarding the door on the first floor.

Damn it. She must have escaped. He gritted his teeth as he envisioned the lady's guards leading her through the tunnel.

He was about to open the chamber door to make sure it was empty when Brian, one of his best men, came down the stairs.

"Laird, I checked all the chambers while ye were in the hall," he said.

David's jaw ached from clenching it.

"There's one door on the floor just above us that wouldn't open with the latch," Brian said. "Shall I break it down?"

David waved him aside and pulled the ax from his belt as he raced up the stairs.

"Open it!" he shouted and pounded on the door.

He did not wait. She could be escaping through a secret door this very moment. Three hard *whacks* with his ax, and the door split. He kicked it until it swung open, then stepped through.

At his first sight of the woman, his feet became fixed to the floor. He felt strange, and his vision was distorted, as if as if he had swallowed a magical potion that narrowed his sight. He could see nothing in the room but her.

She was extraordinarily lovely, with violet eyes, pale skin, and shining black hair. But there was something about her, something beyond her beauty, that held him captive. She was young, much younger than he expected, and her features and form were delicate, in marked contrast to the violent emotion in her eyes.

David knew to the depths of his soul that a brute like him should not be the man to claim this fragile flower, even while the word *mine* beat in his head like a drum. He had no notion of how long he stood staring at her before he became aware that she held a sword. It was longer still before he noticed the two wee lasses peeking out from behind her like frightened kittens.

Anger boiled up in his chest. Every Blackadder man in the castle who could still draw breath should have been here, standing between him and their lady. Instead, she faced him alone with a sword she could barely lift with both hands.

It was a brave, but ridiculous gesture.

There was no defense against him.

CHAPTER 5

Alison had started to scream when the blade of the ax split the door with a sound like crunching bones, but sheer terror closed her throat as the huge warrior who wielded the ax stepped through the splintered remains of the door. He halted just inside the room, his ax still raised as if ready to strike.

By his menacing stillness, she recognized him as the man on the black horse she had seen from the tower. This was the Beast of Wedderburn himself. Her heart beat so hard that the sound seemed to fill the room.

Dirks, a sword, and sundry weapons hung from leather belts and straps across his hips and chest. Unkempt hair of bronze and gold brushed impossibly broad shoulders that were covered in chain mail. What frightened her more than all his weapons were his fierce green eyes, which were fixed on her like a wolf that had found its prey.

Her daughters began to whimper behind her, and it tore at her heart.

"Stay back or I shall strike ye dead!" she shouted, holding the sword in front of her. She would die protecting them if she must.

"Drop the sword," he said, his voice a deep rumble that reverberated in her belly and made her knees shake.

"Nay! I'll not let ye touch us!"

"Drop it *now*."

His ferocious green eyes stole the breath right out of her. She could not speak, so she shook her head.

He moved so quickly that she did not know how it happened. And yet her hands were empty, and he held her sword at his side. He had disarmed her as easily as he had taken her castle.

He stood so close to her that the wall of his chest filled her vision. She felt the heat radiating from his body. Terror gripped her as she waited to find out what he would do next, knowing there was nothing she could do to stop him. Would he slice her in two with his ax as he had the door, or would he force her to the floor and rape her in front of her daughters?

Alison squeezed her eyes shut and prayed for a quick death.

***

David stared down at the lady of the castle, a wisp of a lass whose head did not even reach his chin.

He prided himself on how carefully he had planned each step to avenge his father and to protect his family and clan. Blackadder's widow had always been the key. And yet he had never given the woman herself much thought. Belatedly, he realized he was wholly unprepared to deal with her.

Hell, he did not even know what to call her. Not "Blackadder's widow." Nay, he would not call her by his enemy's name, as if the dead man still had a claim on her. He had heard her Christian name before. What was it? Alison? Aye, that was it. Lady Alison.

He should speak to her, tell her what her fate was to be. Before he could form the words, she tilted her head back and opened her eyes. He was struck dumb, lost in eyes the color of violets. He felt as if he'd stepped into a warm summer day. He could almost feel a light breeze on his face, hear the birds singing, and smell the wildflowers on the hillside.

Good God, was he going mad?

"Please," she said in a choked voice. "Not in front of my daughters."

Her words jarred him from his trance. *Not in front of her daughters?* Did she think he meant to harm her? God forbid, that he would *rape* her?

He was insulted. While he had set out to create a fearsome reputation, he had never violated a woman, nor did he permit his men to do so. Yet this lass was clearly terrified of him. Her whole body was shaking.

He felt the need to reassure her. Instinctively, he lifted his hand to her cheek—and the lady crumpled at his feet.

Faith, what had he done? The two wee girls sprawled on the floor beside their mother in a feminine heap of ribbons, glossy black hair, and silk skirts. They were crying, reminding him again of mewling kittens.

"Hush," he told them, and knelt to feel Lady Alison's pulse. "She's only fainted."

Christ, he'd barely touched her. This did not bode well. What would he do with such a delicate creature?

He heard a cough behind him and turned to find several of his men hovering in the doorway. Did they think he could not manage a senseless woman and two bairns alone?

"Secure the rest of the castle," he ordered them.

When he turned around again, the older of the two daughters was glaring at him with her hand on her hip.

"My mother does not faint," she said.

He raised an eyebrow at her, then shifted his gaze to her younger sister, who was sucking her thumb. Both were dark-haired and pretty, like their mother.

"Stand back," he told them, and slid his arms under Lady Alison.

The older girl pounded on his shoulder. "Don't ye hurt her!"

"I'm only carrying her to the bed," he said, though he was not accustomed to explaining his actions. "I'll not harm her."

"Promise?" the smaller girl asked.

David took a deep breath and reminded himself that they were just wee girls.

"I will protect your mother with my life," he said. "Just as I will protect you."

Both girls' eyes went wide.

"You're my responsibility now," he told them.

That silenced them for the moment. Carefully, he lifted Lady Alison from the floor. She weighed nothing at all, which made him feel like an ox, but her slight frame was soft and curved in all the right places. As he laid her down on the bed, his fingers brushed the side of her breast, and his throat went dry.

He had not expected the widow to be anything like this. As he looked down at her pale, perfect skin and angelic face, he was incensed at the thought of her sharing a bed with Blackadder, a dull, brutish man of nearly fifty. She must have been barely of age when she married the bastard. He imagined how she must have looked on her wedding day, fresh as a dew-kissed morning, with a soft glow in her cheeks.

And now, David was the brutish, undeserving man who would take her to bed.

After a long moment, he realized that the sounds of fighting had died. His men would be waiting for him to give them orders.

He pulled the coverlet over Lady Alison and checked her pulse again. It was strong and her color was returning. Yet she looked so fragile that he felt uneasy about leaving her.

He watched her chest rise and fall with shallow but steady breaths, then his gaze drifted to her parted lips. He shook his head, wondering how long he'd been standing beside the bed staring like a fool. By the heavens, what was wrong with him?

"You," he said, pointing to the old woman who was huddled in the corner and had not made a single peep. "Are ye able to look after your mistress?"

The old woman nodded.

"Then do it." He turned abruptly to leave, but halted when he saw the two girls, who were standing between him and the door holding hands. These two bairns were the heiresses of Blackadder. He had definite plans for them once they were of age—but he had no notion what to do with them in the meantime.

And judging by the size of them, the meantime would last for years. Ach, this was another gap in his plans. He'd helped raise his brothers, but he'd not been around little girls a day in his life.

"Your lady mother is fine," he said, dropping to one knee to speak with them. "She only needs a bit of rest."

The younger girl's dark curls bounced as she tilted her head to the side and examined him with wide blue eyes. After a long moment, she said, "I'm hungry."

David relaxed. Perhaps little girls were not so different from lads after all.

"Come, I'll take ye down to the hall to get something to eat."

When he started for the stairs, the younger girl startled him by slipping her tiny hand in his. He would need to watch this one closely, for the wee thing was entirely too trusting.

"Margaret, don't!" her sister hissed, apparently sharing his concern, but she followed them down the stairs all the same.

Strange how a tiny hand could make the weight of his new responsibilities feel like a boulder on his chest.

CHAPTER 6

David's reaction to Lady Alison irritated him more with each passing moment. His mood was already sour when he entered the hall with the two girls in tow and saw the serving women huddled together in a corner.

"One of ye go upstairs and see to your lady," David told them. "The rest of ye bring us food and drink."

The women looked at him as if he'd ordered them to kill their firstborn children. By the saints, these Blackadder women were easily frightened.

"Take a couple of these women to the kitchens," he told Brian, who was nearest at hand, "and come back with some food."

Brian returned a short time later. "There's not a scrap to be found."

"None?" Anger surged through David's veins. Lady Alison was beautiful, but she was a poor manager of her household or they would not have run out of food so quickly. Her ineptitude was not, however, what made him furious.

He sent men to fetch their wagon of supplies from outside the gate. Soon after, he watched the two girls fall on their meal of dried beef and stale bread as if it were a grand feast.

Why in the hell did Lady Alison not submit sooner? If she had half the sense God gave her, she should have seen that holding out was hopeless. Instead, she let her household, including her wee daughters, go hungry out of pure stubbornness.

***

Alison dreamed someone had tucked her in, something no one had done since she was a child. In her dream, she felt safe. The feeling left her the instant she opened her eyes. For a long moment, she lay still, unable to pinpoint the source of her anxiety.

She bolted upright. The Beast of Wedderburn had been in this very room. The last thing she remembered was him standing over her, his hard green eyes drilling into her…and then he had touched her.

She ran her hands over her body, but she felt no blood, no injury. Her clothes were all in one piece. She looked around the room and saw only Flora, who was staring at nothing. Panic surged through Alison's limbs.

Her daughters were gone. That vile man had taken her precious little girls.

"What has he done with them?" she shouted at Flora, but the old woman just looked at her with glazed eyes.

Alison leapt out of bed, and her vision went black. She held onto the bedpost to keep from falling and forced herself to take slow breaths until she could see again. Then she went to find her children.

Not fully trusting her legs, she kept one hand against the wall as she went down the circular stairs. The rumble of male voices echoed up the stairwell from the hall, but she heard no screams. She felt guilty for sleeping through the violence that must have occurred in the wake of the castle's fall and grief for those she had not been able to protect. Had she been spared because of her noble status?

Or was her turn yet to come?

She steeled herself to find broken furniture and debauchery in her hall. The need to save her children gave her the courage to continue down the stairs on wobbly legs. When she reached the bottom, she surveyed the hall through the low, arched doorway. Her home was filled with scores of men she did not know, rough warriors with weapons tied to their backs and belts, but they were sitting at the long trestle tables in an orderly fashion that seemed so incongruous as to be bizarre.

She drew in a deep breath and stepped inside the hall. Silence fell over the cavernous room as every one of the Hume warriors turned to look at her.

When she saw Wedderburn in the laird's chair at the high table with her daughters trapped on either side of him, a blind rage took hold of her. She tore across the room and stood before the high table, clenching her hands.

"Touch one hair on my daughters' heads, and I'll murder ye, I swear it."

Wedderburn showed no reaction beyond a slight lift of one eyebrow. After a long pause, he spoke in a mild tone.

"That's the second time ye threatened to kill me. I suggest ye not do it again," he said. "As for your daughters, all I'm doing is feeding them."

"Feeding them?" With the blood pounding in her ears, she was not certain she had heard him correctly.

She shifted her gaze to her daughters. They were stuffing bread and dried beef into their mouths with both hands, as if they feared she would tell them they could not have it.

"Aye, feeding them," Wedderburn said, drawing her attention back to him, "something you neglected to do."

"*I* neglected?" she said. "How dare you. If they're hungry, 'tis because ye cut off our supplies."

"It tastes good, Mama," Beatrix interrupted, speaking around the food in her mouth. "Ye must have some."

The smell of the bread made her suddenly lightheaded, and stars sparked across her vision. She gripped the table to steady herself, determined not to show weakness in front of this man again.

The next moment, she found herself leaning backward and staring up into Wedderburn's hard, handsome face. She blinked several times, attempting to clear her vision. Had Wedderburn truly bounded over the table and swept her into his arms? The heat and strength of the body encircling hers told her she had not imagined it.

For a fleeting moment, his brows were drawn together in what looked like concern. Then his eyes darkened with an intensity that stole her breath away. His gaze dropped to her mouth, and she had the wild notion that this stranger was going to kiss her right here in the hall in front of his men and her entire household.

***

David lost himself in fathomless violet eyes. Her body felt deliciously soft and compliant in his arms, and he sank into her, pulled as if by a lodestone to her red lips. But before he reached them, he felt her stiffen in his arms.

"Remove your hands from me," she said, and pushed at him.

He never forgot himself like this. He was always in control. This lass was dangerous.

"Stop struggling," he commanded, and under his glare, her limbs wilted. He carried her around the table and sat her down between him and the younger girl. "Ye should be grateful I saved ye from falling. Ye were fainting again."

"I was not."

Why did she find it necessary to dispute an obvious fact? *Females.*

"Mama's weak from hunger." The older girl, whose name he'd learned was Beatrix, spoke up.

Once again, fury flooded through him at the unnecessary suffering caused by the lady's stubbornness.

"Eat slowly or you'll be sick," he said, and pushed the platter in front of her.

He needn't have warned her. Even starving, Lady Alison ate with the delicacy of a wee bird. It annoyed the hell out of him.

"When did ye run out of food?" he demanded.

The lady gave him a scathing sideways glance but did not answer.

"We've had nothing but thin broth the last two days," Beatrix said. "But Mama refused her portion."

Lady Alison gave her daughter a quelling look.

"When was the last time ye ate?" he asked her.

She shrugged and continued nibbling at her food.

"*When?*" he repeated, keeping his voice low, though he was so furious he saw red around the edges of his vision.

"She didn't take her share yesterday," Beatrix said, blithely ignoring her mother's glare. "Or the day before."

David clenched his jaw so tightly it ached, but he waited to speak again until the three of them had eaten their fill.

"Escort the ladies upstairs and guard their door," he said, pointing at two of his men.

As soon as they disappeared up the stairs, he strode out of the keep and into the courtyard, where the captured Blackadder warriors were being held. He ordered them on their feet and paced up and down before them.

"What kind of men are you," he thundered at the prisoners, "filling your bellies while your mistress, the lady ye were supposed to protect, went hungry?"

He could have dismissed, though not excused, their failure to protect her door as a grave error made in the confusion of battle. But taking their meals while she sat at the table having none showed a blatant disregard for her well-being. No matter what Lady Alison had done to earn their ire—and she must have done something—there was no excuse for their dishonorable treatment of the lady of the castle.

"I should have all of ye whipped within an inch of your lives," he shouted at them. "As your laird's widow, ye *owed* her your protection."

"She's a Douglas, not one of us," one of the prisoners muttered under his breath.

"By God, I will teach ye respect," David said, and hauled the Blackadder warrior forward.

The man was as big as an ox and proved he was no brighter by sneering at David.

"Give him a sword," David called out as he brandished his.

As soon as one of David's men gave the big Blackadder warrior a sword, he charged at David as if he expected to cut him down with his first swing. When David spun, the blustering fool lost his balance, and David slammed him to the ground on his arse. David let him get up and try again, just to have the satisfaction of hitting him once more.

He backed the Blackadder warrior across the courtyard with their swords clanging. When he had him pinned against the wall, David took one last powerful swing and knocked his opponent's sword out of his hands. The man dropped to his knees, acknowledging defeat.

David turned to the other prisoners. "Who will be next?"

He fought half a dozen Blackadder warriors, one after another, pounding them with his sword until each submitted and no more would come forward.

When he was finished, every Blackadder man knew that he lived only because David Hume, Laird of Wedderburn, had shown him mercy—*this time*.

"Take them to the dungeon," he ordered. "I shall decide their fate later."

And now, it was time to tell the lady of the castle hers.

***

Alison's head throbbed from the clank of swords. And yet she had been unable to tear herself away from the window until Wedderburn defeated every Blackadder warrior willing to raise a sword against him. What in heaven's name was the point of that display?

Admittedly, she felt some satisfaction when she first looked out of the window and saw Wedderburn fight Walter, the huge, black-haired warrior who refused to deliver her message, and defeat him with lightning speed. The Hume laird exhibited a violent grace with his sword and never showed any sign of tiring, though he fought man after man. He must have grown warm from the effort, however, because after a time he removed his tunic and shirt.

Alison continued watching him as he rinsed off with a bucket at the well in the courtyard. Though he was a vile brute, she understood why other women might sigh over the sight of him shirtless. How different his lean, muscled torso looked from her husband's. She shuddered at the memory of Blackadder's sagging belly and his barrel chest covered with gray hair. Praise God she would never have to see her husband's flesh, feel his touch, or hear his voice again.

She shook off the bitter memories and joined her daughters, who were playing with their rag dolls on the bed as if this were a day like any other.

She brushed their hair back from their foreheads and kissed them.

"Did that man hurt you?" she asked them again.

"No, Mama," they said in unison as they continued their play.

Her children believed the danger was past. They did not understand that they were now at the mercy of a violent man, the Beast of Wedderburn.

When word of their plight reached her brothers, they would come to her rescue with so many Douglas warriors it would not matter how well Wedderburn fought. They would drive him and all the Humes out of Blackadder Castle.

Alison's task was to make sure that she and her daughters survived until then.

At the sound of the broken door scraping across the floor, she spun around. Alarm shot through her with the force of a lightning bolt as Wedderburn entered her chamber without knocking, as if he had a right to. He looked even more dangerous with his shirt plastered to his damp skin and molded to the muscles of his chest.

His gaze traveled over her slowly, from her head to her toes and back again. "I see you're feeling better."

His remark might have seemed civilized, but his eyes had the feral look of a hunter.

"'Tis best we discuss our business alone," he said with a glance toward Beatrix and Margaret, who had forgotten their dolls and were staring at him wide-eyed.

By "business," she assumed he meant ransom. She did not want to discuss her daughters' worth in front of them, so she did not argue.

"I brought the nursemaid," he said, nodding toward the door, "though I can't see that she's much use."

Alison saw the skirt of Flora's drab gown through the splintered door.

"She'd be fine if ye hadn't frightened the poor soul half to death," Alison said, startling herself with her boldness. "Girls, go with Flora to one of the other chambers."

Beatrix and Margaret looked at her over their shoulders as they trailed out of the room. Alison attempted to give them a reassuring smile, then swallowed hard when Wedderburn shut the door behind them with a thump.

She was alone with her captor.

CHAPTER 7

Wedderburn's unwavering stare made Alison feel like a rabbit caught in an open field beneath a circling hawk. When she realized she was still sitting on the bed and leapt to the floor, Wedderburn stopped staring at her long enough to carry a chair from the hearth and bang it down in front of her.

"Sit."

She had an overwhelming urge to run, like the rabbit when the hawk drops from the sky with its talons out.

"That was not a request," he said. "We must talk, and I can't have ye fainting again."

Escape was impossible, so she sank into the chair and folded her arms across her waist. He pulled the other chair up and sat facing her, uncomfortably close. She scooted back to keep her knees from touching his. If he was trying to intimidate her, he had succeeded.

His silent scrutiny strained her nerves until she had to speak.

"Since ye haven't murdered me and my daughters, I take it you've decided to hold us for ransom." She licked her dry lips and prayed that he had not merely delayed murdering them. "My family will expect ye to treat us well until the ransom is paid."

"A ransom," he said, his hard green eyes assessing her. "Is that what ye think I want?"

"It would be foolish to harm us," she said. "I am the queen's sister by marriage."

"From what I hear, the queen is none too fond of Douglases these days." He tilted his head to the side. "I suspect the only way she'd like to see her husband is hanging from a rope."

Alison had hoped word of the queen's disenchantment with Archie had not reached Wedderburn's ears, but clearly it had. No wonder he did not fear royal retribution.

"Ye make too much of a lovers' spat," she said. "I assure ye the queen loves my brother most passionately."

"She did once, and that is the problem, aye?" Wedderburn gave a dry, humorless laugh. "Violent love slips easily into violent hate."

In the queen's case, that appeared to be true. Alison drew in a deep breath and decided to try a different tack.

"The Douglas clan is powerful in its own right," she said. "My brothers will arrive soon with hundreds—nay, thousands—of warriors to rescue me."

"I doubt that," he said, leaning back in his chair.

"Then ye are mistaken, Laird Wedderburn," she said, annoyed that he did not appear the least bit concerned by the prospect of hordes of Douglas warriors coming to wreak vengeance upon his head.

He leaned forward and rested his elbows on his knees. His coldly handsome face was so close to hers that she could see flecks of gold in his green eyes and drops of water from the well glistening in his hair.

"Perhaps I should tell ye," he said, "I caught your messenger."

"Ye caught Garrett?" Despair washed over her, quickly followed by guilt. "What did ye do to the poor man? Murder him?"

Wedderburn drew in a deep breath before answering. "Nay, I didn't kill him."

"Then what did ye do to him?" She would never forgive herself. "How could ye hurt Garrett? He's an old man."

"He's unharmed," he said.

"I don't believe ye." She turned away and blinked back tears.

"I am guilty of a great many transgressions, lass," he said, "but I'm no liar."

He got up and went to the door, where he spoke in a low voice to someone outside. Unease settled in her stomach as he leaned against the wall with his arms folded and once again examined her at length. The man's capacity for stillness was unnerving.

"I'd prefer that ye leave my chamber now," she said.

"You and I are far from finished, Lady Alison."

Her pulse jumped at the implied threat. "Then I beg ye to say what ye will and be done with it."

She barely got the words out when Garrett stumbled into the room, pushed by the guard at the door.

＊

"I praise God that you're alive," Lady Alison said, taking Garrett's hand and squeezing it.

David watched her greet the old man. Though he was a servant, she treated him with a warmth that put David on edge. She was too soft-hearted. Not the sort of woman who should be with him.

And yet there was no denying he wanted her. Badly.

"I am well, m'lady," the old man answered.

"Though ye did not succeed in reaching my brothers," Lady Alison said, "I am exceedingly grateful that ye tried."

"But I did, m'lady," the old man said, bobbing his head.

"Did what?" Alison asked with a puzzled expression.

Old Garrett displayed several broken and missing teeth in a wide grin. "I took your message to 'em, m'lady."

He was still clinging to her hand and gazing at her with calf eyes as if he were a lovesick lad of twelve.

"That's enough," David said. "Release the lady."

The old man dropped her hand as if it were a burning pot on the fire.

"Leave us," David told him, and waited to speak again until the door closed behind the old man. "Ye made a good choice with Old Garrett. Though I had all the roads watched, he got by us the first time."

David had been sitting on his horse on a hill above the Edinburgh Road when he spied the lone figure crawling on his hands and knees through the tall grass. For days, he had expected the Lady of Blackadder to attempt to get a message through to her Douglas kin. He and his men kept watch on the road, hoping to catch the messenger on his way to Edinburgh, or failing that, to see the Douglas warriors galloping out of Edinburgh in time to withdraw and postpone their attack on Blackadder Castle.

What had puzzled David about the fellow sneaking through the grass was that he was traveling in the wrong direction. He'd nearly let the old man go.

"The first time?" Lady Alison asked. "I don't understand."

"I caught him on his return from Edinburgh," David said.

"Garrett got through!" Lady Alison said, triumph flashing in her eyes.

"Aye." He waited for her to realize what that meant, but she had too much faith in her brothers to see the truth.

"If ye have any sense," she said, "you'll make your escape before my brothers arrive with all their men."

"When I caught Garrett," David said, speaking slowly, "he was carrying a message for you."

Her violet eyes went wide as David handed her the parchment from the leather pouch at his belt. The seal was broken—he had read it, of course—but it was clearly recognizable. From the way her hand trembled as she took the letter from him, she must have an inkling of what was in it.

He watched her closely as she read it. She drew her delicate brows together, forming a slight crease. Then she drew in a sharp breath, and the color drained from her face.

"Come, sit down," he said and took her arm.

She showed no awareness of his presence as he guided her back to her chair. Her gaze was unfocused, and she sat down hard. He took the chair opposite, where he could watch her face to gauge her reaction.

"My brothers knew of my plight and did not come," she said in a whisper. A single tear slid down her cheek.

David prided himself on his steady nerves, but that tear sent panic racing through his veins. *Merciful God, don't let her fall to weeping.*

She should have known not to expect better of the Douglases, being one herself. Perhaps now she would be ready to accept her fate.

"They could have saved me," she said, her voice so low he could barely hear her. Finally, she raised her gaze from the parchment, and the pain in her beautiful eyes struck him like a fist in the chest.

"It would make no difference, lass, if your brothers had come," he said, lifting her chin with his finger. "Once I made up my mind to take you and your castle, no one could have saved ye."

***

Alison was vaguely aware that Wedderburn's finger was under her chin, but she did not push him away. After the shock of her brothers' abandonment, it took all her strength just to remain upright.

The words on the parchment still burned across her vision.

Have patience, dear sister, and take heart. Every day, more men join our side, and I am certain we shall soon restore our family to our former glory. Once our success is assured, I will send help at the soonest possible moment.

Until then, hold fast.
Archie

George's scribbled note across the bottom of the letter hurt her even more than Archie's callous refusal to come to her aid. George had always been her ally. If Archie showed some initial reluctance, George was supposed to persuade him. Archie listened to him. George *could* have persuaded him.

My darling Allie, be brave. If the worst should happen, do not underestimate the power of a pretty and clever lass to bend a man's will.

Your most affectionate brother,
George

Her life and the lives of her daughters were at stake, and her brothers advised her to "hold fast" and bat her eyelashes.

She pushed Wedderburn's finger away and tried to gather herself. Because her brothers were too busy to protect them, she and her daughters had already lost their home. And now this glorified night raider would calculate their worth and demand a ransom. Fortunately, a ransom would not require her brothers to divert their precious warriors.

"My brothers do not place as high a value on me as I thought," she said, her voice wobbling just a bit. "Nonetheless, they will pay a reasonable ransom. May I ask how much ye intend to demand for us?"

She prayed her brothers would not dither over the cost and leave her at the mercy of the murderous Humes for long.

"I'll not seek a ransom," Wedderburn said, his eyes never leaving her face.

"No ransom?" Alison blinked at him. "You'll simply let us go?"

Hope soared in her heart. This ordeal would soon be over. She would pack at once. What would she be allowed to take with her? Not her jewels, but perhaps a few gowns. Beatrix and Margaret would weep bitterly if they had to leave their ponies. Was there any hope the Beast of Wedderburn would let the girls keep them?

"Nay." Wedderburn's deep voice interrupted her thoughts.

For a moment, she thought she must have spoken aloud and he was refusing her request. Her heart sank to her feet as she realized he was saying nay to more than the ponies.

"I cannot let ye go," he said, his tone as unrelenting as the north wind.

"But why?" she asked. "If you're not holding us for ransom, what other reason could ye have for..." Her voice trailed off as the only other possibility came to her.

She could not breathe. Nay, this could not be happening to her. Not again.

And yet Wedderburn was looking at her as if he thought he already owned her.

CHAPTER 8

"I'm taking ye for my wife," David informed her, though he could see that she already understood.

"I will *not* marry you." She stood and backed away from him with her hands clenched. "I refuse."

David chastised himself again for his lack of foresight. Since the day of his father and uncle's execution, he had planned every step that brought him here. Wedding the widow was always a part of his plan—the central piece. And yet he had failed to consider that she might be obstinate about accepting her situation.

Not that it made a damned bit of difference to the outcome, but he should have anticipated this complication.

"I cannot permit ye to refuse," he said. "The wedding will take place as soon as my brothers arrive."

"Brothers?" She looked horror-struck. "There are more like you?"

By the saints, David wished he'd refilled his flask with whisky before starting this conversation with her.

"My brothers should be here tomorrow," he said between his teeth. "That gives ye a full day to accustom yourself to the notion of being my wife."

"An entire day? How very considerate," she said, folding her arms. "But I assure ye that a year and a day would not suffice."

As irritating as he found her tone, he preferred her temper to the despair she had shown earlier. He hoped anger sharpened her wits, as it always did his, so that he could reason with her now.

"As there's no avoiding this marriage," he said, "I suggest ye reconcile yourself to it."

"Reconcile myself to it?" she said, her voice rising. "I'd rather be boiled in oil."

Now she was truly annoying him.

"Many marriages are made under similar circumstances," he said after pausing to take a deep breath. "Once ye think it over, you'll see that this arrangement can benefit us both."

"Oh?" she said, raising her eyebrows. "What possible benefit could this marriage bring to me?"

"For one thing, you'll have a better man than Blackadder to warm your bed," he bit out.

She blushed to her roots. "Don't be disgusting."

David was not accustomed to being thwarted—or to being called disgusting. Though he was aware of his appeal to the lasses, he was not vain about it, probably because he never cared much one way or another if a particular one said aye or nay.

Until now.

"Ye cannot make me do this." She went to the window and turned her back to him. "Please go."

He considered the two obvious means of persuading her. Both were distasteful, but she was forcing his hand. The first one he discarded immediately. Though he was certain she would crumple if he threatened her daughters, he could not make even a pretense of doing that.

That left him with the second obvious method, which he did not like much better. She jumped when he came up behind her and rested his hands on the wall on either side of her, trapping her with his body. Heat seared through him when he leaned forward and his chest touched her back.

"You're not the first lady to wed her captor," he said next to her ear. "How do ye suppose that's usually accomplished?"

"Ye can stick a blade in my heart," she said, "but I will not say vows to you."

"Ah, lass, I fear stabbing ye would thwart my goal."

"Nothing less will persuade me to wed ye," she said.

David sighed inwardly. Why did the lass have to be so damned stubborn?

"I don't need a marriage contract to take ye to bed," he said, hating himself. "'Tis up to you which we do first."

"What?" She whirled in his arms. "Are ye threatening to degrade me?"

Despite the fury in her eyes, her closeness made it difficult for him to concentrate. She smelled like heaven, and her breasts were touching his chest.

"What I intend is to make ye my wife." He made himself say the rest. "If ye don't agree to it now, ye will once ye carry my babe."

"Once I...once I..." She made an ineffectual attempt to shove him away. "Oh, you are a vile, vile man!"

"I am," he agreed. "And one way or another, you shall be this vile man's wife."

***

David pondered his next move as he stomped up and down the courtyard, waiting for his brothers' arrival. Threatening his future wife yesterday had not been his wisest decision. All it had accomplished was to make her more obstinate and make him feel like shite.

What in the hell was holding his brothers up? He wanted to get this wedding over with. He was not as confident as he led Lady Alison to believe that the Douglases would not arrive in force. Her brothers could have sent a false message for him to intercept in the hope of surprising him. And if the Blackadders learned he was here, they would come with every fighting man in their clan to try to thwart his plan.

Once the contract was signed and the marriage consummated, there was not a damned thing the Douglases or the Blackadders could do about it.

Except kill him.

He could not wait another day to bind the lady to him. The risk was too great. But how was he to accomplish it without holding a blade to the stubborn lass's throat? He was at ease leading men, confident in his skills and judgment. As for women, they'd always come to him with little effort on his part. When one became troublesome, he moved on to another.

None of his experience helped him know how to persuade a lass to become his wife when she did not want to. He'd given the lady a day to calm down, so perhaps she had thought it through and was prepared to accept him. Whether she was or not, the marriage would take place today.

As he paced across the courtyard again, his attention was diverted by a charred patch of earth. Odd, how it burned in the shape of a rectangle. He was about to ask someone what had caused it when the guards shouted that his brothers were nearing the castle.

A short time later, the gate creaked open, and David was relieved to see Robbie and Will ride in with a guard of twenty Hume warriors. He always felt better having his brothers close by where he could watch over them—and he wanted to get this wedding over and done with.

"I'm marrying Blackadder's widow today," David told his brothers as soon as they dismounted. "Come, ye shall meet the lady and her daughters before ye change for the wedding."

His brothers stood in place with their mouths gaping open like baby birds.

"Ye brought your best clothes, as I ordered?" he asked.

"You're marrying her?" Robbie asked, his eyebrows almost reaching his hairline. "Why?"

"'Tis all part of the plan," David said, and waved for them to follow him.

"But isn't she old?" Robbie asked as the two boys trotted beside him across the courtyard. "Ach, I'll wager she's ugly as well."

"If David wants to wed her," Will said, "she must be verra pretty—and kind, too."

She *must be kind*? Where in the hell did Will get these notions?

"You're to be courteous to Lady Alison and her daughters," he warned his brothers as he charged up the steps. "Don't behave like ill-bred heathens."

"We're not ill-bred heathens," Robbie said.

"Just pretend your mother is watching," he said, "and act accordingly."

David was going to follow his own advice and be goddamned pleasant.

CHAPTER 9

"I hate stitching," Beatrix said. "Why can't we leave our chamber?"

"Needlework is an important skill," Alison said, doing her best to hide her anxiety behind a smile. "And I've already told ye that I cannot allow ye to run loose with all the strange men in the castle."

She was finding it increasingly difficult to divert the girls, and it did not help that she was exhausted after lying awake all night trying to think of a way to escape the castle—and Wedderburn. By dawn, she had come to the conclusion that her only hope was to delay the marriage long enough to be rescued.

"How much longer will the strange men be here?" Beatrix asked, resting a plump cheek on the heel of her hand.

"I don't know, sweetling," Alison said. "Not long, I hope."

Panic closed her throat when she considered just how long it could take Archie to settle his dispute with the queen. She forced herself to push the thought aside. She must hold out hope.

At the sound of a knock on the door, she bolted to her feet, sending her needlework tumbling to the floor.

"My brothers have arrived," Wedderburn's deep voice came through the door. "I've brought them to meet ye."

Her heart raced as she imagined being encircled by half a dozen warriors in Wedderburn's image. If she did not unbar the door, which had just been repaired, he would only break it down again. At least he had made a pretense of knocking this time.

After drawing a deep breath, she shoved the bar back and opened the door. She barely had time to step aside before Wedderburn strode into the room.

His physical presence overwhelmed her. Though he was a young man, perhaps in his mid-twenties, he exuded an air of authority that made him seem even larger than he was. And he was a big man, a foot taller than she was, muscular, and broad-shouldered.

It was a long moment before she noticed the two others who came into the room behind him. Instead of the dangerous-looking warriors she expected, all she saw was a pair of lads.

"These are my brothers, Robert and William," Wedderburn said.

Neither bore a strong resemblance to him, though the older lad had something of Wedderburn's fierceness in his eyes and stance. The younger one was still a child and had warm brown eyes.

"Robbie is fourteen, and Will is ten," Wedderburn said, pointing at each in turn.

"Ye look like a fairy queen," Will said, and gave her an open smile that was hard to resist. "I told Robbie you'd be pretty."

Before she could respond, Robbie jabbed an elbow into his side.

"But she is!" Will said.

"Enough." Wedderburn's voice caused both boys to snap their attention to him.

Evidently he ruled his young brothers with an iron hand. Alison prayed that if she married him, he would ignore her daughters as their father had.

If she married him?

She was startled to realize she had begun to believe it might actually happen. Unless help arrived quickly, she would, indeed, become the fearsome Beast of Wedderburn's wife.

Alison could not find her voice to introduce her daughters, who had scrambled to her side and were gawking at the boys. Robbie took a step back, as if the girls' blatant interest made him uneasy.

"These wee lassies are Beatrix and Margaret," Wedderburn said, and gave the girls a smile, not the cold one she had seen before, but a flash of warmth that she could almost swear held a trace of affection.

Was it possible that this warrior who broke down doors and threatened to dishonor her had a soft spot for her daughters? In that brief moment when the smile reached his eyes, he was not so frightening, and she was able to see that he was a remarkably handsome man.

When the girls made pretty curtsies, the older boy looked over his shoulder toward the door, evidently wishing to escape.

"I brought you girls a gift," the younger boy said as he lifted the leather bag off his shoulder and dropped to one knee.

Wedderburn cast a questioning look at Robbie, who made a face and shrugged. When Will reached inside the bag, Beatrix and Margaret crowded around him, blocking Alison's view. A moment later, their squeals and shrieks pierced her ears. Before she could move, Wedderburn had picked up both girls and stood with one dangling from each arm.

"'Tis only a puppy, David," the boy said, looking up at Wedderburn. "I promise he won't hurt them."

From this, Alison drew two startling conclusions. Wedderburn must have believed the girls screamed out of fear and acted instinctively to protect them.

And his name was David. She tried it on her tongue. *David*. A strong name, but not one that suited a harsh man.

"Mind your hands," he commanded the girls. "A pup's teeth are razor sharp."

As soon as he set the girls on their feet, they began petting and cooing over the wiggling bundle of black and white fur in Will's arms.

"I know ye lost your da," Will said, "so I brought Jasper here to cheer ye up."

Alison bit her lip. What a thoughtful boy.

"Take them all outside," Wedderburn told Robbie, who gave him a pained expression.

"We can't go," Margaret said, her bottom lip coming out. "Mama says it's not safe for us."

Beatrix glared at her sister.

"Your mother needn't worry," Wedderburn said, placing his large hands on top of her daughters' heads. "Remember what I told ye?"

"That we're your responsibility now," Beatrix said, smiling up at him, "and you'll protect us."

"Aye," he said, shifting his gaze to Alison, "as will my brothers and every one of my men."

Questions swirled in Alison's head. How in heaven's name had he won over Beatrix? Could she trust his word? Could he ensure her daughters would be safe with his men?

She drew in a sharp breath as Wedderburn stepped next to her.

"Do ye believe," he said next to her ear, "that the women of this castle would have been left untouched if I had not ordered it?"

Her hand went to her throat as she considered what could have happened—what she, in fact, had expected to happen—when the castle fell. As a highborn lady, she would have been spared violent rape by the common men, but the serving women surely would have suffered that harsh fate if Wedderburn had not commanded his men not to harm them.

"May we go?" Beatrix pleaded.

Alison nodded her assent, and her daughters ran down the stairs, laughter and barks echoing behind them.

In the end, it was not Wedderburn's words that persuaded her to entrust her daughters' safety to their captor as much as his instinctive act to protect them when they screamed. Her daughters would suffer no harm while Wedderburn held the castle.

The same could not be said for her. She remembered his threat well. *One way or another, you shall be this vile man's wife.*

***

"We must talk seriously now about this marriage." Wedderburn signaled for her to sit on the bench beneath the window. When she hesitated, he said, "Would ye prefer the bed?"

She dropped onto the bench and folded her hands in her lap. "There's nothing to discuss."

He settled next to her, crowding her, and stretched out his long legs. Though the servants had lit no fire and the room was chilly, his body radiated heat, warming her side from shoulder to thigh.

"Ye need a husband who is strong enough to protect you and your daughters," he said.

"And who will protect us from you?"

"Why fight this?" he said, ignoring her question. "Few women of your station can choose who they marry."

"Aye, but their families—people who care about their well-being—choose for them."

"And your family cared so much about ye that they wed ye to Blackadder?" He folded his arms across his chest. "God save me from such a *caring* family."

He had a point. Though her grandfather was in his grave, she had yet to forgive him for marrying her to Blackadder.

"My circumstances are different now," she said. "As a widow, the choice of whom to marry, or whether to marry at all, is mine."

"Ye believe your brothers would allow ye to remain unwed?" he asked, raising one eyebrow. "Ye can't be that naïve."

Archie's parting words came back to her with like a slap across the face. *I'll find ye a husband.*

"Believe me, your brother the earl has no intention of leaving ye unwed for long," he said. "He'll want this castle in the hands of a strong ally who can defend it."

"Then he'll not take kindly to your stealing it."

"Once we're wed, your brother will see the wisdom of the match," Wedderburn said with a shrug. "I am feared and respected in these parts. He'll come to view me as an asset."

"An asset?" she said, her voice rising. "After ye laid siege to my castle and forced me to wed ye?"

"Aye, I'm certain of it."

With all her heart, she wanted to believe that her brothers would respond to the wrong done to her and her daughters with fury, not cold calculation. They did care for her. And yet she would not be in this predicament if they had put her interests above their ambitions.

Now that Archie was the chieftain and earl, would he use his family members as pawns in his power games just as their grandfather had? She pushed the question aside, determined to maintain her composure and argue for her future.

"You've told me why ye believe this marriage would be to my advantage," she said. "But I fail to see what benefit it holds for you."

His eyes darkened. "Several come to mind."

Oh my. She licked her dry lips and did not ask him to elaborate.

"Ye already hold the castle, so ye don't need us," she said. "Why not let me and my daughters go?"

"The cost of keeping Blackadder Castle—and I will keep it—will be far less if I'm perceived to have the *right* to hold it," he said, giving her a smile that did not thaw the ice in his eyes. "Our marriage will save much bloodshed."

Alison felt as if the ground were shifting under her.

"Some of the blood ye save will be Douglas blood," Wedderburn continued. "If I am your husband, 'tis unlikely your brothers will attempt to remove me from Blackadder Castle by force."

He was trapping her with his words, each one another link in the chain he was tightening around her. And the hard lines of his handsome face told her he would never relinquish the castle without spilling blood.

"Most of the other lairds will see that they've missed their chance," he continued, "so I'll not have to fight them either."

"Missed their chance?"

"I am not the only man who wants to gain control of these lands and castle, just the first to act," he said. "If it were not me, lass, it would be someone else."

Alison leaned her head against the stone wall behind her and stared at the ceiling. It had been a foolish dream to believe she could have her freedom. Why had she not seen it? She was the granddaughter of chieftains, the sister-in-law to the queen, the widow of Blackadder and the mother of his heirs. A woman with her blood connections was valuable property. Wedderburn was right. If it were not him forcing her into marriage, it would be someone else—if her brother did not barter her away first.

She would never be allowed to remain unwed or to choose her husband, never have the chance of finding true love. Not that she believed in true love, though she had once, a very long time ago. Her girlish hope for love had disappeared like a wisp of smoke in the wind when she married.

"I know this is not fair," Wedderburn said, "but let's make this arrangement as agreeable as we can."

Wedderburn startled her by laying his hand over hers. His was so large that only the tips of her fingers showed beneath it. She did not jerk her hand away because she did not want to chase away the unexpected kindness she saw in his eyes.

A tiny light of hope began to burn in her chest. But then the kindness left his eyes like a door slamming shut, and the light of hope flickered out.

***

David cursed himself for his momentary lapse. Lady Alison's soft and sweet femininity brought out a dangerous longing in him for something he should not want, and most definitely could not have. He could never permit himself to be weakened by a woman the way his father had. Never.

Men spoke of his father as a great leader, but his mother had been harder, colder, more determined. David took after her.

He reminded himself that he was not marrying Lady Alison because he wanted to or because she was breathtakingly beautiful or because she needed protection, though he could give her that. And it did not make one damned bit of difference what she wanted or how she felt about becoming his wife.

He was marrying her for the sake of his brothers and clan and to carry out his promise of vengeance. She was a means to an end, and that was all she could be to him.

"I hope we can have a cooperative union and be useful to each other," he told her.

"A practical arrangement, then?" she asked.

"Aye."

"I'll ask the servants to prepare a bedchamber for ye," she said, and stood as if to dismiss him.

"You'll ask them to prepare *our* bedchamber."

She arched her eyebrows. "That is beyond the practical arrangement ye suggested."

"'Tis exceedingly practical," he said. "I am the chief of the Humes, and I need heirs."

She dropped her gaze to the floor, and her shoulders drooped on a slow exhale.

"There are benefits to marriage that we shall both enjoy." He brushed his knuckles against the softness of her cheek and brought her eyes back up to his. "I'm looking forward to them verra, verra much."

"Well, I am not," she said with a flash of anger in her eyes. "This is far too soon. Ye must respect that I am newly widowed and grant me time."

Her rejection stung more than he wanted to admit.

"What I *must* do," he said, "is wed and bed ye before anyone attempts to thwart me."

"How dare ye be so indelicate as to speak of bedding me," she said.

"I dare do more than speak of it." He let a slow smile curl the corners of his mouth. "And while no lass has ever accused me of being delicate, I'll try to be gentle, *if* that's how ye like it…"

She slapped his face. While she did not have the strength to hurt him, the lass did put all she had into it.

He grabbed her wrist to prevent her from slapping him a second time and leaned down until they were nose to nose. "We shall be husband and wife before the sun sets."

"I shall not do it," she said, holding his gaze.

"Did ye hear me say ye had a choice?" he asked. "Be in the hall in one hour."

"Or what?" she asked, tossing her head.

"Or I shall carry ye down."

CHAPTER 10

David stomped down the stairs. Why did every conversation he had with Lady Alison leave him feeling like a brute?

Taking the castle was a simple matter compared to taking his bride. While he could not afford to become attached to her, he did not wish to make her miserable either. He wanted her content—and in his bed, where he'd make her more content.

Leave it to Will to think of bringing a gift. At ten, his brother had the wisdom to win females over with honey, rather than threats. Of course, Will had not brought the pup for that purpose, but because he had lost his father and thought the lassies must be grieving too. Will was probably right about that. Though Blackadder was a foul man who deserved a worse death than he got, he had been their father.

Damn it, David should have brought a wedding gift for his bride. He'd had more important matters on his mind. Besides, what in the hell would he give her?

He had informed the servants about the wedding, and they were scurrying about the hall when he entered, cleaning and such. He collared one of the men and pulled him aside.

"I want my bedchamber prepared for the wedding night," he told him. When the servant gaped at him as if he did not understand, David waved his hand. "Flowers, whatever a bride expects."

"The laird's bedchamber?" the servant asked, unease pinching his face.

"Aye, *my* bedchamber," David said, glaring at him. "And move Lady Alison's things into it at once."

Best she know from the start how it would be. Her former husband may have been content to let her sleep in a chamber with her daughters, but he would not.

A useless wave of fury seized him at the thought of Blackadder bedding Alison first and for all those years. He added that injury to the list of the dead man's crimes.

Had their marriage been a close one? Had she slept with her daughters while Blackadder was alive, or did she move there after his death because she could not bear to sleep in their marriage bed without him?

God help him, he was insanely jealous of a dead man. This was not like him, but then, he had never had a wife before.

"Perhaps you'll want to see the laird's chamber first?" the servant asked, interrupting his black thoughts.

"Aye," he said. "I'll have a bath and dress there for the ceremony."

He followed the servant back up the stairs to the floor just above the hall.

"Here it is," the servant said in a cracked voice. He pushed open the door and stepped back quickly.

David's boots echoed as he entered the room. Rich tapestries covered the walls, and the furniture included a chest, a small round table with two chairs, a bench, and a narrow table with a pitcher and bowl on it. David stood in the middle of the room and turned in a slow circle where the bed should have been.

"Where is it?"

The servant had gone pale and sweat glistened on his forehead. "The lady burned it."

"She did what?"

The man sidestepped to the arrow-slit window, keeping his eyes on David, and pointed. "There."

David joined him at the window and looked down into the courtyard. The fellow appeared to be pointing at the charred rectangle David had wondered about earlier. When he realized what it was, he burst out laughing. Apparently, Alison shared his low opinion of her former husband.

"The lass has spirit, aye?" he said, slapping the man on the back. "Shame Blackadder wasn't in it at the time."

He was still chuckling to himself after he shooed away the servants who prepared his bath.

But as he soaked in the steaming tub in his bed-less bedchamber, his amusement faded. What had Blackadder done to make Alison so angry that she would burn his bed? Such strong emotion suggested a fiery passion gone bad.

***

Pride made Alison put on her best gown, a midnight-blue velvet that matched her eyes and showed off her fair skin. Beatrix knelt on the bed behind her to fasten the hooks in the back, a task that had become too difficult for Flora due to her failing eyesight and painfully swollen knuckles. Despite Flora's shortcomings, Alison had not allowed any other servant to help her dress since the first year of her marriage.

When she first arrived as a new bride of thirteen, the servants tested their new mistress and took advantage of her inexperience. Blackadder turned a deaf ear to her complaints, and once the servants saw how little power she held, their lack of respect grew more blatant.

Alison was never sure which of them terrorized her with pranks and worse, safe in the knowledge that her husband would blame her for the loose hem that caused her to trip, the ring from her father that went missing, and the poor dead cat she found beneath her favorite gown in the chest. After that first terrible year, Alison was harder to frighten, and the malicious pranks were replaced by a lazy disregard.

Without a competent maid, an elaborate coif and headdress were a challenge, and Alison did not have enough time in any case. She decided to wear her hair simply, in a single braid with a silver ribbon woven through it. Blackadder had laughed at the makeshift headdress she had made from a piece of the leftover blue velvet and embroidered with silver thread, but it would have to do. She held it in place with a silver circlet.

"Ye look lovely," Flora said, blinking her filmy eyes.

Not very reassuring, coming from a nearly blind woman. But why should she care? She did not want this marriage, and Wedderburn would wed her if she looked like old Flora.

"Why did ye change your gown and fix your hair?" Beatrix asked.

Alison sat on the bench and patted the smooth wood surface on either side of her. When the girls clambered up beside her, she put her arms around them. If she wanted to tell them before Wedderburn came pounding on the door, she must do it now.

"Unless your uncles arrive quite soon," she said, glancing at the door, "I'll be marrying the Laird of Wedderburn today."

"Why?" Beatrix asked.

"'Tis a bit hard to explain." She did not want to tell her daughters how little choice a woman had in this world and hoped Beatrix would not press her for a better answer.

"Does that mean Will and Robbie will be our brothers?" Margaret asked. "I'd like to have brothers."

"No, sweetling." Alison was about to add that they would share a household, until she realized she did not know if the two lads had come only for the wedding or if they would live at Blackadder Castle.

"Will our new laird make ye cry like Father did?" Beatrix asked, her sweet face clouded with worry.

Alison had tried to hide her misery from her daughters, but Beatrix was an observant child.

"I'm certain he will not," she lied, and kissed Beatrix's forehead before her smile faltered.

"Where will he sleep?" Beatrix persisted.

Beatrix must have been awake some of those nights when she returned from Blackadder's bedchamber and cried herself to sleep. Alison should have been more careful.

"For now, you two and Flora will move to the Tower Room," Alison said, combing her fingers through her daughter's hair.

Wedderburn apparently had discovered that the laird's chamber lacked a bed because he had sent a man to inform her that he would make this his bedchamber until it could be replaced.

"I'll sleep here with Wedderburn tonight," she said, fighting to keep her voice calm, "for at least a little while before I join ye in the Tower Room."

Her body tensed with the urge to grab her daughters' hands and blindly run as fast and far as she could. But with the castle filled with Hume warriors, they would not even reach the gate. They would not escape today, and tomorrow would be too late for her.

"I'm scared to sleep in the Tower Room without ye," Margaret said, and leaned against her.

"Would ye feel less afraid if I let the puppy sleep with ye tonight?"

Her daughters jumped off the bench and shouted with joy.

If only it was so easy to resolve her own fears of the coming night.

Alison got to her feet and smoothed her gown with sweaty palms. The hour Wedderburn had given her was gone, and she intended to avoid being carried into the hall over his shoulder like a prize hog. That would only frighten her daughters and humiliate her, and it would not save her from this marriage.

She touched the black quartz pendant her mother had given her, though the only luck it had brought her so far was bad luck, and went to meet her fate.

***

Patrick Blackadder's anger was cold and hard like a piece of ice lodged in his chest.

"*I told ye it was a mistake to order half our men to desert Lady Alison and leave the castle vulnerable,*" *he said to his father.* "*Now Wedderburn has taken what belongs to us.*"

This was just the latest in a series of miscalculations that jeopardized Patrick, their family, and their clan. His father should step aside before he ruined them all.

"*I meant for her brother to see that she and the castle needed our protection,*" *his father said.* "*I expected him to agree to a quick marriage.*"

"*David Hume took her without the Douglas chieftain's permission,*" *Patrick said.*

Wedderburn had taken a calculated risk, wagering that Archibald Douglas would not divert his attention from his fight to gain control of the royal heir. Patrick would have done the same as Wedderburn if he sat in the laird's chair instead of his father.

"*He humiliated us,*" *Patrick said between his teeth.* "*Good God, Father, he released our warriors as if he had nothing to fear by letting them go.*"

The Blackadder men had straggled in without their boots or weapons, and each one spoke in awe of the Hume laird's skill with a sword. Patrick had been tempted to cut them all down.

"*Damn that young Wedderburn,*" *his father said.* "*Who would have guessed he'd dare affront both the Douglases and us, and so soon after his father and uncle were executed?*"

"*I warned ye about him.*"

The Humes were known for their fierceness and opportunism, and Patrick had seen David Hume fight at Flodden. The heir to Wedderburn had fought at the front on the Hume vanguard with impressive ferocity and a foolish lack of concern for his own safety. Against the odds, the Hume vanguard had succeeded in their part in the battle while others failed.

When the two Hume lairds saw that the battle was lost, they ordered their men to quickly collect supply wagons and what valuables they could from the dead, English and Scots both, and abandon the field. They were only robbing the English victors of a portion of their spoils, but that was not how most of the defeated Scots saw it.

"*If Wedderburn took the castle yesterday,*" *his father said, shaking his head,* "*then ye can be sure he's already wedded and bedded Lady Alison.*"

Patrick's control nearly snapped. At the thought of another man touching her, his hands shook with the need to sink a blade into his enemy's heart.

Alison was meant to be his.

He had wanted her since he was sixteen and saw her for first time at her wedding to his kinsman. In the years since, his desire for her had grown to a fever. He had suffered every time he saw her with his Blackadder cousin, an old warrior who was past his time like Patrick's father.

His only comfort was that Alison suffered too. Every time she looked at her husband, Patrick saw the distaste on her face. If she'd been happy with the old goat, he could not have borne it.

When she was finally his, they would make up for those lost years.

"Wedderburn believes he's won, but he's underestimated us, just as his father and uncle did," his father said with a self-satisfied smile. "'Tis not the end of this."

That was the one thing Patrick and his father agreed on.

CHAPTER 11

The hall was utterly silent as three hundred Humes waited for their chieftain's bride to appear. David's temper was rising by the moment. *Where was she?*

He felt like smashing furniture, but a strong leader controlled his emotions, so he remained still. As time crawled by, his men cast uneasy glances his way when they thought he was not looking. The only Hume who appeared at ease was Will, who was staring at the ceiling as if he could see the stars through the roof. Sometimes David found it difficult to believe they shared any blood at all.

He was steeling himself for the odious task of hauling his screaming and wailing bride down the stairs when a low rumble traveled across the crowded hall like a wave. His men parted, and there she was, standing under the arched doorway like an angel descended from the heavens.

Alison was breathtaking in a rich blue velvet gown that clung to her lithe curves. Instead one of those fussy headdresses he hated, she wore a simple, elegant one that framed her face like a portrait.

He was relieved she had come to the hall on her own, but she remained frozen in the doorway like a frightened doe ready to spring away at any sudden movement. With slow, deliberate steps, David crossed the room to her.

"I appreciate your coming down," he said to her in a low voice, and grasped her hand before she could take flight.

He tucked it firmly into his arm and led her back across the room to the small table where the marriage contract was laid out. As she glided on light steps beside him, he took in his bride's delicate profile and the dark braid laced with silver that fell enticingly to the small of her back.

As soon as they reached the table, he scrawled his signature at the bottom of the marriage contract. He held out the quill to her and hoped to hell he would not have to grasp her hand and force her to sign. When she reached for it, he let out the breath he was holding. Her fingers brushed his and sent a jolt of desire through him.

How long must he wait before he could take his bride to bed? The vows and the wedding feast were all that stood between him and what he wanted.

As Alison leaned over the table to sign her name, her braid fell over her shoulder. His gaze followed its path along the ivory skin above her bodice and over the curve of her breast. He imagined loosening the silky strands of the braid with his fingers and kissing the side of her neck as he unfastened her gown...

He was so caught up imagining the coming night that he forgot where he was, what he doing and why. It all came back to him with a start when Alison set down the quill and turned to him with all the color drained from her face. She had decided to accept this marriage with dignity because she could not avoid it, but the prospect of having him as her husband obviously horrified her.

She flinched when he took her wrist, and David told himself it did not matter that she detested him. The marriage was necessary to serve his goals.

When he placed their hands together palm to palm in preparation for the vows, the significance of how this marriage would change his life struck him like a thunderclap. He chose her out of duty, as chief of the Humes, but he would live with her as a man.

He had been so focused on his goals of protecting his family and punishing the Blackadders that he had not considered he would be sharing his table, his hearth, and his hall with this woman. Since laying eyes on her, he had, of course, devoted a great deal of thought to bedding her for the first time. But this black-haired lass with an angel's face would share his bed for years to come, bear his children, and, if they both survived, grow old with him.

And she would rather be boiled in oil.

What troubled him even more than her aversion to him and their marriage was this dangerous longing he had to fight to hold at bay when he imagined a lifetime with her.

***

Alison felt woozy as she watched David Hume, Laird of Wedderburn, wrap the symbolic binding around their joined hands as he recited the words that would bind them together as man and wife. His hand dwarfed hers, and his palm was rough with callouses from swinging sword and ax.

She glanced to the side until she found her daughters and was relieved to see Will standing between them and holding their hands. How did Wedderburn get such a sweet brother? Wedderburn had insisted the girls attend the ceremony, knowing she would put on a brave face for them. She smiled at her daughters, just as he expected her to, and pretended she was content to become the wife of the Beast who had stolen their lands and castle.

The ceremony brought back a flood of terrible memories. Although she was just as powerless to stop her marriage now as then, she was not the naive thirteen-year-old girl she had been ten years ago. At least this time she already knew the groom was a monster.

Unlike her first husband, however, Wedderburn was undeniably handsome. She would give him that. His striking features were harsh and forbidding, reminding her of the old stories of the Norse warrior god Thor. He wore his sun-streaked bronze hair loose, except for two braids on either side at his temples—probably to keep his hair out of his eyes while he was swinging his murderous weapons. Though he had traded his chain mail for a clean linen shirt and fine tunic, he remained every inch the warrior.

She stared at their hands, bound together now, and felt the tension flowing between them. When she looked up, she realized Wedderburn must have stopped speaking some time ago and was waiting for her to say her part. He had three hundred witnesses who would swear she made her vows freely. It would be pointless to provoke his temper by refusing.

Alison looked into the eyes of the most dangerous man she had ever met and pledged her body, heart, and loyalty to him, until death.

The ritual was complete. So why did Wedderburn continue to stare down at her, unmoving, as if there was something more to say?

"As soon as I can," he finally said in a low voice meant for her ears alone, "I'll find a priest to bless our union."

Unfortunately, the church's blessing was not required to make a valid marriage.

"Would a blessing ease your guilt?" she asked.

He turned abruptly to face the hall and raised their bound hands into the air as if proclaiming victory. The shouts of his men thundered in her ears as he led her to her usual place at the high table. He sat next to her in the ornately carved chair that had belonged to Blackadder chiefs for generations.

In the absence of a priest, Wedderburn signaled to one of his men to say grace.

"God bless this food and all of us Humes."

The Humes must be accustomed to such brevity, for they immediately began filling their trenchers from the platters.

"Ye must eat," Wedderburn said, glaring down at her untouched meal.

She did not answer. How could he expect her to eat?

"I apologize that there was no time to prepare a grand wedding feast," Wedderburn said, "with lavish dishes, music, and dancing."

Though the quickly prepared meal was paltry for a wedding feast, it seemed bountiful after their days of want. He must have sent for the additional food to be brought with his brothers.

"I had a grand feast at my first wedding." She fixed her gaze on the wine cup clenched between her hands. "I don't need another."

"Well, this is my first wedding, and the only one I'm likely to have, so I do wish it could be different." Wedderburn tilted his head back and drained his cup.

"Ye wish it to be different?" she snapped, her anger making her forget her fear momentarily. "Ye *chose* to do this and got precisely what ye wanted, while I must suffer to do as ye command."

He pressed his lips into a tight line and did not speak for a long moment.

"I forced ye to wed me because I *must*," he said beneath the noise of the hall. "But I will protect ye better than your own family did."

"So you've told me," she said.

She jumped when he slammed his cup on the table.

"Let us finish this," he said. "'Tis time for the bedding ceremony."

CHAPTER 12

The bedding ceremony. Alison squeezed her eyes shut.

"I understand I cannot avoid…what will happen this night," she said. "But must we observe this particular custom?"

"Aye. I will have witnesses to say we were properly bedded," he said. "There can be no doubt as to whether we are fully and irreparably wed."

Her cheeks were hot with shame and her head pounded. No woman should have to go through the humiliation of the bedding ceremony twice. She remembered vividly the ribald jokes, the men gawking at her, almost drooling. They made no effort to hide that they were imagining touching her most private places and doing the vile things to her that her new husband had the right to do.

"If ye wish your daughters to miss it, bid them goodnight now," Wedderburn said.

She was surprised it occurred to him that she would not want her daughters to witness the bedding ceremony, but she was grateful. She would be unable to hide how much it upset her, and they would fret.

"Thank you for that," she managed to choke out.

Though he spoke of the bedding as if it were just another formality, she knew his thoughts were on what he would do after the others left them alone in the bedchamber. David Hume, Laird of Wedderburn, desired her. It was in his eyes every time he looked at her.

She felt them on her now as she left her seat to kiss her daughters and send them off to bed with their nursemaid.

"Sleep well, my sweetlings," she said, forcing a smile. "Be good for Flora and don't argue over the puppy."

After returning to her seat, she gulped down the rest of her wine to fortify herself and kept her gaze on the table. When Wedderburn stood and held his hand out to her, the hall erupted in shouts. Panic squeezed the air out of her lungs as he led her from the hall. The floor and walls seemed to vibrate with the clapping, stomping, and shouting of the Hume men.

She must have been lagging behind, for Wedderburn turned to give her a penetrating look and tucked her hand more tightly into the crook of his arm. The noise grew still louder inside the stone stairwell, and she felt as if it were pounding against her skull. When she stumbled, Wedderburn picked her up without pausing and took the remaining stairs three a time.

His expression was shuttered, revealing nothing, as he carried her inside the bedchamber and set her on her feet.

Her two least favorite serving women were waiting and led her behind a screen, where they stripped her of all her clothing except for her plain linen shift. In a flash of memory, she saw the dark bloodstain on the finely embroidered night shift she had worn on her first wedding night, and she felt ill.

From the other side of the screen, the hum of voices, shuffling of feet, and barks of laughter filled the bedchamber. The two women unfastened her braid and combed out her hair, jerking her head with rough, impatient hands. After applying lavender water to her throat and wrists, they signaled that she was ready.

But she was not ready. It had all happened too quickly.

When she did not move, the women took her arms and pulled her out from behind the screen. She let her hair fall forward to hide her face and kept her gaze on her bare feet as the two women led her across the room to the bed. Still, the buzz of male voices filled her ears, and she felt their eyes on her, stripping her of the thin shift.

The women folded back the bedclothes and scattered dried flower petals on the sheets. An odd gesture, as if there was a grain of romance to this forced marriage or what would happen in this bed tonight. She risked a glance at Wedderburn, who stood still fully clothed on the other side of the bed. His expression was stony, as if he were already displeased with her.

At least she was not a thirteen-year-old virgin this time. Nothing could be as terrible as that. *Nothing*. She had been wrong to believe that memory was safely buried beneath the later years of Blackadder's tedious but demeaning routine in the bedchamber.

He had used her body without a hint of affection, as if she were just another possession he owned, an instrument he could do with as he pleased. She knew other women suffered worse at their husbands' hands. Blackadder never beat her. But he berated her and made her feel dirty, humiliated.

Would Wedderburn treat her the same way? Perhaps worse?

Her hands shook as she climbed into the bed. When she quickly pulled the bedclothes up to her chin, hoots of laughter filled the room. The bed sank under Wedderburn's weight as he climbed into it from the other side, and she squeezed her eyes shut.

Alison fought to keep from weeping as she waited for the public humiliation to end—and the private one to begin.

***

David had witnessed beddings before, but he'd been too drunk to notice if the bride was upset. And if every man had looked at the bride with lust when she was put in the bed, well, he had not seen anything wrong with that. But this time the bride was his, and David found that he did not like the ritual one damned bit.

Alison's prickliness during their wedding feast had irritated him, but seeing her lie beside him looking frightened and vulnerable choked him with frustrated fury.

No man should see his woman in bed but him. His men had the sense not to make remarks loud enough for him to hear, but from the moment she stepped out from behind the screen, they were whispering and elbowing each other. They stared at his bride with open lust while the two serving women took their damned time spreading her rich, dark hair over the pillow.

"Leave her be," David snapped when he could not bear the tortured look on his bride's face another moment.

The two women straightened and stared at him wide-eyed.

"Out!" he shouted at them, then he turned to the others. "You've seen enough! Everyone out! Now!"

They emptied the room as quickly as captured wild horses escaping through a broken gate. David got up and barred the door behind them.

At last, he was alone with his bride.

He paused to calm his temper before turning around. How did this lass provoke such unwieldy emotions in him? Not only rage at those who upset her, but a throbbing desire that threatened to rob him of his reason.

He told himself it was damned lucky he found her appealing since he was stuck with her for life. But he should not want her this much. Alison's beauty had a fragile quality that reminded him too much of his stepmother.

He thought of how his father's blind affection for his second wife had caused him to make decisions that endangered the clan and ultimately cost him his life. Surely David was not at risk of that fate. Love would never find him. What he felt for his bride was only lust, and lust could be sated.

He had all night to do it. His breath grew shallow and his cock hard as he anticipated the hours ahead. Finally, he turned around to join his bride.

God help him. Alison was holding her hands over her face as if the sight of him was past bearing. When he lifted the bedclothes and climbed in next to her, she made a high-pitched squeak.

He stretched out on his side, propped his head up on his elbow, and examined his reluctant bride. Though he was not even touching her, she was trembling.

He had the sense to realize that how he started this marriage could set how things would be between them for a long time. While he could not abide a woman who fawned over him, he wanted a wife who welcomed him into bed—not just tonight, but every night.

Alison presented a problem, another challenge to overcome. He would succeed, it was just a matter of how.

As he watched her, he thought long and hard about that burned bed.

"Alison, look at me."

She jumped when he ran a finger across the back of her hand. Ach, she was drawn tighter than a bowstring.

"I won't hurt ye." He would try his best not to, but she was such a frail thing.

When she finally dropped her hands from her face, his breath hitched and hot desire flooded through him. He was a healthy young man in bed with an absurdly lovely woman. And this was his wedding night. He had imagined being in bed with her from the first moment he saw her.

He could not wait any longer to touch her. Her violet eyes went wide as he enveloped her small hand in his and pressed his lips to her knuckles.

"You'll become accustomed to me in time," he said.

Though it would take all his control, he would make love to her slowly. He wanted to discover how she liked to be touched, to learn the meaning of her sighs, to explore every inch of her.

She bit her plump bottom lip, sending another surge of lust pulsing through his veins. Yet the terror in her eyes warned him to be cautious. Lord above, he wanted her so badly his teeth ached. But not like this. Nay, he wanted her hot and wet and willing.

He was a determined man.

He would make her want him.

CHAPTER 13

Strange, but there was something inexplicably comforting about the way Wedderburn's huge hand engulfed hers. If only he would stop at that.

"No need to be frightened." His lips turned up at the corners in a slight smile that made him look somewhat less forbidding. "Since ye have two children, we both know you've done this before."

Just because she had done it did not mean she wanted to do it again. *Ever.* She glanced at his chest and shoulders, which were all rippling muscle, and her heart beat frantically.

"We're married, no matter how it came about," he said. "We both have needs."

Alison refrained from rolling her eyes. She knew whose needs he was concerned about.

"Why not give each other pleasure?" he asked in a husky voice.

Pleasure? At least Blackadder had never required her to pretend to enjoy what he did to her. She swallowed and stole another glance at Wedderburn. He really was quite handsome. Not that it made any difference.

"Alison is a bonny name," he said, edging closer to her. "It suits ye."

"Thank you," she said, her voice coming out high.

He was so close now that she felt his breath on her cheek and the heat of his body all along her side. The waiting, not knowing how horrid the act would make her feel, was difficult to bear. Her throat was so tight she could not swallow.

"I want to please ye," he said.

She sucked in her breath as he brushed a loose strand of hair from her cheek.

"It would please me to be done with it," she said when she could bear the tension no longer. "Just do what you're going to do to me and let me leave."

He lifted his head from the pillow. "Do *to* ye?"

In the long silence that followed, her nerves were so taut she felt as if she might snap in two.

"Do to ye?" he said again, but this time his tone was teasing. "If ye wish me to pleasure ye first, I'm happy to oblige."

She was going to ask what he meant, but the words died in her throat when he whispered in her ear, "*Exceedingly* happy to oblige."

She could barely think with his warm breath tickling her ear—and then his tongue! The man was far too unpredictable. She clutched the bedclothes as he kissed her temple, the side of her face, and the sensitive spot below her ear. Strange how a murderous man's touch could be so gentle, almost tender.

What game was he playing? She feared he would lure her into letting down her guard so that she would be unprepared when he began his assault in earnest.

***

David had gone to a great deal of effort to make a fearsome reputation for himself. Until now, it had never been a detriment with the lasses. Plenty of women were drawn to danger, judging by how many showed up in his bed uninvited.

He sighed inwardly as he looked at Alison's white knuckles gripping the bedclothes. Clearly, his bride was not one of those lasses who found his darkness intriguing.

Why did it trouble him so much that she feared him, nay, loathed the very sight of him? He told himself he merely wanted a peaceful home and a ready bed partner. Yet as he looked into his bride's pale face, an unfamiliar tenderness swept over him—and it worried him.

He set that concern aside to deal with the problem at hand.

He had never set out to seduce a woman before. He did not have time to waste chasing women. If a lass was not interested enough to come to him, he had not bothered with her. But Alison was his wife, and he was determined to break down her barriers and make her want him. The question was, how to begin?

A memory came to him from when he was Will's age, shortly after his father remarried. He was passing his father's chamber and heard his new stepmother's laugh coming from inside. Curious as to why she was there in the middle of the afternoon, a time his father usually spent training his men, David pressed his face to the crack in the door. He was amazed to see his warrior father, laird of his clan, running a comb through his wife's hair as if he were a servant. She sat on a stool with his father standing behind her, and she was smiling at whatever his father was saying. When his father paused to kiss the top of her head, she leaned back against his chest and ran her hand up his thigh.

David's heart had lurched as he watched the intimate scene, and he felt disloyal for the longing their warm affection stirred in him. Even at ten, he had known with utter certainty that such a scene had never occurred between his father and his own mother.

After Will and Robbie were born, they were enveloped in the warm bond between their parents. Though David would die for his brothers, he had never been part of that tight circle. He did not resent being on the outside—at least, he hadn't since he was Will's age. It kept him strong and focused, unlike his father, who had lost his strength to a woman, like Samson under Delilah's scissors.

David was his mother's son, not the sort of man a gentle lass could love. But neither would he risk the lives of those who depended upon him out of weakness for a lass. Nay, he was not like his father.

And yet he could learn something from that scene he had observed through the crack in the door. He could mimic that affectionate gesture to soothe his bride and get what he wanted.

"Come sit on the stool, lass," he said, "and I'll comb your hair for ye."

***

The Beast of Wedderburn wished to comb her hair? Alison did not know what to make of it. By this time on her first wedding night, Blackadder had ripped her shift and was pawing all over her. She was not at all sure what Wedderburn actually intended to do, but she took his proffered hand and let him lead her to the stool.

After retrieving her ivory comb from the narrow table against the wall, he stood behind her doing nothing except make her nervous.

"I've not done this before," he said, "so tell me if I pull your hair."

Was he jesting? With Blackadder, she had known what to expect, but Wedderburn was a paradox, by turns threatening and considerate.

He lifted the weight of her hair over his arm and slowly drew the comb through it from her scalp to the ends.

"How was that?" he asked.

"You've a gentler touch than the women who combed it earlier," she said.

He chuckled, a deep, reassuring sound. "I do?"

"Aye, though 'tis not saying much," she said, hoping to make him chuckle again.

"If they treated ye roughly," he said, "they will be punished."

"Please don't," she said quickly. "I am sure they didn't mean to." Of course, they had, but the women would find subtle ways to make her suffer in retribution if they were punished.

His "hmmph" in response could mean anything, but she had greater worries at the moment than disrespectful servants. Despite her fears, she felt her body begin to relax as he combed her hair with smooth, rhythmic strokes.

After a long while, he set down the comb, and she tensed again as he knelt in front of her and placed his hands on either side of her head. She tried to control her panic, but he could crush her head between those powerful hands. When he began to rub her temples, she drew in a shaky breath.

Why was he doing this? His handsome face was unreadable. After a time, she found it difficult to stay on her guard. As the tension left her body, it was replaced by an overwhelming tiredness, and her eyes drifted closed.

"By the heavens, you're beautiful," he said.

Her eyes flew open, and she found herself staring into piercing green eyes just inches from hers. She could not breathe with him so close.

"I want ye so badly it hurts," he said in a rough whisper, looking as though he would like to swallow her whole.

She braced herself, knowing what would come next.

"But we can take as long as ye like to become…acquainted." His eyes held hers as he spoke, but his fingers drifted down the length of her arm and then encased her hand.

Her breath caught in her throat when he pushed her shift off her shoulder.

"I intend to become well acquainted with every lovely inch of ye," he said, and pressed his lips to the skin he had just bared. "And I'll have ye wanting me when we consummate this marriage."

His pledge to wait until she wanted him was an empty one, unless he was willing to wait for all eternity. Still, Alison was grateful for whatever time it bought her.

He pulled her to her feet. When he cupped her cheek and locked his gaze on her mouth, her throat went dry. Her breath hitched as he dragged his thumb across her bottom lip.

He was going to kiss her. She knew it would be different from Blackadder's kisses, but she did not know how. Her heart beat wildly as he leaned down, inching closer and closer until she felt his breath on her mouth. When his lips finally touched hers, they were surprisingly soft, and hers parted on a sigh. Despite her fears and the harrowing tales she'd heard about him, her only thought was, *This is how a kiss should be.*

Except for his hand on her face, only their mouths touched. His tongue gently probed her mouth, sending darts of pleasure to her toes. His fingers slid through her hair, massaging her head. Her mind grew sluggish, as if drugged by a potion, while her skin became far too sensitive. Every fiber of her body seemed drawn to the heat of his, so near but not quite touching.

She had heard poets speak of kisses that enthralled like a spell, but she had thought they exaggerated, if not outright lied. She had been wrong. Of their own accord, her hands went around his neck, and with the pressure of just her fingertips, she brought his powerful body against hers.

He groaned and pulled her into deeper, wetter kisses, and she sank into him like warm honey over hot bread. When he broke the kiss, she felt dazed and unsteady on her feet. By the heavens, that was nothing like Blackadder's slobbering kisses.

Before she could recover, he swept her up into his arms, carried her to the bed, and laid her down. She could not catch her breath. After barely touching her before, his hands and mouth were everywhere.

"Ye feel so good," he said as he pressed kisses to her cheeks, her eyelids, her hair, her neck.

He paused just long enough to jerk his breeks off, and she got an eyeful of his enormous, pulsing erection. Fear coursed through her as he sprawled half on top of her and locked his arms around her. She felt trapped, suffocated.

She told herself it would be over soon, and she mustn't aggravate him. Still, a small gasp of alarm escaped her lips when she felt his shaft, hard and urgent, prodding her hip. He drew back at once and examined her with a furrow between his brows.

"Ach, I frightened ye." He was breathing hard. "From the way ye kissed me, I thought…Well, it doesn't matter what I thought."

He moved to lie beside her and propped his head up on one elbow. The candlelight played over the hard, handsome features of his face, picked up the gold glints in his hair, and lit his skin with a warm glow.

"I'm not accustomed to a woman like you," he said.

She was tempted to ask what sort of woman he was accustomed to. Instead, she asked, "What do you mean by a woman like me?"

"You're such a delicate lass," he said, brushing her cheek with the back of his fingers. "I'm afraid I'll hurt ye without meaning to."

She blinked against a sudden threat of tears. No one had worried about her in such a long time. Without pausing to think about what she did, she laid her hand on his chest. She felt the steady beat of his heart against her palm.

He covered her hand with his. "Promise you'll tell me if I hurt ye?"

"Aye," she said.

"If I'm slow to hear ye," he said, and gave her a wink, "just hit me over the head to get my attention."

"I wouldn't want to hurt ye," she said, and gave him a small smile. "I'm tougher than I look."

"Are ye, now? We'll see about that," he said with a wicked glint in his eye.

His expression grew serious again as he ran his finger over her collarbone and along her skin above the neckline of her shift.

"I like to touch ye," he said. "I want ye to like it as well."

Alison drew in a shaky breath as his lips followed the line his finger had traced along her bare skin. She could not reconcile this man with the Beast of Wedderburn, who broke down her gate and challenged every warrior in the castle. At least she understood the Beast.

This other Wedderburn who teased her with gentle touches confused her. She suspected he might be even more dangerous.

"I want to hear ye say my name," he said against her ear.

"Laird Wedderburn."

"Nay, my Christian name." He rested a hand on her hip, firm and possessive. "Do ye know it?"

He dragged the tip of his tongue down the side of her throat, and she felt her nipples tighten.

"David," she said on an exhale.

When he leaned back, the heat in his eyes made her heart skip a beat.

"I like how it sounds on your lips," he said, dropping his gaze to her mouth. "Say it again for me."

She swallowed. Her voice came out barely a whisper. "David."

Tension curled in her belly as he leaned over her. A startled yip came from her throat when his chest touched hers, making her all too aware there was nothing between them but the thin shift. But then his mouth was on hers and drove every other thought from her head. Her resistance melted as his soft, warm lips sent tingles of pleasure to her belly and down her limbs.

When he pulled away, a sigh escaped her. The man certainly knew how to kiss a lass.

He laced his fingers in her hair and stared down at her. The intensity of his green eyes was unnerving.

"What do you want from me?" she asked.

"I want to make ye quiver with need until ye can't help crying out my name when I'm buried inside ye," he said. "I want to give ye such pleasure that every day ye long for the night so that ye can come to my bed again."

She snorted. "That will never happen."

"It will," he said.

When pigs fly.

"I want ye willing," he said with a slow smile, "and that ye shall be."

"What difference could it possibly make?" Blackadder had never cared. He took what he wanted. Wedderburn would do the same.

"It matters to me." Wedderburn's smile was gone, and his eyes looked haunted.

The fearsome Laird of Wedderburn, who rained terror on the Borders, stole her castle, robbed her children of their birthright, and risked the wrath of both her powerful clan and the Crown without a second thought, felt uneasy about taking his rights as a husband unless she was willing.

"Ye feel guilty about this part," she said, startled by this unexpected truth. "That's why ye want to seduce me."

He shifted his gaze to the side. Wedderburn had forced her to say vows and to commit herself, her property, and the raising of her daughters to him without a trace of guilt. But forcing her to give him her body crossed a line, violated a code of honor she never would have guessed he had.

The walls she had erected to protect herself cracked and let in a thin ray of hope.

"For what it's worth," he said, "I didn't feel I had a choice about this marriage either."

She sighed inwardly. Men made decisions and pretended it was fate. Of course he could have let her go.

"But from the first moment I saw ye," he said, "I wanted ye."

Her skin grew hot as his dark gaze swept over her.

"I'll seduce ye," he said, and dragged his thumb across her bottom lip, "because pleasuring ye will give me pleasure."

"I believe"—she paused to clear her throat—"that it is your pride that requires it."

"That too," he admitted, and a smile curved his full lips as he leaned closer.

That smile disarmed her and was quite unfair. But it was nothing to the kiss that followed. Instead of grabbing and prodding at her, he enfolded her in his arms and kissed her as if he wanted to do it forever.

She had never experienced anything as sensuous as his kisses. Though they remained unhurried, they grew deeper and longer, his tongue moving against hers in a magical rhythm. She felt as if she was falling into a dream—but she was abruptly awakened from it by his erection jutting against her thigh.

She broke the kiss and turned her head. Although the beginning was far more pleasant than with Blackadder, it would end the same.

She reminded herself that Wedderburn was using his slow kisses, gentle touches, and comforting embrace to win her compliance and assuage his guilt. The desire he evoked in her was as unwelcome as it was unexpected. It would only make the disappointment harder to bear.

"What is it, Alison?"

It almost made her weep to hear him say her name. Blackadder never did when he used her in bed.

Wedderburn kissed her forehead and held her close. "I didn't mean to frighten ye again."

"Ye didn't."

"Then tell me what is wrong," he said. "One moment we're in a fever, and the next ye lie stiff in my arms."

She was not sure she could explain it—or if she should. But his continued silence told her he was waiting for an explanation.

"To Blackadder—" She felt him tense at the mention of the name and stopped speaking.

"Go on," he said.

"To him, I was simply a body to slake his lust," she said, feeling foolish. When Wedderburn did not laugh or chide her, more words tumbled out. "I was a possession he had a right to use, a woman with no feelings that mattered."

Wedderburn still did not speak.

"I don't want to feel like that again," she said in a whisper.

Wedderburn's eyes were dark with a violent emotion, but his hands were gentle as he held her face.

"You'll never be just any woman to me," he said. "I want to know you, Alison Douglas."

***

David watched her face for signs of alarm as he pressed his lips to her palm. Despite what she said, he did not believe for a moment that she trusted him enough to tell him if he frightened her. He cursed himself for falling on her like an animal earlier. He would not forget himself again.

Besides being a betraying weasel and a royal arse-licker, Blackadder had been an utter fool when it came to this lass. Alison was as sweet and delicate as a ripe peach, and Blackadder had trod on her like a loose bull in the garden. David was determined not to make the same mistake. Though he wanted her past bearing, he must first persuade her that she had nothing to fear from him—at least not in bed.

He had a choice to make. If she were a virgin bride, it would be necessary to show blood on the sheets as proof that they were irrevocably wed. But she was a widow, and no man who looked at her would believe David had waited.

His gaze fell to her parted red lips, and his entire body ached with need. Lord above, he wanted her more than any lass he had ever wanted before. But he was a man who had learned to look beyond his immediate wants, to be patient and plan his moves carefully to gain the larger goal, to attain the greater success.

His cock was painfully hard, and he wanted her hand around it. Or better yet, to thrust it deep inside her. Instead, he drew in a deep breath and accepted that he would not have everything he wanted from her just yet.

"We'll not consummate our marriage this night," he said, his gaze fixed on hers, "but I shall make ye mine."

"I don't understand," she stammered.

"Ye will, lass," he said. "Ye will."

CHAPTER 14

"I'm going to take my time," Wedderburn said. "Ye will enjoy it."

That sounded like a command. Did he really think she would take pleasure in this just because he ordered her to? The man's arrogance was boundless.

He tugged on the tie at the top of her shift until the bow came loose and the shift fell open, revealing a narrow V of skin down the middle of her chest. He leaned over and blew on the bare skin in the gap, a surprisingly pleasant sensation that sent a shiver of awareness through her. When his lips followed, making a soft, tantalizing trail between her breasts, she began to suspect his arrogance was justified.

"You're seducing me now?" she asked.

"Aye," he said with a smile in his voice.

He continued pressing light kisses between her breasts, while running his hand up and down her side. His fingers brushed the side of her breast, and she waited, not breathing, for him to do it again. The next time, he covered her breast with his hand, and his breathing changed. She suspected this signaled that the gentle seduction was over.

Instead, he rubbed his thumb over her nipple, sending darts of pleasure through her. When she felt moist heat on her breast through her shift, she lifted her head and saw that his mouth had replaced his hand. *Heavens.* She let her head fall back. Whatever he was doing felt good.

When he stopped, she stifled a groan.

"Let's slip this off," he said, inching the hem of her nightgown up her thigh.

Her breathing grew shallow as his hand slid up her bare thigh, then hitched when he gripped her hip. He eased his hold at once and cast a worried glance at her face. What he saw there must have reassured him. She caught the satisfied glint in his eye before he pulled her up and gave her a long, lingering kiss.

The kiss distracter her, and the next thing she knew he'd pulled her shift over her head and she was naked. She saw him swallow hard as he stared at her. Without uttering a word, he eased her onto her back.

When she reached for the bedclothes to cover herself, he gripped her wrist and shook his head. She felt awkward as his eyes traveled slowly over her nakedness. But when his gaze returned to hers, the heat in his burned her embarrassment away like mist under the hot sun.

"Ach, you're perfect," he breathed.

He shuddered, and she sensed he was fighting a battle with himself. Wild, confusing emotions ran through her. Without knowing what she wanted from him, she reached out to him and said his name.

"David."

He groaned and pressed her into the bed, bracing his weight on his elbows, and his mouth was on hers, hot and demanding, as if he wanted to devour her. He was holding her so tightly she could barely breathe. These kisses were not like the ones before, but hungry, open-mouthed kisses, full of darkness and danger.

She never wanted him to stop.

He broke away and abruptly rolled off her. Her skin prickled as the cold air hit it.

She starred up at the ceiling, too stunned to move, and waited for him to start shouting at her. She had no idea what she had done wrong.

***

Alison's worried expression confirmed his fear that he had been too rough.

"I'm sorry." Was he always going to be apologizing to her?

If he did not learn to control his passion, he would batter this fragile flower. She was so delicate-boned that, even naked, she looked refined. He thought of Gelis, his mistress back at Hume Castle, with her wide hips, full breasts, and strong legs. He had never worried about hurting her in bed. But it felt wrong to think of another woman while he was holding this angel in his arms.

He swallowed when he looked at Alison's breasts. They were small and perfectly shaped, just like the rest of her. What had ever made him think he preferred large-breasted women? Her nipples were hard, begging to be touched.

He kissed her, taking care this time to hold his hunger in check, even when she slipped her hand around his neck. He gently played with her nipples until he drew little high-pitched sounds from her throat that were gratifying but tested his resolve.

He broke the kiss so he could look into her eyes while he dragged his fingers up the inside of her thigh. Her breathing grew shallow as he moved his hand in slow circles, each time drawing closer to his goal. When he brushed her curls, she startled. Then he cupped her, and her eyes went wide.

Oh Jesu, she was already hot and wet for him. When he ran his finger over her damp heat, she sucked in a sharp breath.

"What are ye doing?" she asked.

"I want ye to find your release," he said in her ear.

"My what?"

He thought about that for a long moment. "Have ye never found pleasure in a man's arms before?"

She shook her head.

Was it possible? Ten years married, and not once? It pleased him that in this, at least, he would be her first.

When he began stroking her again, she tried to squirm away, but he held her in place and kissed her. The lass liked to be kissed, and he took full advantage of it. As their tongues moved together in a slow, sensuous dance, her resistance melted like butter in a hot pan. Before long, she sank her fingers into his hair and pulled him closer.

"Tell me this feels good to ye," he said as he kissed the side of her face.

"Mmmm." Her breathing was uneven, and her eyes unfocused.

She shivered when he kissed the peak of each breast. He circled and flicked his tongue, coaxing her nipple, until she arched her back in silent invitation. When he drew her breast into his mouth, he closed his eyes against a rising tide of desire that threatened to pull him under.

He felt her fingers, tentative and light, touch his hair, so far from the violent lust he felt for her. Wanting more from her, he scraped his teeth over her nipple and was rewarded when her hands fisted in his hair. He suckled her breast, relentless in his need, until she moaned and tossed her head side to side. His hand was still between her legs, stroking and circling, as he moved up to kiss her throat and her face.

She was unbearably beautiful like this, with her lips parted and her chest rising and falling in shallow breaths. Her nipples were rosy and taut. When he rubbed his rough thumb over one, she nearly came off the bed. She was close, so close.

"Do this for me, my pretty lass," he whispered.

He clenched his jaw until it ached to keep himself from lying on top of her to share that exquisite moment, to feel her body clench around him as he plunged into her again and again.

"Please…please," she murmured.

Despite the desperation in her voice, he sensed her resistance.

"Trust me, sweet Alison. Trust me."

He buried his face in her neck as her body convulsed.

As her breathing gradually slowed, he wrapped her in his arms, wanting her so badly he shook. He squeezed his eyes shut as he imagined being enveloped in her liquid heat as she cried out his name. He knew if he entered her now, he could send her over the edge a second time. Aye, he could do it, and she would not resist.

But he had given her his word that he would not. He drew in ragged breaths until his heart stopped racing.

"Is this your way of bringing me under your power?" she asked, a sleepy smile curving her lips, which were still rosy from their kisses.

"Aye."

She laughed, a light, musical sound that he had not heard before but already wanted to hear again. Then she looked at him with eyes that were soft and liquid, and his heart clenched.

Ach, he was the one in danger here, not her.

He made himself get out of the bed and leave her.

CHAPTER 15

David lay awake staring at the ceiling and wondering what kind of fool he was. He was lying on the hard floor of the former laird's bed-less chamber, while the lass who drove him senseless with lust lay in their bed in the chamber above him. If that did not make him a fool, then believing she had never found pleasure with a man before probably did.

Had she lied to him about that? Women knew how to play on a man's pride. He found it difficult to believe her when he remembered how she had kissed him back and how slick and hot she had been under his hand. *Ach*, he was hard as a rock again. He would never sleep.

Without even asking, she had somehow managed to persuade him not to take her on their damned wedding night. Was it all a farce to avoid the risk of conceiving a child before her Douglas clan could rescue her? Her brothers' disgraceful letter should have convinced her to give up hope of that, but he understood that disloyalty was a bitter potion to swallow.

He recalled the last line of the letter: *Do not underestimate the power of a pretty and clever lass to bend a man's will.* Was that what she had done?

He was still awake when the gray light of pre-dawn filtered through the narrow window and someone knocked on the chamber door. Out of habit, he sprang to his feet with his dirk in his hand, then he lit the lamp and donned his breeks.

When he opened the door and saw Robbie and Alison, he swallowed a curse. What in the hell was Alison doing wandering around the castle in her nightclothes with his brother? She had a wrapped a plaid around her shoulders but her feet were bare. The lass could catch her death of cold. He stepped back to allow them to come in.

"I came looking for ye upstairs," Robbie said, "but Lady Alison said ye weren't with her."

He looked at his wife again. By the saints, she was lovely with her hair loose and tangled from sleep. He could smell the faint scent of lavender on her skin from where he stood.

"Why are ye sleeping here?" Robbie asked, his gaze dropping to David's plaid on the floor.

Alison's face went scarlet, and she would not meet his eyes. *Damn.*

"What do ye want?" he asked Robbie.

"Brian returned with news, but he didn't want to be the one to wake ye," Robbie said, and glanced again at the plaid on the floor, "it being your wedding night and all…"

David rubbed his forehead. At least it was his brother who found him here. If it was anyone else, he'd be a laughingstock among his men for not lasting the night with his bride.

"Brian says that the Bl—"

"Wait," David told his brother, then turned to Alison. "Upstairs with ye, lass."

He saw the flash of hurt in her eyes before she spun around and hurried out of the room. Ach, could he not tell his wife to leave a room without bruising her feelings?

"Why did ye do that?" Robbie asked.

"Because she can't be privy to what you're about to tell me."

"But she's your wife now, isn't she?" Robbie asked.

"That doesn't mean we can trust her," David said. "She's been a Hume less than a day, but she'll be a Douglas all her life."

Perhaps he could trust her after she bore him an heir. Her loyalty might shift then, not to him but to their child, which would have much the same result.

"Now tell me what news Brian brought."

"He was in Edinburgh watching for the Blackadder kin, as ye told him to," Robbie said. "Tulliallan and his sons came to the Holyrood Palace to whine, claiming one of them is the rightful heir to Blackadder Castle. They're asking for the Crown's help to toss us out."

He had expected as much.

"They are begging for their deaths," David said.

Blackadder's distant male kin should not inherit over the daughters, but in Scotland disputes over inheritance rights were sometimes determined by the political winds. If they persisted in their challenge, David would take no chances. Dead men could not be heirs.

He did not yet know how deep the Tulliallan Blackadders had been involved in the conspiracy against his father and uncle, but they likely deserved to die for that too.

"Will ye go to the Council?" Robbie asked.

"I don't make arguments or threaten with petitions," David said. "These Blackadders are still in Edinburgh?"

"Aye. Brian rode through the night to bring word," Robbie said.

He could not attack them there, so they would live a little longer. Still, he could not let this threat go unanswered.

"Tulliallan believes his own lands are far enough away that he's safe from me," David said. "I want him to feel my breath on his neck."

**

The wind was howling, and the maids had let the fire go out again, knowing that the laird would not return tonight in this storm. Alison rubbed her arms for warmth as she looked out into the black night and wondered where her new husband was. She had not seen him since his abrupt dismissal two days ago, in the early hours after their wedding night.

She blushed every time she thought of how he had touched her that night. Despite the intimacy, what he'd done did not constitute the joining that was required to complete a marriage. If she escaped before he returned, could the marriage be undone? Not that she could escape with his men watching the gate, and it would be her word against his. David Hume was a brawny man in his prime. One look at his muscled body and fierce expression, and no one would believe he had been unable to perform the task—or that he had been willing to wait.

Why did he wait? And what had she done to so displease him that he'd left her to spend the rest of the night sleeping on a hard floor? Regardless, she doubted he would wait a second time. The way he touched her was so different from Blackadder, she could not help wondering what it would be like…

A crash above her sent her racing out the door and up the stairs to the Tower Room, where her daughters were. Angry shouts came through the open door. She flew inside, not knowing what she would find.

Robbie had his younger brother pinned against the wall while her daughters, who were half Robbie's size, were clutching at his arms and legs in an effort to pull him off Will.

"Stop this at once!" Alison said, and the room went quiet.

Robbie released his brother and stepped back. Defiance shone in his eyes, but she suspected the flush in his cheeks was embarrassment.

"Will, are you all right?" she asked, resting her hand on the lad's shoulder.

He nodded without looking at her.

She lifted his chin and looked into his dark brown eyes. "What happened here?"

"Nothing."

"I saw it all," Beatrix said. "Robbie—"

"I don't want to hear it from you, Beatrix," Alison said. "Robbie, let us discuss this alone."

"But what if he lies?" Beatrix asked, looking as if she was bursting to tell the tale.

"I'm sure Robbie is too big a man to do that," Alison said, shifting her gaze back to him. "Follow me."

She turned and started down the stairs and was relieved when she heard footsteps behind her. Why was this falling to her? She had not expected her marriage to Wedderburn to bring her responsibilities toward these two lads. No matter how she handled this tiff between his brothers, he was bound to disapprove.

She returned to the bedchamber she'd shared, however briefly, with Wedderburn, and sat in one of the two chairs by the hearth. Robbie halted just inside the door and folded his arms across his chest.

"Please sit with me." She smiled and motioned toward the other chair.

After a pause, he stalked across the room and dropped into the chair. She sighed inwardly and prayed for wisdom.

"I don't know ye well, of course, but I've noticed that ye seem to have anger eating at your heart." She regretted being too preoccupied with her own distress to speak to him sooner.

"Will is such a…such a…"

She was certain he had been about to use a foul word but thought better of it.

"I don't mean only this incident with Will." She leaned forward and touched his arm. "I know something is troubling ye. Will ye tell me what it is?"

He pressed his lips together and blinked furiously, fighting tears. Her heart went out to him. Fourteen was a difficult age, when a lad was neither man nor child, and Robbie had lost his father not long ago.

"He treats me like a child," he spat out.

"Who does?" she asked. "The laird?"

"David was raiding and fighting when he was my age," he said. "But he leaves me here with the bairns and old men."

Alison was relieved to learn David was attempting to protect his brother from the violence.

"He says 'tis my job to watch over you, your wee lasses, and Will," he said. "As if I'm a nursemaid, not a warrior!"

Tears of rage were threatening again, and she feared Robbie's pride would not survive it if he succumbed to them.

"I practice hard," he said. "I'm as good with a sword as most of the men."

"I understand ye feel mistreated," she said. "But ye mustn't take it out on Will. 'Tis not his fault."

His shoulders drooped, and he looked at the floor. "I know. Ach, but he is so irritating."

"Irritating? He's a sweet lad."

"Exactly!"

"You're bigger than him, and he's your brother," she said. "The laird is right in saying that it's your duty to protect him."

Robbie sank lower in his chair, and she felt she had made her point, but then he sat up straight again.

"Are ye going to tell David?" he asked with a frantic look in his eyes.

She was tempted to ask just what David would do, but she suspected Robbie had too much pride—and loyalty to his brother—to tell her.

"This won't happen again?" she asked. When he shook his head, she said, "Then I see no need to trouble the laird with it."

He nodded his thanks and stood, ready to leave.

"Your time will come," she said, and smiled at him. "I'm certain you'll be a great warrior like your brother."

"I'm ready now, and I'm tired of waiting."

Fourteen and he was tired of waiting. What could she say to that?

"Will ye speak to David for me?" he asked.

"And tell him what?"

"That I can't play nursemaid forever," he said with a fierceness in his eyes that reminded her of his older brother. "I want to fight for my clan."

What made him think she could influence David? And even if she could, she certainly would not encourage him to take his brother on his violent excursions.

"Will ye be upset with me if I tell ye that I'm glad he left ye here to watch over us?" she said, taking his arm as she walked him to the door. "I don't know your brother's other men, and 'tis a comfort to me to have a man here I can trust."

Robbie gave her a sideways glance and his mouth curved up on one side in a slight smile that told her he knew exactly what she was doing, the clever lad. She was glad to discover he had bit of humor in him, though it was buried as deep as his brother's.

"Please," he said, earnest again, "speak to David for me."

***

Patrick Blackadder stormed into his father's chamber to confront him.

"Writing more petitions?" Patrick bit out when he found his father at his table with his clerk.

His father dismissed the clerk and put his hand up for Patrick to be silent until the man closed the door behind him.

"Did ye hear?" Patrick asked him, containing his rage with an effort. "While we were in Edinburgh, the Humes stole two hundred of our cattle."

"Of course I know," his father said, giving him an icy stare.

"The Beast stole them from the fields within shouting distance of the castle," Patrick snapped. "He's made a laughingstock of us."

"If he hopes to taunt me into doing something foolish, he'll not succeed," his father said in an irritatingly calm tone. "We'll get the better of him in the end, you'll see."

"How long must we wait?" Patrick said leaning across the table. "Surely, you'll agree that we must exact retribution."

"Oh, aye, we'll crush this young Wedderburn," his father said. "But we cannot do it alone. He's gained too much strength. We must have either the Douglases or the Crown's forces on our side."

"I want him dead now."

His father came around the table and put his arm around Patrick, making him want to vomit.

"You're to do nothing, ye hear me?" his father said. "I'm laird, and we'll do this my way."

His father's way led to one humiliation after another. Patrick was so frustrated he wanted to throw his father bodily across the room. Instead, he gritted his teeth and reminded himself that the old man would not live forever.

When his father dismissed him, he stomped up the stairs to his own chamber, where he had a woman waiting for him.

"Come here," he told the woman.

She had dark hair and blue eyes, as they all did. He shoved her to her knees.

How many times had Alison been forced to submit to Wedderburn already? The thought tormented him. Patrick could forgive her if

Wedderburn did force her, but the idea that she might give herself willingly had taken hold of his imagination.

Perhaps the Beast had been her secret lover even before he took the castle. Patrick shook his head. Nay, the Blackadder warriors who had been there all said that Alison refused to surrender even when the food ran out. Wedderburn had to break down the gates to get in.

She was loyal to Patrick.

He fisted his hands in the woman's dark hair to hold her as she sucked his cock and tried to imagine she was Alison. It made him furious when he could not.

"Not like that, ye fool," he said and hit her when she released him.

She was a poor substitute. They all were. Alison would know just what he wanted.

"Get out before I slice your throat."

The woman was weeping and slow to gather her clothes. He could not stand the sight of her another moment and shoved her out his bedchamber naked with his boot at her back. The only lass who could truly satisfy him was Alison.

Patrick would have his vengeance on Wedderburn for stealing what belonged to him—Alison, the castle, and the Blackadder lands. He would be watching for Wedderburn to make a mistake. One day soon, he would make the Beast suffer for what he'd done.

CHAPTER 16

When Alison returned to the Tower Room, she found Will and the girls attempting to teach the puppy Jasper to roll over with comic results. The children's fits of giggles made her worries recede.

"Time for Beatrix and Margaret to go to sleep," she told Will.

He sniffed loudly as she kissed his cheek, then reported, "Ye have a good smell."

"Goodnight, Will," she said, stifling a laugh. She was quickly growing very fond of both of David's brothers.

"I'll send Flora up," Will said as he left.

"Ask one of the maids to come as well," Alison called after him. "My fire is nearly out."

Flora came upstairs as quickly as her old legs could carry her. After they tucked in the girls, Alison returned to her freezing chamber. She changed quickly into her night shift and wrapped a blanket around herself.

She had been pacing the room to keep warm for some time before two maids finally sauntered in with a basket of peat.

"Restart the fire, please," Alison said.

"Feels warm as a fresh dung heap to me," one of them said. "Must be that weak Douglas blood."

"Why isn't that new husband of yours here keeping ye warm?" the other said. "Does he not like ye any better than our last laird?"

Though Alison should be immune to their insolence by now, she was tired and cold. And the remark stung. Why had Wedderburn left their wedding bed and stayed away two more nights? She wondered what price she would pay for offending him.

"Please just do as I ask," she said, and was annoyed at the pleading tone in her voice.

"Certainly, m'lady," the first one said, holding her skirts out in a mocking curtsy.

"Right away, m'lady," the other said, and the two exchanged amused glances.

When Alison turned and saw Wedderburn looming in the doorway behind the two serving women, her heart went to her throat. His towering frame and dark expression reminded her that she had far more serious concerns than surly servants.

"You shall not disrespect my wife!"

Both serving women jumped a foot as David's voice thundered through the room. Then they clutched each other as he came toward them.

"How dare ye accept the shelter of my roof, the protection of my men at arms, and the food I provide," he said in a low, menacing voice, "and repay me with insolence."

A warm glow of gratitude spread through Alison. No one had defended her in a long time.

"We meant nothing by it, laird," one of the women said.

"We'd ne'er dream of doing anything against ye, laird," the other added.

"When ye mock my lady, ye mock me," he said, his eyes glimmering like an angry lion's. "Ye shall not spend another night under my roof. Pack your things and go."

Alison's pleasure over his defense of her evaporated. This punishment was too harsh.

"M'lord husband"—Alison licked her dry lips and took a step closer to him—"they would surely die in this storm."

"What do I care," he said, turning his ferocious gaze on her, "if they wander the hills in the rain and sleet till death finds them?"

The women gasped.

Alison folded her hands to hide how they were shaking. "I beg ye to forgive them."

"My forgiveness must be *earned*," he said, then he turned back to the two women. "I'll wait until the storm ends before I decide what to do with ye."

"Bless ye, m'lord," the two said, dipping their heads.

"Do not give me cause to regret showing ye mercy. I shall not give it again," he said. "Now get out of my sight."

After the women fled from the room, David went to the window and stared out at the black, howling storm.

"I am grateful ye wouldn't permit them to speak to me that way," Alison said to his back.

"Then why did ye interfere?"

She felt her courage slipping away as she was flooded with memories of

Blackadder's angry criticisms. *Why did ye do that, ye empty-headed fool? Can ye do nothing right?*

"I asked ye why ye did it," David said, turning to face her.

"I didn't want the women turned out because of me," she managed to say.

"It was what they deserved." His eyes burned into her. "Never dispute my decisions before others again."

***

David hated when Alison looked afraid of him.

"Do not cower," he commanded her.

Her eyes grew wider still, and though she stood her ground, he could see that it cost her.

"Please," he said, the word foreign on his tongue, "sit down while I get this fire lit for ye."

He knelt by the hearth and retrieved his flint from the bag attached to his belt. A wave of tiredness hit him as he leaned over to gather the peat the serving women had spilled on the floor when they saw him. He had not slept much on his wedding night—for the wrong reasons—and none at all the two nights since.

The dramatic raid fed his men's pride and his reputation, but bringing so many cattle all the way from Tulliallan Castle in stormy weather was a miserable task. And he had returned to the news that his aunt had died of a fever at Dunbar Castle, leaving Robbie and Will's mother alone in her captivity. All he wanted to do would sleep. Nevertheless, he would get to the bottom of this trouble with the servants now. Ignoring a problem would not solve it.

After he got the fire burning, he settled himself in the chair opposite Alison. She was dressed just as he last saw her, as if no time had passed—in her shift with her feet bare, her hair loose, and a blanket wrapped about her shoulders. This image of her had been his constant companion through the endless hours of riding in the rain and wind, yet the memory did not capture the radiant beauty of the real woman.

How he regretted leaving their bed on their wedding night. He'd had a good reason, but as tired as he was he could not recall it. When Alison fidgeted in her seat, he realized he had been staring at her for some time. He shook his head and forced his mind to the task at hand.

"I've seen how the Blackadder servants treat ye, and I'm puzzled how this came to pass," he said. "Ye carry the blood of chieftains and must have been raised to expect deference."

Her cheeks flushed and she dropped her gaze to the floor. His intention was not to embarrass her, but neither would her embarrassment deter him.

"Why is it," he pressed, "that the granddaughter of the famed Bell the Cat, the man who dared to take down a king, is not respected in her own home?"

"My husb—Laird Blackadder—said I failed to inspire the respect of his household because..." She paused and her voice dropped to a whisper. "Because I was unworthy of it."

"God damn him to hell." David slammed his fist on the arm of his chair. "I knew it!"

From the way the servants appeared to act out of habit, he had suspected that Blackadder not only failed to require them to accord her proper respect, but had encouraged their disgraceful behavior.

"I'll not tolerate my wife being disrespected." He leveled his gaze at her. "If any of the servants give ye difficulty, you're to tell me."

"I can't promise to do that if ye mean to turn them out."

She licked her lips, a nervous gesture that distracted him so that it was a long moment before he took in her words and realized she was refusing to follow his order.

"Are ye suggesting I excuse their insulting behavior?" he demanded.

"Nay, but frightening the devil out of them is probably sufficient," she said, glancing at the door through which the maids had fled. "You're verra good at that."

If he wasn't mistaken, the lass was having a wee bit of fun with him. It had been a long time since anyone had teased him.

***

Why in heaven's name had she not bitten her tongue? That was just the sort of remark that would send Blackadder into a rage. When a smile twitched at the corners of David's mouth, she breathed a sigh of relief.

"Ye spoke of the servants," she said, feeling more sure of herself now, "but what about your men?"

His momentary humor vanished, and he narrowed his eyes at her. "What about my men?"

"What if they should disrespect me?"

"They won't."

She thought of how Walter and his close companions had mistreated her. "But if they did..."

Wedderburn leaned forward and spoke in a low, dangerous voice. "Has one of them done something?"

She shook her head.

"Understand me, lass," he said, his eyes sparking green fire. "I'll not let anyone mistreat ye, no matter who they are."

"My brothers said much the same," she said. "Their noble intentions meant naught when they became inconvenient."

Wedderburn grabbed her by the shoulders, and his fierce expression made her swallow.

"I am not like your brothers or Blackadder," he said. "I am a Hume, and I protect my family."

Alison should have felt terrified with Wedderburn holding her in an iron grip and speaking with such ferocity just inches from her face. Instead, she found the notion of his employing all that brawny muscle to protect her rather gratifying.

She did, however, feel a bit breathless locked in his intense gaze. He had the greenest eyes she had ever seen.

Frowning, he looked down to where his thumbs were digging into her shoulders and abruptly released her.

"I didn't mean to hurt ye," he said, and moved back to the window.

"Ye didn't," she said, though he had a little.

"Or to frighten ye."

He was looking out into the stormy night with his arm propped against the wall, which gave her the opportunity to examine his strong profile and tall, powerful frame.

"Ye didn't frighten me either," she said.

"Hmmph," he grunted, and cast her a sidelong glance.

"Don't worry," she said, venturing a smile. "I'm sure ye can still scare any misbehaving servants witless."

This time her attempt at humor failed utterly.

"The Blackadders are poisonous," he said, clenching his hand against the wall into a fist. "I don't like having any of them in the castle. I won't toss them out in a storm, but their days here are numbered."

"What of my daughters?" Alison could not help asking. "Are they not Blackadders?"

"Ach, those wee lasses are sweet creatures," he said, his expression softening. "There's none of *him* in them."

"None at all," she agreed. Blackadder had ignored their daughters, for the most part. She thanked God she had borne only girls, for Blackadder would have tried to mold a boy to be like him.

Wedderburn stared out the window again for a long while, and she wondered what he was thinking.

"Did ye care for him once?" he asked.

She sensed the question was important to him and hesitated, uncertain how best to answer. No matter how low his opinion was of her previous husband, David Hume placed a great value on loyalty. *I protect my family.* He would surely disapprove if she told him that she loathed the man who was the father of her children and her husband for ten interminable years. In truth, she had not realized the depth of her animosity toward Blackadder until she was free of his constant presence shadowing her days like a black thundercloud.

Wedderburn returned to stand in front of her, increasing her unease. Finally, she settled on an honest, but incomplete answer.

"I disliked how Blackadder made me feel."

He ran his finger along the edge of the neckline of her night shift from her shoulder to the valley between her breasts, sending little shivers of pleasure along her skin. "How do I make ye feel?"

Distracted by his touch, she blurted out the truth. "Confused."

"I confess I was hoping for better than confused," he said with a soft laugh. Then he leaned forward and blew in her ear, sending another thrill of awareness through her. "I see I shall have to work harder."

***

Alison stiffened at first when he pulled her into his arms, but she softened like butter as he gave her a slow, lingering kiss.

When she slid her hands around his neck and leaned into him, the weariness and frustrations of the last two days melted away. He would have her now. He was almost certain of it.

Somewhere in the back of his mind, David was aware of the gate creaking, followed by the snorts and hoof beats of horses in the courtyard. But no one sounded the alarm, so he dismissed it and gave all his attention to how good this dark-haired angel felt in his arms. *His* dark-haired angel.

"Ye smell like heaven," he said, burying his face in her hair.

Her breathing grew shallow as he ran kisses along the side of her throat. Aye, his wait was over. Alison wanted him. He would take his time and make love to her all night.

He nipped at her earlobe while he eased the blanket off her shoulders. It dropped to the floor with a soft *whish*. Now the only barrier between him and what he wanted was her thin night shift. Desire burned like fire through his veins as he anticipated seeing her naked and feeling her soft, seductive curves beneath his hands.

He was inching the night shift up her thigh when someone knocked on the door. He ignored it, but the fool only pounded harder.

Bang, bang, bang!

When he pulled away, Alison's lips were rosy from their kisses and her eyelids were half closed. Ach, he was going to murder whoever was beating on that door. He stomped across the room and flung it open to find Brian.

"Ye have a visitor," Brian said.

"Unless it's our dead king come to life," David said between clenched teeth, "he can wait."

"'Tis Laird Cochburn," Brian said before David could slam the door. "He's anxious to speak with ye."

Cochburn was a neighboring laird and an old friend of David's father. His arrival in a storm at this late hour suggested a matter of secrecy as well as importance. Despite that, David was having a hell of a time persuading himself to put duty before pleasure.

"Pour the whisky," he said, finally resigning himself to it. "I'll be down shortly."

He closed the door and returned to Alison. By the saints, he wanted her. And in his current state, he would not need much time at all. Temptation sang through his veins as he imagined taking her fast and hard against the wall. He forced himself to suck in a slow breath. He should not even think of taking his delicate and refined wife like that—and most definitely not the first time.

He kissed her lips again and left the bedchamber before he could change his mind.

Damn Cochburn.

CHAPTER 17

"We are good Scots—we fought at Flodden with our last king," Cochburn sputtered. "Yet we're made to suffer insult after insult!"

Cochburn paused in his diatribe to toss back another draught of whisky and slam his cup on the table. He was a good man, but too excitable for David's liking.

"How dare the regent appoint D'Orsey, that French outlander, over us as Warden of the Eastern Marches. That position belongs to you," Cochburn said, pointing his finger at David. "A Hume laird has been our warden since my grandfather's time."

Taking the wardenship was the least of the offenses Regent Albany and his friend D'Orsey had committed against the Humes. It was D'Orsey, the famed French commander, who Albany sent to attack the Hume castles and take the wives of the two lairds captive while the Hume men were raiding across the border. Upon the Hume lairds' execution, Albany declared their lands forfeit. David had taken possession of the Hume lands and badly damaged castles, but his right to them was not recognized.

And D'Orsey still held his stepmother hostage at Dunbar Castle.

"That Frenchman has lands in his own damned country," Cochburn continued. "He should be home minding them, not ruling over us Scots!"

David shared Cochburn's outrage, but he was careful to show no reaction. Cochburn had come to ask something of him. David sipped his whisky and waited to hear what it was.

"And now the King's Council has taken advantage of my nephew's worthless guardian to quarter a royal garrison—a royal garrison of *French* soldiers, mind ye—at Langton Castle."

"Ach, I hadn't heard that." David understood now why Cochburn was so upset. Placing a minor's property under royal "protection" was the first step toward claiming it for the Crown. "What do ye plan to do about it?"

"Lay siege and take it, just as ye did here with Blackadder Castle," Cochburn said. "I don't have enough men to take Langton on my own if the

Crown sends help to the royal garrison that holds it. I've come to ask for your support."

"I sympathize, but as ye know, I have enemies and battles of my own to fight just now," David said, though he was already inclined to do it.

"Helping me will give ye a chance to do battle with one of those enemies," Cochburn said. "That cursed D'Orsey is bound to see it as his duty as warden to break the siege."

David tensed, afraid to hope his chance had come.

"You've wanted to catch D'Orsey outside Dunbar Castle," Cochburn said. "I'll wager that he'll come himself."

D'Orsey was famed throughout Europe for his fighting skills, and he liked to flaunt them. *The pompous arse.* David heard that D'Orsey loved to joust, for God's sake. While it was true that Scottish kings sometimes held jousts for the court's amusement, in this part of Scotland there was so much violence that men did not need to play at fighting. Here it was never a game, with ladies dropping lace handkerchiefs.

The Douglases spent a good deal of time at Court. Alison might well have been one of those admiring ladies, which only added to his irritation.

"I'll send some of my men to support the siege," David said, and poured them both another drink.

"I knew I could count on ye." Cochburn slapped him on the shoulder. "You're a good man, like your father."

"When will ye need them?" David asked.

"Perhaps a week," Cochburn said. "I'll send word."

"If D'Orsey does come," David said, "I mean to capture him."

"*Capture* the bastard?" Cochburn said, raising his eyebrows.

"If I take him prisoner, I can trade him for my father's widow," David said. "Killing him will have to wait for another time."

That time would come. David would not rest until he had fulfilled both of his father's dying wishes.

***

Alison had to sit down to recover her wits. Wedderburn's kisses had left her entire body tingling and her knees weak. The kisses sparked vivid memories of how he had touched her on their wedding night, which made it even worse. If Brian had not interrupted them…

She pushed those thoughts aside as best she could while she got dressed, brushed her gown, and re-braided her hair. Though the hour was late, she wanted to welcome her new husband's first guest at the castle. David had just told her he expected the servants and his men to respect her. Obviously, it was important to him that she be the kind of laird's wife who managed her household with grace and authority—the kind her mother had raised her to be.

After years of being treated like dirt under Blackadder's boots, her confidence was low. Perhaps she would have been better able to withstand Blackadder's efforts to crush her spirit if she had not wed him so young. Before going out the door, she took a deep breath and reminded herself that she came from a long line of chieftains and strong women. She was not meant to be that sad, meek lass Blackadder had made her into.

The hall was quiet when she entered. The two lairds sat alone at the high table at the far end of the long room, while most of the other men were asleep or talking in low voices in other parts of the room. A few of the men who had been away from the castle with David for the last two days wore fresh bandages. She wondered whom they had fought and why. The Humes had already taken Blackadder Castle. What more did David want?

She recognized Cochburn, though she did not know him well. With his thickening middle, bald head, bulbous nose, and jagged scar down the side of his face, he suffered by comparison to Wedderburn's hard, masculine beauty.

After noticing no food had been brought to their guest, she gently shook one of the servants awake and sent her for a platter of cold meats, cheese, and oatcakes, as well as another jug of whisky. The woman rose at once and went to do as she bid with a courteous "Aye, m'lady." Evidently, David's threat to toss out anyone who disrespected her had already spread among the servants. Though he had done her many wrongs, she was grateful for that.

As she approached the two lairds, who were in deep conversation, she caught a familiar name: Lord D'Orsey.

"A thousand welcomes to ye, Laird Cochburn," she said.

"My friend here is a verra lucky man," Cochburn said. "Blessings on your new marriage."

He spoke as though their marriage was a happy event arranged by their families, rather than one accomplished through siege and capture. She could not quite thank him, but she nodded to acknowledge his good wishes.

"May ye have many children," he said, and raised his cup.

She smiled at the thought of a new babe in her arms. She had given up on having more, another fault Blackadder had laid at her door.

"May that blessed event come soon," Wedderburn said, and raised his cup to her too. Over the top of it, he gave her a sizzling look that left no doubt he was thinking of the act of conception rather than the babe it might bring.

"Ah, here are the refreshments." She smiled her thanks to the sleepy servant who arrived with a generous platter and a jug of whisky.

Cochburn had his eating knife out before the platter was on the table. "Thoughtful of ye, Lady Alison," he said as he stabbed a slab of beef. "'Twas a long ride here."

She had intended to exchange a few pleasantries with their guest, then leave the men to their talk, but they appeared to welcome her presence. With Blackadder, silence had always been the safest course, but she wanted to show Wedderburn—and herself—that she could be an engaging hostess.

"Did I hear ye mention Lord D'Orsey?" she asked. "I'm pleased to say that I met the famed French nobleman several times at court."

"Did ye now?" Wedderburn kept his eyes on her as he paused to take a long drink of his whisky. "I'm surprised, as he is Regent Albany's man."

"'Tis true that we Douglases have had our disputes with Albany over the years," she said, giving the men a bright smile. "But my sisters and I couldn't hold that against D'Orsey. He's every bit as charming as everyone says."

"Charming?" Wedderburn said, and poured another drink for himself and Cochburn.

The two were going through the whisky at a rather alarming pace, and that hard look was back in Wedderburn's eyes. Alison hoped to God her new husband was not a mean drunk. That was something a wife needed to know.

With her mind on Wedderburn's drinking and how little she knew about him, she almost forgot that he had asked her about D'Orsey.

"Aye, D'Orsey is charming and unfailingly courteous as well." She felt a trifle nervous under Wedderburn's silent gaze and found herself babbling on. "I saw him on the lists once, and he is most impressive with a lance. He won the tournament, of course. None of the other men stood a chance. Ye should have seen how all the ladies were sighing over him and dropping their handkerchiefs…"

She was about to add that she had been Beatrix's age and thought the ladies all very silly, when she realized that her husband's eyes had gone from cold to icy and that Cochburn's smile was gone as well.

"You'll excuse me if I lack D'Orsey's exceptional manners," David said between clenched teeth, "but Laird Cochburn and I have important matters to discuss."

She blinked at him. The conversation had started off so well. What had she had done to deserve his none-too-subtle reprimand?

"In private," he added when she was too surprised to move, as if he thought she was too slow-witted to understand she had been dismissed.

She felt as if she had been punched in the stomach. So much for his worthless remarks about respect.

"Good evening to ye, Laird Cochburn," she said, fixing her attention on the older man. "I'm delighted to have ye as a guest in *my* home."

Without sparing a glance for Wedderburn, she spun around. She quelled the urge to run, held her head up, and refused to let a single tear fall before she reached the stairs.

***

Alison awoke with a start when Wedderburn came stumbling into the bedchamber reeking of whisky. Her mother had taught her to avoid drunken men, and Wedderburn could be frightening enough stone cold sober. What violence might he be capable of drunk?

She lay still as death and pretended to be asleep. If he chose to force her now, there was nothing she could do. She hated this feeling of helplessness.

The mattress sank as he flopped down atop the bedclothes and flung one heavy arm over her. She turned her back on him and wondered if she could slip out. He did not appear to notice she was there, but then he mumbled something, rolled onto his side, and nuzzled her neck. Panic seized her when he pulled her against him and pressed his erection against her backside.

When Blackadder died, she believed she was done with being treated as no more than a body to accommodate her husband's needs. That brief taste of freedom had changed her.

"I won't have this!" She shoved Wedderburn's arm off her and scrambled out of the bed.

Unfortunately, she was on the far side from the door. She clenched her hands, fear coursing through every muscle, and prepared to defend herself, though she was aware that the effort would be utterly useless. She knew better than to fight. From Blackadder, she had learned it was far less humiliating and painful to submit at the outset. And yet she could not do it.

She waited, but nothing happened. When her heart stopped beating so loudly in her ears, she heard a snore coming from the bed. She put her hand to her chest and tried to calm herself as she listened to Wedderburn's steady breathing. When she was certain he was sound asleep, she tiptoed to the chair where she had draped her gown. Then, keeping an eye on his still form sprawled across the bed, she dressed in the near darkness and fled.

CHAPTER 18

Alison lay awake the rest of the night, squeezed between her daughters and snoring Flora, dreading the coming day. When morning finally came, damp and dreary, she was tempted to send the girls and Flora down to breakfast without her and spend the day with the bedclothes pulled over her head. Instead, she kissed her daughters good morning, helped them dress, and steeled herself to face Wedderburn.

When they went downstairs, she was surprised to find that their nocturnal guest had departed before breakfast. Wedderburn was not in the hall either, *praise God*.

Several of the men who had been gone the previous two days with Wedderburn were still asleep on benches, despite the usual morning activity going on around them. During the meal, she overheard bits of conversation from the others about how many they had fought and riding through the night.

She wondered again where they had gone and why. Her new husband appeared to have plans beyond taking the Blackadder castle—and her.

When he did not appear at the noon meal either, she took a tray of food to leave outside their chamber door. Though Wedderburn would come downstairs eventually and find her, ready food might buy her more time. Balancing the tray on one hip, she pressed her ear against the freshly mended door. When all seemed quiet inside, she heaved a sigh of relief.

The door suddenly opened, and she screamed as she fell into Wedderburn with her tray. The expanse of his bare chest filled her vision. A quick glance downward revealed that at least he wore his breeks. Slowly, she lifted her gaze to his face. With the dark shadow on his unshaven jaw and his hair falling across his eyes, he looked startlingly handsome.

And even more dangerous.

***

Alison's scream pierced David's skull like a hot spike through his eye. He'd only crawled out of bed because of his growling stomach, and he had no notion why she was staring at him as if she'd discovered a demon haunting her bedchamber.

He was a starving man, so he took the tray from her before she dropped it, then searched his mind for an explanation for that look she was giving him. He was groggy after three nights of little sleep and then waking up in the middle of the day. The whisky had not helped either.

Slowly, memories from the night before began to churn through his head. They went from good to bad, to worse, to still worse, starting with an image of Alison's eyes half closed and her lips red from kissing him, and ending with a vague recollection of a drunken attempt to bed her.

Well, that explained the look. He had lost ground in his battle to win her, but he was not a man to let adversity stall him for long. The smell of savory stew made his stomach rumble again, reminding him of another pressing need.

"Thank ye for bringing this. I'm near death with hunger." He stopped himself from ordering her to come in and asked, "Will ye keep me company while I eat it?"

Alison looked wary, but after a brief hesitation, she nodded. As she sidestepped past him, he caught a tantalizing whiff of lavender.

She sat primly in one of the chairs and folded her hands while she watched him work his way through the bowl of steaming venison stew. When he finished, he set the bowl aside and sat back. With his hunger for food satisfied, his craving for her took hold of him. He did not understand why he found her primness so alluring, but he did.

"I have some things I wish to discuss," she said, sitting up straighter still.

Talk was not what he had in mind, but he could see that it was unavoidable and nodded for her to proceed.

"First, I'd like to ask ye a question," she said.

He took a long drink of the ale she had brought. He was thirsty as hell after all the whisky he'd drunk with Cochburn last night.

"Was last night unusual," she asked, "or do ye make a habit of becoming falling-down drunk?"

He nearly spewed a mouthful of ale. "I wasn't that drunk," he said once he recovered. "And nay, I don't make a habit of it."

Alison gave him a skeptical look, which annoyed him. Hearing his mother's voice in his head, lecturing him that strong drink was a vice of weak-willed men, did not improve his mood. If he had not been exhausted, the whisky would not have affected him like that.

"A man who has as many enemies as I do cannot afford to dull his mind with drink," he said.

That seemed to satisfy her. *Christ.*

"Anything else ye wish to ask me?" he said.

She ran her tongue over her lip, that nervous gesture of hers that made him forget for a moment why he was annoyed.

"What did I do to upset ye when we were speaking with Cochburn last night?" she asked.

"Ye didn't upset me," he said. "I don't get upset."

She arched an eyebrow.

"I merely suggested ye leave so that Cochburn and I could finish our business."

He had suggested it strongly, but what was wrong with that? He was the laird, for God's sake. He did not owe her an explanation. But then he remembered how he'd made her look like a puppy that had been kicked last night and decided to explain himself anyway.

"Ye spoke well of my enemy, D'Orsey," he said.

"The charming French knight?" she asked. "What could ye have against him?"

"He holds my father's widow hostage."

Alison drew her brows together. "You're speaking of Will and Robbie's mother?"

"Aye," he said. "My father's second wife."

"I assumed she was at Hume Castle," she murmured, then she looked up sharply. "Surely ye don't fear D'Orsey will harm her?"

"Not permitting her to return home to grieve for her dead husband with her family is harming her," he said. "And not permitting her to comfort her young sons is harming them."

Alison was quiet for a long while, and David's thoughts turned to his stepmother, whose delicate health worried him. His duty to free her weighed heavily on him.

"Ach, the poor lads. I suppose that is one of the reasons Robbie seems so troubled," Alison said, shaking her head. "He's the other subject I wished to discuss with ye."

"My brother?" Good God, why?

"He asked me to speak to ye on his behalf."

Why would his brother confide in Alison? Robbie hardly knew her. If his brother had something to say to him, he could damn well say it himself.

All the same, David kept silent and waited for her to tell him what this was about.

"Robbie wants ye to treat him like a man—which, of course, he isn't," she said. "I was relieved when he told me that ye refuse to take him...wherever it is that ye go."

He almost smiled. Robbie had made a mistake in choosing Alison as his emissary.

"In truth, I cannot keep him from the fighting and raiding much longer," David said. "Robbie will be a man soon."

"Be that as it may," she said in a tone that suggested she disagreed, "I hate to see him so unhappy. And he's a bit hard on Will."

"If Robbie's done something he ought not, tell me and I'll punish him."

"He's done nothing," she said a mite too quickly. "But I am worried about him."

"Robbie is right that Will acts in ways that invites jests from some of the young warriors." He leaned on his elbows and ran his hands through his hair. "I fear I've been too soft on him."

David was not accustomed to discussing his problems—especially problems involving his brothers—with anyone. But Alison was not going to mock the lads, so he saw no harm in it. And hard as it was to admit, he could use some advice.

"Will is just fine as he is," Alison said with a flash of fire in her eyes.

He liked that she defended his brother, though she obviously did not know a damned thing about what it would take for a lad to gain respect from the men.

"Ye needn't worry about Will," she said. "He's kind, but he's not weak. That lad has a mind of his own."

That was true enough. "All the same, I can't have my brother being ridiculed. In the long run, it will do both him and the clan harm."

"I have an idea..." She looked up at him from beneath her lashes as if waiting for him to object. When he didn't, she said, "I understand Robbie has become rather good with a sword."

"He has," David agreed, though he had no notion why she was mentioning that now.

"Why not give him the task of training Will?" she asked.

"I should train Will, just as I've trained Robbie."

All the experienced warriors helped train the younger ones, but his brothers' training merited his personal attention. One day they would fight at his side and play important roles in the clan. He owed it to them and to the clan to see that they became the most skilled and cunning warriors they could be.

"I've been preoccupied with other matters, but that's no excuse." He had spent countless hours training Robbie, and Will deserved no less.

"Ye weren't laird when ye trained Robbie," she said. "When Will is older and more skilled, he'll need your instruction. But surely he could learn a great deal from Robbie now."

The more he thought about it, the more David saw the merit in Alison's suggestion. Will would gain warrior skills, and Robbie would feel recognized for his.

"Lord knows I don't know what else to do with them," he said, rubbing his face. "'Tis worth a try."

Alison blessed him with a smile that lit up her eyes and made his stomach flip. Odd, how she seemed to reward him when he showed weakness. Ach, women.

Regardless, a clever warrior took advantage of an opening when he saw one. With one sweep of his arm, he pulled her onto his lap. Her eyes went wide, but when he was careful to do nothing more to alarm her, she stayed put. Her soft bottom felt good resting on his thigh. He would content himself with that for the moment.

She ran her tongue over her lip again, and he nearly forgot his resolve to wait to kiss her.

"I was surprised Cochburn was gone before breakfast," she said. "That was a short visit."

"Hmmph." She obviously wanted to know what brought Cochburn to the castle, but David saw no good reason to share Cochburn's plans with her—and plenty of reason not to.

"Odd, his coming and going in the night," she said, though she must have read David's silence. "What did he want?"

Why did she persist? Had she found a means to send word of his activities to her brothers? Or worse, was she spying for the Blackadders? Perhaps she only pretended to share his contempt for her former husband and his kin. True, the women servants treated her with disdain, but David had seen how the men looked at her. With little effort, she could have any one of them eating out of her palm.

"What is your interest in Cochburn?" he asked, keeping his tone even.

"I'm merely curious," she said, which told him precisely nothing.

"We've more pressing matters than Cochburn to discuss…" He cupped the back of her neck and dropped his gaze to her mouth. "…or not discuss."

He felt her giving in to the powerful pull of the attraction between them as he leaned in.

"But I want to be the sort of wife who is a good helpmate to her husband." She spoke in a husky voice and her eyes were drifting closed.

"I'm certain ye can be verra helpful in many ways that we'll both find exciting," he murmured when his lips were nearly touching hers, "but ye needn't concern yourself with Cochburn."

He was so close that he could almost taste her kiss when she shoved her hands against his chest and jerked away. Before he knew it, she had slid off his lap and was halfway out the door.

Damn. What happened?

He was still staring after her long after she slammed the door.

***

Alison was so upset that she kicked the door after she slammed it. She had hoped for a very different marriage, but apparently Wedderburn wished to keep her in the dark as much as Blackadder had. Would she be reduced to listening at doors and bribing servants to have any notion of what dangerous schemes he was involved in?

Ach, it was so unfair. If a man committed treasonous acts, his wife and family suffered for it. Lands were forfeited, reputations tarnished. No one knew that better than a Douglas.

And she wanted to be more to her new husband than a convenient bedmate. He had pretended to listen to her advice about his brothers, but then he deliberately attempted to divert her from the subject of Cochburn—and very nearly succeeded.

As she marched down the stairs, she came to a decision. He said he would wait until she was willing. Well, she would use what little power she had and not give herself easily to David Hume, Laird of Wedderburn. He was a confusing man, alternately intimidating and seductive. Regardless of which side he showed her, she would not give in until he gave her what she wanted.

She did not fool herself that it would be easy. When he put his mind to seduction, he was hard to resist. But no matter how much she thrilled to his touches and kisses, she would make him wait until she was not just another woman to him, not just a body he had a right to use. He could take her against her will if he chose.

But, damn it, if he wanted her willing, David would know who she was when he was inside her. It would *matter* to him who she was.

He would want *her*.

CHAPTER 19

Alison regretted her display of anger, fearing what her punishment would be. If she had slammed the door and walked out on Blackadder like that, he would have chased her down and pulled her back by her hair.

She shook her head to clear it—she would not permit herself to spend one more moment recalling the despicable things Blackadder had done to her. If God was just, he would burn like his bed.

To avoid Wedderburn, she spent most of the afternoon in the kitchens discussing menus and checking food stores with the cook, who had grown less surly now that their supplies could be replenished.

"You've outdone yourself with this stew," she said, after taking a taste from the spoon he held out.

His permanent frown eased into what was probably a smile for him. Winning him over was not as difficult as she thought, and she regretted not trying harder sooner. Blackadder had made such a mouse of her.

"We've plenty of beef, thanks to these Humes," the cook said with a nod of approval.

Alison knew better than to ask where the beef had come from. One did not ask that in the Borders, where cattle thieving was a point of pride.

The cook turned to shout another order at one of the kitchen maids. "Fetch more onions, ye lazy lass."

The kitchen was growing busier, with pots bubbling and the kitchen maids scurrying in preparation for the evening meal. Alison was reluctant to leave the safety of the undercroft, but she could see she was getting in the way.

"I'll leave ye to your work," she told the cook.

Hoping to avoid Wedderburn a little longer, she passed through the hall with her head down and hurried up the stairs. She tiptoed past their bedchamber door and continued up the wheeled stairs to the Tower Room to find her daughters. As she neared the top, she heard the rumble of a deep voice intermingled with her daughters' giggles. She paused outside the partially open door to listen.

"Baaa, baaa."

Who was that bleating like a sheep? The sound was followed by another burst of giggles.

"Moooo."

She opened the door and was stunned to find the infamous Beast of Wedderburn sitting on the floor with her daughters playing with carved wooden animals. Shy Margaret sat on the laird's lap petting a wooden pig with her finger while Beatrix bounced a wooden horse across the floor. All three looked up at Alison at once.

"Look what David made for us!" Beatrix bounded over to her, holding out the carved horse for her inspection.

"Ye cannot call the laird by his Christian name," Alison quickly chastised her daughter.

"I told them to." David rubbed the top of Beatrix's head with his knuckles, making her squeal with laughter. "Ach, this one's a wee rascal, aren't ye?"

Confused, Alison dropped her gaze and examined the carving Beatrix had handed her.

"'Tis beautifully made," she said as she ran her fingertip over the smooth wood. It was simple and yet captured the essence of the animal.

Wedderburn was a complex man, full of contradictions. He was a fierce Border laird who struck terror in the hearts of his enemies—and probably his friends as well. And yet here he was playing with her children, making silly animal noises. He was lethal with a sword and made beautifully carved toys with a small blade.

"Make the piggy sound again," Margaret said, leaning against his shoulder. "P-l-e-a-s-e."

Alison felt a rush of warmth toward him as he made an awful snorting sound that sent the girls into gales of laughter.

She was struck by the realization that Beatrix and Margaret had never been at ease around their father. It was not just that they had no joyful moments like this with him, but that they had sought to avoid his notice. With the instinct of small animals, they had hidden in the corners and shadows whenever he entered a room.

Alison thought she had protected them from seeing the evil in their father, but she had failed.

David stood and brushed the stray shavings from his breeks to cries of "Don't go! Please!"

"I must speak with your mother now," he told the girls. "You two behave yourselves."

Both girls ceased their begging and gave him solemn nods.

Alison's eyes stung as she watched him lift Margaret over his head, and her daughter's peal of laughter filled the room. No matter what evil acts Wedderburn might be guilty of committing, a man who showed such kindness to her young daughters had much good in him too.

"I can see that you're a verra fine mother," he said, taking her arm as they descended the stairs. "Beatrix and Margaret are remarkable lasses."

Nothing could have touched her more deeply, and she felt herself blush with pleasure. Her resolve to resist him was weakening by the moment. Worse, she was beginning to fear that guarding her heart could prove to be an even greater challenge than resisting his passion.

Ach, he was a dangerous man.

***

As soon as David had Alison inside their bedchamber, he kissed her slowly and thoroughly. He wanted to see that look again—the one she'd had on her face when he looked up from playing with her daughters to find her standing in the doorway. Her expression had been soft and held no trace of fear or resentment.

He was gratified when she kissed him back. Her fingers gripped his tunic, and she rose on her toes to meet him. Without lifting his lips from hers, he felt for the pins holding her head covering.

"I love your headdresses," he murmured between kisses.

She laughed and leaned back. "They're so plain. How can you like them?"

"They're easy to remove."

She laughed again, a sound that somehow made him feel lighter. This was going far better than he expected after the way she had run off earlier. He kissed the side of her neck and the sweet spot below her ear as he loosened her braid. When he had it undone, he buried his fingers in her thick hair and breathed in her scent.

He captured her mouth again and began unfastening the hooks at the back of her gown. Their kisses grew deeper, their tongues moved together in a rhythm suggestive of what would come later. Aye, surely it would this time. He reminded himself to go slowly, to savor every moment and every touch along the way. Their first time joining as man and wife would happen but once, and he wanted to make it memorable.

He covered her breast and groaned at the sensation of the soft flesh filling his hand. Unable to help himself, he pulled her against his throbbing shaft. God in heaven, she felt good.

She made a startled, high-pitched sound when he gave into another urge and dropped to his knees to press his face between her breasts. He paused to revel in this slice of heaven before wrapping his arms around her hips and lifting her up as he stood.

"What are ye doing?" she squealed.

"I'm carrying ye to the bed," he said, "where I'm going to pleasure ye until you're begging for me to take ye."

And I'll do it again night after night until you're so pleased to share my bed that you're content to be my wife, despite who I am, despite the wrongs I've done to you, and despite what I can never give you.

He would never say these things to her, of course. Alison must never know it had become important to him that she not regret becoming his wife.

That she not despise him.

He laid her down on the bed and kissed her until they were both senseless. When he slipped her loosened gown off, she lifted her hips to ease his way. Aye, she wanted him this time.

Her nipples were hard, rosy peaks, and her breathing grew ragged as he brought his fingers in slow circles up the inside of her thigh. He groaned when he found how hot and wet she was for him. She closed her eyes, concentrating on the movement of his hand. As he watched her face and soft parted lips, he swallowed against a surge of emotion. She had never been more beautiful, more desirable. *And she is mine.*

He felt drunk on her scent, and the little sounds she made sent bolts of desire shooting through him. He wanted her more than he had ever wanted any woman before.

In a thrice, he shed his clothes. He thought he would die of pleasure when he covered her and felt her bare skin against his. Leaning on his elbows, he eased her legs apart with his knee. He bit his lip against the rush of sensation as his cock rubbed against her silky inner thigh. Ach, he needed to be inside her now, to feel her liquid heat around him. *Now.*

"Say ye want me," he said against her ear, unable to keep the desperation from his voice. She had to say aye.

"Nay."

Why? What in God's name was she waiting for? He had told her he would wait to consummate their marriage until she was willing, but she did desire him. Her body did not lie.

"Not this." She lifted her hand and rested her palm against his cheek. "Not yet."

He was choking with frustration, but he told himself that *not yet* meant *soon.*

And *not this*, meant everything else was fair game... He smiled to himself. Nay, she would not hold out long.

CHAPTER 20

Alison could barely draw breath under David's dark, lustful gaze, which promised sinful pleasures beyond her ken. She was acutely aware of every inch of his long, muscular body that touched hers, from where his chest brushed the sensitive tips of her breasts, to his hard, flat stomach flush against hers, to his muscular legs stretched along the length of hers.

Her attention focused on his hard shaft between her legs, one tantalizing inch from where he had brought her such pleasure with his hand. Her body throbbed there, and she wanted to pull on his shoulders and urge him forward.

She forced herself to remember why she had made her resolution and what she needed from him after their lust was spent. Blackadder had shattered her pride and self-respect, and she wanted them back even more than she wanted Wedderburn right now.

"Not yet, David," she said again.

They both gasped when he moved forward and pressed his erection against her. Despite all her intentions, *aye* was on her lips when he covered her mouth with his and rolled to the side.

He began working his magic with his fingers. *Heaven help her.* She was unable to think of anything except the sensations coursing through her body. This time, as the tension built inside her, she knew what it was leading to, and her anticipation only served to intensify the blinding burst of pleasure when it came.

She was sprawled loose-limbed on the bed, trying to catch her breath when David began kissing his way slowly down her body. As he moved lower, his lips and tongue trailing over her hip and abdomen, a prickle of unease ran through her. Her disquiet grew when he settled between her legs. Her body was still so sensitive that she twitched when he kissed the inside of her thigh.

Good heavens, what was he doing now? She rose up onto her elbows and confirmed that he was, in fact, running his tongue over that most sensitive spot between her legs. She was so shocked that she could not find her voice.

He looked up and gave her a wicked smile that made her nipples harden and sent tingles all the way to her toes and back again.

"Trust me, lass," he said. "You'll like this even more."

As it turned out, he was right.

***

When Alison came in spasms that shook her body and made her cry out, David's entire body tightened and pulsed, demanding his own release. He wanted to be inside her with every fiber of his being. Yet pride and something else he could not name required that she want that too. He needed to feel her pull on his shoulders, to lift her hips, to lock her legs around him.

He needed to hear her say the words. *I want you, David.*

Would she ever?

He moaned as his body moved of its own accord, thrusting his erection against her side.

She trailed her fingertips down his chest, her light touches igniting sparks, and said, "Let me."

He gasped when she wrapped her fingers around his throbbing cock. This was not what he hoped for, but it did feel good. Exceedingly so. And he was beyond ready. He gritted his teeth to prolong the pleasure as long as he could.

Though she was inexperienced with receiving pleasure, she had clearly done this before. He kissed her hard on the mouth to keep himself from thinking about how she had gained her expertise.

He bit back her name and buried his face in her hair as he came in an explosion of pleasure.

But afterward, as Alison lay in his arms, he tortured himself with thoughts of her pleasuring Blackadder with her hand. And, far worse, letting that foul man do what she denied him. He stared at the ceiling while the black thoughts swirled in his head.

She had disliked Blackadder—or at least she professed to—so perhaps she had taken a lover. She would never choose a man like him, the Beast of Wedderburn. Nay, if Alison took a lover, he would be a courtier dressed in brocade and velvet who flattered her with flowery poetry and strummed on a goddamned harp.

David clenched his teeth until his jaw ached.

"If ye ever let another man touch ye again," he said, "I'll kill him."

***

Wedderburn's harsh words cut through Alison's languid drowsiness like a sword. She rolled away from him and out of the bed. How could he say such a thing to her?

"You insult me," she said, clenching her hands. "I welcome no man's touch—though I must tolerate yours."

He leaned back on his elbows and let his gaze travel over her. Suddenly aware that she was stark naked, she snatched her night shift from the floor and jerked it over her head.

"I'd say ye more than tolerated my touch," he said with a smirk on his handsome face that made her want to slap him. "'Tis only right that I give ye fair warning I won't tolerate another man so we can avoid unnecessary bloodshed. Ye know how killing troubles me."

The wretched man actually winked when he said this.

"I am not free with my favors," she said, glaring at him. "I've given ye no cause to suggest it."

"A man who trusts easily doesn't place sufficient value on his pride or his life," he said with a shrug, "and he's bound to lose one or both."

"Hmmph." She folded her arms and turned her head.

"Trust, like forgiveness, must be earned."

"Well then," she said, "you've yet to earn either from me."

Alison never would have risked speaking with such insolence to Blackadder, and she had no notion why she had the nerve to do it now. It was not as if David's accusation of immoral behavior was worse than Blackadder telling her she was inept and weak-minded. And yet David's insult had set a fire under her.

His eyes held a dangerous glitter as he got out of bed and came toward her. Standing her ground was not easy, but she did.

"Ye can be damned irritating when ye let your spirit show." He cupped her neck, preventing her escape, and leaned down until she felt his breath on her face. "But I find it verra appealing."

She barely had time to realize he was not angry with her before he pulled her into a fiery kiss that made her head spin and her knees weak.

CHAPTER 21

Alison awoke encircled in David's arms, snuggled closer, and let her eyes drift shut again.

Another night like last night and she feared she would not be able to hold out. She had been powerless for so many years in her marriage to Blackadder that she clung to this bit of control that her new husband had granted her over her body.

The joining had been the very worst part with Blackadder. She had loathed it so much that she had learned to divert him with her hand and mouth. Though she was still a wee bit fearful, she expected it to be different with David—so different that she found herself looking forward to it rather fervently.

The man had sensual weapons that he wielded with as much skill as he did his weapons of war. Nothing had prepared her for this. While her body's responses were thrilling, the emotions they stirred overwhelmed and frightened her.

Each time, she felt as if she revealed a secret part of herself that left her vulnerable in a way that she had never been with Blackadder. And, as satisfying as the sexual release was, she was left with a hollow feeling, as if she had a hole in her heart, a void that cried out to be filled.

Love was a girlish notion that she and her sisters had spoken of for hours on end when they were young and foolish. She did not hope for love, but she wished she could have the sort of marriage her parents had. She remembered how they shared their burdens, how her father sought her mother's counsel on important matters.

She sighed to herself. The prospect of having that sort of marriage with Wedderburn seemed unlikely. Outside the bedchamber, he spoke little to her, beyond a few banal words at meals. When he saw her about the castle, he followed her with his eyes, his desire fairly scorching her skin. As much as that excited her, she'd come to the conclusion that he desired her that much precisely because she denied him.

Once she gave in she would lose the only leverage she had to draw him closer.

She sighed as David slid his hand along her side, a simple gesture that twisted her heartstrings. In truth, it would take so little for him to persuade her.

***

Damn, she was a stubborn woman.

Three more days had passed and still Alison resisted the inevitable, just as she had when he laid siege to the castle. David watched her sleep in the dawn light slanting through the narrow window. One would never guess that such a sweet face hid an iron will. He kissed her forehead, careful not to wake her.

Each time they were in bed, he felt closer to his goal. And each time something caused her to retreat. Usually he had no notion what he had done or said that led her to hold back.

For a man who had never had to work to win over a lass, it was a humbling experience.

But Alison did want him. He could tell that from her sighs and moans, the way she clung to him, the desire in her eyes. She had her reasons for making him wait—for making them both wait. He just needed to overcome them.

It had become almost a game between them, one that was both frustrating and tantalizing. Alison satisfied his physical need with her hand or, *dear God*, her mouth. And yet he never felt satisfied. He wanted to make her his, utterly and completely. He found it difficult to think of anything else.

She was weakening. They both knew she could not resist much longer. Once she finally gave herself to him, he would lose this constant, raging desire and be himself again. In a way, he would miss the heart-stopping anticipation. After imagining it so often, the simple act of sexual congress could never meet his expectations.

He twined a silky strand of Alison's midnight hair around his finger and tried to quell his unease about leaving her. Cochburn had sent word that he was ready to lay siege to his nephew's castle. The wiser course would have been for David to consummate the marriage at once—and repeat the act as often as he could. The sooner Alison conceived, the better.

Many a marriage had been annulled at the behest of a well-connected family who claimed, rightly or wrongly, that the marriage had not been consummated. Once Alison carried his child, however, she would be good and truly bound to him in the eyes of the world—and in hers.

The realization that this was the reason she continued to resist him hit him like a fist to the chest. Ach, he was a fool. Alison still hoped to escape the marriage. Why else would she allow him to pleasure her in every way but the one that led to conception?

She does not want to bear my child.

David could not completely stifle the hope that there was a different explanation for her continued resistance, but he must keep up his guard.

If Alison gave herself to him freely, if she risked conceiving a child with him, perhaps then he could trust her.

But not before.

***

Alison opened her eyes to find David staring down at her and rested her palm against his cheek. A few days ago his stern expression would have frightened her, but not now. She wanted him to tell her his secrets, to share his troubles, to tell her everything that made him the man he was.

Instead, he rolled on top of her and gave her a fevered kiss.

"Let me make love to ye like I want to this time," he said, his breath hot on her skin. "Don't torture me any longer, lass. Surely I've given ye enough time."

He had been more patient than she had a right to expect. And his passionate kisses, stroking hands, and erection jutting against her thigh were quite persuasive. Why was she waiting for something he might never give her?

"I must leave today," he said, desperation in his voice. "Don't let me go unfulfilled."

He was leaving?

He was peppering her face with kisses, but she managed to ask, "Where are ye going?"

"It doesn't matter," he said into her hair.

"How long will ye be gone?"

"Not long." He groaned as he pressed his erection against her. "Too long. I can't wait. I want ye so much."

With an effort, she pushed him off her and sat up.

"You're my husband," she said. "What ye do affects me and my daughters."

"I told ye I will keep ye safe," he said, gripping her arm. "That's all ye need to know."

"But I *want* to know more," she said. "I've a right to know what dangers lie ahead." Dangers he was bringing down on their heads.

"I'd never throw ye to the wolves like your conniving relations." He thumped his chest. "I protect what is mine."

"Ye think I belong to ye?" she said, getting angry now. "I'm not some horse ye own."

"I don't treat ye like a damned horse, though perhaps I should, as my horse has learned to do as I tell it," he said. "'Tis time you accepted that you're my wife and that ye have a duty—in God's own eyes—to share your body with me gladly and bear my children."

"Ach, I don't recall the priests telling me the part about doing it *gladly*."

"Must ye be so damned stubborn, lass?" he said, raising his hands as if beseeching the heavens. "Ye know ye want me."

"You're a vain man, besides being a vile one," she said, tossing back the covers. Of course, it was true that she desired him, but he should not have said it like that.

"I didn't say ye could leave," he shouted after she slid out of his reach and out of the bed.

"I'm not a child," she said as she threw her clothes on willy-nilly, "and I won't be treated like one."

Before she knew it, he was out of bed and had her backed up against the cold stone wall. He was the Beast of Wedderburn again, towering over her with rage glittering in his eyes. She felt her courage seeping out of her.

"Believe me, I know you're a woman." A vein in his neck pulsed. "Is there another man? Is that the reason?"

She shook her head. How could he think that was possible? Blackadder would have killed her, and no man would dare approach her now and risk Wedderburn's wrath.

"Like it or no," he said in a tone as cold and hard as a shard of ice, "when I return, ye shall be a dutiful wife, warm my bed, and give me heirs."

His words formed a black cloud over her hope for a different kind of marriage, a different kind of life. Her shoulders slumped under the weight of her disappointment.

Without sparing her a glance, David pulled on his clothes and started to leave. Then he paused and turned back to her.

"What is it ye want from me, Alison?" he asked in a voice that had gone quiet.

Without waiting for an answer, he turned and went out the door.

More. I want more from you, David Hume.

CHAPTER 22

Alison went upstairs to find David, hoping to ease the tension between them before his departure. Though she was not ready to give up her hope of being treated as more than a bed partner and brood mare, it seemed unwise to quarrel with a man she would be tied to for decades.

Her hand was on the latch of their bedchamber door when she heard an angry voice coming from inside. It sounded like Robbie. She put her ear to the door without a shred of guilt about eavesdropping. If David would not share what he was doing, how else was she to find out?

"I'm not man enough to go raiding with ye, but ye expect me to do *this*?"

"I do." David's voice was calm.

"Well, I won't do it!" Robbie shouted. "Ye can't make me!"

What on earth was David making his brother to do? She found herself silently cheering for Robbie, who apparently did not like David forcing decisions upon him any more than she did.

"This is for your benefit and Will's," David said with an edge to his voice. "Ye should be grateful."

"Keep your bloody *gift*," Robbie said. "The price is too high."

"You'll see it differently in a few years," David said.

See what differently? Alison strained to hear, but they had lowered their voices and she could not make out their words. Frustrated, she pushed the door open a crack.

"I'm taking some of our men to assist Cochburn," David said. "I'll leave them there and return on the morrow."

At least she had learned something about his plans, though she did not know where he was going or what he was helping Cochburn do.

"I want to go," Robbie said.

"I need ye here," David said. "I'm entrusting the safety of my wife and stepdaughters to ye while I'm gone."

"You're making me their nursemaid again?" Robbie said, his voice going high with outrage.

"Protecting them is an important responsibility."

Alison pushed the door open, and the two spun toward her with black expressions.

"I fear 'tis too late to protect us," she said. "We've already been taken captive and our castle overrun by Humes."

She was relieved to see the glint of amusement in David's eyes after how they had parted. Her attempt at humor was lost on Robbie, however, who bolted past her like a storm.

"I see my suggestion did not help matters with Robbie," she said, glancing toward the door.

"Will's training is going well, and it has succeeded in easing the trouble between my brothers," he said. "Robbie is just angry because I won't allow him to go with me today."

She noted that David omitted saying where he was going, but it was pointless to press him. He seemed willing to talk about his brother, if nothing else, and she wanted to know what David was forcing him to do.

"Is that all Robbie was angry about?" she asked, since she could not ask him outright or he would know she had been listening at the door.

"Aye, that's all it was," David said in tone that did not invite further questions.

Why he was lying? And why was he suddenly unwilling to discuss his brother?

"I'm concerned about him," she said. "He seems—"

"'Tis his age," David said. "He'll grow out of it."

"With his mother gone, perhaps it would help if I spoke to him again while you're away," she said. "If I could persuade him to confide in me about what's troubling him—"

"Don't," David said. "I'll deal with my brother when I return."

"I see." She dropped her gaze to the floor so he would not see how much his words hurt her.

In brief moments, David allowed her to see behind the stone wall he had erected between them. But every time she began to trust him, he showed her how unwise that was. His passion and occasional kindness had caused her to lose sight of who he truly was.

She would be wise to remember that her new husband was the Beast of Wedderburn, a ruthless man who would do whatever he believed necessary to achieve his ends.

***

David had no cause to hope Alison would come out to see him off, and yet he found his gaze returning to the door of the keep again and again as the men prepared to ride. He went to speak to Robbie, who was only here because David had ordered it and stood apart looking sullen.

"I'll not have the men think of my wife as a prisoner and give them authority over her," he said. "I've told them you're responsible for her and her daughters' safety in my absence."

Robbie scowled but had the good sense not to give voice to his thoughts.

Will, the only member of David's family who was not angry with him, brought him his horse. After squeezing Will's shoulder, he took the reins.

He had one foot in the stirrup when he caught sight of Alison emerging from the keep with the girls, her delicate beauty like a shaft of sunlight breaking through dark clouds.

She had come, but she did not look any happier about it than Robbie. The girls ran down the steps and made their usual happy squeals when he picked them up. When Alison joined them, she remained silent and aloof.

"Remember," David said to Beatrix and Margaret, "none of you ladies are to leave the castle while I'm gone."

"Not even a wee ride on my pony?" Beatrix asked.

Ach, this lassie thought she could wheedle anything from him.

"Nay," David said, giving her a hard look. "But if you're good, I'll take ye when I return."

"Can we have a picnic too?"

A picnic, for God's sake. "When the weather's good," he said, which seemed to satisfy her.

Both girls giggled when he set them down and rubbed their heads with his knuckles. His wife's expression, however, remained stony.

"I see no reason I can't take them on short rides," Alison said, after he drew her aside. "Surely you've terrorized the entire countryside sufficiently that no one will attack us if we stay close to the castle."

"One day you'll be able to take them riding again," he said "'Tis not safe for ye to do it now."

"Do ye think I'll attempt to escape?" she said. "I'm no fool. I know I wouldn't get far with two bairns on small ponies."

Ach, she was being obstinate again.

"This is important," he said, gripping her shoulders. "You're never, under any circumstances, to leave the castle without my permission."

"Let go of me." She tried to twist away, but he held her firmly.

"When I'm away," he said, leaning closer so that they were eye to eye, "I need to know you're safe behind these castle walls."

"Safe or safely imprisoned?" she snapped, and turned her face away.

"Damn it, Alison," he said, taking her chin and forcing her to look at him. "I must have your word on this."

"As ye command me to give my word, *Laird Wedderburn,* then of course ye have it."

She spun around, leaving him to watch her stiff back as she climbed the steps to the keep. Ach, she was being as difficult as Rob. He would protect his family whether they liked it or not.

Yet, deep down he knew it was not his order to stay within the castle walls that had upset her. It was not enough for her that he would lay down his life to protect her. She wanted more from him—his trust and perhaps even his heart.

These were things he would not give her, even if he could.

CHAPTER 23

"Robbie! Will ye play hide and seek with us?"

Alison cringed as Beatrix's voice carried across the length of the hall to where Robbie was sitting with a group of men.

"Hush," she said as she intercepted her daughter and grabbed her hand.

Her admonition came too late. The men were snickering, and Robbie's face was scarlet.

"Nursemaid duty calls," one of them said.

"Will ye carry my doll for me?" another said in a high-pitched voice, which caused another burst of guffaws.

"Ye mustn't bother Robbie now," Alison whispered to her daughter. "He's busy."

"But Robbie's not doing *anything*," Beatrix persisted in a too-loud voice.

"Upstairs," Alison said. "Now."

Robbie stormed out of the hall. She wanted to go after him, but she had to deal first with her daughter, who was oblivious to the fact that she had humiliated Robbie.

As soon as she had delivered Beatrix to Flora in the Tower Room, given her a brief but stern lecture, and told her not to leave her chamber until supper, Alison hurried out to find Robbie. On her way through the hall, she saw the group of men who had been laughing at Robbie. Her temper snapped, and she decided to do something she never would have dared with Blackadder's men. She was about to find out if her new husband's assurance that his men would respect her was true.

"The laird ordered Robbie to look after my daughters, and ye ridicule him for it?" she said, so angry that her voice shook. "Ye should be ashamed of yourselves having your fun at the expense of a fourteen-year-old lad."

The men dropped their gazes and shifted in their seats.

"'Twas just a wee bit of teasing," one of them said.

"I suspect you've been torturing the lad for some time," she said, putting her hands on her hips. "Ye know Robbie has too much pride to tell the laird, but don't think I won't."

The men looked worried, which Alison found quite satisfying. That task done, she marched out of the hall to find Robbie.

As she crossed the courtyard, she saw him galloping out the gate. She shouted and ran after him, but she was too late to stop him. She stood at the gate breathing hard and watched him disappear over the horizon. An older warrior with steel-gray hair began to close the gate.

"Shouldn't someone go after him?" she asked.

"Ach, the lad just needs to cool his temper," the guard said. "He's never gone long. Our laird did the same when he was Robbie's age."

"Will he be safe riding alone?" she asked.

"A lad needs to feel a bit of danger," the guard said with a wink.

And Alison had thought raising daughters was difficult.

"Don't fret, m'lady. The laird's brother has a good head on his shoulders," the guard said. "He'll come back fine, you'll see."

Alison took comfort in the old guard's assurances. All the same, she did her mending by the window in the Tower Room that overlooked the gate so that she could watch for Robbie. When he did not return by supper, she went back to speak to the older warrior who stood guard at the gate.

"I expect his horse went lame and he's walking back," the old guard said with a shrug.

"Has he been gone this late before?"

"Aye," he said, and stretched. "I'm sure he'll turn up, and there's naught we can do before daylight anyway."

If a horde of screaming banshees appeared, she suspected this old warrior would pick at his teeth and tell her he had seen it all before.

"I don't like it," she said, hugging herself.

"The laird said he'll be back tomorrow," he said. "If Robbie's gotten himself into trouble, the laird will find him and bring him home."

"How can ye be so sure?" she asked.

"Our laird is the best tracker I know," he said. "And the Devil himself would be wise not to stand between him and one of his brothers."

***

"You're leaving already?" Cochburn asked. "Thought ye were waiting till morning."

"Changed my mind." David mounted his horse and signaled to Brian, who was returning with him. It would be dark in a couple of hours and he was anxious to be on his way.

"Can't say I blame ye," Cochburn said. "I'd ride hard for home if I had a bonny bride like yours waiting for me."

"I brought what men I can spare," David said, ignoring the remark. "Send word if D'Orsey arrives."

"I'm grateful for the help, but ye should take a few of your men back with ye," Cochburn said. "'Tis no secret that the Blackadders want your head."

David was not concerned. He had a sixth sense that told him when he was being followed, and it was easier to disappear with one companion than with twenty. While he could fight off an attack if he took more men with him, he preferred to choose the ground and circumstances for the inevitable confrontation with the Blackadders.

"Haven't ye heard?" David said, cocking an eyebrow. "I can call up a black mist from hell to hide me from my enemies."

Cochburn was still laughing as David and Brian rode off. They were halfway home and the sky was growing dark when David spotted a lone rider coming toward them.

"That's Robbie's horse," Brian said.

"Aye, and that's my brother on it." He spurred his own horse to a gallop, fear rushing through his veins. Something dreadful must have occurred for Robbie to disobey his order. Visions of Blackadder Castle filled with smoke and the sounds of battle filled his head.

When he met his brother, David pulled his horse up hard, causing it to rear.

"What's happened?" he shouted.

"Ye said ye weren't coming back till tomorrow," Robbie said.

Was the lad in shock? David forced himself to wait for Robbie to gather himself and say what disaster had befallen their family and clan. He imagined Alison and the girls screaming while enemy warriors flooded the castle.

"I came to join the siege," Robbie said.

David stared at his brother, unable to accept what his ears heard. "The castle has not been attacked?"

Robbie shook his head. The frantic beat of David's heart slowed, and his fear turned to anger.

"Ye disobeyed me for no cause?"

"I'm ready to fight as a man," Robbie said.

"I gave ye a man's duty when I placed the care of our family in your hands," David ground out.

"Laird," Brian said, and nodded toward the horizon.

A large band of riders were cresting the hill, their outlines silhouetted against the orange sunset. They must have recognized Robbie and followed him all the way from Blackadder Castle, hoping to catch them both.

"Ach, ye wee fool," David hissed at his brother as he turned his horse around. "Ye had two dozen men behind ye, and ye didn't notice ye were being followed?"

Robbie's face finally showed a smidgen of shame.

"This way," David said, and spurred his horse into the valley below them.

Without being told, Brian fell in behind Robbie, knowing David wanted his brother protected at all costs.

***

David was still fuming when they finally rode into Blackadder Castle after a long night of hiding in muddy ravines and risking good horses riding over rough terrain in the dark.

"We had thirty men chasing us all night, and we lost them!" Robbie shouted to the guards at the gate, and shook his fist in the air.

David held his tongue until they had dismounted and were walking their horses to the stable.

"That was no damned game," he said through clenched teeth. "Ye could have gotten us all killed."

"We weren't," Robbie said.

"By luck," David said. "I ordered ye to stay here."

"With the bairns and old men," Robbie said.

"Keep your voice down," David ordered.

They had reached the stables, where a couple of young lads were waiting to take their horses.

"Give them a good brushing and extra feed, lads. We pushed them hard," David said, patting his horse's neck. "If ye notice any sign of lameness, be sure to come find me."

"If ye don't need me, laird," Brian said, "I'll be off to find my bed."

Brian was covered in mud and looked as tired as David felt.

"I'm grateful ye were with us," David said, resting his hand on Brian's shoulder. "You're a good man."

Brian's eyes shone. "'Tis an honor to serve ye, laird."

David was anxious to see Alison and set matters aright with her.

Leaving her upset had nagged at him from the moment he left. But before he sought her out, he needed to soak off the mud and his irritation with his brother in a steaming tub.

Robbie should know to leave well enough alone, yet no sooner were they out of the stable than he picked up their conversation.

"I did as well as Brian," Robbie said.

"Brian did not disobey my orders." *Nor did he lead thirty Blackadder warriors to us.*

A number of men had come out of the keep to greet them. David gave them a warning look to keep their distance.

"I am your laird," David said, "and ye will follow my orders, same as any Hume."

"Even when you're wrong?"

"Aye," David said without breaking his stride. His patience was too thin to have this conversation now with his brother.

"Ye ought to treat me like a man."

"A man must follow orders for the safety of all." David stopped and turned to face his brother. "I warned ye that next time ye disobeyed me I would punish ye, as I would any other man."

"So punish me," Robbie said, glaring back at him.

He suspected Robbie had forgotten that the usual punishment for disobeying an order was a lashing. If Robbie would just keep his mouth shut, David could still avoid imposing it.

"I will punish ye, but right now I'm tired and I'm starving," he said. "If ye have even a wee bit of sense in that thick head of yours, you'll stay out of my sight until I call for ye."

David turned his back on his brother and started up the steps of the keep.

"What must I do to make ye see that I'm not a bairn anymore?" Robbie called after him.

Barely holding his temper in check, David ignored him and kept walking.

The familiar *swoosh* of a sword being drawn from its scabbard stopped him in his tracks. He prayed to God he was mistaken and that Robbie had not done what he thought he had.

"Let me fight you!" Robbie said behind him.

Damn it to hell. Slowly, David turned around. His brother had indeed drawn his sword on his laird and chieftain, a grave offense. Several of their clansmen rushed toward Robbie to disarm him. David put his hand up to stop them without taking his eyes off his brother.

"Chieftain or no, pulling a sword on me is a mistake," David told him. "No man has done that in many years and walked away."

Robbie swallowed and David could see that he regretted his rash move, but he was too stubborn to drop to his knee and beg forgiveness. *Damn that Hume pride.*

"Drop your sword," David said in a low voice, wishing to hell they did not have an audience. "We both know you're no match for me."

Robbie's eyes were still angry, but he seemed to realize the depth of the hole he had dug himself into and laid his sword on the ground.

"Ye know ye must be punished," David said.

"Aye," Robbie said, his tone defiant.

David could have had his brother muck out the stables for disobeying his order not to leave the castle if that was all he'd done. But challenging his laird in front of all the men required a severe penalty. Robbie wanted to be treated like a man, and so he would be.

"How many lashes would ye say ye deserve?" David asked him.

CHAPTER 24

Alison was in the kitchens with the cook when she heard running feet coming down the stone steps to the undercroft. A moment later, Will burst into the kitchen.

"Alison! Help me!" The usually implacable lad was frantic and out of breath.

"What is it?"

"David is going to flog Robbie," he said, fighting tears. "Please, ye must stop him."

Alison dropped the wooden spoon she was holding and hurried out of the kitchen with him. "Where are they?"

"In the courtyard," Will said. "Robbie challenged David in front of all the men."

They raced up the stairs and across the hall.

The moment Alison pushed through the outer doors, she saw David and Robbie at the center of a large circle of men. They stood too close together, and she could feel the fury radiating from their bodies from thirty yards away. Whatever was about to happen, Will should not see it.

"Go back inside," she told him. "I'll do what I can."

She watched from the top of the steps of the keep for a moment, uncertain what to do. They were nose to nose, glaring at each other, but they had not come to blows yet. Perhaps their good sense would prevail.

She saw a sword on the ground beside Robbie and remembered how quickly David had disarmed her. How foolish of the lad. He was nearly as tall as David, but gangly and thin as a long-legged colt, while David had the build and grace of a Celtic warrior god.

Despite how angry David appeared to be, surely he would not have his brother flogged? She gasped in horror as Robbie's hand shot out and he shoved his chieftain in front of half the Hume warriors.

Alison picked up her skirts and ran.

***

A bloodcurdling scream filled the courtyard. David knew it was Alison before he turned to see her flying down the steps of the keep and across the courtyard. The men leapt out of her way as if she were a raging banshee.

"Don't touch him!" she shrieked, and threw her arms around Robbie.

Robbie was as startled as David. His eyes went wide and a scarlet blush crept up his neck.

"Alison, go inside!"

Alison turned around to face him, but instead of obeying his command, she stood in front of Robbie with her arms stretched out to the sides, as if she meant to protect him with her body.

Christ! David was in the grip of such rage that he did not trust himself to touch her.

"Remove her." At his nod, two of his men gingerly took her by the arms.

"The devil take ye, David!" she shouted, as they had dragged her kicking and screaming to the keep. "Ye cannot do this! I will not let ye!"

His rage was suddenly gone, replaced by utter desolation.

He steeled himself to do what he must, and repeated the question he had put to Robbie before Alison's dramatic interruption.

"How many lashes would ye say ye deserve for disobeying and disrespecting your chieftain?" Drawing a sword amounted to more than disrespect, but David deliberately downplayed the offense.

He saw a flash of fear in Robbie's eyes at the mention of lashes, but his brother did not flinch. The tension was like a taut rope between them as David waited for his brother's answer.

"Ye could start by apologizing," David said, hoping Robbie would give him an excuse to minimize the punishment.

"A hundred," Robbie spat out. "A hundred lashes."

"Ye won't survive a hundred," David said, keeping his voice even.

He knew damned well what his brother was doing. A hundred was the number of lashes the English had given David when he was not much older than Robbie. At least, that was the story the other prisoners who witnessed his flogging told afterward. David himself had no notion what the true number was because he'd passed out before they were done. He never confirmed nor denied the number when asked, but it had become another tale that enhanced his reputation and served his clan.

"Then give me half the lashes today," Robbie said, meeting his gaze.

"And finish the job in a second round."

The pigheaded little bastard. Robbie was suggesting that David whip him within an inch of his life and then let him heal, only to do it again. That was exactly what the English had done to David, and everyone in the clan knew it.

The worst part of that flogging had been waiting for the second round, when his body was bloody and battered from the first. It would break most men. David could not bear to see his fourteen-year-old brother break, and he surely did not want it to happen at his hands. Damn Robbie for cornering him with his defiance.

His brother wanted to prove he was as tough as David. But Robbie had been raised by a kinder, less demanding mother, in a circle of affection. One day, he might be as strong as David. But he was not yet.

Grief washed over David. He should do it now, but he gave himself a reprieve.

"You'll have your punishment tomorrow at daybreak."

***

David sat alone in his chamber drinking. How could he flog his brother? He remembered Robbie's first step and teaching him to ride. But he had no choice. Robbie had first defied him and then openly challenged him in front of the men.

At the sound of the door creaking, he reached for his dirk. Alison glided in like a moonbeam in his dark sky. He recalled her screams when his men dragged her away and took another swallow of his whisky.

"If you've come to curse at me and wish me to hell again, it will do no good." He was already in hell.

"I'm begging ye not to go through with this."

"Ye waste your breath," he said. "I have spoken. The matter is settled."

He fixed his gaze on the bottom of his cup and waited for the sound of the door slamming. But she did not leave. Though he did not look at her, he was so aware of her in the quiet room that he could hear her breathing, as soft as a butterfly's wing.

"It doesn't have to be settled," she said. "You're the laird. Ye can change your mind."

"'Tis because I'm the laird that I cannot change it," he said. "Men don't respect a leader who makes idle threats or tolerates disobedience."

He felt her approach as if she held a line attached to his heart. He closed his eyes against the steady pull.

She halted a foot away, within easy reach. All he wanted in the world at this moment was to rest his head against her breast, to listen to the soothing beat of her heart, to feel her fingers comb through his hair.

God help him, but she brought out a weakness in him.

"Ye must not flog your brother," she persisted, "for your own sake as much as his."

He flinched at the thought of the lash marking his brother's tender, unscarred back. His cup was empty so he took a long pull from the jug.

"You're a better man than this." Her voice was strained.

He turned to look out the narrow window at the moonless night, which was as black as his heart.

"I never claimed to be a good man," he said.

"I believe ye are," she said, "or at least ye could be."

"What use is a good man?" he said. "'Tis a strong man who serves his people."

"Ye can be both," she said. "'Tis not weak to show kindness or mercy."

"Ye think our neighbors respect kindness?" he snapped.

She rested her hand on his shoulder. God, he needed her touch.

"I know ye love your brothers," she said.

She did not understand that it was because he loved his brothers that he had to do this, no matter what it cost him.

"Robbie and Will worship ye," she said. "You're the example they strive to meet, and that they'll judge themselves by as men."

"I never asked for that," he said.

"If ye do this, they'll never feel that way again." She brought her face in front of his and looked at him as if she were trying to see into his soul. "I am telling ye, David, that if ye do this, you'll lose them both."

"As Robbie told me repeatedly, he's becoming a man," he said. "He must learn the consequence of not following orders."

"Even if it destroys his spirit?" she said. "The cost is too high. Why can ye not see it?"

"I cannot appear weak and still protect my family and clan." He slammed his fist on the table. "My reputation is all that stands between all of you and destruction by our neighbors."

"I hoped that ye were not as terrible as your reputation, I hoped…" Her voice caught in a strangled sob, and she stamped her foot. "I wanted to believe in ye!"

"I am a lost cause, Alison." He tilted his head back and took another long drink as she slammed the door behind her.

He was alone again, as he had always been.

CHAPTER 25

Robbie shook off the men who were leading him to the post in the center of the castle courtyard and crossed the courtyard with his head up in a show of bravado. When he reached the post, he turned and met David's gaze. David knew his brother so well that he could see the fear Robbie hid behind the proud defiance of his stance.

"Go inside," he said to Will, who stood beside him. "Ye don't have to watch this."

"I'll stay for Robbie," Will said, giving him an accusing look.

Alison's words echoed in his head. *You'll lose them both.*

At David's nod, the men stripped Robbie of his shirt. His brother had shot up to six feet, but he had not filled out yet. The sight of his narrow shoulders and thin arms made David's head pound and his chest feel hollow.

Sweat broke out on his palms as he watched the men tether his brother to the post.

He would reduce the sentence to fifteen lashes. Nay, ten. Any lad should be able to stand ten. At his age, David had withstood far more. And David would not wield the whip as viciously as his English captors had.

"Give me the whip." David took it from the man who held it for him and marched to the center of the courtyard. He could have asked another to give the punishment, but it was David's decision and his duty. Besides, he would never allow one of his men to hurt Robbie. And he believed he should suffer with his brother.

He drew in a deep breath and cocked his arm.

He remembered the crack of the whip and the effort it took not to cry out when it cut through his skin and tore at his muscle. After twenty lashes, he had given in and screamed like a lass. After forty, he had passed out. He heard that they cut him down that first time after fifty or so.

Sweat rolled into his eyes, and the cold wind whipped his shirt against his damp skin. He reminded himself that the flogging the English gave him had served a useful purpose. It had hardened him, had helped him learn to withstand pain and fear and never show it.

And yet, he could not do it to his brother.

He tossed the whip to the ground. Pulling his dirk from his belt, he went to cut his brother down. He waved the others away.

As he sliced the ropes that bound his brother like an animal, he hated himself.

"You're not going to flog me?" Robbie asked in a strained voice.

"I was wrong to do this," David said. "I'm sorry."

"I thought a man never apologizes," Robbie said.

"I don't feel like much of a man today," David said, and clenched his teeth as he cut through the last rope.

Panic flashed through Robbie's eyes as his knees started to give way, but David had seen it coming and held a steadying arm around Robbie's shoulders.

"They'll think I'm a coward for being weak-kneed when ye didn't give me a single lash."

"Ye showed courage facing your punishment," David told him. "Just keep your feet until we get through the door, and that courage is all they'll remember."

That, and their chieftain's weakness.

"Davey," Robbie whispered, "I'm not certain I can walk that far."

"Of course ye can," David said. "You're my brother, and I won't let ye fall."

***

David dragged his sorry arse up the stairs, feeling like hell. All he wanted was to be left alone.

When he opened the door to the bedchamber, he was surprised to find Alison standing at the window with her back to him. He thought she would be in the kitchens, where she usually went when she wished to avoid him. She must have watched the entire miserable scene.

She whirled around, and for one breathless moment, she stared at him, unmoving. Then she stunned him by running across the room and leaping into his arms. He was so caught off guard that he staggered backward.

He buried his face in her neck, needing to hold her more than he could ever admit.

"Ye did the right thing," she said. "I'm so proud of ye."

After all the daring feats for which he was famed—or infamous—*this* is what earned him her praise?

"I showed weakness in front of the men," he said, resting his forehead against hers. "That can only lead to trouble."

"Ye put your brother before your pride," she said, her voice choked with emotion. "They should respect ye for that."

He gave her a faint smile. "Ach, ye don't understand men."

"What ye did was brave."

He was going to ask her what in the hell was brave about making a fool of himself, but then she kissed him. And it was not a sweet kiss. Nay, this was a hot, hungry kiss that sent shocks down to the soles of his feet and emptied every thought from his head.

Her tongue was in his mouth, and she had one hand in his hair and the other around his neck, pulling him closer. He felt lightheaded from all the blood surging to his cock, and that was before she began rubbing her thigh up and down against his.

He cupped her sweet bottom and groaned as he pulled her against his erection. When she responded by wrapping her legs around his hips, he feared he would explode then and there.

He had no notion why his reluctant bride was suddenly behaving as if she wished to eat him alive, but he needed her to want him like this.

Without lifting his mouth from hers, he carried her to the bed and they fell across it. Her hands were all over him—under his shirt, over his bare chest and down his belly, driving him to madness. He was sucking on her tongue when her hand found his cock through his breeks.

"*Jesu.*" He flopped onto his back to give his full attention to the sensation of her stroking him.

When she snatched her hand away, he groaned in disappointment.

"I'm sorry," she said, her face turning pink. "I'm behaving badly."

"Sorry?" he said in a ragged voice. "I wanted to die that felt so good."

A purely feminine smile curved up the corners of her mouth. "Truly?"

"Aye," he said. "I haven't seen this wild side of ye before."

"I haven't either."

Her breath hitched when he cupped her cheek and ran his thumb over her swollen bottom lip.

"Don't misunderstand me. I like ye when you're sweet and shy," he said. "But when you're like this, I'm at your mercy."

Though he had made his admission in all seriousness, she laughed and proceeded to cover his face with kisses. Ach, this lass was a mystery. Yesterday she cursed at him in front of his men. But now that he'd made an utter arse of himself, she was kissing him as if he was a hero returned from battle.

He pulled her on top of him so that she was sitting up straddling him. She looked so lovely with her cheeks flushed and her hair falling loose that she took his breath away. He ran his hands up her thighs under her gown. *Ach*, he could feel her heat through their clothes.

How far would she let him go this time…

"I'm ready," she said, sounding determined.

"Ready?" His heart hammered in his chest. He was afraid to hope. Yet all the signs pointed to the answer he'd wanted to hear since the first moment he saw her.

"To truly become your wife," she said, looking straight at him with her wide violet eyes.

He held his breath and waited, still afraid he mistook her meaning.

"I want to consummate our marriage." She paused and wet her lips. "I want ye, David Hume."

God, yes! How long had he waited for her to say those words? He felt as if he'd suffered a lifetime of longing.

"Are ye certain, Allie?" He had tried to ignore the quaver in her voice, but he couldn't.

She gave him a slow nod. "Aye."

He wanted her so badly his hands shook, but he must not frighten her. No matter what it cost him, he would be gentle and go slowly.

"Does this mean you've given up on your brothers rescuing you?" he asked, though he should not care why she was willing.

"I have, but that's not the reason," she said, her gaze unwavering. "Ye were right when ye said if it wasn't you, I'd be forced to wed some other man."

He tried to ignore the stab of disappointment that she had simply accepted the inevitability of marriage and the loss of her freedom.

"If the choice were mine to make," she said, "I'd choose you."

His foolish heart wanted to believe her, but the truth was that she'd had no choice.

"Ye prefer the devil ye know?" he said, forcing a smile.

"Today I saw what was in here," she said, and placed her hand over his heart, "and you're no devil, David Hume."

She was wrong. But he would do his damnedest to protect her from the darkness in his soul.

***

Alison was startled by her own boldness. After the unbearable tension of waiting to see if David would go through with the punishment, and then the burst of joy when he tossed the whip aside, all her pent-up emotions had turned quite suddenly—and unexpectedly—into flaming desire the moment she flung her arms around David.

If he had not halted their headlong rush into passion, the bedding would be over and done with by now. She wished it were. Now that she had time to think, she was losing confidence.

Though David would never rant at her for failing to please him, she feared she would disappoint him. With Blackadder, the joining had often been painful, and always unpleasant, so that made her a tad nervous as well.

"I want to take this slowly." David lifted her to her feet beside the bed. "Let me undress ye."

She would miss this naked hunger in his eyes. Whether he was disappointed or not, one thing was certain. Once she gave David what he wanted, he would never desire her this much again.

His hands, which were usually so sure, shook as he unfastened the hooks down the back of her gown. Her skin was overly sensitive and her breasts felt heavy. With each hook he released, the tension mounted between them.

After he unfastened the last one, he pushed her gown off one shoulder and kissed her bared skin. His lips felt warm and soft as they moved across her collarbone and up the side of her throat. He eased the gown off her other shoulder, and it fell in stages, catching on her breasts and hips before cascading into a pool around her feet. Taking her hand as if she were descending from a carriage, he helped her step out of it.

He swept her shift over her head in one motion. She felt awkward to find herself suddenly naked before him in the firelight, but it was too late to turn back now. And she did not want to.

"Ah, lass, you're so verra beautiful."

He stared at her, his gaze scorching her skin and making her nipples taut. When he finally pulled her into his arms, his tunic felt deliciously rough against her breasts. He gave her a slow, deep kiss that made her forget her embarrassment.

As they kissed, he moved one hand to cup her breast, and she moaned into his mouth when he found her nipple. When he broke the kiss and leaned back, he looked sinfully handsome with his hair falling over one eye.

"I should get naked too, aye?" he said, a smile curving up the corners of his mouth.

She smiled back at him. "Aye."

Before the word left her lips, he had pulled his tunic and shirt over his head and tossed them across the room. He managed to discard his boots and breeks nearly as quickly, so that he now stood before her in all his naked glory.

He had called her beautiful, but by the heavens, he was the beautiful one. Her gaze slid over his muscular shoulders and chest, traveled down over his rippled stomach, and came to a halt on his huge erection. When he lifted her chin with his finger, she realized he had caught her staring at his manly parts and flushed.

"You've nothing to fear from me," he said, his green gaze locked on her face. "I promise I won't hurt ye."

"I know ye won't." She rested her palms against his chest. "I trust ye."

***

David swallowed. She trusted him not to hurt her when, despite his promise and his best intentions, he did not fully trust himself. The storm of passion brewing inside him felt too dangerous to unleash.

But then Alison rose on her toes and brushed her lips against his, and the sweetness of her kiss calmed the wild beast in him just enough. He would be the gentle lover she needed him to be.

Even if it killed him.

CHAPTER 26

Alison expected David to accomplish the act with quick determination, now that she had finally agreed. Instead, he touched her in all the ways he'd done before when he was trying to persuade her. Long before he was poised over her, prepared to complete their marriage, her anxiety had burned to ashes in the flames of their passion.

"Are ye ready?" David asked, his gaze fixed on her face as if watching for any sign of distress.

"Oh, aye."

She sank her teeth into her bottom lip as he eased inside her, inch by inch, with excruciating slowness. *Oh.*

"I didn't know..." she said between unsteady breaths, "it would feel...this good."

David pressed more deeply inside her. *Oh my.*

The muscles of his face and neck strained as he pulled out most of the way and then slowly thrust inside her again. *Oh my, oh my.*

She forgot to breathe as she focused on the sensation. She wanted to hold David's gaze, to stay lost in those deep green pools, but as he increased the rhythm, her eyes closed and little high-pitched sounds came from her throat.

Of their own accord, her hips lifted to meet his thrusts. She dug her fingers into his shoulders as the now-familiar tension rose inside her. She wrapped her legs more tightly around him, and yet he seemed to be deliberately holding back, keeping her on the edge.

"Harder" and "faster" escaped her lips. He groaned and kissed her deeply, then he did as she asked.

Aye, aye, aye. Sparks crossed her vision. Their bodies strained against each other and yet they were as one.

"You're mine," he said, holding her face between his hands as he moved inside her.

She could no longer tell where he ended and she began.

She cried out as spasms of pleasure pulsed through her body.

"Alison," he called her name.

His body answered hers, thrusting more deeply still, and she fell into a liquid fire with him.

As the storm of sensations subsided, she held on to David as if he were all that kept her afloat in an endless sea. She surreptitiously wiped away the tears streaming down her face. Her emotions were raw and jumbled and far too strong to contain.

When he started to move off her, she resisted.

"I'm too heavy," he said, though he held most of his weight on his elbows. "I fear I'll crush ye."

"Not yet." She wanted to keep him inside her, to stay as one with him as long as she could.

He brushed her hair back from her face and looked at her with an expression she could not read. Had he felt the same wonder, the extraordinary closeness that she had?

"You're mine now," he said again, his green eyes intent on hers. "Now and always."

"I am," she said.

But are ye mine, David Hume?

***

David stared up into the darkness and tried to make sense of what had happened to him.

He listened to Alison's soft breathing as she slept in his arms, amazed at how it felt as if she had always belonged there. When she sighed in her sleep, a rush of tenderness overwhelmed him.

She was *his wife*. He was caught by surprise by the feelings that stirred in him. He wanted to protect her from every harm, to keep her beside him no matter what came, to see her belly grow with his child. He knew to the depths of his soul that so long as he could have her he would never want another woman.

He had believed that making love to Alison would slacken the lust that had tortured him from the moment he met her, but nothing more. They had given each other sexual release in other ways before. Why had this been so different?

When he was inside her, he felt as if he had found a home for his lost soul, an answer to his longing.

And that worried the hell out of him.

***

"*I was this close to catching Wedderburn and his brother,*" *Patrick Blackadder said, holding his finger and thumb an inch apart for his father to see.*

Time and time again, he caught their trail, despite the black, rainy night, and despite all the tricks his prey employed, from crisscrossing burns to backtracking. But always, Patrick was one step behind Wedderburn and missed him.

All night long he had imagined dumping the bodies of Wedderburn and his brother before the gates of Blackadder Castle and demanding entry. If he had succeeded, he would have possession of the castle and Alison this very night. He'd be bedding her now.

"*Wedderburn led ye on a merry chase, did he?*" *Patrick's father said with that smug look on his face.* "*And there were only three of them to your thirty?*"

"*If he'd had more, I would have caught him,*" *Patrick said.* "*'Tis easier to hide with three.*"

His father snorted. "*If I were a younger man—*"

"*Don't flatter yourself,*" *Patrick said.* "*Wedderburn would have lost ye in the first hour.*"

"*Mind how ye speak to me,*" *his father said, slamming down his cup.* "*You've much to learn. 'Tis fortunate I'll be laird for a good long while yet.*"

"*At least I attempted to kill Wedderburn and right the wrong he's done us.*" *Instead of sitting on my fat arse boring everyone with tales from my youth.*

"*I want vengeance as much as you, and I promise we shall have it.*"

Patrick ground his teeth as his father patted his shoulder, as if he were a lad of twelve.

"*While ye were roaming about the countryside on your fool's errand, I set a plan in motion,*" *his father said.*

After listening to his father's plan, Patrick had his doubts, but his father was set on it.

"*'Tis all arranged,*" *his father said.* "*Just do as I told ye.*"

"*I'll do my part,*" *Patrick snapped.*

"*Good.*" *His father touched his cup to Patrick's.* "*Blackadder Castle, Lady Alison, and those wee heiresses will be ours verra soon.*"

"*Until the day Alison's daughters are wed to men in our family, they*" *pose a threat to our claim to Blackadder Castle,"* Patrick said. *"Given how long before they are of age to marry, keeping them alive creates an unnecessary risk."*

"They're our kin and innocent bairns," his father said. *"Once we have them in our hands, they'll be no threat."*

How dare his father speak to him in that insufferable self-righteous tone, when they both knew the other, darker reason his father wanted those two lassies alive.

As soon as his father left him, Patrick sent for Walter, the former captain of the guard at Blackadder Castle.

He looked the big black-haired warrior up and down. Walter was utterly ruthless and had been spouting venom against Wedderburn since he arrived. He was the perfect choice for the task.

"Walter," Patrick said, leaning back in his chair, *"how would ye like to wreak some vengeance on the Humes?"*

CHAPTER 27

Alison was astonished by how quickly and unexpectedly her life had changed. Every meal with Blackadder had been a misery, fraught with opportunities for him to criticize her before the household. But sitting between David and her daughters at supper now, she felt giddy.

Dare she trust this happiness?

David squeezed her thigh beneath the table. When their eyes met, the heat in his made it hard to breathe. She never would have guessed a man could give her such intense physical pleasure.

"I thought this meal would never end," he said in her ear, and brought her hand to his lap to feel his erection. "I'm dying to get ye upstairs."

"Beatrix, Margaret, time for bed," she said, and sprang to her feet. "Come, Flora and I will take ye upstairs."

David caught Alison's arm and said, "I'll join ye shortly."

She felt her cheeks turn pink with a mix of pleasure and embarrassment. For an astute man, David seemed oblivious to the fact that the conversation in the hall dropped to a low hum as every person in the room paused to watch their laird. She was well aware that his men were amused by their early retirement each night and frequent disappearances at odd times during the day.

As she entered the stairwell, she looked over her shoulder and caught David watching her. She smiled to herself, assured that he would follow soon.

Still, she was grateful to have a little time alone after bidding her daughters goodnight and leaving them in Flora's care. She looked at the bed and imagined David lying on it, unselfconscious of his nakedness, his powerful body and hard features reminiscent of the ancient warriors of legend.

Sometimes when he made love to her, he was all need and passion. Other times he was so tender that she could almost believe he cared for her. But the feeling never lasted. Most of the time outside of bed, he was that other man—the hard, relentless laird.

The physical pleasure they shared was a gift. She should be satisfied with that. Instead, the strong feelings he evoked when they made love only seemed to make her long for something more.

She did not want to love her new husband.

But she feared that, whether he wanted it or not, David would steal her heart.

***

Alison awoke at dawn with a sense of foreboding, and her hand went to the pendant at her throat. Whether the black stone was magical or no, it reminded her of her mother and gave her comfort.

"I saw ye send Brian off yesterday," she said when she saw that David was awake. "Has something happened?"

She had waited to ask, hoping David would tell her on his own. Brian was David's most trusted man, so the errand must be important. Still, she did not care where or why he'd sent Brian so much as she cared that David share it with her.

"Nothing to trouble yourself about," David said, and kissed the tender spot below her ear.

"I know your responsibilities weigh on ye," she said. "My mother always said that sharing your troubles makes them lighter."

He leaned down and circled her nipple with his tongue. If he was trying to distract her, he succeeded.

"Tell me the tale behind this," he said, running his finger over the smooth black stone that lay between her breasts.

Though she was disappointed he would not tell her about Brian's errand, at least he was showing an interest in her beyond her breasts.

"How do ye know there's a tale?" she asked.

"The stone is unusual and ye always wear it." He paused. "Was it Blackadder who gave it to ye?"

"Nay." Ach, she wanted to gag at the thought. She wished she could burn everything of hers that Blackadder had ever touched.

"Who gave it to ye, then?" He raised an eyebrow. "One of your admirers?"

"I was far too young before I wed to have admirers."

"Beautiful women have admirers," he said, "married or no."

He'd managed to give her a compliment and an insult all at once.

"My mother gave the pendant to me," she said. "She had one made for me and each of my sisters from a single stone that she believed had protective powers."

"So there *is* a tale," David said.

"Aye, one of royal politics, love, and murder."

"Ach, the best kind," he said with a glint in his eye.

This was the unexpected, playful side of David that made her defenses melt like butter in a hot pan.

"When our late king was a young man, everyone knew that he must marry a foreign princess to make an alliance for Scotland," she began. "The only question was whether the princess would be French or English."

***

David should get an early start on the day. And yet he found himself entranced by Alison's melodic voice and the faraway look in her eyes as she recited what he guessed was an oft-told story in her family.

"A royal mistress, however, could bring lucrative posts and other favors to her family," she continued. "So all the Scottish nobles paraded their bonny daughters before the young royal in the hope that one of their own would catch his eye."

No doubt David's family had played in that game, though the thought disgusted him.

"The Drummond sisters, my mother included, were renowned beauties," she said. "The king fell deeply in love with my mother's sister Margaret and made her his mistress. That in itself did not endanger her."

Something nagged at David's memory about a tragedy in the Drummond family.

"The king installed my aunt in Stirling Castle and lived openly with her as if she were his queen," she said. "Rumors began to fly that the king wished to make her his wife."

David did not need to be told that this would have upset every powerful faction in Scotland, not to mention the kings of France and England.

"What did your grandfather Drummond do to protect his daughter?" David asked.

"Protect her?" Alison gave a short, humorless laugh. "He imagined his grandchild with a crown on his head and persuaded our besotted young monarch that a king could do as he pleased."

"What happened to your Aunt Margaret?" he asked, knowing it could not have ended well.

"The four Drummond sisters were all visiting their father at Drummond

Castle when the tragedy occurred," she said. "Though it could never be proven, we believe my mother's sisters were poisoned at breakfast. In any event, all three fell ill and were dead by supper."

"Ach, I'm sorry, lass." He brushed her hair back and kissed her forehead.

"My mother took a walk by the river that morning instead of joining the household at breakfast," Alison said. "She found a large black quartz beside the river. When she picked it up, an old woman appeared through the mist and told her the stone held magical powers."

David raised an eyebrow. This sounded like fanciful imaginings to him. No one ever seemed to meet these mysterious folk on a clear day.

"The old woman told my mother that she would bear four daughters and instructed her to give each daughter a piece of the stone," Alison continued. "She said that there would be a time when each of us would be in dire need of whatever luck and protection the stone could bring us."

"I suppose the old woman disappeared into the mist?"

"Aye," she said in a hushed voice. "When my mother looked again, the woman was gone."

"Hmmph."

"She feared the old woman could be a fairy in disguise bent on causing mischief, as they so often do," Alison said. "But when she saw the fate that befell her poor sisters, she knew that she had narrowly escaped the same death and that the stone held good magic."

Alison's piece of the "magical" stone had not brought her much luck—first Blackadder, and now him.

"I lost it the day I wed Blackadder," Alison said, absently rubbing her finger over the opaque black stone. "I only found it again after I had the bed taken out."

David lay back and stared at the ceiling, thinking of that burned bed again and what a damned shame it was that Blackadder died before he had a chance to kill him.

"Why did your father choose Blackadder for your husband?" he asked, though he should not blame her father for showing such poor judgment, when his own father and uncle had not seen that Blackadder was a snake.

"My grandfather was chieftain of the Douglases for fifty years, and he was the one who deemed a marriage alliance with Blackadder would be of value," she said. "My father agreed to it because he and my mother preferred Blackadder to the alternative my grandfather proposed."

"There was someone else he wished ye to marry?"

"Not marry," she said, giving him a sidelong glance. "My sisters and I bear some resemblance to our aunt, the king's great love. Our grandfather hoped that would lead the king to make one of us his mistress."

"He was willing to put you in that kind of danger after your aunts had been murdered?" The thought infuriated David.

"The king was wed to Margaret Tudor by then, so there was no danger—or hope—that the king would want to marry one of us," she said. "It was the fervent wish of both my Douglas and Drummond grandfathers, however, that the king would take one of us into his bed long enough to bear a royal bastard."

Did they care nothing for the lasses? Making their granddaughter the king's whore was not even the worst of it. While a royal bastard did bring a great many advantages to both the child and his family, the royal blood that ran in the child's veins could also endanger them due to the threat the child posed to the king's legitimate heirs.

"My grandfathers decided their best hope was my sister Maggie," Alison said. "And I was married off to Blackadder."

David pulled her closer and kissed the top of her head. What a miserable family she had, on both the Drummond and Douglas sides. He wished he could have protected her from all of it.

"Ye see why my mother wanted to give us a bit of magical protection?" She held the pendant up and smiled.

Ach, it did something to his heart to see her hold the pendant as if all she had against the evils of this world was a wee bit of stone.

"Ye have my sword, and my life if need be, to protect you," he said, holding her chin and looking into her eyes. "I'll allow no harm to come to you or your daughters."

He ran his gaze over her ivory skin, red lips, and violet-blue eyes framed by sooty black lashes. After barely leaving their bed for a week, he still could not get enough of her. He longed to taste her skin again, to hear her sighs, to feel her legs locked around him as they moved together.

He should have gone with Brian to Hume Castle to see how their clansmen in that area were faring. Brian was more than happy to go, as he was courting a lass in one of the villages there, and David had plenty to keep him busy here. But the real reason he did not go was that he did not want to miss a night with Alison.

For the first time, he had a glimmer of understanding of how his father could be so foolish over his second wife. He recognized the danger and saw how easily it could happen. But he had learned from his father's mistake that vulnerability in a laird endangered the entire clan.

He could enjoy his bride, but he must never allow Alison to become his weakness.

***

"I can't remember the last time I was on a picnic." Alison leaned against David and smiled up at him. "'Twas kind of ye to remember your promise to Beatrix."

"As if the wee devil would let me forget it," he said, squeezing her shoulders.

Alison snuggled closer as she watched the girls and Will, who were throwing rocks in the burn and arguing over who had thrown their stone the farthest or made it skip the most times. After years of suffering Blackadder's constant criticism and mistreatment, her spirit felt light.

A bond was surely growing between her and David, and hope blossomed in her heart that he was coming to truly care for her.

"I'd like to make love to ye in this bonny spot," he said in her ear, "with the birds singing and the sunlight on your bare skin."

"Can we return without the children and the guards?" she asked.

"Those rain clouds are headed this way," he said, frowning at the horizon. Then he turned back to her and winked. "We'll have to make do with our bed. But if we leave soon, we'll have time before supper."

"I'll fetch the children," she said, and grinned at him.

As she got to her feet, Margaret emerged from the brush that grew along the burn.

"Where are Beatrix and Will?" Alison asked.

"That way," Margaret said, pointing upstream.

Alison lifted her skirts and made her way through the scrub brush. She heard the two children before she saw them.

"I don't like being told what to do," Beatrix said.

Alison chuckled to herself. That was certainly true. Curious, she took a few steps closer until she could see them through the branches.

"I'd let ye do whatever ye want. I wouldn't care," Will said, and tossed a stick into the burn. "But I expect you and Robbie will have rows that shake the roof."

"I don't want to marry him," Beatrix said. "I don't want to marry at all."

Unease tightened Alison's stomach. What had the children overheard that inspired this talk of marriage?

"I like Margaret nearly as much as I like Jasper," Will said, and patted the pup's head, "but I don't want to marry her either."

"Then we won't do it," Beatrix said, crossing her arms.

"David told Robbie that we must do it for the good of the clan," Will said. "And when David says something must be done for the clan, 'tis a waste of breath to argue."

Alison was so upset she was shaking. She told herself not to panic, that she must give David a chance to explain. Surely he would not plan her daughters' marriages without consulting her. Whatever the children had heard, they must have misunderstood.

***

David felt a rare contentment as he lay back and watched the passing clouds while wee Margaret sat beside him playing with the wooden pig he'd carved for her. He could not recall ever whiling away the afternoon like this. His mother would have beat him for it. *A laird's heir has too much to learn to waste time on frivolity.* His stepmother often took his brothers on outings like this, but he was too old by then to be included.

His breath caught as Alison appeared through the trees, looking as beguiling as a wood nymph. Would he ever become accustomed to the effect she had on him? While he had enjoyed spending time with Will and the girls, all he wanted now was to have his wife alone and naked in their bedchamber.

With his mind on that, he did not notice at first that Alison was unusually quiet on the short ride back. He took a closer look. Her back was stiff, and she was clutching the reins.

"What's wrong?"

"It can keep until we're alone," she said, then she spurred her horse and trotted ahead.

He let her go and fell back to ride beside Will. "Do ye know what this is about?"

"I think she overheard me and Bea talking about the betrothals."

"By the saints, Will, why could ye not keep it a secret?"

"Bea is my friend." Will shrugged. "It felt wrong not to tell her."

David cursed under his breath. Alison was right about Will having a mind of his own. How could David rule his clan with authority when his wife and young brothers challenged his commands?

"Why didn't ye tell Alison?" Will asked.

David felt a twinge of guilt. He had intended to inform her, but the time was not right yet.

"It was my decision to make," he said. "My wife ought to be grateful I've done well by her daughters by arranging for their future."

Will gave him a long sideways glance. "Ye don't understand lasses much, do ye?"

CHAPTER 28

David told himself that Alison was a reasonable lass who would accept his decision, as she ought, and even see the wisdom of it in time. All the same, he drew in a deep breath before he opened their bedchamber door. Alison stood waiting for him with her arms folded and a strained expression.

"Ye haven't taken it upon yourself to arrange my daughters' marriages, have ye?" she asked with a brittle smile.

He thought women were supposed to confuse a man with subtlety. Her direct question caught him off guard, and he hesitated too long.

"Then it's true," she said, her voice rising.

"As their stepfather, 'tis my responsibility to secure their future," he said, attempting to sidestep the question.

"What precisely have ye done?" she said, looking at him as if he were the devil's serpent.

"I've betrothed them to my brothers."

"Ye did this without a word to me?" she said with fire in her eyes. "Ye know my daughters are *everything* to me. *Everything!*"

"Their welfare is my responsibility," he said.

She propped a hand on her hip and glared at him. "When did ye plan to tell me?"

"I would have shared my plans with ye, but I knew ye would react poorly—as ye have."

"My daughters are little more than babes," she said. "Ye had no need to act so quickly and when everything is uncertain."

"Uncertain?" he said, his own temper rising. If she still harbored some notion of being able to leave him, he meant to set her straight. "There's no uncertainty about this. You, your daughters, and these lands are mine to do with as I see fit."

"Don't ye dare speak of my daughters as if they're your property to dispose of as ye please," she snapped. "They are *my* daughters. *My* responsibility. Ye have no right."

"I have every right, and ye damn well know it," he said. "What I do is for their benefit."

"Their benefit? Ye use them as pawns and tell me it's for their benefit?"

"I'll do far better by them than either the Blackadders or your family would," he said. "I'd never see them harmed, but I *shall* bind them and these lands to my brothers and my clan."

"This is unforgivable."

"You're a Douglas, for God's sake. Ye knew from the time they were conceived that their marriages would be arranged to bring lands and great families together."

"If you'd left me a widow, it would be *my* decision," she said, thumping her hand against her chest. "*I* would put their happiness first."

"Ye speak as if I'm giving them to foul men who'll mistreat them," he said. "What is your complaint? I've betrothed them to my only brothers. You're fond of Will and Robbie, and they'll make your daughters fine husbands one day."

"Ye haven't known Beatrix and Margaret a fortnight. How could ye have any notion of who would be appropriate husbands for them?" she said. "And we both know it would make no difference what sort of men your brothers become. Ye did this for the Blackadder lands."

"Of course I didn't take the castle just to give it up," he said. "But I could find no better husbands for the lasses in all of Scotland."

"It wasn't enough to control my daughters' property until they were of an age to marry," she continued as if he had not spoken. "All ye care about is giving their lands to your own blood and making them Hume lands forever."

"That is not all I care—"

"Ye had me fooled. I hoped my feelings mattered to ye, yet in my heart I didn't truly believe it." Her voice wobbled and she looked dangerously close to tears. "But I did believe ye cared for my daughters."

Before he could say another word, she turned and ran out the door.

"I do care for them," he shouted after her. "I'd protect them with my last breath!"

***

As if the heavens reflected David's dismal mood, ominous clouds rolled in before supper, bringing driving rain and a wind that howled outside the windows.

The discord between him and Alison left David unsettled.

"'Tis quiet without them," Will said.

Alison and the girls had taken their supper in the Tower Room, and the meal was indeed a morose affair without their light voices and sweet smiles. Ach, he was behaving like a sentimental old woman.

Tonight, he would set matters aright with Alison. He had no notion how to soothe her with words, but once he got her clothes off, he knew how to soften her defenses.

Would she be so angry that she would avoid sharing their bed tonight? God, he hoped not.

He had just left the table and started for the stairs when Brian charged into the hall with rain dripping off his cloak and mud splattered on his boats. He made a straight line for David.

Brian had news. And it looked like bad news.

"I was on my way to Hume Castle to see how our clansmen fare, as ye told me to," Brian said, still breathing hard. "Before I reached it, I met one of our men riding hard this way."

"And?"

"He said one of our villages was attacked two nights ago."

"Their cattle was taken?" David did not like losing cattle to raiders, but they had plenty and could replace what the villagers lost.

"Aye," Brian said. "He couldn't tell me who was responsible."

Brian was not a man easily rattled. The loss of cattle did not explain the distraught look on his face.

"What else?" David asked.

"He said that several of the village men were murdered." Brian struggled to get the words out. "And some of the lasses may have been raped."

"God, no!" David clenched his hands in rage.

Stealing cattle was a respected skill, and stealing a lass to wed her, as David had done, was part of their way of life. But raping and killing innocent villagers violated the code.

Which of his enemies had committed this heinous act?

"What village was attacked?" David was anxious to be on his way.

"Eccles."

That was the village where the lass Brian was courting lived with her grandfather. Brian had been working up the courage to ask for the lass's hand for months.

"We'll gather the men and ride to the village at once to lend what help we can," David said, gripping Brian's arm. "Then we'll make whoever did this pay in blood."

"We both know this was done to provoke ye," Brian said. "They'll expect ye to ride to the village in a rage. I'll wager they've laid an ambush along the way."

"Gather the men," David said.

CHAPTER 29

"I know your blood is hot, laird, and so is mine," Brian said. "But we've a better chance of slipping past an ambush if we wait until it's full dark."

Though David was usually the one with the cool head, he ground his teeth, impatient to act. The harm to the village, however, was already done.

"You're right. 'Tis better we arrive a couple hours later than not arrive at all," David said. "Have the men ready to ride as soon as night falls."

As he turned to leave the hall, his gaze fell on Robbie. His brother would never again beg him to come along, but David could see the desperate hope in his eyes. The other men would come to view his brother as weak if David continued to coddle him.

"Ye can come," David told him, "but stay close to me and do *exactly* as I say."

"I will," Robbie said, eyes shining. "I promise."

David's mind was on the attack on the village as he went upstairs. When he opened the bedchamber door, he found Alison dressed for bed in a thin robe with her shining black hair loose about her shoulders.

He had intended to gather his things and immediately return to the hall until he saw her. Before he faced the harshness of the night to come and the horror in the village, he needed to be surrounded by her softness, to breathe in her feminine smell, to lose himself in her sighs, to hear her say his name when he was deep inside her.

She had become his haven in this violent world.

***

When David appeared in the doorway, his face was so shadowed that Alison had to fight against the urge to comfort him.

"I thought ye might be too angry to sleep here tonight," he said.

"I am still angry."

She had been too upset to risk a confrontation in front of the household earlier, but she had nothing to gain by refusing to speak to him. Though he had the right to do what he did, she had expected greater consideration from him. He had hurt her badly.

"Having a wife is new to me," he said. "I did what I thought best. Perhaps I should have let ye have your say before I contracted your daughters to Will and Robbie."

Perhaps? "Could I have changed your mind?"

"I'm trying to apologize, Alison."

"But ye would have done it regardless," she said, folding her arms. Still, his apology meant something. God knew, Blackadder had never apologized once for his abhorrent behavior, and she suspected it was a rarity for David.

"I care for Beatrix and Margaret," he said. "I would die before I let any harm come to the wee lassies. Ye must know that."

She did, but his failure to add that he also had feelings for her was salt in her wound. "Protecting my daughters from harm is not the same as caring for their happiness."

"They must be safe before they can be happy." He held out his arms. "Come, lass, let's put this behind us."

She longed to take the comfort he offered, but she held back.

"I need to know," she said, "that you'll consult me before making any other decisions about my daughters."

"I will," he said with no hesitation.

It was a small victory, but it was enough to allow her to step into his arms without sacrificing her pride. Her heart was already lost.

***

An hour later, David lay with Alison in his arms, dreading having to leave her.

It was good that he must go. He needed distance to clear his head. When he was in bed with her, he felt as if he was drowning in lust and desire—and he never wanted to come up for air.

Wanting her was one thing, needing her quite another.

He could not afford weakness. Too many lives depended upon him to act wisely on their behalf and not be ruled by his own needs and desires.

He forced himself to get up, pull on his breeks, and look for his boots.

"You're leaving?" Alison's voice behind him was sleepy.

"Aye."

David stole a glance at her over his shoulder. When he saw her sitting on the edge of the bed with her hair tumbled down, all he wanted to do was climb back under the warm bedclothes with her.

"But it's late," she said.

"Aye." It was nearly full dark— time to leave. He found his chainmail shirt and put it on.

"Where are ye going at this hour?"

He shook his head at her and proceeded to gather his weapons. Though Alison seemed too innocent to scheme against him, it was far too early to trust her.

He had already made one costly error in judgment. By not flogging his brother, he had shown indecision at best, and weakness at worst. He could not help but wonder if that perceived weakness had led to the attack on the village. Though he could not regret releasing his brother from his punishment, he should have foreseen the trouble and dealt with Robbie's anger earlier. He could not afford another mistake.

"How long will ye be gone?"

"Can't say," he said as he slid a dirk inside his boot. Would she not leave it alone?

"Can't or won't?"

When he did not answer, she got out of bed, wrapped her robe around herself, and stood between him and the door.

"Why can't I know?" she asked, folding her arms. "I'm your wife."

"There's no need for ye to know." Even if he'd been certain he could trust her, he would not want to burden her with the tale of raped and murdered villagers.

"No need?" she said. "So ye just came up here to use me and leave?"

Use her? Why in the hell would she say that?

"Does this mean nothing to ye?" she asked, waving her hand toward the bed. "After all that's passed between us, ye still don't trust me?"

It meant too much to him. *She* meant too much.

"Ye enjoy what I do in bed," he said, letting his gaze travel over her body with deliberate meaning.

"Pleasuring me is not enough," she said. "I could find another man to do that."

His vision blurred with rage. "Find another man to pleasure ye?"

Instead of backing up in fright as she should have, she rolled her eyes.

"It shouldn't be difficult," she said, lifting one delicate shoulder.

She was baiting him! He clenched his hands to keep from shaking her.

"So long as I draw breath, there will never be another man." His head felt as if it would explode.

"I want a man who respects me," she continued as if he hadn't spoken.

"In and out of bed."

"Ye can't accuse me of failing in that," he said. "Unlike Blackadder, I insist that every member of my household accord ye the respect due you as my wife and the lady of the castle."

"Not *every* member of your household," she said.

"Name one who has failed to respect you, and I'll have him killed, if that's your wish," he said. "Ye know I will."

"Ye make a great fuss—"

"I am laird and chieftain," he ground out. "I do not make fusses."

"Ye fuss about how everyone else must give me respect, but you…" Her cool veneer finally cracked.

"But I what?" he said, standing over her with his hands on his hips.

When she looked up, there were unshed tears in her violet eyes. "But you give me none."

"Laird," someone shouted through the door. "The men are ready. Nightfall is upon us."

***

With David away, Alison felt unsettled as she got into bed. Odd, how quickly she had come to feel safe when he was in the castle. She slept in fits and starts, waking with every rustle of wind outside her window and every creak inside the keep, thinking David had returned.

The chamber was still dark when she was awakened by a light rap on the chamber door. *David is home.* A burst of relief coursed through her before she remembered she was angry with him. The chamber was freezing, so she pulled on a robe as she rushed to unbar the door for him.

When she swung it open, her relief fled, and fear crept up the back of her neck. The torch in the wall sconce outside her door cast an eerie light over the form of a man in a monk's brown habit. His hood was pulled low, obscuring his face in darkness and making him look like the angel of death. She quickly closed the door most of the way.

"Who are you?" she asked, peeking through the crack. "And how did ye get in?"

"I come from the abbey," the monk said in a gravelly voice, then paused to glance over his shoulder. "I have a message for ye."

"A message? From whom?"

"I was told you'd recognize the seal."

He reached inside his sleeve and handed her a folded parchment of fine quality. As soon as she turned it over, she recognized the seal: a cross superimposed over the flames of the Douglas crest. The message was from her uncle, the bishop, a man of considerable power in the church as well as her clan.

After all this time with no word from her family, why were they finally contacting her now? And why was it the bishop, and not her brothers?

"Does the sender await an answer?" she asked.

"Aye, m'lady," the monk said, and looked over his shoulder again.

She felt uneasy about letting a man into her bedchamber, but he was a monk and sent by her uncle. Pulling her robe more tightly about her, she motioned for him to come in.

After lighting a candle, she turned her back on the monk to read the letter. She broke the seal and unfolded the stiff parchment.

I await you at the nearby abbey. Come at once with your daughters. Tell no one that I sent for you and avoid disclosing your destination.

Do not fail to follow my instructions. Your life and the lives of your daughters are at stake.

"What say you, m'lady?" the monk asked, interrupting her thoughts.

David had ordered her not to leave the castle in his absence, but what was she to do? She could not refuse the bishop. He issued orders with the authority of both the Church and her clan. And his message warned that her daughters' lives were at stake. Regardless of David's wishes, their safety must come first.

Besides, the abbey was so close by—little more than a mile away—that it hardly counted as leaving. She could be there and back before breakfast.

And yet she felt uneasy about going. She did not doubt that the message was from her uncle, but why did he not simply come to the castle to speak with her? Surely he did not fear that David would harm a bishop.

She sighed. Given David's ruthless reputation, her uncle would be justified in fearing exactly that. She wished he had told her what he wanted instead of sending a message clearly meant to frighten her. The Douglas inner circle, however, had a long habit of secrecy born of their involvement in rivalries and schemes at the highest levels.

She read the last line of the message again. *The lives of your daughters are at stake.* If David was here, she would not lie to him. No matter her uncle's instruction, she would tell David why she must go to the abbey.

But David was not here.

CHAPTER 30

Alison narrowed her eyes at the monk. "I don't believe ye told me how ye got inside the castle."

"A servant feigned a sudden, grave illness in the night and begged the guards to send a request for help to the abbey," he said. "As ye know, we're famed for our healing potions and remedies."

"Which servant did this?" she asked.

"The prior would not wish me to say, but ye needn't fret, m'lady," the monk said with a smirk. "I expect the ill servant will have a miraculous recovery. In fact, the servant was already recovered sufficiently to show me your door."

She did not like the deceit or her servant doing the prior's bidding. Apparently she would not get an explanation as to why this ruse was necessary until she spoke with her uncle.

"I'm anxious to see my uncle and return," she said. "I'll fetch my daughters."

"We can't be seen leaving together, m'lady," he said. "You're to wait until daybreak, just before the guards on the night watch are relieved, but no longer."

That would be wiser. Persuading the guards to let her leave at all would be a challenge, but they certainly would not let her go at night.

"I don't know what I'll tell the nursemaid," she said, speaking her thoughts aloud.

"The old woman was given a sleeping potion," the monk said.

"A potion?" she said, alarm racing through her veins.

"Nothing that will harm her," he said. "Now, I must be gone. The household will awaken soon, and the fewer folk who know of my presence, the better."

Alison felt increasingly uneasy as she paced the floor and watched for the first signs of dawn through the window. The servant who feigned illness, and whoever gave Flora a sleeping potion, had received some sort of message hours before she did. It troubled her that there were spies in the castle, even if they were helping her uncle.

After weeks of dank and dreary winter mornings, the sunrise was glorious, filling the horizon with a glow of pink and gold. Telling herself this was surely a good sign, Alison hurried up the stairs to fetch her daughters.

Flora was snoring loud enough to shake the bed, but she looked no worse than usual. Alison kissed the old woman's forehead before shaking her daughters awake.

"I don't want to get up yet," Beatrix complained, as Alison hurried her sleepy daughters into their clothes and heavy capes.

"Hush," Alison said. "We must be quick."

"Why?" Margaret asked, rubbing her eye.

Alison felt guilty for rushing them out of bed, but her uncle's message sounded urgent—and one did not keep the bishop waiting.

"'Tis a lovely morning," Alison said. "If we hurry, we can take a ride before breakfast."

"But David said we're not to leave the castle while he's away," Beatrix said. "He'll be angry."

"Let me worry about that," Alison said. "Now, no more arguing."

If David found out, he would, indeed, be furious. And he would be even angrier if he remembered that the prior of the abbey was a Blackadder.

Well, she was none too pleased with him either. He refused to tell her where he was going or why. If he could keep his goings and comings secret, then so could she.

*　*　*

David's heart sank as he surveyed the ruins of the village. The blackened stone walls of the cottages and the singed remains of their thatched roofs were stark against the pink dawn sky.

A few villagers were poking through the ruins looking for anything they could salvage. Most of them had fled to Hume Castle, where he and his men had stopped for the night to deliver food. Though Hume Castle had been badly damaged in the fighting between his uncle and Albany's forces, it offered better protection from rain and marauders than these roofless cottages.

David had stayed up most the night listening to the villagers' tales of horror. By all accounts, the band of men who rode into the village in broad daylight brandishing swords and torches were Blackadders.

David glanced at Robbie and wished he had spared his brother this.

"Why did they commit this outrage against villagers?" Robbie said. "They're just farmers and shepherds, not warriors."

That was precisely the question running through David's mind. Guilt and rage vied with sorrow in his heart. He was certain this attack was aimed at him. Yet there had been no ambush along the road.

What did his enemy hope to gain by this atrocity?

He steeled himself for more bad news as Brian emerged from a burned-out cottage. The lass Brian hoped to wed and her grandfather had not been among the villagers who fled to Hume Castle, and they had hoped to find them here. But Brian's expression as he strode toward David was blacker than the soot that covered his hands.

"I can't find Leana anywhere," Brian said.

"We'll keep looking," David said, though he was losing hope that they would find her alive.

Unable to find any other words, he rested a hand on Brian's shoulder and stared off at the horizon.

"Wait, isn't that her grandfather there?" He pointed to an old man walking through a field next to the village with his head down.

Brian set off at a run across the field. When Robbie started to follow, David caught his arm.

"I'll go with Brian," he said. "See what help ye can offer the others."

Seeing the burned village was grim enough. He did not want his brother to hear this tale.

"The men who did this made no secret of who they were," the grandfather was saying as David joined him and Brian. "It was the Blackadders, and they wanted us to know it."

"We'll make them pay for this, I promise ye," David said.

"That won't bring my granddaughter back."

David looked at Brian's face, which was drained of color, and feared the worst.

"I've looked in all the cottages and the fields," the old man said. "I can't find her."

David organized his men into lines to make a methodical search of the fields and nearby wood. He hoped he could at least give the old man and Brian her body to bury.

He kept Brian at his side as he joined the search for the missing lass. At the sound of ducks, he turned to see them taking flight from a low marshy area some distance away and caught sight of a bit of bright color amidst the cattails and reeds.

Leana had vibrant red hair.

David took off running, with Brian hard on his heels. When he reached the marsh, David found the lass face down, her body cast aside in the reeds and mud like a discarded bone that had been picked clean.

Gently, David turned her over and cradled her in his arms. Brian wept openly as he pulled her torn skirts down over her blood-smeared thighs and wiped the mud from her face. David had no words to comfort him. Vengeance was all he could offer.

But wait. Did he see her draw a shallow breath? He felt for her pulse.

"She lives," he said, looking up at Brian. "She lives!"

Moving quickly now, they wrapped her in Brian's plaid. While Brian held her on his lap, David retrieved the flask from his belt and lifted it to her lips. He sent up a prayer of thanks when she moaned and took a sip.

Though the lass was weak and badly hurt, she would survive.

"Ye will see her through this," David said, squeezing Brian's shoulder. "I know it."

His heart bled for his friend. He could not imagine what he would do if anything like this happened to Alison.

Thank God she and the girls were safe behind the strong walls of Blackadder Castle.

***

Alison herded her daughters down the stairs. They were nearly to the bottom when Beatrix tugged at her hand.

"I have my wooden horse," she said, holding up the carving David had made for her, "but Margaret forgot her pig. I'll run back and fetch it for her."

"Nay—"

"My piggy!" Margaret wailed, her eyes going wide with panic. "I can't go without my piggy!"

The girls had carried the carvings with them everywhere since David made them. Recognizing that she would lose this battle, Alison dropped to one knee and put her arm around Margaret.

"All right, your sister will get your pig," she said, then turned to Beatrix. "We'll wait here, but hurry."

Alison wanted to be gone and back as quickly as possible. Anxiety thrummed through her as she waited for Beatrix, who was dallying. When she finally returned with the carving, her hands were covered with soot.

"I couldn't help it," Beatrix said. "Her pig was behind one of the chairs by the hearth."

The men in the hall were beginning to stir. Alison kept her head down as they passed through, hoping no one would ask where they were going so early. She hated to lie, and she was poor at it as well. When they stepped outside into the cold air, she drew in a deep breath.

The stable lad looked surprised when she asked him to saddle her horse and the girls' ponies, but he did as she bade him. The guards would be more difficult.

But luck was on her side. The two warriors who stood by the gate were young. One had carrot-red hair and freckles, and the other was making a courageous attempt to grow a beard.

"Good morn to ye, Lady Alison," the red-haired guard said, dipping his head. "May I ask where you're going?"

"I'm taking my daughters for a short ride before breakfast," Alison said, giving them a bright smile. "After all the damp weather we've had, it would be a shame to waste such a lovely morning."

The guards exchanged uneasy glances.

"I don't like it," she heard the red-haired guard whisper.

"But what can we do?" the one with the weedy beard whispered back.

"Open the gate, please," Alison called out.

"I'm not certain Laird Wedderburn would approve," the red-haired guard said. "Let me take your horses back to the stable for ye, and you lasses can enjoy the morning with a stroll around the courtyard."

"I don't want to disappoint my daughters," she said, waving her hand toward the girls on their ponies. When that did not appear to sway them, she put her hand on her hip. "Did the laird tell ye to bar the gate against me?"

"Nay," the redhead admitted, "but that doesn't mean he'd want us to let ye ride off."

"I am the lady of the castle and your laird's wife," Alison said. "He's spoken to ye about treating me with respect, now hasn't he?"

"Aye," the two answered in unison.

This confirmation that David had ordered his men to respect her made her feel all the worse for her deceit.

"We'll just ride in circles around the castle," she said, softening her tone.

"I'll come with ye," the redhead said.

"No need," Alison said, knowing full well they would be tired after standing duty all night. "Ye can watch us from the tower if ye like, but we'll be close enough to shout for help if we need it."

With obvious reluctance, the young guards opened the gate wide enough for them to ride their horses through. Alison led the girls around the castle twice, waving at the two guards each time they passed the gate.

"We're changing guards soon," the guard with the weedy beard called to her on their third time around.

"One more time round, and we'll come in," she called back.

When she and her daughters reached the back side of the castle, it took only a few moments to gallop across the open field and slip away under the cover of the trees along the river. Alison felt guilty about fooling the young guards. Hopefully, this meeting with her uncle would not take long, and she and the girls would return before their absence caused any worry.

CHAPTER 31

Alison held her daughters' hands as she waited to be admitted to the prior's quarters, which had a separate entrance and was the only part of the abbey where females were permitted. She was anxious to be done with this and return to the castle.

The same monk who had brought her the message answered her knock and waved them into a small vestibule with a wooden bench on either side.

"Our prior has little fondness and less patience for children." The monk looked at Beatrix and Margaret with a pinched expression that suggested he shared the prior's view. "I'll mind your daughters while ye go inside."

Alison didn't like leaving the girls, but her uncle and the prior would not want to discuss important matters in front of them.

"I won't be long," she told them, then turned to the monk. "We left before breakfast. I'm sure they'll behave like little angels if ye bring them something to eat."

"I'll see that your *angels* are fed, Lady Alison."

Beatrix stuck her tongue out behind the monk's back, and Alison gave her a warning look.

"They're waiting." The monk put his finger to his lips before opening the door to the next room, then signaled for her to go in.

The two high-ranking churchmen ignored her entrance and continued speaking in low voices with their heads together. While she waited for them to acknowledge her, Alison examined them and the room. The two men sat in ornately carved chairs with matching silver cups at their elbows. The prior wore the plain robes of his order, which contrasted sharply with the richly furnished room. Her uncle, who had no need for an outward show of humility, wore a heavily jeweled cross and a fur-lined cloak over his purple cassock.

She had met the prior, who was her former husband's uncle, many times, and she did not like him the better for it. She doubted that he was drawn to the Church by his devotion to God any more than her uncle was.

For men from great families, the Church was another road to power.

Finally, her uncle turned toward her and held out his hand.

"Greetings, Your Grace." She made a deep curtsy and kissed his ring, then turned to the prior and curtsied again.

"How do you fare, my dear?" her uncle asked.

"I'm well, thank you."

"You poor child," he said, shaking his head. "'Tis abhorrent to think of a niece of mine being forced to give herself to that foul Beast of Wedderburn."

"Quite distressing," the prior agreed. "Has the vile man mistreated you *very* badly?"

The prior fixed his beady eyes on her and leaned forward, evidently hoping for a gruesome tale.

"My daughters and I have been well treated," Alison said.

"No need to put a brave face on it," her uncle said. "This has been dreadful for all of us."

"If my being captured was disturbing," she said, "why did no one come to help me when we were besieged?"

"Other matters took precedence at the time." Her uncle stared down his long, pointed nose at her. The bishop was not accustomed to being challenged, particularly by a female. "However, this unfortunate situation can yet be remedied."

Remedied? What could he mean?

"I suppose it is too much to hope," the prior said, his eyes on her breasts, "that Wedderburn has not bedded you yet?"

She dropped her gaze to the floor as thoughts of what she and David had done in bed went through her head. This was not a subject she wished to discuss with a bishop and a prior.

"A minor issue," her uncle said, waving his hand dismissively. "We can praise God that she was not a virgin."

Alison's cheeks grew hotter still.

"There will be no bloody sheets to contend with," her uncle continued. "No proof."

Understanding dawned on Alison as she looked from one churchman's stern, unyielding face to the other.

"But there were many witnesses to the bedding ceremony," she said, knowing now why David had insisted upon it.

"Unless Wedderburn had the witnesses remain in your bedchamber to watch him accomplish the deed," the prior said, raking his gaze over her again, "'tis your word against his as to whether he succeeded in the task."

"And I can say with some certainty that the Church will choose to believe you, my dear," her uncle added with a smug smile.

"But Wedderburn did succeed." Repeatedly.

"Regardless, you shall swear that the marriage was never consummated," her uncle said in a tone that conveyed he thought her slow-witted, "so that it can be annulled."

"I don't want an annulment," Alison told them.

She had initially accepted the marriage because she had no choice. Now that her uncle and prior threatened to take it away, she realized just how important the marriage—and David—had become to her. Though she had known him but a short time, images of him flooded her mind. *David, stern and formidable as he pledged to protect her with his life...at ease on the floor amidst her squealing daughters and wood shavings...impossibly handsome as he lay naked beside her with his hand on her cheek and his eyes dark with desire...*

Nay, she did not want to give him up. Though she wished he cared as much for her as she did for him, that did not change her resolve.

"I've had the petition to Rome prepared," her uncle said to the prior. "We needn't wait for it to be formally granted to move ahead with our plans."

Panic rose in her chest as the two churchmen discussed her future as if she were not in the room.

"I cannot agree to this," she said, raising her voice.

The two men abruptly turned toward her.

"I have shared a bed with my new husband, and I'll not lie about it." She was shaking. It was not easy to stand up to her uncle, but she would not let him do this. "I am David Hume's wife, and I shall remain so."

"The matter has been decided," her uncle said in a firm tone. "The Douglases and the Blackadders have come to an agreement. This false marriage shall be dissolved, and you shall marry a Blackadder."

"That is not possible," she said. "I could already be carrying Wedderburn's child."

"All the more reason to act quickly," the prior said. "My brother will not be happy about claiming the Beast's spawn, but he'll do it."

"As will my niece," her uncle said, glaring at her.

"I will not." Alison took a step backward, in the direction of the door.

She had made a grave mistake in coming. Worse, no one at the castle knew where she was.

CHAPTER 32

Relief coursed through David's veins when he crested the last hill and saw the solid stone walls of Blackadder Castle. After finding Leana, his unease over the Blackadders' motive for the attack grew into a pulsing urgency to return home and see that his family was safe. Though he had left enough men at the castle to defend it, a warrior survived by trusting his instincts. He had set out at once.

He saw no sign of trouble as they approached the castle. Hume men stood on the wall and waved. All was well. Still, he did not regret pushing his men to ride hard. He was glad to be home.

Odd that he thought of the castle that had belonged to his enemy such a short time ago as his home. That was because of Alison. She filled an emptiness inside him.

He regretted the harsh words between them before he left. On the ride back, he'd given a good deal of thought to her and their argument. Trust was hard for him, but she deserved better.

Anticipation swept through him as he led his men up to the open gate. He imagined Alison and the girls running out of the keep to greet them. One night away, and he missed her.

He needed to talk to her about Leana. He had left Brian with Leana, but suggested he bring her to Blackadder Castle when she was well enough to ride. Alison had a big heart and would know what to do to help the poor lass.

The household was gathering in the courtyard. David scanned their faces, looking for his wife. Was she still so upset with him that she would not show him the courtesy of greeting him upon his return? It seemed unlike her.

He dismounted and tossed his reins to a stable lad, then climbed the steps of the keep. Inside, the servants were clearing the remains of breakfast from the tables.

Alison was not in the hall, but Will ran up to him with the girls' pup on his heels.

"I've been teaching Jasper tricks," Will said. "I wanted to surprise Bea and Margaret."

"Where are they and Lady Alison?"

"I was just looking for them," Will said.

"They must be upstairs," David said, and started for the stairs.

He took them three at a time, with Will and the pup behind him.

"I'll check the Tower Room," Will said, and continued up the stairs while David pushed open the door to his and Alison's bedchamber.

He stood in the empty room. "Damn it, where is she?"

Moments later, Will appeared in the doorway. "They aren't in the Tower Room, either."

"When did ye see them last?"

Will scrunched up his face in thought, then said, "Last night."

"What about breakfast?"

"I was working on the tricks with Jasper and forgot to eat."

Just then, Robbie came running up the stairs, shouting, "David!"

"What is it?"

"Everyone's saying Lady Alison and her daughters are gone."

"Gone?" David asked, hoping he had heard misheard.

Robbie nodded.

"How could they be gone?" Fear clenched David's stomach as the image of Leana face down in the mud and reeds filled his mind. "Where did they go?"

"No one knows," Robbie said.

***

"I'll give you a moment alone with your niece," the prior said, casting a murderous look at Alison. "I'll be in the chapel praying that God grants her wisdom."

Her uncle pulled her to his side with a grip that hurt her arm. He tilted his head toward the door and pressed a finger to his lips to indicate that the prior or one of his minions could be listening.

"The Blackadders have gone to the King's Council," he said in a hushed voice, "and argued that your dead husband's male relations have a higher claim to inherit his lands and castle than your daughters do."

"Surely their blood tie is too distant?"

"Not too distant when the political winds blow against us," he whispered. "Your marriage to the Laird of Tulliallan, however, will resolve the dispute to both families' satisfaction."

"Tulliallan?" she hissed. How could he think she would *ever* wed that disgusting man?

"A child of yours will still inherit the Blackadder lands," he continued, as if it should not matter to her that he was speaking of a child she would conceive with the despicable Blackadder laird—or that Beatrix and Margaret would be disinherited.

"More importantly, this will ensure that the Blackadders support your brother Archibald as the rightful guardian of his stepson, the king."

"David Hume would make a far stronger ally in that fight than the Blackadders," she said, knowing that arguing for what would be best for her and her daughters would be useless.

"*If* he chose to be an ally," her uncle said.

"Let me speak to him."

"Wedderburn is too unpredictable," he said with a sour expression. "He prides himself on being his own man."

"Ye must let me try, because I refuse to pretend this marriage never happened," she said.

"Our chieftain will be gravely displeased to learn you've refused to do your duty as a Douglas."

"My brother knows of this?"

"At whose behest do you think I came here?" When she did not respond, he rolled his eyes heavenward. "I negotiated this agreement with the Blackadders at your brother's request."

Archie had done this to her? "Does George know?"

"Of course he does," he said with an impatient sigh.

She was devastated to learn that her brothers had once again put their ambitions above her well-being. They expected her to submit to being used as a pawn, and they could not even be bothered to tell her to her face.

"I'll take you and your daughters home to Tantallon now," he said, referring to the massive Douglas fortress on the edge of the sea. "You can speak with your brothers there."

"My home is at Blackadder Castle with my husband," she said. "'Tis growing late. I must collect my daughters and return. When ye see my sisters, please give them my warm regards."

Her brothers could go to hell.

"Be forewarned," her uncle said, his face turning a blotchy red, "this is not the end of it."

Alison had all she could stomach of the arrogance of the men in her family, starting with her uncle.

"I'm saving ye from making a grave mistake," she said, shaking her finger at him. "I know the Blackadders better than you do, and they cannot be trusted."

"'Tis not your place—"

"David Hume is ten times the man that any of the Blackadder are," she said. "Tell my brothers that they'd be wise to make him their ally—and damned foolish to make him their enemy."

With that, she whirled around and headed for the door.

***

"Surely the men who accompanied my wife left word as to where they were going," David said, gripping Robbie's shoulders.

"She refused an escort," Robbie said. "She told them she was only letting the girls circle the castle with their ponies."

David wanted to strangle the guards for not going with them. "When was this?"

"At daybreak, shortly before the guards changed," Robbie said. "I woke up the men who were at the gate at the time, and that's all they could tell me."

"That was at least an hour ago," David said.

"Do ye think they were taken, or…" Robbie's voice faded, leaving unsaid the alternative—that she had left him of her own accord.

"I don't know," David said, though the timing just before the guard changed certainly suggested she had planned it. "Whether she and the lassies left on their own or were taken, they are in danger. We must find them, and quickly."

"But we don't know where to look," Robbie said.

"They can't have gotten far." David tried to make himself think. Where would Alison go?

Or to whom?

CHAPTER 33

Alison was frantically helping her daughters into their cloaks when the prior returned.

"You're not letting her leave, are you?" the prior asked, glaring at Alison's uncle.

"For now," her uncle said. "She was a pliable child. I don't know what's happened to her."

Under her breath, Alison said, "I have a husband who values a lass with spirit."

"The children are Blackadders," the prior said. "I insist they remain with me."

"You insist?" her uncle said in his most haughty tone. "Let me remind you that these children are my blood relation and nieces of the Earl of Angus, the king's stepfather."

Alison felt immediately safer with her powerful uncle taking her part, though she was well aware that he spoke in her defense not out of affection, but because the prior had insulted his pride.

"Thank you, Your Grace." She dipped him another curtsy, then took her daughters' hands. "Hurry, girls. We're going home."

She told herself that the prior would not dare cross her uncle by attempting to obstruct their departure. All the same, she did not take an easy breath until the abbey disappeared into the trees behind them. Beatrix and Margaret were unusually silent, sensing her unease, and rode at a trot without her asking.

Ominous thunderclouds darkened the sky and a strong wind whipped the trees, making the usually pleasant ride along the river seem eerie.

She tucked her chin into her cloak and revisited her meeting with the clerics, which had been a revelation in more ways than one. Chief among her discoveries was that she was hopelessly in love with her new husband.

She felt a prickle on the back of her neck and her thoughts scattered. She felt as if someone was watching them. The meeting at the abbey had made her jittery and must have fueled her imagination. But the horses seemed edgy too.

"What's that sound?" Beatrix asked.

"A deer, perhaps," Alison said, and signaled for the girls to stay quiet.

It sounded like a large animal moving through the trees, but it could just be the wind rustling the branches. She was anxious to get home.

Not long now. There was a small clearing around the next bend, and a quarter-mile past that they would be in sight of the castle. They would be safe then.

They rounded the bend, and her heart went to her throat.

A dozen riders were in the clearing, and she knew at once that they were waiting for her and her daughters. She turned her horse, but more riders appeared through the woods behind them, blocking her path. In a matter of moments, they were surrounded.

"Lady Alison, 'tis always a pleasure." The man who spoke had a pointy beard and hard gray eyes and bore a remarkable resemblance to her late husband.

Patrick Blackadder. She recognized several of the other men as well, including his brother.

"You ladies should know better than to be out riding alone," Patrick's brother said with a nasty smile. "It could be dangerous."

"'Tis fortunate that we've come to escort ye to safety," Patrick said.

"We're not going anywhere with you," Alison said, lifting her whip. "Get out of our way."

One of their men grabbed her reins, while another snapped the whip from her hand, pulled her off her horse, and pinned her arms behind her back.

"You'll ride with me," Patrick said, holding his hand out to her. "After all, you're going to be my wife."

"Ye know very well I already have a husband," she said through her teeth as she struggled against the man who held her.

"No need to pretend loyalty to the Beast," Patrick said. "Wedderburn will be dead soon. They'll find him lying in a field with crows picking at his eyes."

The certainty with which Patrick spoke made Alison shudder. What did Patrick know that made him so confident?

"Ye can't kill David," Beatrix said. "He's a hundred times stronger and more clever than any of ye."

"Mind your mouth, lassie, if ye don't want it bloodied," Patrick's brother said.

"Don't you dare!" Alison shouted at him. Looking into her daughters' terrified eyes, she said, "David will come for us."

She prayed with all her heart that it was true.

"Wedderburn is many miles away, but we've dawdled here long enough." Patrick held out his hand to her again. "I don't think we need to wait for him to die to share a bed, do you?"

"I'd die first."

"Shame to make us wait for what we both want," Patrick said, raking his gaze over her. "But you're not truly necessary for this. Ye may remain here if ye wish."

This had to be a trick. The Blackadders would not give up this easily.

"'Tis your daughters who are the heiresses," Patrick said with a smile that sent a chill up her spine. He turned to his men. "Take the wee lasses."

"Don't touch them!" Alison cried. She fought to get to her daughters, but she was held fast. "Nay, ye can't take them!"

Her daughters' screams rang in her ears as two men wrested them off the ponies and onto their horses. The breath went out of Alison. *Please, God, no!*

"Ye can't do this!" She kicked and bit the man who held her, but she couldn't break free.

"I'll take the mouthy lassie," Patrick's brother said.

"Mother!" Beatrix cried out as from he lifted her from the other man's horse, plopped her in front of him, and fastened one beefy arm around her.

"Patrick, take me instead," Alison pleaded. "Take me and leave my daughters!"

"Ye must know I can't leave the wee heiresses behind—at least not alive," Patrick said, then turned to her daughters, who were wailing their hearts out, and said in a falsely pleasant voice, "Ready to ride?"

"Don't leave me here!" Alison cried. "I'll do anything ye say. *Anything.* Just take me with my daughters."

"And the good prior said ye were an unbiddable lass," Patrick said. "But then, he doesn't know much about women."

CHAPTER 34

"David, wait," Will called from the floor above.

"I can't," David said over his shoulder, and continued down the stairs two at a time, with Robbie close behind him.

"But I know where they've gone!"

David came to an abrupt halt and leaned back to look around the curve of the wheeled stairs at his youngest brother.

"Bea left a message," Will said. "Come see!"

A short time later, David stood with his brothers examining a childish drawing scrawled on the stone wall.

"Bea must have used this blackened stick from the fire," Robbie said, picking it up from the floor.

"Her mother will be angry—" David started to say, but then he remembered that both mother and daughter were gone.

"She signed it so we'd know it was from her," Will said, pointing at the large smudged "B" beneath it.

"'Tis only a drawing," David said, disappointment weighing him down like a boulder.

"Will's right. See, that's the three of them riding," Robbie said, pointing to the three longhaired stick figures on four-legged creatures. "They're going to this building with a wall around it. Do ye suppose it's a castle?"

Perhaps the child did mean to leave them a message. David was afraid to hope.

"Isn't that a cross on the building?" Will said.

"Then 'tis not a castle, but a church..." David thought aloud as he examined the scrawled drawing more closely. "Those are trees there, and that wavy line must be a burn."

He ran his hands through his hair. *Think! Where did Alison take them?* It was obviously a place the child had seen before. There were only the three of them in the drawing. No matter how anxious Alison was to leave him, she would not take the girls very far on her own. It had to be nearby.

The answer came to him like a bolt of lightning: the abbey, where the prior was her late husband's kinsman.

Alison had left him, and she could not have chosen a refuge that hurt him more.

She had gone to the Blackadders.

"We must ride hard for the abbey," he said, though he suspected the Blackadders would have moved Alison and the girls by now.

That's what he would have done in their place.

***

Alison's fear mounted as they rode farther and farther away. Would anyone even look for them before Patrick had her and her daughters locked away inside Tulliallan Castle? And Patrick was well on his way to becoming as loathsome as her former husband.

She did her best to ignore his erection pressing against her backside, but when he attempted to cup her breast, she slapped his hand. "Stop it."

"No need to play coy with me. We'll be man and wife soon," he said against her ear. "I've waited years for this, and I know ye have too."

Was he mad or so vain that he had deluded himself into believing she desired him?

"Ye should have been my wife from the start," he said. "I wanted to kill my kinsmen every time I saw him with ye. When he died, it was my turn."

Patrick had always made her uncomfortable, but she had not realized he harbored such notions about the two of them.

"My uncle and the prior said nothing about my marrying you," she said. It seemed unlikely he would let them go if he knew his father had a different plan, but that was the only card she held.

"I know they told ye we would wed," he said. "That was the agreement my father reached with the Douglases."

"'Tis not what I was told."

"Don't lie to me," he said. "The prior told me they discussed the annulment with ye, and ye refused. Why would ye do that?"

"They did speak of an annulment," she said, "but they said it was your father I must wed."

"That bastard!" Patrick whipped his horse so hard that they jolted forward.

She gripped the horse's mane to keep from falling and glanced over her shoulder at her daughters, who looked so frightened she could not bear it.

"So my father and the Douglases expected me to wait, like my idiot brother," he bit out, "and wed one of your daughters when she comes of age."

She squeezed her eyes shut and prayed. *Please, God, don't let this happen.* Unfortunately, the betrothals could easily be broken. Without David's protection, her daughters were in very real danger of falling victim to the Blackadders and her brothers' schemes.

"Since your family did not deliver ye as promised, we Blackadders will change the terms to suit ourselves."

"How so?" she asked, though she did not expect to like the new terms any better.

"You'll be mine, of course," he said, pressing against her. "My father will be happy to take one of your daughters. He has a weakness for verra young lasses."

Alison felt nauseous. "Wedderburn will murder all of ye for even thinking of touching my daughters," she said. "He's verra fond of them."

"The Beast is *fond* of them?" Patrick laughed. "He'll be in a rage for certain, but not because he cares for them."

"He does," she insisted, emotion making her choke on the words, "as much as if they were his own daughters."

She imagined David returning to the castle to find them gone. Why had she not told someone where she was going?

"What Wedderburn cares about is that we've ruined his own plans for the wee heiresses."

"He's not like you Blackadders or my family," Alison said. "He pledged to protect my daughters with his life."

Alison turned again to see her daughters, who rode behind them, each in the clutches of a Blackadder. They looked so small and helpless that she wanted to weep. She held back her tears and gave them what she hoped was a reassuring nod.

"Believe me, the Beast is no different from us," Patrick said. "He'd sell those lassies to the devil to keep the lands he stole."

She thought of Robbie and Will, who already had a bond of friendship with her daughters and would grow up to be the best of men. Her objection to the betrothals seemed trivial now. As David said, his brothers would make fine husbands, unlike the vile men her family and the Blackadders would have them wed.

"When I get my hands on Wedderburn, I'll make him suffer for every time he touched you," Patrick said, his lips against her ear. "I'll punish him until he begs for death."

CHAPTER 35

Alison's hope that David would somehow find them faded with each mile they traveled. Most likely he had not even returned home yet to discover they were gone.

Yet she would not accept this fate. Escape was not possible now, while they were accompanied by a dozen armed warriors and she and her daughters were each held by a different rider. She would have to wait until after they reached Tulliallan Castle. But no matter how long it took, she would escape with her daughters and find her way back to Blackadder Castle.

And to David.

She heard the drum of galloping hoof beats and turned to see a group of riders appear at the top of the hill beside them. A moment later, the riders swept down the hillside like a wild river. Alison recognized David brandishing his sword at the front of the fast-approaching riders, and she knew her prayers had been answered.

The Blackadders fell into chaos, shouting to each other, while their horses whinnied and reared.

"God damn Humes!" Patrick said as he tried to control his mount.

An instant later, the Hume warriors rode into the Blackadders, filling the air with their war cries. Alison struggled to keep her daughters in sight, but she could only catch glimpses of them through the tumult.

"Mother! Mother!" Over the clank of swords and shouts, she heard them crying for her.

She elbowed Patrick as hard as she could, catching him off guard, and slid off his horse. As soon as she hit the ground, she realized her mistake. All around her, the battle raged on horseback. Swords flashed across her vision, and horses shied and sidestepped. If she did not get out of the midst of this quickly, she was going to be trampled.

She heard a roar and turned around to see David charging his horse through the mêlée toward her. Time seemed to slow and the chaos around her blurred. She saw only David coming for her, swinging his sword on one side and then the other, cutting down every Blackadder man who blocked his way.

She screamed as someone jerked her up from behind by her hair. David's dirk flew above her head. She heard a *thunk* and a wail of agony as her hair was suddenly released. She fell to her hands and knees. Mud from the horses' hooves spattered her face as she struggled to get back on her feet before she was crushed.

David charged forward, cutting down one last man between them. Without slowing his horse, he leaned down over its side and swung her out of the mud and into the air. She landed with a jarring thump behind him on his horse.

"Save my daughters!" she cried, pointing in the direction she had last seen them.

"Ian, follow me!" David shouted to one of his men, and spurred his horse up the hill, away from the raging battle.

He halted under an old oak a few yards up the hill and dumped her to the ground. She was not hurt, but she lost her footing and fell backward on her bottom with her muddy skirts askew.

"Don't let her loose," he told Ian. "Tie her to the tree if ye have to."

Then he turned his horse and rejoined the fight.

Alison scrambled to her feet and strained to see where her daughters were.

"There!" she screamed when she saw a rider galloping off with Margaret down the path through the wood. A moment later, Patrick and his brother galloped off in the opposite direction with Beatrix.

"Ach, he's split the lasses up to make to make it harder for us to catch them both," Ian said beside her. "And he's left the rest of his men behind to hold us off while they escape."

David was the first to break through the Blackadder warriors, and he rode after Beatrix. Though it had not taken him long, Patrick and his brother had gained a good deal of distance.

The other Humes were bogged down in the fight.

"Someone must go after Margaret before it's too late," Alison cried in frustration.

Robbie, who was not in the fight—probably at David's order—was close to the path through the wood. She watched him skirt around the fighting men, then take off at a mad gallop down the narrow path. He disappeared into the wood.

"Robbie is just a lad. Ye must help him!" she said, pulling at Ian's arm. She was frantic.

"Nay," Ian said.

"If ye won't go, let me have your horse, and I will."

"The laird said to keep ye here," Ian said, glaring down at her. "Ye may have fooled those two dimwits at the gate this morning, but I know better."

When she started for his horse, he blocked her path. He fingered the rope around his waist to remind her of David's order to tie her if necessary. She beat on his shoulder, but he would not budge. There was nothing she could do but wait.

She felt as if she had died a thousand deaths before Robbie emerged from the brush. When she saw Margaret clinging to him on the back of his horse, tears welled in her eyes. *Praise God!*

Robbie rode up the hill to her. She saw the blood-soaked sleeve of his sword arm as he handed Margaret down to her from his horse, and she wanted to weep for what this fourteen-year-old lad had to do to bring her daughter back.

"You're a good and brave young man, Robbie," Alison said. "I'm forever in your debt."

Robbie's cheeks flushed. He gave her a quick nod, then turned his horse and rode into the fight.

Alison covered Margaret's eyes to prevent her from seeing more bloodshed and hummed to block out the men's screams as they died. Dear God, what had she done? The blood spilled today was on her hands. None of this would have happened if she had not left the protection of the castle.

Margaret lifted her head and asked, "Where's Beatrix?"

"Don't worry," Alison said, and brushed her daughter's hair from her face. "David's gone after her."

Margaret dropped her head against Alison's chest, as if that was all she needed to hear.

Many things had become clear to Alison today. She had learned who she could trust and who she could not. And she knew with absolutely certainty that David would not return without her daughter.

***

A murderous rage coursed through David's limbs, pulsed in his chest, and tinged the edges of his vision blood red. The Blackadders would pay for taking his wife and stepdaughters with their miserable lives.

Riding at a breakneck gallop, he was steadily closing the distance between him and the two horses. Patrick Blackadder was on one while his brother rode with Beatrix. All David could see of her behind the brother's bulky frame was a bit of bright skirt and a tangle of dark hair blowing in the wind.

He'd never let them take her.

He spurred his horse to go faster still. Patrick Blackadder looked over his shoulder and saw him coming.

Aye, I'm going to catch and kill you. You've committed your last misdeed against me and mine, Patrick Blackadder.

David was close enough now he could almost taste revenge.

Patrick shouted something to his brother, then suddenly veered sharply to the right. *Damn him to hell.* David could only follow one. He stayed on the brother's trail, as Patrick must have known he would.

He ground his teeth in frustration as he watched Patrick ride off, his image growing smaller and smaller on the horizon. The man was even lower than David had believed. Rather than take a chance that the two of them could prevail against him in a fight, Patrick had abandoned his brother to make his own escape.

His horse's mane whipped David's face as he leaned low over its neck and pushed the animal harder still. As he drew up beside the other rider, Beatrix turned wild eyes on him. Their horses' hooves thundered over the ground. Letting go of his reins, David rammed his dirk into the man's thigh and grabbed Beatrix with his other hand while his enemy screamed and reflexively reached for his wound.

The bastard was quick, though, and caught David's arm. Beatrix screamed in his ear and galloping hooves blurred before his eyes as he was nearly wrenched off his horse. He slammed his fist against the hilt of the dagger in the man's thigh. When the man let go of him with a howl of pain, David quickly righted himself.

He saw terror in his enemy's eyes. *Aye, death and David Hume have come for you.* Holding Beatrix against his chest with one arm, he unsheathed his sword with the other and cut his opponent down with one sweeping motion.

He slowed to a trot and watched the Blackadder horse drag the brother's limp body, which was caught by one foot, along the ground.

Battle rage still pumped in his veins. He stared off in the direction Patrick had ridden. Beatrix was safe now. He could set her down to await his return while he rode after Patrick.

David needed to see Patrick's blood on his sword, to hear the sharp sound of steel ringing this enemy's death song in his ears. But then he looked down at Beatrix, who had buried her face in his chest and was gripping his shirt in her wee fists, and knew he could not leave her.

Patrick would face his wrath another day.

***

David had returned with Beatrix, the fighting was over, and the bodies of the dead lay on the ground.

"'Tis all right now," Alison said, holding her daughters in her arms. "You're safe. You're safe." She repeated the words over and over, but her children wept inconsolably.

The Humes herded the four Blackadders who had not been killed or escaped into a circle. Alison prayed they meant to take them captive, but the hard expressions on the faces of the Hume men made her fear the worst. Killing in battle was one thing, but this would be murder. She could not bear for David to incur this black mark on his soul because of her misjudgment.

CHAPTER 36

David stood before the Blackadder prisoners, his body tense with the need to punish them for the affront to his pride, the fear that had shaken him when he thought Alison was lost, and the pain of knowing she had gone willingly.

The Blackadders had come far too close to succeeding. If David had not returned early or had not discovered Beatrix's message, he never would have seen the trampled meadow along the path to the abbey and found the Blackadders' trail in time to catch them.

A message must be sent. Every man in Scotland must know that an attack on his family would lead inexorably to death.

"Kneel," he commanded the prisoners, "and face your death with what courage ye can muster."

Another chieftain would give the grisly task of execution to another, but David would not burden one of his men with it. The affront had been personal and the responsibility was his.

He unsheathed his sword.

A twinge of guilt broke through his rage when he saw that the first prisoner was not much older than Robbie. In his mind's eye, he saw the burned village and Leana's discarded body in the reeds again. He had good reason to believe a different party of Blackadders—a party led by Walter—had attacked the village. But whether these four men had participated in that crime or not, they were Blackadders and guilty.

Killing a man on his knees turned David's stomach, but it must be done. These men did not merit a warrior's death. He wiped the blood and sweat from his hands and approached the first prisoner.

Suddenly, Alison was between him and the four Blackadders.

"I beg you," Alison said, falling to her knees like the prisoners and clasping her hands. "Don't kill them!"

David looked down at his wife, a woman he would die for. What he would not give to have her defend him. Instead, she judged him. She would fall on her knees to beg for these foul men who meant her harm, but she despised him for the lengths he would go that she might be safe.

He had learned as a boy that life was rarely fair. And still, the injustice of it cut deep.

"Get away from the prisoners," David hissed.

"I can't let ye do this," she said. "When your temper cools, you'll regret slaughtering men who are already defeated."

They deserved to die. The consequences of endangering his family must be made clear to all.

"Look at them, David. See how young they are," she said, flinging her arm out toward the prisoners. "Do ye believe they had a choice about riding with Patrick Blackadder today?"

They were enemy warriors, not lads playing games. And yet, looking down into Alison's pale face, he hesitated. If he did this, he would be even more of a monster in her eyes than he already was. Why did that still matter to him after what she'd done?

"Please," she said. "My daughters have seen enough bloodshed today."

He turned and called to Beatrix and Margaret, who were being guarded by Ian. As soon as Ian released them, they ran to him. When he knelt down to speak to the lassies, they threw their arms around his neck.

"I knew ye would find us," Beatrix said.

"Me too," Margaret said close to his ear.

His heart hurt a little less knowing that they trusted him.

"Did any of these men hurt you?" he asked, pointing at the four prisoners. If they had, nothing could save them.

The girls' black curls bounced as they shook their heads in unison.

"Ye were verra brave, and I'm proud of ye."

They hugged him again, and he wondered if Alison had been as easy to please when she was a wee girl.

"You lassies will ride with Robbie and Ian to the castle," he said, and signaled for his brother and Ian to take them.

While the two helped the girls onto their horses, David returned to stand before the prisoners. It was against his better judgment to spare them.

"Ye may thank my lady wife for your lives, but heed my warning." He let his gaze travel slowly along the row so that each man would see the depths of his rage in his eyes. "If ye ever set foot on Hume land again, I shall cut ye to pieces and feed ye to the crows."

David's fingers itched on the hilt of his sword, and he hoped one of the prisoners would give him an excuse.

"Gather your dead and ride before I change my mind," he said, and turned his back on them.

***

David tied the reins of Alison's horse to his, snapping the knot tight, then looked at her with an expression of such cold fury that a shiver went up her spine. He motioned for one of his men to help her onto her horse, as if he were too angry to risk touching her himself.

David did not turn back to look at her once on the long ride back to the castle. The other Hume men were subdued. Alison felt their disapproval in their silence and surreptitious looks. Miraculously, none of them appeared badly injured, but most had cuts and bruises.

When they finally rode through the castle gates, the entire household poured into the courtyard. But after seeing the men's hard expressions, no one spoke a single word. Will alone gave her a friendly look.

"Take care of the horses and mind Beatrix and Margaret," David ordered his brothers, then he turned and pointed a finger at Alison. "You, come with me."

Those were the first words he had spoken to her since the rescue. As she followed him up the stairs to their bedchamber, she could feel the heat of his anger pulsing from his body, as if she were standing too close to a raging bonfire.

As soon as he closed their bedchamber door behind them, he turned on her.

"At the first opportunity, ye chose to go to my enemies," he ground out between clenched teeth.

"I—"

"The Blackadders!" he shouted. "If ye were going to leave me, did ye have to stab me in the heart by going to them?"

"I didn't. My uncle sent for me—"

"Don't lie," he said, clenching his hands. "I saw no Douglases there."

As quickly as she could, she told him about the monk delivering a message in the night, what happened at the abbey, and being taken by force on their return.

"I had no choice but to go to the abbey," she said. "He's my uncle and a bishop, and he said my daughters' lives were at stake."

"Neither your family nor the Blackadders have ever given a damn about you or your daughters. But I," he said, pounding his chest, "I would give my life to protect you. And this is how ye reward me?"

"David—"

"I should never have expected loyalty from a Douglas," he spat out.

He turned his back on her and went to the window.

"I did not choose them over you," she said. "I was not disloyal. I feared for my daughters and felt I must heed my uncle's warning to come."

"Lies pour from your mouth," he said, still with his back to her. "Ye knew damned well what your family and the Blackadders wanted."

"I swear I did not."

"Any fool would know they meant to take you and the girls from me, and you're no fool, Alison Douglas," he said. "Ye wanted to leave me."

"Nay, I did not," she said, tears blurring her eyes. "That's what they wanted me to do, but I refused."

"Easy to say after your scheme failed," he said.

"I did not know their plan."

"If that is true, then ye blindly put your trust in men who have proven time and again that they are unworthy of it." He paused. "Ye withheld that trust from me, despite all I've done to try to earn it."

"You haven't trusted me, either," she said.

"And I was right not to."

He was so angry that she hesitated to go to him, but she needed to touch him, to somehow reassure him. He flinched when she rested her hand lightly on his shoulder.

When he turned around to face her, his eyes glittered with danger. "I suggest ye keep your distance."

"I'm not afraid of you," she said, and brushed her trembling fingers against his rough, unshaven cheek.

"Ye should be."

His expression was so fierce that it took all her courage not to step away from him. But her heart heard the pain behind his anger and harsh words.

CHAPTER 37

"I'm sorry I hurt you," Alison said.

David's eye twitched when she rested her hand against his chest.

"I'd advise ye not to touch me," he said.

"I want to comfort you."

"Comfort is the last thing I want from ye now," he said.

The dark, raging lust in his eyes stole her breath away. Her body reacted to it with a violent need that pulsed through her veins.

"Go while ye can," he said in a rough voice.

When she shook her head, he pulled her against him.

"I see there's one way that ye still want to be my wife." He thrust his hips against her, making her fully aware of his erection. "And that's with my cock servicing you."

She jerked back. "Don't be crude."

"Crude is what ye expect from me, aye?" He held her chin and fixed eyes like green fire on her. "I'm the Beast. I don't merit your respect or your loyalty."

"I don't think that."

He spun her around and pressed her back against the stone wall.

"A good pleasuring is all ye want from me," he said, and curled his hand around the back of her neck. "God knows ye don't want anything else from me."

"I do—"

"Not my protection, not my fealty, not my crude conversation. But *this* ye do want," he said, thrusting against her again. He leaned down until his face was an inch from hers. "Because when I'm inside ye, ye forget who I am and what ye think of me."

***

"I don't forget who ye are," she said, but David knew she lied.

She was the one person he wanted to choose him, and she never would.

Despite everything he did and all that he felt for her, she ran away from him the first chance she had. She risked her life and the lives of her daughters to abandon him.

And yet he had never wanted her more than he did now. His body thrummed with the need to touch her, to claim her, to make her his in the only way she would let him.

"I cannot be gentle this time," he warned her.

Instead of running from the room, she touched his cheek, and lust roared through him.

He kissed her with all the anger and anguish that was raging through him in a torrent. He had feared for her life so many times in the past hours. That fear roiled with fury and the wrenching pain that had torn his heart in two.

His hands sought desperately for her bare skin, pulling at her gown until the hooks ripped from the cloth. He jerked her bodice down, then lifted her higher to bury his face between her breasts, while he tried to push her endless skirts out of his way.

He had to have her. Now. He didn't want to give himself time to think. Didn't want to remember that she cared nothing for him, that she tried to leave him, that she fled to his enemies.

In a fever, he stroked and kissed her, drowning himself in his need for her. He grazed his teeth along her throat and tasted her skin. When he finally freed her skirts from between them, he ground his pelvis against her, his erection rubbing against her heat.

He was a man blinded with pain and lust.

**

Alison was thrilled by the strength of David's passion. For once, he was not treating her as if he feared she would break. He was holding nothing back.

When the Blackadders took her, she had feared she might never see him again. Never touch his face, never hear his voice, and never have the chance to show him how she felt. Now she wanted him as desperately as he wanted her. When David crushed his mouth against hers, she dug her fingers into his shoulders and kissed him back, matching his passion.

No matter how tightly she held him, she could not get close enough. She wanted to leap into the flames with David Hume. Her husband, her lover, the man who had earned her trust and stolen her heart.

She slid her hand between them to unfasten his breeks. "I want ye inside me."

Instead, he unhooked her legs from around his waist and stood her on her feet while he tore her gown and chemise down over her hips until they fell around her feet. He dropped to his knees, and she gasped even before his mouth touched her.

God have mercy! She fell back against the wall and gripped his hair in her fingers under the sensual assault of his mouth and tongue, circling, sucking and licking until she came in a pounding climax. Her knees were so weak she would have fallen, but he held her against the wall. In one motion, he rose to his feet and thrust inside her.

She gasped as another orgasm hit her with a burst of blinding light. She did not know if she was dying and glimpsing heaven. And still he pounded into her. She sank her fingernails into his shoulders and screamed his name.

His release came in a cry of anguish.

He dropped his forehead against the wall, and she felt the pounding of his heart against her chest. They were both gasping for air, and sweat glistened on their skin. Though her limbs felt weak, she kept her arms and legs wrapped around him. She wanted to stay joined like this forever.

She was so depleted that her mind was sluggish. Words, even if she could have formed them, seemed inadequate after such intense lovemaking.

She had hope that all would be well between them now.

He carried her to the bed, and they collapsed onto it. Though it must be the middle of the day, she had not slept the night before and the ordeal with her uncle and the Blackadders had taken its toll. She hooked her arm around David so she would know if he tried to leave and fell into an exhausted sleep.

She had no idea how long she'd been sleeping when he woke her to make love again. The first time had been in anger, but this time he shattered her with his tenderness. He kissed her as if he might never get the chance again.

With every touch, every kiss, every murmured endearment that escaped from his lips, he exposed his heart to her. The connection between them was too deep for him to deny it.

Though David did not want to be, he was hers again.

***

David got out of bed and gathered his clothes, which were scattered on the floor with hers. When he saw the ragged edge of her torn shift, he felt a surge of guilt for ripping her clothes off and taking her like an animal.

Then, the second time, he'd let her see his bleeding heart. He would not make that mistake again. He had his pride.

He looked at Alison lying on the bed, looking as innocent and vulnerable as ever. Despite her disloyalty and his fury, he had to fight the temptation to lie back down and hold her in his arms.

He had become as weak as his father.

David had hoped she would say something that would change what had happened. But there were no words she could say that would not be false. Her actions had spoken so forcefully that only a desperate fool could find a way to ignore them and believe in the soft looks she gave him.

He was desperate, but he was never a fool.

CHAPTER 38

Patrick Blackadder watched his father drink his ale and waited.

"I've sent a message to D'Orsey," his father said. "He fought the Humes on Albany's behalf before, and he owes us his position as warden."

His father had conveniently forgotten that he had betrayed the Hume lairds, expecting a grateful regent to appoint him as warden. Patrick did not bother reminding him. It did not matter now.

"Once D'Orsey learns that Wedderburn is supporting Cochburn's siege of Langton Castle, he'll have to act." His father paused to cough and thump his chest. "He'll break the siege and bring the perpetrators to justice. And we'll be rid of Wedderburn for good."

His father sputtered and coughed again, then dropped his cup. Patrick watched it roll across the floor.

"Help me!" his father wheezed, clutching at his throat.

"There's nothing that can be done," Patrick said. "You're dying."

Curious as to how long it would take, Patrick leaned back and sipped his wine. The old man fell to the floor and rolled on his back, making ugly sounds through his closing throat.

As usual, his father sought help from the wrong quarter and grasped Patrick's ankle. Good God, the old dog was strong. Patrick had to pry his fingers loose.

"Father," Patrick said, leaning over him, "you've made your last miscalculation."

His father's attempt to wed Lady Alison himself had been the last straw.

A flash of confusion clouded his father's eyes, then his body convulsed and his eyes turned into blank, bulging orbs.

Patrick had not even finished his wine yet. Hell, that took no time at all.

***

Alison awoke to an unearthly keening and reached for David, but he was gone.

Fearing someone in the household had died, she dressed quickly and opened the door. The wretched sound was coming from upstairs. She followed it to the Tower Room, where she discovered that Flora was the source of the wailing.

The nursemaid sat on a stool weeping, while Old Garrett stood beside her, patting her back and looking distraught.

"What's wrong?" Alison sank to one knee and took Flora's hand.

"I can't do without my Garrett," Flora said with tears running down her face.

Alison was too stunned by the revelation that the two elderly servants had formed a romantic attachment to speak.

"The laird ordered all the Blackadder servants to leave the castle," Garrett said. "Says he'll flail us if we're not gone in an hour."

Alison closed her eyes. This was her fault.

"I'll speak to the laird, but come with me first," she told Garrett. "I have something I want to give ye in case I can't change his mind."

Alison looked away while Garrett murmured something to Flora and kissed her cheek, then she led him back to her bedchamber, where she rummaged through her trunk. At the very bottom, she found the leather bag that held the few silver coins she had managed to squirrel away over the years without Blackadder noticing.

"'Tis not much, but here are two for you and two for the cook." She put the coins in his palm and closed his fingers over them. "Please tell Cook I am sorry to see him go."

She found David sitting on the keep steps sharpening a long dirk with a whetstone and wearing a hard expression. He looked very much as if he was preparing to make good on his threat to skin someone alive.

"I must speak with ye," Alison said.

"I've other matters to attend to." He pressed his lips into a firm line and drew the whetstone across the blade with unnecessary force.

"Why are ye sending all the servants away?" she asked.

"If the part of your story about the monk delivering a message is true," he said, drawing the stone across the blade again, "then one or more of the servants was party to the scheme."

"Every word I told ye is true," she said. "Can't ye question them and find out which ones were involved?"

"I don't care which ones did it," he said. "I want every one of them gone."

"Surely ye can spare Old Garrett and the cook?" she said. "I've no doubt both are loyal."

David wiped his blade and held it up to examine the razor-sharp edge, which gleamed in the sunlight. Then he stood and rammed it into the sheath at his belt. Finally, he looked at her, and the cold fury in his eyes made her draw in a sharp breath.

"Loyal to you, perhaps," he said. "But I don't trust them. Or you."

She had been mistaken in thinking he'd spent his anger in their fierce lovemaking and was well on the way to forgiving her.

"Patrick Blackadder took us by force on our way home," she said, though she had explained this before, "because I refused to do what they wanted."

Without a word, David turned away from her and started down the steps.

"I told them nay!" she said, gripping his arm.

"Ye shouldn't have been there," he said, and shook her off. "Ye shouldn't have gone. I told ye not to leave the castle."

"And I've told you why I did it, but ye don't want to hear."

"Ye gave me your word," he said. "I won't trust ye again."

"Ye never did!" she said to his back.

***

David leaned over the map he'd rolled out on the head table and contemplated the final steps he needed to take to avenge his father and uncle. He had allowed himself to be diverted by his wife for too long.

It pained him that his father's widow continued to languish in Dunbar Castle, but until her captor, Lord D'Orsey, exposed himself, there was nothing he could do. That left the Blackadders. After the events of the last two days, he regretted that he could only kill Patrick Blackadder once.

"The Laird of Tulliallan and his son Patrick sent those men to attack the village as a diversion," he said to his senior men and Robbie, who were gathered around the table. "They wanted me away from the castle when they lured my wife to the abbey."

Was Alison lured or was she part of the scheme? Even if she was complicit in the beginning, it had not gone as she expected, for she had clearly been frightened for her daughters.

Regardless of her guilt, he would not speak ill of her in front of the men.

Now that his temper had cooled somewhat, he realized that it had been unreasonable for him to expect loyalty from a woman he had forced to wed him. And he could not fault Alison for not wanting to be bound to him. She had, however, done her best to deceive him into believing that she did.

That she had succeeded was his own fault. He had wanted to believe it.

David brought his thoughts back to the business at hand and nodded to Brian, who had just returned from Hume Castle and looked as if he'd aged ten years in the last two days.

"We know for certain that the men who committed the attack on the village were former guards at this castle." Brian's haunted gaze traveled over the other men. "When we find them, Walter Blackadder is mine."

Brian had told him earlier that Leana had named the former captain of the guard as her attacker.

David looked up as one of the guards from the front gate entered the hall and approached the head table.

"Laird," the guard said, "we've got a fellow outside who rode in alone and says he carries a message for ye."

"What clan is he?" David asked.

"He's an outlander. Talks funny and is verra"—he paused as if searching for a word— "clean-looking for a fighting man."

"Invite our guest inside."

The tall, well-built stranger who entered the hall wore gleaming armor and a neatly trimmed beard. David guessed he was a French knight, and his heartbeat quickened.

"I am Sir Francoise Guinard," the man said with an elaborate bow and an accent that confirmed he was French. "Lord D'Orsey has asked me to convey a message to you."

"May I offer ye some refreshment first?" David did not wish to appear anxious to hear D'Orsey's message, and a Scot always offered hospitality in his home.

"*Non, merci*," the man said with another crisp bow. "My lord awaits your reply."

"What is the message?"

"Lord D'Orsey wishes to parlay with you."

"Where and when?" David asked.

"Tomorrow at dawn, in the place where the Blackadder and Whiteadder rivers meet."

David allowed himself a small smile. D'Orsey was finally leaving the impregnable Dunbar Castle. Better yet, they would meet on David's territory.

"What assurances do you require for your safety?" the knight asked.

"I don't rely on other men's assurances," David said, which caused the

French knight's eyebrows to go up a fraction. "But ye can tell Lord D'Orsey I'll be there."

"I am instructed to inform you that, as the meeting place is but a short ride from here," the knight said, "Lord D'Orsey will extend the protection of the parlay to you for only one hour after the parlay ends."

"I'll grant Lord D'Orsey the same," David said, and was amused when the knight's eyebrows shot up still higher this time.

"That should give you and your men adequate time to return to Blackadder Castle."

It would, if that was what David intended to do.

"*Bon nuit*," the knight said, and made yet another bow before turning on his heel. His shining spurs made soft clinks as he left the hall.

"Do ye think you'll be able to persuade Lord D'Orsey to release my mother?" Robbie asked as soon as the doors closed behind the messenger.

"I hope so," David said.

"He could be setting a trap for us, instead of a parlay," Brian said.

"Ach, ye know these Frenchmen set great store by their rules for fighting," David said. "All the same, we'll go tonight so we can scout the area and set up lookouts."

In Scotland, men who trusted their enemies' word alone could end up with their heads on pikes or hanging by their necks in burned buildings.

"Why did he set the parlay on Blackadder lands?" Robbie asked.

"Marching an army of men across our lands, especially so close to the castle, is meant as a threat," David said. "He's telling me he's warden and has authority here."

"Arrogant son of a bitch," one of his men said.

David smiled to himself. He would take advantage of that arrogance.

"Why didn't ye tell him to stay off our lands?" Robbie asked.

"Because," David said, putting his arm around his brother's shoulders, "this is right where I want him."

***

Alison's heart lifted when David entered their bedchamber, but fell again when he donned his shirt of mail and strapped on weapons without so much as a glance at her.

"Talk to me, David. Please."

"I've nothing to say to ye." He continued to gather his things without looking at her.

"I don't want it to be like this between us," she said.

"You're my wife," he said, "and ye don't have to like it."

"Let me understand the terms of this marriage," she said, becoming irritated.

"What don't ye understand?" he asked, turning eyes like green ice on her.

"Am I to warm your bed, bear you an heir, and that is all?"

"Aye," he said, holding her gaze as he shoved another dirk into his belt.

Without another word, he turned and strode out of the room.

A short time later, Alison stood on the steps of the keep watching the men prepare to ride out.

"Do ye know where they're going?" she asked Will when he appeared at her side.

"To meet the Frenchman."

"Lord D'Orsey?"

"Aye," Will said. "David is going to force him to release my mother."

Alarm ran through her.

"I asked to go," Will said, "but David said my turn will come later."

"What does he intend to do?"

"I don't know," Will said, "but I heard the men say 'tis a bold plan. Perhaps his boldest yet, though it would be hard to surpass what he did in Edinburgh."

Alison flew down the steps. She had to stop him. Even her brother, with all his men, had not challenged the Crown's forces directly.

When David saw her coming toward him, he clenched his jaw.

"Please, let me have a word in private." She glanced at the others who were preparing to ride out with him. "I don't want to embarrass ye in front of your men."

"By the saints, woman," he hissed, "ye don't think running off with my enemy did that? For God's sake, these are the same men who had to help me chase ye down."

Well, she couldn't undo that now.

"Listen to me," she said, desperate to persuade him. "D'Orsey acts with the authority of the Crown, and he'll have hundreds of warriors with him."

David looked at her as if he were waiting for her to make her point. Ach, he was a stubborn, prideful man.

"Besting D'Orsey will take more than sneaking into Edinburgh in a dark cloak."

Blurting that out was a grave error, judging by the withering glare David gave her.

"I didn't mean that," she said quickly. "Going into Edinburgh alone as ye did took great courage—far more than good sense would allow. But courage will not be enough to defeat D'Orsey. I'm afraid you'll get yourself killed."

"No wonder ye left me," he said. "Ye have no faith in me at all."

"I do. But even if ye prevail, what then?" she asked. "Ye know what happened to your father and uncle when they crossed the Crown's forces."

"No one knows that better than I," he said in a cold voice. "It will not happen to me."

CHAPTER 39

D'Orsey was waiting in the meadow by the river with twenty mounted warriors on either side of him and as many as five hundred men blanketing the hillside behind. As David rode closer, he was glad to see that only a score of the men with D'Orsey's were members of his elite French guard. The rest were Scots.

David rode into the meadow with only a dozen men, including Brian and Robbie. Since D'Arcy hadn't given him time to gather a large force himself, his best course was to bring so few as to show a reckless fearlessness and brazen disrespect.

Naturally, he'd had men scour the area earlier for traps. Even now his lookouts were hiding in the lone oak across the river and on the surrounding hills. Living next to their powerful English neighbor, Scots learned long ago to be both bold and devious fighters.

"I don't see the Blackadders," Brian said in a low voice. "I expect they're at the back."

The Blackadders would stab a man from behind, but they were never the first to run into battle.

David halted his horse in front of D'Orsey. Everything about the Frenchman offended him, from the pristine white tunic he wore over his chain mail to the gleaming silver inlay on his saddle. What had his blood boiling, though, was the horse D'Orsey was riding.

"*Bonjour*, Laird Wedderburn," D'Orsey said, inclining his head in greeting.

"You insult me by riding my father's horse," David said. "I've no patience for false courtesy."

"Then let us come straight to the matter at hand," D'Orsey said with a tight smile.

"What matter is that?"

"You know very well," D'Orsey snapped, and David was pleased he had pricked the Frenchman's cool demeanor. "You're participating in the siege of Langton Tower."

"As ye can see," David said, spreading his arms, "I'm here, not at Langton."

A few suppressed chuckles came from the Scots behind D'Orsey. David knew this valley and was well aware that his voice would carry up the hillside.

"I'm told you hold sway with men of these parts," D'Orsey said. "From what I hear, Cochburn would not have besieged Langton without your tacit approval."

"Border men are free to make their own choices," David said, letting his gaze travel over the Scottish warriors behind D'Orsey.

"In fact," D'Orsey said, "it's said that no one crosses through these parts without your leave."

"And yet, you're here."

Snorts of laughter erupted from the Scots.

"I am the royally appointed Warden of the East Marches," D'Orsey said through tight lips. "It is my duty to keep order here."

"We don't need a foreigner to keep order," David said, letting his anger show this time. "I'd advise ye to follow Albany back to France and tend to your own lands. Leave the tending of Scottish lands to Scots."

"Damn your insolence," D'Orsey said. "In the name of the king, I command you to remove your men from the siege at Langton Castle at once."

David was on the verge of commanding D'Orsey to remove his head from his arse when his brother coughed to catch his attention.

"Ask him to return my mother," Robbie said in a low voice.

"I'm willing to discuss the fate of Langton Castle," David said, "*after* ye release my father's widow, Lady Isabella."

"Ah, that lady is a treasure," D'Orsey said. "I assure you that she receives every courtesy at Dunbar Castle."

"The only courtesy she wishes from you is to be returned to her family," David said.

"Such a refined lady is surely better off in my care than in the care of a man known as *the Beast*."

"She is an ill and grieving widow," David said, letting his voice carry to the men gathered on the hillside behind D'Orsey. "My father is dead. What purpose can it serve to hold her hostage now?"

"As the widow of a traitor," D'Orsey said, "she serves as a warning to all Scots that the families of traitors will pay a price for their treachery."

"With the constant shifts in power as scheming men seek to control our child king," David said, "who can say what counts for treason? It changes day by day."

There was a rumbling murmur of agreement from the men on the hillside.

"I ask you again," David said, "release my father's widow."

"I cannot," D'Orsey said. "I am a reasonable man, however, and am willing to negotiate a resolution of the siege to avoid spilling blood. What else do you want? A few dozen cattle, perhaps?"

Did the fool not know who stole his cattle? Some of the Scots laughed aloud, but David was past humor.

"What else do I want?" David said, raising his voice to a thunder. "I want justice for the murder of my father and uncle."

"They weren't murdered, but executed for treason," D'Orsey said.

"They were murdered through treachery!" David shouted. "They were invited to Edinburgh as the regent's guests and promised safe passage."

"I see I was mistaken in believing we could discuss our differences civilly."

"My father and uncle agreed to discuss their differences with Albany civilly." David spat on the ground. "I've seen what comes of that."

"For the last time, I command you in the name of the king to cease the siege at Langton Castle," D'Orsey said.

"When our Scottish king is old enough to speak for himself, I shall gladly follow his commands." At least, he would if the king gave sensible commands.

D'Orsey's face turned a darker shade of red, but David had never expected to persuade D'Orsey to release Isabella. He had spoken for the benefit of the Scots who rode at the Frenchman's back, prodding their natural resentment against a foreigner's authority. He also had reminded them that he had legitimate grievances, ones that could only be satisfied by blood vengeance, something they all respected.

David turned his horse, and his men did the same. As he rode away, he felt five hundred pairs of eyes on his back and hoped he had been sufficiently persuasive.

"I shall end the siege at Langton," D'Orsey shouted after him, "and I shall make you and all who follow you pay for your insolence."

David turned his horse abruptly back around.

"And I promise you before God and every man here," he said, fixing his gaze on D'Orsey and raising his fist in the air, "that the next time we meet, I shall see you dead or in chains."

CHAPTER 40

"Laird, come take a look," one of the Hume men on the ridge called over his shoulder.

David crawled through the grass and rested on his elbows to watch D'Orsey's forces as they traveled west on the far side of the river that cut a valley between the hills. He and his men had been following them for the past hour.

"D'Orsey's still got three or four hundred men," his man reported, "but the Scots have been quietly disappearing over the hills by the score."

This was just as David hoped. The Scots would ride with D'Orsey for silver coin, but they were not so willing to fight the Laird of Wedderburn for the Frenchman. Most of them believed David was in the right and that the same injustice could easily befall their own families.

More than that, they knew D'Orsey would either die or return to France one day. But as long as the rivers flowed, there would be Humes in the Borders. In a land where blood was paid for in blood and grievances were remembered for generations, men did not cross the Humes lightly.

David glanced up at the sky. It was time. They didn't have much daylight left, and they were close to the castle should they need to make a quick escape. As the saying went, *leave the backdoor unlocked.*

He crept back down the hill and gathered the men he would take with him in a circle. They were thirty of his fastest horsemen, for speed was essential. If all went well, a small, fleet group, similar to a raiding party, would serve his purpose.

If not, they'd ride like hell for the castle.

"Remember," David told them, "I want D'Orsey captured, not killed, so I can trade him for Lady Isabella."

He sent Robbie to stand watch halfway to the castle, which would keep him out of harm's way.

"If ye see us galloping in your direction, ride ahead to the castle," David instructed him. "Tell them to open the gate and be prepared to close it fast behind us."

David led his thirty riders up to the ridge and paused, giving the men below time to see them. Then he gave the signal, and the Humes rode down the long hillside like a pack of running wolves.

D'Orsey appeared to be shouting at his forces to form a line. Instead, hundreds of Scots began crossing the stream to join the Humes. Others who wished to avoid taking sides disappeared.

This was what David hoped for, but it was happening too quickly. There were too too many well-meaning Scots between his group of fleet riders and D'Orsey.

D'Orsey did not lack for courage, but he was not a fool. As soon as he realized he would be fighting with only his French guard, he spurred his horse to make his escape.

It was a magnificent horse and had been his father's pride.

David and his men were caught in the midst of all the Scots who were joining their side. *Damn it!* When they finally broke free, D'Orsey had too great a lead. He was going to escape, and all this would be for naught.

From the corner of his eye, David caught sight of a rider ahead and to his left, coming from the direction of Blackadder Castle. The rider was small for a man, and he was racing toward D'Orsey with the apparent intention of cutting him off.

***

Alison sat with her daughters by the great hearth in the hall, pretending to stitch. She was so tense awaiting the outcome of David's encounter with D'Orsey that when one of the guards approached her she jabbed herself with the needle.

"Sorry to trouble ye, Lady Alison," he said. "But with the laird gone, I thought I should tell you."

"What is it?" she asked, pleased that someone wished to consult her, even if her husband never did.

"'Tis about Will."

Unease settled into the pit of her stomach.

"I was up on the wall on duty," the guard said. "Will was with me, talking about birds and such."

"That's our Will," Beatrix piped up. "Is he still there looking at birds?"

"Ye know how that lad gets odd notions in his head," the man said. "One moment he's yapping about bird songs and wingspans. Then he halts mid-thought and races down the ladder. Next thing I know, he's riding out the gate like a streak of lightning."

Good God. For all she knew, there could be a battle raging nearby.

"There are fresh apple tarts in the kitchen," she told the girls, hoping to divert them so they would not see how worried she was. "Go have one while they're warm."

"I want Will to come home," Margaret said.

"I'll send him down to join ye as soon as he returns," Alison said with a firm hand on their backs. Once she had them on their way, she hurried out of the keep with the guard.

"I expect the lad's just chasing a bird and will give up soon," the guard said, but he looked worried. "I would've rode after him, but the laird said we were to stay here and keep watch. I shouldn't have left my post this long."

"I'm going up on the wall with ye." Alison gathered her skirts in one hand and started up the ladder. "I need to watch for Will and the others myself."

***

David did not want to believe the rider streaking across the distant field was who he thought it was.

"Will's gone mad!" Brian shouted. "That's him, chasing after D'Orsey."

David's heart nearly stopped beating. *Mary, Mother of God. Please, no. Not Will.* He would rather die a thousand deaths than see Will harmed.

David spurred his horse until they were flying over the ground. Fear clutched at his gut.

Another rider appeared ahead, racing across the field a quarter-mile behind Will. David cursed. It was Robbie. Positioned where he was, he would have seen Will first.

David gritted his teeth in frustration as Will curved his horse's path and fell in beside D'Orsey's in a mad race. What in the hell did he think he was doing?

By the saints! He could not believe his eyes as he watched his foolish brother slash at D'Orsey with a sword while riding at breakneck speed. He prayed that D'Orsey would not knock Will off his horse or pull his own sword and slice his brother in half.

They were still too far ahead. David grasped hold of his horse's mane and leaned low over its neck. There was a bog ahead that the locals knew to avoid. His only hope was that D'Orsey would become mired in it so that he could catch up before his brother got killed.

At the last minute, Will found the solid path through the bog. But

D'Orsey, being unfamiliar with the terrain, forced his horse to ride straight into it. The Frenchman fell off as his horse struggled valiantly in the sinking ground, and David thought luck had finally gone his way.

Though he was riding at a full gallop, time seemed to slow to a crawl as he watched D'Orsey reach the path and pull Will off his horse.

With all his attention on Will, David did not notice until now that Robbie had reached the edge of the bog. Robbie dismounted and ran to Will's aid.

With all his heart, David regretted provoking D'Orsey and risking his brothers. D'Orsey was a famed knight, skilled in battle, said to be unmatched with a sword. Robbie and Will would not last long against him.

David was finally nearing the bog when he saw D'Orsey raising his sword over Will's head.

"D'Orsey!" David shouted as he urged his horse over the uneven ground.

Robbie charged into the Frenchman. D'Orsey sent Robbie flying into the muck, and Will fell backward onto the ground. Looking straight at David, D'Orsey raised his sword high over his head again to strike the deathblow to Will.

David's horse found a patch of firm ground and sprang ahead as D'Orsey's blade began to fall.

Leaning to the side, David swung his sword with all his might and sliced through D'Arcy's neck as his horse thundered past them.

Over his shoulder, David watched as D'Arcy's blade continued to fall, its sharp point on a path to Will's heart. Will rolled to the side just before the blade struck the ground where he had lain.

David slowed his horse to a trot and turned around. Robbie reached Will first and was helping him up when David pulled his horse up beside them.

He dismounted and fell to his knees. Now that it was over, David could not breathe, and his hands shook. *Thanks be to God for saving Will, for he is the best of us Humes.*

He watched his brothers embrace for the first time in years.

"No one will make jests about him now," Robbie said as he squeezed Will's shoulders. "If not for you, Will, D'Orsey would have gotten away."

David was drenched in a cold sweat. He had nearly lost both his brothers. The image of D'Orsey's blade over Will would haunt him for a long, long time.

He looked down at the severed head. He had no hostage now to exchange for his father's widow, and he'd killed the Crown's warden, a treasonous offence. Somehow, he must turn this to his advantage.

He must ensure the safety of his family, and he knew only one way to do that. His very name must strike terror in the hearts of his enemies. Even the Crown's forces must fear him.

"What are ye doing?" Will asked, turning wide eyes on him.

"Legends are made by acts such as this," David said. "And I must be a legend."

CHAPTER 41

"Praise God, they've returned!" Alison pressed her hand to her chest as she watched the riders approaching the castle.

David was at the front, with his brothers on either side. Somehow, he had found Will. The worry that had weighed down her chest, making it hard to breath, suddenly lifted, and she feel light as she raced down from the wall.

"David!" Ignoring decorum, she shouted and waved to him as he rode into the yard through the open gate.

He looked magnificent astride his horse and dressed for battle in his chain mail shirt. She picked up her skirts and ran to meet him.

When he reined in, his horse turned to the side, and Alison came to an abrupt halt.

A grizzly head was tied to David's saddle by its long hair. Her hands flew to her face, and she heard herself scream, as if it the sound were coming from someone else.

"I know who this is," she said, pointing at the bloody head. "'Tis Lord D'Orsey."

She tore her gaze away from the horrible sight and looked up at her husband. David's expression was hard and distant.

"Nay, ye couldn't have done this," she said, backing away and shaking her head.

His eyes were as cold as death. Who was he? She thought she knew him. How could the man she loved be capable of such gruesome brutality?

He looked past her and proceeded to ride his horse in a circle around the courtyard while the entire household watched.

"This is what any man, no matter how powerful, can expect if he crosses the Humes!" David shouted.

Everyone except Alison raised their fists and cheered.

"I go now to place my enemy's head on the market cross at Duns as a warning to others," he said in a voice that filled the courtyard. "Who will ride with me?"

Again, shouts filled the courtyard.

Then, as suddenly as the courtyard had filled, it emptied, except for a few serving women and guards.

Alison was so stunned that she was unaware that Will and Robbie had remained in the courtyard until Will ran to her and threw his arms around her waist.

"I won't let him turn ye into an animal like him," she said. Tears ran down her face as she held Will and ran her hand over his hair.

Over the top of his head, she met Robbie's gaze, and the hardness in his it reminded her too much of David's.

"You've no right to judge him," Robbie said. Before he could say more, her daughters' arrival stopped him.

"You're back!" Margaret called out as she ran up, then her face fell. "What's wrong? Why is Will crying?"

"He's not," Robbie snapped, then he put his arm around his brother and stomped off with him.

***

David wished he could have avoided returning to the castle before riding to the market cross in the town of Duns. He had no choice. After Will's ordeal, he needed to see his brother safe inside the castle walls. Besides that, it was important that the entire household bear witness and spread the word of his ruthlessness toward his enemies.

But he had paid a high price for it. Alison had looked at him as if he were one of the damned from hell. Until that moment, he had, despite her betrayal and all good sense, retained the foolish hope that he might in time earn her forgiveness for capturing her and her lands and gain her true affection.

When he saw the sheer horror on Alison's face, that hope froze and died inside him.

But he'd be damned if he'd make excuses for what he'd done. Alison could not love him for what he was, but only a ruthless man could keep her safe.

***

Alison listened to the male voices drifting up from the hall as she paced the bedchamber, waiting for her husband. Apparently, David was in no hurry to see her. She had seen him ride in an hour ago, after she sent the children to bed. Will was not himself, so she told him he could sleep on a pallet in the girls' chamber tonight and left Flora to put them to bed. No doubt seeing the severed head had upset the poor lad.

That was nothing to how upset he'd be when the Crown forces came to take David away. She was frightened out of her mind for him. And how could he do it? She had persuaded herself to dismiss half of what people said about him, but she wondered now if every sordid tale was true. Had she been blinded by love?

She had meant to choose her words carefully, but by the time David deigned to come upstairs, she had worn out the floorboards with her pacing and worked herself into a state.

He closed the door and stood in front of it with his hands on hips, but he said nothing.

"How could ye commit such a vile act?" she asked.

"It was necessary."

"Cutting off his head and tying it to your saddle by his hair was *necessary*?" she said, her voice rising. "Do ye not fear God will punish you for murdering and desecrating the body of a man like D'Orsey? Ach, there was no man in all of Scotland so esteemed for his chivalrous conduct."

"Men who live by the sword die by it," he said in a belligerent tone.

"What good could your act of barbarism possibly bring?" she asked, raising her hands in the air. "Except to bring the Crown's wrath down on you?"

"I told the crowd that gathered around the market cross that so long as my father's widow remains a prisoner, any man who ventures from Dunbar Castle can expect the same."

"Ye believe such threats will achieve anything?"

"I don't make idle threats," he said, with ice in his eyes. "They'll free her soon. This sort of news travels faster than horses."

"My God," she said, shaking her head, "you're a cold, bloodthirsty barbarian."

David moved with the swift grace of the lions in the royal menagerie. He stood over her, his body vibrating with emotion.

"Just remember, this cold, bloodthirsty barbarian," he said through clenched teeth, "is all that stands between you and those who would use you and your daughters for their own ends."

"And you're different from the Blackadders and my family, are ye?" she said. "You haven't used us?"

"If you'd rather put your daughters into their hands, then do it," he snapped. "Ye know they're safer with me. Ye should be grateful that men fear me."

"What I fear is that you'll bring the Crown's forces down on us," she said. "By the saints, David, could ye not have shown some restraint?"

"D'Orsey led the forces that took my family's home and my father's widow," he said, his chest rising and falling with labored breaths. "After losing her husband of fifteen years, his head displayed on a pike for ridicule, the woman is ill with grief, and yet D'Orsey still refused to release her."

"I understand that—"

"Ye understand nothing! A price had to be paid, a lesson given," he said in a low, menacing voice. "Justice demands blood for blood."

Despite herself, she took a step back. He was showing her his wounds, but he reminded her of a wild beast whose wounds enraged him and made him more dangerous.

"They cut off my father's head and displayed it on a pike on the Tolbooth for all of Edinburgh to see. *My father's head!* And you suggest my response should have been measured?" He stepped closer, his eyes burning fire. "Nay, Alison, restraint was not possible."

He left the room without a backward glance. Alison sank to the floor, shaking.

CHAPTER 42

For the first time since their wedding night, David slept in the former laird's bed-less chamber—and he slept just as poorly as he had that night. When he was not imagining his wife naked in their bed in the chamber above him, he was plagued by images of her face horrified by the sight of him.

Something had snapped inside him when Alison accused him of using her and her daughters and being no better than her family and the Blackadders. Perhaps it was the element of truth to her accusation that made him lose control of his temper and frighten her.

In the morning, the tension was so thick between them at breakfast that even Beatrix was quiet. It pained him to see the shadows beneath Alison's eyes and how pale her face was against her dark hair.

He got up and left the table to spare her his presence.

A short time later a message arrived from Dunbar Castle. Evidently, word of D'Orsey's death had traveled quickly indeed. The captain of the garrison advised him that Lady Isabella "was ill" and invited him in the most stiffly cordial terms to fetch her as soon as he may. Though he knew the illness was a pretense that her release was an act of mercy, it worried David.

He would set out at once with Will and a large guard. Robbie was out riding patrol with some of the men, so he would have to wait to see his mother when they returned.

David did not bother bidding his wife goodbye. She would be glad to see him gone. As he took one last look at her across the length of the room, he felt as if a fist squeezed his heart.

***

An unexpected swell of emotion filled David's chest when the drawbridge at Dunbar Castle was lowered and Isabella walked across it, followed by her maid and two servants carrying a trunk. At long last, he had fulfilled his father's dying command to free her.

He stood back while Will embraced his mother.

"Forgive me for taking so long to obtain your release," David said, going down on one knee before her. "Robbie will be at the castle when we return."

"I'm grateful," Isabella said, touching her fingertips to his cheek. "I feared my sons would be grown before I saw them again."

"We need to be gone from here," he said, looking up at the row of guards on the castle's gatehouse, "lest they change their minds."

He helped Isabella mount, and none of them spoke again until Dunbar Castle was a good distance behind them.

"Are ye well?" David asked Isabella. She looked thin and drawn, but her health had always been delicate.

"I'm going home," she said, smiling, "so I feel grand."

"We're not going home," Will piped up. "I mean, we're not going to Hume Castle. We have a new home."

David sighed. This was not how he wished to break the news to her.

"New home?" Isabella asked, turning to him.

"Aye, we laid siege to Blackadder Castle," he said. "It's ours now."

"And David has a wife too," Will said.

"You? Married?" Isabella said, looking as if she'd seen a pig fly.

David's head was aching.

"Her name is Alison—Lady Alison," Will said. "She's pretty and kind, and we all like her verra much."

"Then I'm sure that I shall like her as well."

David spurred his horse and rode ahead.

The journey to Dunbar had taken half a day, and he'd had hoped to return by nightfall. Despite Isabella's assurance that she was well, she tired easily. He was glad he'd had the foresight to order a tent brought along for her.

Will ate supper with her in the tent, then came out to join David and the men around the fire.

"Mother wishes to speak with ye," Will said.

"Now?" David asked.

When Will nodded, David took a drink from his flask and got up. There was no door to knock on, but he felt uneasy simply entering her tent.

"Lady Isabella," he called from outside. "Ye should be resting. Shall we speak in the morning?"

"Come in." Her voice was so faint he barely heard it.

He stepped inside and looked at the woman who had caused the downfall of his father and nearly his clan as well. Yet he could not blame her for his father's weakness. Isabella had never meant to cause harm.

"My son has grown fond of your bride and her daughters in a short time," she said with a warm smile. "Will spoke of little else."

"Hmmph," David grunted, and hoped that would be the end of it.

"What about you?" Isabella asked.

"What about me?"

"How do you feel about your new bride?"

Why was she asking? She'd never concerned herself much with him before.

"We've spoken little, you and I, for having lived under the same roof for so many years," she said, seeming to read his thoughts. "After losing your father and being kept away from all of you, I don't want this distance between us anymore."

All David wanted to do was leave the tent.

"I could never have replaced your mother in your heart," she said, "but I should have tried harder to mother you. You were still young enough to need it."

"I was *ten*." For God's sake.

"As I said." She sighed. "I do regret it."

"You've nothing to regret with regard to me." It was not her fault that he was difficult to feel affection toward, even as a child.

"I was young and so in love. And then the babes came," she said, sounding wistful. She paused, then asked, "So tell me, how did you acquire this wife?"

"She came with the castle," he said, which caused his stepmother to laugh.

"Then I assume this is Alison *Douglas* we're talking about," she said. "That was a bold move."

"Aye, it was."

"You sound as though you regret it," she said, pinching her brows together. When he didn't respond, she said, "Naturally, the circumstances make for a difficult start to a marriage, but Will thinks so well of her. You should give the lass a chance."

"I don't regret making Alison my wife," he said in a tight voice.

"What is it, then?" She startled him by leaning forward and touching his hand. "Come, tell me."

"What I regret," he said after a long silence, "is forcing her to wed me."

He didn't know why he confessed this to Isabella, with whom he'd never had an intimate conversation in his life.

It had been necessary for him to marry Blackadder's widow and gain control of the daughters, and he would make the same decision if he had it to do over again. Yet, in his heart of hearts, he wished Alison had become his wife under different circumstances. Ridiculous as it was, he wished he could have given her the choice, and that she had wed him because she wanted him.

"You care for her," Isabella said.

"Aye," he admitted, shifting his gaze to the roof of the tent.

"Why does that make you unhappy?" she asked. "Does she not care for you?"

He wanted to believe that, for a brief time, Alison had cared. She knew him for what he was now, and any affection she might have felt before had been replaced by revulsion.

"My nature offends her," he said.

"You're a fine man, one any woman would be proud to call husband."

"My wife does not agree." He got to his feet. There was nothing to be gained by discussing it further.

"Give her time," Isabella said, looking up at him.

"Time won't change this," he said. "I'm the wrong man for her."

And Alison was the only woman for him.

He made up his mind on the ride back. He would give her what she had wanted all along.

***

Alison felt at loose ends and took a walk around the castle grounds. David was furious with her, and she did not know how they would mend things between them.

She thought back to the day of the picnic and how happy she was then. Nothing had been right between them since, and she had made them worse by her reaction to D'Orsey's death. But heavens, what woman wouldn't be upset by that gruesome head?

Once David was no longer standing over her like an enraged bull, she had been able to give more thought to what he'd said about it. She had not fully appreciated before the magnitude of David's smoldering rage over his father's death.

Though she could never condone what he'd done to D'Orsey—she shuddered again at the thought—she could admit there was justice to it, given D'Orsey's role in his father's beheading. And to her surprise, it apparently had persuaded the new garrison commander at Dunbar to release

Will and Robbie's mother. David had been right about that.

Alison turned the corner of the keep and found Robbie leaning against the wall, watching her daughters play with their wooden toys. Knowing Robbie, he must be bored senseless.

She felt him tense as she leaned against the wall next to him. "You've developed a sudden interest in carved animals, I see."

He folded his arms and continued watching the girls with a serious expression.

"Your friends are on the other side of the keep practicing," she said.

"When David's gone, I'm responsible for these lasses' safety." He gave her a sour sideways glance. "And yours."

"Why are ye upset with me?" she asked.

"I'm not," Robbie said, keeping his gaze on her daughters.

Alison blew out a breath in exasperation. "Something's happened. I want ye to tell me what it is."

"Ye want to know?" Robbie said, turning fierce green eyes on her that were so much like David's. "Truly?"

"I do."

"Nay, ye don't," he said. "Ye want to believe what ye want to believe."

Her mind had been on her troubles with David, but she realized now that Robbie had been stone-faced around her since David paraded the head around the courtyard and Will cried. But why would he be angry with her for that?

"Come," she said, "tell me what this is about."

"Ye acted disgusted by what David did to that French bastard, but ye don't know why he did it," he spat out. "And ye don't care why."

David had already told her why. *Blood for blood, a lesson had to be given.* Apparently Robbie felt the need to explain that to her too, so she'd let him.

"I do care," she said, "so why don't ye tell me."

"D'Orsey was going to murder our Will," Robbie said. "I tried to save him, but D'Orsey knocked me sideways and sent me flying, as if I was one of those wooden toys."

Robbie paused to wipe at an angry tear that slid down his cheek.

"He had his sword raised over Will." He swallowed. "I saw David coming on his horse, but he was too far away. He could never make it. I thought my little brother was dead."

Alison touched his arm, but he jerked it away.

"D'Orsey's blade was no more than a breath away from slicing Will in two," Robbie said. "But David came riding up at a full gallop and struck with such force that it lifted D'Orsey backward off his feet."

Her hand went to her throat. Tears sprang to her eyes at the thought of how close they'd come to losing Will.

"Why did David not tell me?" she asked.

"Loyalty is everything to him," Robbie said. "He expected ye to trust him, to believe in him, without requiring an explanation."

She had failed David, and he could not forgive her.

***

Alison watched with a lump in her throat as Robbie picked his mother up off the ground in an embrace and spun her around.

"My, you've grown so tall," Isabella said through her tears.

All through the introductions, Alison's gaze strayed to the door. David must have stopped to talk to the guards at the gate or to give instructions regarding the horses to the stable lads.

"Will spoke so much of you, that I feel as though I already know you," Isabella said to her.

"Mmmhmm." Alison smiled and leaned to look past her. She feared she was being rude, but she was distracted, waiting for David. It was pouring rain. What was keeping him?

She was anxious to apologize to him and set things right. He'd saved Will's life and rescued Isabella, and she had upbraided him.

"Pardon me," she said, touching Isabella's arm, "but I must find David."

She opened the outer door and squinted against the driving rain. She spotted David walking his horse through the muddy courtyard. Why was he leading it *away* from the stable?

"David!" she called, but he didn't hear her.

She picked up her skirts and ran after him. Though the distance was short, her skirts were heavy with mud and rain soaked her back by the time she reached him.

"David," she said, catching his arm. "Where are you going?"

"I'm leaving for Hume Castle," he said, his face expressionless.

Disappointment weighed down on her chest.

"So soon?" She wiped at the water streaming down her face with her sleeve. "When will ye be back?"

He shrugged, and she noticed a raindrop caught on his lashes. He had such beautiful eyes. But he looked tired, and she longed to brush her palm against his unshaven cheek.

"When?" she asked again.

"I expect I'll be back from time to time," he said. "But I'll be living at Hume Castle now. I've left Brian in charge here."

"*Living* at Hume Castle?" She blinked against the rain pouring into her eyes as she tried to absorb this news. "Can't we leave tomorrow? I need a bit of time to pack my things. And shouldn't we wait for this storm to pass?"

"You'll be staying here. Brian's a good man and will keep ye safe." He started to reach for a dripping strand of hair that was stuck to her cheek, but dropped his hand. "Go inside before ye catch your death."

"I don't want to go inside," she said. "Tell me what ye mean. Say it outright."

"We'll remain married," he said, turning his gaze away from her. "But I think it best we live apart."

"Why?" she asked, stunned. Was he that disappointed in her?

"Ye wanted your freedom," he said, still not looking at her. "I'm giving it to ye."

"But...but..." she sputtered, "what if I don't wish to live apart?"

"I can't be the man ye want," he said.

Before she could find any words that might change his mind, he mounted his horse.

"I wish ye happy," he said, and dipped his head.

She could have been content with her freedom if she had never met him, never become his wife. But not now. Why did David steal her heart only to leave her?

"Why did you ever come here?" she said, clenching her hands. "Could ye not have let me be?"

Alison stood, soaked to the skin, and stared after him long after he rode out the gate.

CHAPTER 43

"I'm your mother, Beatrix," Alison said, folding her arms as she stood over her daughter. "You'll have to speak to me sometime."

She was not sure which was worse, Beatrix furious and glaring at her, or Margaret looking pitiful as she sat on the floor rubbing her wooden pig against her cheek.

"Why did ye make David leave?" Beatrix said, stamping her foot.

At least Beatrix had finally spoken to her, but Alison felt too weary to deal with her daughter's anger. She could barely crawl through the days since David left.

"If ye think I have the power to make the Laird of Wedderburn do my bidding," Alison said, "you're mistaken."

"Ye haven't even tried to bring him home," Beatrix said, her voice thickening with the tears she was holding back. "You've done nothing! Nothing!"

He doesn't want me.

Beatrix held out her hand to Margaret and led her sister out of the room. Alison watched them leave, then dropped onto a stool facing the narrow window. She stared out at the dark clouds that were gathering on the horizon, like a reflection of her dismal future.

The next morning, the hall was nearly empty by the time she dragged herself downstairs. She sank into a chair beside Isabella near the hearth and picked up the needlework she'd left there.

"Ye missed breakfast again," Isabella said.

She had lain in bed missing the warmth of David's body next to hers and risen too late.

"Ye should go down to the kitchens and get something to eat," Isabella said. "While you're there, ye can give your new cook instructions."

"I'm not hungry."

Alison should become acquainted with the new members of her household Brian had brought from Hume Castle to replace the servants David had sent away. Not long ago, she would have relished training new servants, but she let Isabella do it for her because she simply did not care.

"Blood for blood is a sacred duty here in the Borders," Isabella said. "David could not hold his head up as a man, and certainly not as a laird, until retribution was exacted."

"I understand that now." Alison stifled a sigh. Isabella had said that so often in the last days as to be a trifle tedious.

They stitched in blessed silence for a time.

"Ye do know he has a mistress at Hume Castle?" Isabella asked.

Alison felt as if the wind had been knocked out of her in a hard fall and could not draw breath.

"At least, Gelis *was* his mistress," Isabella said, continuing with her stitching as if this was nothing. "I imagine she's still there. Waiting."

"You're speaking of *David's* mistress?" Alison said, her mind slow to accept what she was hearing.

"David's not the sort of man to go from bed to bed," Isabella said.

Never once had Alison heard of him disappearing with one of the serving women, though more than one had given him the eye. She had taken his fidelity for granted.

"So naturally, he kept a mistress," Isabella continued. "Same one these past two years."

"He wasn't married at that time," Alison said.

"Aye. Did I say her name is Gelis?" Isabella tied a knot and bit her thread. "Can't say I like her much, but she has the sort of curves that leaves men with their tongues dragging on the floor, if ye know what I mean."

Alison felt as if a blade had been stuck in her heart.

Isabella gave a small sigh. "I assume he'll take up with her again now."

"He wouldn't," Alison said.

"A man has needs," Isabella said, giving Alison a sideways glance, "particularly a *vigorous* young man such as David."

The thought of David touching another woman, *vigorously* or otherwise, made her feel sick to her stomach.

"What are ye going to do about this?" Isabella's voice broke into her thoughts.

"What can I do?" Abandoning the pretense that she was stitching, Alison tossed her needlepoint across the floor.

"Well, the first thing ye can do is not leave him alone with that Gelis,"

Isabella said.

"David ordered me not to leave the castle," she said, blinking back tears. "The last time I did, it ended verra badly."

"A wife must have the good sense to know when to ignore her husband's orders."

"David doesn't want me. He wouldn't have left if he did," Alison said. "And he'll *never* trust me."

"He told me he cares for ye," Isabella said. "And God knows that's not something David would admit to lightly."

"He did?" Alison asked, sitting up straight.

"As for not trusting ye, well, running off certainly didn't help, dear," Isabella said and patted her arm. "But I suspect that the true reason David mistrusts your loyalty is because, in his heart, he doesn't believe he's worthy of love."

Alison's hand went to her heart. What Isabella said struck a chord of truth. Despite David's devotion to his family and clan, he stood apart. There was a core of loneliness deep inside him. She felt sure that she had breached the walls around his heart to reach it before she had gone to the abbey.

Surely she could do it again. She had to.

"I'll ask Brian to arrange an escort for me and leave at once." Alison stood and leaned over to Isabella to kiss her cheek. "Thank you."

Isabella gave her a knowing smile.

Before Alison had taken two steps, Flora entered the hall, waving her hands in the air.

"I can't find them! They're gone! They're gone!"

***

David refilled his cup with whisky, tossed it back, and wiped his mouth on his sleeve.

He did not miss her. And he most definitely did not need her.

But when he closed his eyes at night, all he saw was Alison. He had to drink himself into a stupor to sleep at all. Even blind drunk, he heard her voice, her laugh, her sighs. He remembered exactly how her fingertips felt on his cheek.

The woman's hand on his shoulder was familiar, but it was not Alison's. Her scent was not Alison's either.

He felt warm breath in his ear.

"Come to bed," the woman said. "I'll make ye forget her."

"'Tis not possible." Even if it were, he did not want to forget Alison.

Memories were all he had, and he clung to them like a man lost at sea grasping a broken plank from his sunken ship.

"I'm willing to try," the woman said in a throaty voice.

David shook his head, which made the room spin and blur. "Just pour me another."

Soon after, his forehead hit the table and his vision went blissfully black. He had no idea if hours or days had passed when next he woke, but his neck was stiff from the awkward angle his head lay on the table.

"How long has he been like this?"

David heard Alison's voice as though through a thick fog. But he'd heard her voice in his head so often that he knew better than to believe it was truly her. She was miles away in Blackadder Castle, out of his reach, enjoying her freedom and hating him. Which was what he deserved.

"Someone should have sent for me."

He smiled at the irritation in Alison's tone. Usually he thought of her in her softer moments, but he liked to see her riled, too, with her violet eyes flashing.

"David!"

Her voice in his ear and the touch of her hand on his shoulder were so real this time he wanted to weep. Ach, what a ruin of a man he was.

"Get up," she said, and shook his shoulder hard. "I need ye, David Hume."

She needed him? Not likely.

All the same, he risked spoiling the illusion by cracking one eye open. Her lovely face was just inches in front of his. Her violet eyes were startlingly beautiful this close.

"Is it really you?" he asked, his tongue thick in his mouth.

"Aye," she said, and brushed his hair back from his face with her fingers in a soothing gesture he never thought he'd feel again.

He should lift his head off the table, but it was heavy, and he still suspected he was dreaming. But when he focused his eyes and saw fine lines of distress pinching her brows, he sat up. The abrupt movement gave him a blinding headache and roiling stomach, but he ignored them.

"What's happened?" he asked. "Are my brothers safe?"

"They are. But David," she said, her bottom lip quivering, "our girls are gone."

David had been drinking for days, but he was suddenly stone cold sober. The image of Beatrix's and Margaret's sweet faces was as clear in his mind as if they stood before him.

"Sit down," he said, taking Alison's hand, "and tell me all ye know."

"Flora woke to find them gone from their bed. She thought nothing of it at first, but when they missed breakfast, she went to look for them."

"They must be somewhere in the castle," he said.

"I had the entire household looking for them," she said. "Will knows all their hiding places, but they were nowhere to be found."

What mishap could have befallen them inside the castle? David's heart lurched as he thought of the castle's deep well.

"Then one of the guards found their pup barking outside the gate," she said.

"Outside?" Good God, the lassies must have left the castle. The guards who let them pass would feel his wrath. "They couldn't have gotten far on their own."

"We called and looked for them," she said, wringing her hands. "Others are still looking, but I came for you. I fear someone has kidnapped them from the castle."

It was possible. The guards checked carts coming in, but not those going out. The pup must have followed the cart or horse with the lassies out, but he was too young to keep up for long.

"I am so sorry, love." He enfolded Alison in his arms and kissed her hair. "I will get them back. No matter what it takes. If I have to move heaven and hell, I will get them back."

"I know ye will," she said. "But I'm so frightened."

This time, she had sought his help, not her brothers'. He hoped he was worthy of her faith. She leaned back, and the warmth in her violet eyes made the ice around his heart melt.

"I intended to come for ye even before I knew the girls were missing," she said, brushing her fingertips over his cheek. "I love ye, David Hume, and I want ye to come home."

David pulled Alison against him and buried his face in her hair. With her in his arms, he was already home.

***

Patrick could not believe his luck.

"'Tis a pleasure to see you two lasses again," he said, smiling down at them.

A couple of the Blackadder women Wedderburn had thrown out of the castle were in the village, probably asking for handouts, when they saw this pair. They caught them and brought them straight to Patrick, expecting a reward.

"*I can't help but be curious. How did ye happen to be walking on the road from Blackadder Castle to the village all on your own?*"

The two exchanged a look, and the older one shook her head.

"*I asked ye a question.*" *The smaller one was already weeping, so he picked her up and gave her a shake.* "*Tell me.*"

"*Put my sister down and I'll tell,*" *the older one said.*

"*See, I can be verra agreeable if ye do as I say.*" *He set the sniveling bairn on her feet, then sat down in the ornate chair that had belonged to his father and propped his feet up.* "*So, lassie, tell me the tale.*"

"*We sneaked out when the gates were opened for carts bringing supplies for the kitchens,*" *the older girl said.* "*It was early and still half dark, so no one saw us.*"

Patrick threw back his head and laughed. After all the trouble Wedderburn had gone to, the pair of wee lassies had walked out the front gate on their own.

"*Ach, I'd love to see Wedderburn's face when he realizes he's lost his heiresses.*" *Patrick had not been this amused since he watched his father thrashing on the floor.* "*Where in God's name did ye think ye were going?*"

The girls exchanged another look instead of answering. But when he started to reach for the younger one, the older girl spoke up quickly.

"*To Hume Castle,*" *she said.* "*To bring our laird home.*"

Patrick leaned forward. "*Wedderburn is not at Blackadder Castle?*"

Both girls shook their heads.

"*But your mother's still there?*"

They nodded. More good news.

"*I answered your questions,*" *the older girl said.* "*Can we go home now?*"

"*Home?*" *He laughed again. They were such idiots.*

But what should he do with them? He drummed his fingers. Killing them was the simplest solution to eliminating their inheritance claim. He could dump their bodies by the village, and the blame would never fall on him.

That, however, would not satisfy his need for vengeance against Wedderburn. He smiled at his puny captives as a plan formed in his head. For now, at least, they were more valuable to him alive than dead.

CHAPTER 44

"I see you're awake, Laird," Gelis said, leaning in the doorway.

David watched Alison eye her and wondered how in the hell she knew who Gelis was. He'd heard that women could sense that sort of thing, but he had not even thought of touching Gelis since he returned.

"Now that you're awake," Gelis said, and sauntered over, swinging her hips, "a message came for ye earlier."

She was doing her best to make Alison believe there was something still between them, judging by the suggestive look she was giving him. Ach, he did not need Gelis making trouble for him now. Not when he finally had Alison here.

He pulled Alison tight against his side and kissed her cheek.

"Gelis, this lovely lass is my wife, Lady Alison." His voice thickened with emotion at the word *wife*. "Ye can take the whiskey away. I've no need of it now."

He heard the door shut, but he could not take his eyes off Alison. He could not imagine wanting anyone else.

He forgot about the message until Alison picked it from the table. He broke the seal and looked for the signature at the bottom.

"It's from Patrick Blackadder," he said. Patrick signed it as laird, so his father must be dead.

"I knew it," Alison said, her hand going to her throat. "He has Beatrix and Margaret, doesn't he?"

David took the letter to the window to read it in the fading light. There was nothing subtle about the message. He had let Patrick see his weakness, and his enemy was taking advantage of it.

Lady Alison swore to me that the Beast of Wedderburn truly cared for her daughters. Pretending affection toward her daughters to win the mother's was a clever trick, but now you must make a choice. Will you keep all that you've gained and cause Alison to hate you? Or will you prove as foolish as your father and give up everything?

"What does he want?" Alison asked, leaning over his shoulder.

David scanned the rest of the letter. Patrick was demanding he give up everything he had fought for.

"I will relinquish one daughter," David read aloud, "in exchange for possession of Blackadder Castle."

"For only one of them?" Alison said.

"In exchange for the second daughter," David continued, "you must submit yourself to my custody so that I may deliver you to Edinburgh to face charges of treason for murdering the Crown's warden."

Alison sat down hard. "Oh, David, what will we do?"

"We'll meet his terms," he said. "We've no choice. We can't risk the girls' lives."

"Surely we can find another way," she said. "Ye can't put yourself in that man's hands."

"The exchange is to take place tomorrow," David said. "That doesn't give us time to plan a subterfuge, even if I were willing to take the risk, which I'm not."

He glanced again at the last lines of the message, which he had not read to her.

Alas, the health of children can be so precarious. Remember that before you consider attempting to take the daughters from me by force or trickery during the exchange.

"With Albany gone, I've a good chance of fighting the treason charge," he said, trying to reassure her without actually lying. "The English king is threatening to invade. The Council will want a strong man on the border to keep English troops from reaching Edinburgh."

"I don't trust Patrick to stand by the bargain and take ye to Edinburgh," she said. "Do you?"

He shrugged and said, "We'll see."

There was no chance in hell Patrick would give him up. He was as set on revenge as David was—or rather, as he once was. He looked at Alison. Now that he had so much to lose, vengeance was not worth the cost.

"We must find a way around this," she said. "We'll offer the castle for both girls."

"Patrick won't accept that."

"Then I'll beg my brothers for their help."

He raised an eyebrow at her. They both knew how likely that was to meet with success.

"Things are different now," she said, clinging to his arm. "They will have heard that when ye confronted D'Orsey hundreds of Scots crossed to your side. They'll want ye on their side for their fight with the Hamiltons."

"I'll send an escort to ride with ye to your brothers."

Even if her brothers did send help, which he doubted, they would never arrive in time. The ride to Edinburgh, however, would keep Alison safely away from the exchange. If she were there, he feared Patrick would be tempted to add her to his list of demands.

"I'll not be parted from ye so soon," Alison said. "I'll send a message to my sister, Sybil. If anyone can browbeat my brothers into coming, she will."

David was relieved when she agreed to wait at Hume Castle for their arrival.

As soon as she finished writing her letter and sealed it, he sent for one of his men to carry it the Douglases.

"Lady Sybil must receive it tonight," Alison told the man. "Tell the servants to wake her if need be."

After the messenger left, David bolted the door and took Alison into his arms.

"Ach, I missed ye so much," he said.

"Why did ye leave me?" she asked in a small voice.

"I thought that's what ye wanted," he said. "I'm a rough man who doesn't deserve ye."

"You're a good man," she said. "What I wanted was your trust and your heart."

"I should have trusted ye," he said, "but you've had my heart from the start."

He felt like a beast to want her so desperately when they were both filled with such fear for Beatrix and Margaret. Yet he could not help his body's reaction with her breath on his neck, her scent filling his nose, and her soft curves pressed against him.

"I've been a fool to waste the time we could have had together," he said as he ran his fingers through the thick strands of her midnight hair.

"I'm glad we have tonight," she said, leaning back to look at him. "Make love to me, David. I need ye."

"We'll make the most of this night," he said. "It may be a while before we have another."

He knew it would be their last.

"I'm sorry I never told ye how verra much I love you," he said. If by some miracle he survived this, he would tell her every day.

***

Alison cursed the birdsong and the gray light coming through the window, sure signs of dawn—and David's imminent departure. From David's breathing, she knew he was awake too.

"Patrick would take me in your place," she said, running her fingers over his chest.

"Ach, ye can't think I could live myself if I let ye do that." David cupped the back of her neck with his hand and traced the line of her jaw with his thumb.

"But he wouldn't kill me," she said. "He's always wanted me."

"Nay!" David took a deep breath, then spoke more calmly. "Besides, Patrick wouldn't agree to take ye in my place."

"Why not?"

"Because he expects he'll get ye in the end anyway," he said. "With the castle in his possession, your daughters disinherited, and me out of the way, he'll have every reason to believe your brothers will agree to a marriage."

"But I'd never do it." She would die first.

"I can face whatever comes so long as I know you're safe from him," he said, his eyes fierce on hers. "You're strong enough to stand up to your brothers. Stay with my men, and they'll protect you."

"Don't worry about me," she said, and brushed a long, sun-bleached strand of hair behind his ear. "I'll be waiting for ye."

"The time grows late," he said. "I must get dressed and go."

She crawled out of bed and fetched his shirt for him.

"While ye were sleeping, I used the tip of your dagger to pry the black stone from my pendant," she said as she helped him put it on, "and I sewed it into the hem of your shirt."

She took his hand and showed him where the bump in the hem was. The stone was flat and only an inch in diameter, so she did not think it would be noticed.

"I know they'll take your weapons." She swallowed. "But I couldn't let ye go in there with no protection."

David smiled at that.

"I know ye don't believe the stone holds magic, but it's brought me the best of luck since I found it again." She paused, fighting tears. "It brought me you."

"I'll bear this burden lightly, knowing I have something of yours with me," he said, and patted the hem of his shirt where the stone lay. "Now, lass, we must say goodbye."

"This is not goodbye," she said.

He brushed her cheek with his fingers, and the sad resignation on his face frightened her more than anything.

"From something Patrick told me," she said, "I don't believe he'll kill ye right away."

David did not speak, but she could see in his eyes that he believed the same.

"That gives us time," she said, gripping the front of his shirt. "Promise me you'll hold out until we can get ye released."

"Dying easy isn't in my nature, lass," he said with a bittersweet smile.

"Trust me, my love," she said, and gave him one last kiss. "This is not the end."

If her brothers did not come soon, she had another plan.

David would not like it.

CHAPTER 45

As David rode into Blackadder Castle as the laird and a free man for the last time, the memory of entering Holyrood Palace with his father and uncle on that fateful day made him break in a cold sweat. It was not that he feared death, but that he wanted to die with a sword in his hand, not chained and beaten.

This was not the death he would choose, but he would give his life a hundred times over to save Beatrix and Margaret—and to spare Alison the pain of losing them.

His time with her had been far too short. He wanted to have half a dozen children with her and to grow old together. Still, he counted himself a lucky man. He had been truly loved for a time by a dark-haired angel.

He dismounted and patted his father's horse. One of his brothers could have the stallion now.

In short order, he called his men into the hall and told them about Patrick's message and the exchange that would take place. The hall filled with raised voices as the men made their objections known. David raised his hand to silence the uproar.

"'Tis been an honor to lead you," he said when they quieted. "But I've made my decision, and you'll all follow it."

He took Brian and Robbie aside. Time was growing short.

"Brian, I'm counting on ye to take Alison's daughters to safety at Hume Castle after the exchange," he said. "Ride fast. The Blackadders may try to follow."

"I'll get them and your brothers to Hume Castle," Brian said. "But can we not rescue the lassies some other way?"

David remembered Patrick's threat and shook his head. *Alas, the health of children can be so precarious.* He turned to Robbie.

"I may not return from this," he said, putting hand on Robbie's shoulder. "You're young to take up this burden of leading the clan."

"Lead the clan?"

"Brian will make the decisions and train ye for the next two years," David said. "Listen well to him and Alison. With their guidance, you'll be a wiser laird than I."

"No one could match you," Robbie said, blinking back tears. "Ye must come back to us."

"I'll certainly try," he said, and put his arm around his brother's shoulders.

"Don't do this," Robbie said.

"Patrick Blackadder wants my blood," David said. "I can see no other way to persuade him to release Beatrix and Margaret."

"Then put him off until we can think of one."

"If we delay, he'll murder them." David thought of what happened to Alison's aunts. With the right poison, it would be impossible to prove the wee lasses did not simply fall ill.

He called Will to him next. Ach, this was hard. He felt he already knew the man Robbie would become, but Will was still a half-written page. Though David could not divine precisely how this brother would turn out, Will was special and was sure to become a man worth knowing.

"I want ye to keep my sword for me," he said, then he picked his brother up and gave him a bear hug like he used to when Will was a wee bairn. "Look after your mother."

"They're coming!" someone shouted.

David went up on the wall to watch his enemy's arrival. Relief swept over him when he saw the small figures of Beatrix and Margaret riding with two of the Blackadder men. Until this moment, he had not been certain they were still alive.

"David!" The girls shouted and waved when they saw him.

They looked bedraggled but unharmed. *Praise God.* When the Blackadders halted, the girls were taken off the horses and held by a familiar, black-haired warrior.

"Ye cannot act on it now," David said in Brian's ear, "but that is Walter."

Brian stared at Walter, as if memorizing his image. "I will kill him one day verra soon."

"Good," David said.

"What is your decision, Wedderburn?" Patrick shouted from below.

"I accept your terms," David called back. "All of them."

"Empty the castle and hand yourself over," Patrick shouted, "and I'll release the two lasses."

Neither side trusted the other, and David left it to Brian to argue the timing. In the end, it was agreed that the Humes would empty the castle first but that the gates would remain open until one girl was handed over.

David gave the order, and the Humes filed out. To ensure the agreement was followed, the Blackadder archers had arrows aimed at the girls' hearts, while the Humes had arrows aimed at Patrick.

David was the last Hume to leave. The loss of this castle, which had been so important to him once, meant nothing compared to losing his brothers, his stepdaughters, and most of all, his wife.

Patrick and all but thirty of the Blackadders trooped into the castle. After conducting a search to make sure David had not left men hidden inside, Patrick appeared on the wall.

"Let one of them go," Patrick called down.

Walter released Margaret. She ran across the thirty yards that separated the Humes and the Blackadders who remained outside the gate, straight into David's arms.

He held her for a moment, squeezing his eyes shut, then handed her to Robbie. "Keep her hidden behind the men," he said.

"Now for the moment of truth," Patrick said in a loud voice. "Will the Beast give himself up for a useless lassie?"

Beatrix, who was still held by Walter, looked at David and shook her head. She was as brave as her mother.

"I've pledged to deliver your laird to the Council," Patrick shouted to the Hume men. "But one wrong move, and we'll kill both the lass and your laird."

"Brian," David whispered, "protect my family."

"With my last breath," Brian said. "I wish there was another way to do this."

"A man has to die sometime."

And if he must, dying to save those he loved was the best of reasons.

David took a deep breath. Then he did what he had vowed he would never do again.

Just as he had done when he entered Holyrood Palace with his father and uncle on the day they died, he ignored the prickle at the back of his neck and every instinct that told him to fight, and he disarmed himself.

He unstrapped his sword and handed it to Will. Then he removed the dirks from his belt and boot, and the hidden one strapped to his thigh. Finally, he pulled the ax from the back of his belt and dropped it on the ground.

Danger hung in the air and death awaited as he walked with steady steps toward his enemy. Two-thirds of the way across the divide, he halted. He stood alone and weaponless.

"Let the other lass go!" Brian's voice rang out.

For an instant, David considered whether it was possible to fight, rather than give himself up. When Beatrix ran to him, could he protect her with his body until his men reached him? Nay, the risk of her being hurt was too great to attempt it.

Apparently, the Blackadders had considered this same possibility. Instead of releasing Beatrix as he had Margaret, Walter walked her across the divide to the Hume warriors with the point of his blade at her back.

David was surrounded by a dozen Blackadder warriors, who tied his hands behind his back and shoved him toward the gate. Up on the wall, the Blackadder archers still had arrows aimed at his heart. He looked over his shoulder and saw Beatrix pulled into the protection of the Hume warriors.

All of his family was safe. No matter what happened now, he had no regrets.

CHAPTER 46

Alison's joy in embracing her daughters was bittersweet.

"Praise God I have ye back." She broke down weeping as she held them.

"They've taken David," Beatrix wailed.

"I know, I know," Alison said, patting their backs. After they quieted, she asked, "How did the Blackadders manage to take ye from the castle without any of us knowing?"

"They didn't take us from the castle," Beatrix said.

"What?" Alison turned to Brian, who had brought the girls and was standing nearby with Robbie and Will.

"They've quite a tale to tell ye, Lady Alison," Brian said and nodded at Beatrix. "Out with it, lass."

"We were almost to the village when they caught us," Beatrix said. "It was those two hateful maid servants. Jasper got away, but we didn't."

"Are ye telling me ye left the castle on your own?" Alison was beside herself. The girls had brought all this on them.

"We wanted to find David and tell him we needed him to come home," Margaret said, her bottom lip trembling.

"Quick, tell her how ye left," Robbie said, poking Beatrix's arm.

"We found the secret tunnel out of the castle," Beatrix said.

Alison's heart almost stopped in her chest. Could this be the miracle she had prayed for? If there was a tunnel, their warriors could surprise the Blackadders and free David.

"What secret tunnel?" she asked.

"Will told us that the day the Humes took the castle David was afraid we'd escape through the castle's secret tunnel," she said. "We've been looking for it ever since."

"We only found it because of Jasper," Margaret piped up. "He ran into Father's old chamber, and that's where the hidden door is."

The girls never would have gone into the laird's chamber when their father was alive. In the ten years Alison had lived in Blackadder Castle, she had been in that room hundreds of times, but never a moment longer than she had to.

"Where exactly is this secret door?" Alison asked.

"In the wall, behind where the bed was." Beatrix went to explain how they had been trying to catch the puppy, and she dove for him and fell against the wall. "The bottom stone behind the tapestry moved, so I stood up and kicked it."

That was so like Beatrix.

"We felt cold air, so we crawled behind the tapestry," Beatrix continued. "And there it was. An opening in the wall, just our size."

"Is it big enough for me to fit through?" Brian asked.

"I think so," Margaret said, tilting her head back to take in his full height, "if ye mind your head."

"Where does this tunnel come out?" Alison asked.

"By the river," Beatrix said, "not far from where we had our picnic."

"The Blackadders were watching to make certain we left the area, and we needed to get these lassies to safety," Brian said. "But after dark, I'll take some men and go back."

"Wait," Alison said, and turned to her daughters. "Did ye tell Patrick how ye left the castle?"

Both girls shook their heads.

"I told him everything else," Beatrix said. "But I knew the tunnel was a verra important secret, so I lied about how we left."

"Good," Brian said. "We'll sneak in through the tunnel tonight and have our laird and the castle back by morning."

"Ye can't," Beatrix said, her shoulders slumping. "The tunnel is only for coming out, not going in."

"Why do ye say that?"

"We got scared in the tunnel and tried to turn back," she said, "but the secret door closed behind us and wouldn't open."

"Probably the lassies weren't strong enough to open it. I'll sneak back on my own now and check," Brian said, then turned to Beatrix. "Ye must try to tell me exactly where ye came out of the tunnel. It must be well hidden."

"I can show ye," Beatrix said.

"Nay," Brian said. "David was verra clear that I was to bring ye to Hume Castle and keep ye here."

"Bea is good at drawing," Will said and ran to fetch a charred piece of kindling from the hearth.

***

It was late afternoon before Brian returned. Alison knew from his defeated expression that he had not succeeded. She drew him and Robbie into a corner of the hall where they could speak alone.

"I found the tunnel. My guess is it hasn't been used since the time of our grandfathers' grandfathers. 'Tis narrow, with piles of loose rock and debris. I reached the door, but the lassies are right. There's no way to open it without breaking through the stone wall, which would take time and cause a great deal of noise."

"What we need is a man on the inside," Robbie said. "Perhaps we can bribe one of their men to open the tunnel door."

"He'd take our coin and betray us," Brian said. "Then we'd have all the Blackadders waiting for us as we came out of the tunnel."

The two argued ideas back and forth, but the answer was obvious to Alison.

"I can get inside," she interrupted. "Patrick will let me in. I'll find the door and open it for the rest of ye."

This was a far better plan than her original vague notion of going in and somehow getting David out by herself.

"Nay," Robbie said, folding his arms just like David. "Ye can't do it. 'Tis far too dangerous."

"I'm the only one who can," she said. "Patrick won't let anyone else in, and ye both know it."

"David would never agree to let ye put yourself into that man's clutches," Brian said. "Wait for your brothers and let them persuade Patrick to release him."

"I waited for my brothers once. I'll not wait again," she said, and stood up. "I'm going to save my husband."

One of the Hume men ran into the hall and called out, "There are riders coming, Lady Alison. Can ye come tell us if they're Douglases?"

Had she misjudged Archie and George? She hurried out of the keep and climbed the ladder to stand on the wall. Despair weighed down her shoulders when she saw the riders. Even if they were Douglases, what good were a dozen warriors?

Archie never rode with so few men now that he was the earl and chieftain. She narrowed her eyes, trying to see if George was one of the riders. One rider wore a gown and looked remarkably like…

Good heavens, it was her sister Sybil.

"Open the gates!" she shouted, then hurried down from the wall.

As soon as her sister rode in, she slid down from her horse and ran into Alison's arms. Sybil was only seventeen, but she radiated confidence and a lively sensuality.

"I'm so glad to see ye," Alison said. "But tell me there are more Douglases coming."

"Archie and George were away, so I came with my guard," Sybil said.

"I hoped Archie would come or send George to negotiate David's release," Alison said.

"I brought something more useful than Archie," Sybil said with a glint in her eyes. She leaned close and whispered, "I stole his seal."

Alison was shocked. A chieftain's seal carried the weight of his authority. "Archie will be in a fury."

"Not if I return it before he notices," Sybil said with a wink.

"How did ye manage to take it?" Alison asked. "Surely he keeps his seal in a locked drawer."

"I've known how to pick a lock since I was fourteen," Sybil said. "I let a lad kiss me in exchange for the lesson."

"Sybil, ye didn't."

"Ach, he was such a handsome lad, I might have kissed him anyway," she said with a wave of her hand. "Now, we'll write this nasty Patrick Blackadder a message. I've been practicing Archie's signature since the day he became earl."

"Whatever for?" Alison asked.

"To survive at Court a lass must learn such things," Sybil said.

From what Alison heard, Sybil was a great success at Court.

"Unlike Archie, who can be shortsighted and difficult," Sybil said, "I'll write whatever ye need our chieftain to say."

The more Alison thought about it, the more she thought it might work.

"Bless ye," she said, hugging her sister again.

They went upstairs, away from the prying eyes of the men, to compose the message. There was no need for the others to know Archie had not written it. When they were done, Sybil signed it with a flourish and set the Douglas chieftain's seal to it.

"I'll go with ye to Blackadder Castle," Sybil said.

"Nay, I need ye to stay here," Alison said. "If this doesn't go as we hope, I want ye to take care of my daughters."

"Me?" Sybil said. "Why not our sister Maggie? Everyone knows she'll make a wonderful mother."

"I dislike her husband," Alison said. "And I want my daughters to learn to be strong like you."

"Nothing is going to happen to you," Sybil said, gripping her arms. "But if it should, I'll teach them to be like their mother. You've changed, Allie. Love has made ye strong."

Alison felt confidence flowing through her. "Aye, it has."

"This might come in handy," Sybil said, holding up a thin piece of metal. "It's a lock pick. Doesn't work on every lock, but most of them."

"How did ye get it?"

"From the same lad," Sybil said with a grin, "for two more kisses."

***

Alison rode up to the gate of Blackadder Castle surrounded by her sister's Douglas guard, whose presence had helped persuade her Hume protectors to go along with her plan. Thanks to Sybil, who never traveled light, she wore a fine gown and elaborate headdress, as befitting her status as sister-in-law to the queen.

Alison drew her horse up a few yards from the gate and waited.

While the guards spoke among each other, she quelled the temptation to rub her sweaty palms on her skirts. A short time later, Patrick himself appeared on the wall, apparently not trusting the word of his men. He disappeared again, and her heart sank.

"Our laird welcomes Lady Alison," one of the Blackadder men shouted down. "But she must enter alone."

Alison swallowed back her panic. She must go inside and open the secret door to the tunnel. She was the only one who could save David.

After signaling to her Douglas guard to leave her, she heard them ride off. She sat still on her horse and kept her eyes fixed ahead. As she had hoped and feared, the gate creaked open. Patrick stood in the middle of the courtyard, his stance wide and his hands behind his back. Instinct urged her to turn her horse and gallop away as fast as she could.

Instead, she rode in alone to face Patrick and a castle full of warriors with nothing but a parchment rolled up her sleeve, a lock pick in her headdress, and a dagger strapped to her thigh.

CHAPTER 47

Alison forced herself to ride at a leisurely pace across the courtyard to Patrick. His resemblance to her former husband struck her anew, bringing her back to the day she had ridden into this castle as a young and frightened bride.

Patrick still thought of her that way. He underestimated her, and she would use that to her advantage.

"This is a surprise," Patrick greeted her, "but a delightful one."

She was relieved that he was choosing to be civil, at least for the moment.

"I'm glad." She tried to hide how nervous she was with a smile. "Will ye help me down?"

She clenched her teeth to keep from cringing when he clasped his hands on her waist. As she dismounted, her heavy headdress started to tilt. She imagined the lock pick lost in the dirt or, worse, falling at Patrick's feet as the headdress rolled to the ground. Heart racing, she shoved it firmly on her head with one hand as she descended to the ground, then gingerly released it.

"I apologize for not admitting your escort," Patrick said. "But circumstances make it difficult to trust anyone these days."

"I trust you," she said, taking his arm, "or I wouldn't have come, and certainly not alone."

From the look of satisfaction on his face, that had been exactly the right thing to say. She breathed a little easier.

"If you're here to ask me to release Wedderburn," he said, giving her a thorough perusal as he led her to the keep, "you'll need to be verra persuasive."

"I don't expect ye to release him," she said. "I understand he must face the Crown's justice after what he did."

Once they were inside, he snapped his fingers at the servants and ordered them to bring refreshments. Patrick clearly relished the outward signs of his new status as laird, which was so unlike David, who exuded a natural authority. David Hume could enter a room in rags, and one would know he was a leader men would follow into battle.

It felt strange to sit in her usual seat with Patrick next to her in the laird's chair that David had occupied so recently.

"I heard your father died," she said. "I am sorry for your loss."

"He was old," Patrick said. "This is fine wine, isn't it?"

Apparently he had forgotten that the wine came from her wine cellar.

"If ye didn't come to beg for Wedderburn's life," he said, "then why did ye come?"

She remembered how insistant Patrick was when he kidnapped her on the way home from the abbey that they were meant to be together and that she had always wanted him. She considered telling him he was right, but she feared she could not play that part well enough and he would see the lie. The safer course was to pretend simple acceptance of her changed circumstances.

"We women must be pragmatic," she said. "I don't wish to give up my home or my children's birthright."

She jumped in her seat as Patrick rested a hot, moist hand on her thigh. Luckily, it was not the thigh with the dirk strapped to it.

"Naturally, my brother, the Earl of Angus," she said, giving Patrick a pleasant smile as she removed his hand, "is also concerned about my and my children's future."

"Your brother?" he said. "If he had an interest, he'd be here."

"Alas, his responsibilities as stepfather to the king and a member of the King's Council make it difficult for him to leave Edinburgh at this time." She withdrew the message Sybil had forged from inside her sleeve and handed it to him. "He hopes you and I can come to an agreement that is satisfactory to both our families."

"Odd," he murmured as he read it, "that he would send a lass to negotiate."

She pasted a smile on her face, but the blood pounded in her ears as Patrick finished reading the missive. Would he guess it was a forgery?

"What makes a marriage alliance between our families acceptable to ye now?" he asked, narrowing his eyes at her. "Ye must admit that fleeing the abbey showed a certain lack of eagerness."

She was prepared for this.

"At the time, I thought I might be carrying Wedderburn's child, who would be the Hume heir." She could not help flushing as she spoke of a matter that should be private between her and David. "But I'm not."

Patrick gave her a stiff nod. As she had anticipated, he understood a desire to maintain inheritance rights.

"The other reason is that, frankly, I did not wish to wed your father."

"And ye feel differently about having me for your husband, aye?" he said with a dangerous smile playing on his lips.

She knew before she came that there was a risk Patrick would disregard the formalities of a marriage negotiation and simply haul her upstairs and rape her. From the way he was looking at her now, he wanted to. She could almost see the calculations going through his head.

***

Patrick drummed his fingers. What was his kitten up to?

"I'd look forward to wedding ye," she said, casting her gaze downward in that demure way that made his blood rise. "With our family connections, it should still be possible to obtain an annulment. That will take time, of course."

Patrick had her here under his roof. He sure as hell was not waiting for their wedding.

"As my brother says in his letter, this situation with Wedderburn must be handled carefully to avoid trouble with the Humes and their allies." Her fingers flitted nervously to her headdress as she spoke. "He thinks it important that Wedderburn be judged for his crime by the Council so that the blame does not fall on you—or on the Douglases. He urges you to bring him to Edinburgh as quickly as possible."

"I already have this castle and my enemy in my dungeon," Patrick said. "I've no need for his cautious advice."

"My brother has extremely high ambitions, as I'm sure ye know," she said, folding her hands. "He'll not agree to the marriage if it hampers his larger goals."

This was odd, indeed. Alison had always been quiet and meek. Though she came from a family that had been involved in royal schemes for too many generations to count, he had never heard Alison speak of men's affairs before.

His kitten had gotten above herself. He would return her to the timid lass of his fantasies and enjoy the process.

He drummed his fingers again. Why was she arguing so fervently for him to bring Wedderburn to the Council? Was it a ploy to save his life?

All the years when she was wed to his kinsman, she had wanted him. Patrick was sure of it. But that was before Wedderburn. The Beast was young and virile, and he had a build and looks that attracted women like flies.

"*Is it true that you and Wedderburn had been living separately?*" He knew it, *but he wanted to watch her face as she said it.*

"*Aye,*" she said. "*I couldn't bear the sight of him after what he did to Lord D'Orsey.*"

Had he seen a touch of sadness in her eyes before she answered?

Alison had said she looked forward to being his wife. But was it Wedderburn who owned her heart?

He knew just how to find the answer.

***

Patrick gripped Alison's arm and jerked her to her feet. She looked wildly around the crowded hall as he dragged her across the room to the stairs that led to the undercroft. But there was no help for her among the Blackadders.

"You've no need to pull me," she said, fighting to keep calm. "I'm happy to come with ye."

He ignored her plea. When she stumbled on the stairs, he lifted her off her feet and carried her to the bottom before setting her down again. Once he hauled her past the kitchens and storerooms, she knew where he was taking her.

The dungeon.

David must still be alive, or Patrick would not bring her down here. Despite Patrick's vicious hold and frightening behavior, relief washed through her.

When they reached the iron grate door of the dungeon, Patrick took the torch from the bracket in the wall and held it up to the grate.

"Take a good look at him," he said, pushing her forward with his hand at her back. "He's not as handsome as he was."

She realized this was some sort of test and steeled herself to see what Patrick had done to her beloved.

"Wedderburn!" he shouted. "Alison is here."

There was no answer, but she heard a soft moan coming from the darkness at the back of the cell. Patrick took the long key that was attached to his belt and opened the lock on the grated door. With one arm around her waist, he dragged her inside the cell and thrust the torch in front of them, lighting the far corner.

David was slumped on the ground and chained to the wall with manacles. Tears sprang to her eyes to see her proud husband, the legendary warrior and laird of his clan, chained like an animal.

As her eyes adjusted to the gloomy light, she saw gashes and dried blood on his feet and legs. Her gaze traveled upward to the bloody pulp that was his hand resting on his knee. *God help me, what has Patrick done to you?* She dug her fingernails into her palms. No matter what she felt, she must not show it.

His head was resting on his other knee, cushioned by his arm, so she could not see his face. His shirt was bloody and torn, but they had not stripped him of it. That meant he still had the stone.

Hold on, love. I'm here. I'm here!

***

David heard his enemy's voice saying her name.

Alison. He could smell the faint scent of the lavender she wore, but his mind was playing tricks on him. He had drifted in and out of wakefulness since the last beating.

"Wedderburn!" Patrick's voice roused him again from his stupor. "I want ye to see who I've taken from you."

Alison could not be in this hellhole. But she had been with him in his heart all along, and he was holding on as long as he could to keep her there.

"Ye were willing to die for her daughters," Patrick said, "and here she is to negotiate her next marriage before you're even dead."

David felt her presence even more strongly than before. His lifted his head, but it was too heavy to hold up, so he rested it against the stone wall behind him. One eye was swollen shut, but if he concentrated he could open the other one a slit.

And there she was. As lovely in his dream as the last time he saw her. The sight of her made him smile, which broke open one of the cuts on his lip.

"Alison." David was not sure if he'd spoken aloud. It was her. He pushed himself up against the wall and staggered to his feet.

"Now you've lost everything ye stole from me," Patrick said. "She's mine now. Mine!"

"Nay." David shook his head, though it sent shocks of pain through his skull.

Patrick pushed Alison out of the cell. Then he stepped closer to David, just out of the reach of his chains.

"I want ye to know that while ye lay here on the stone floor helpless and bleeding," Patrick taunted him in a harsh whisper, "I'll be in your bed with your wife, fooking her all night."

"Nay!" A surge of rage made David's body forget his injuries, and he lunged for Patrick. When the chains around his wrists jerked him back, the pain in his hand made him deaf and blind for a moment. Then, through the ringing in his ears, he heard Patrick's laughter.

"It's me she wants," Patrick said. "It's always been me."

CHAPTER 48

Alison fought to gain control of her emotions before Patrick came out of the cell. She had known he would make David suffer out of sheer hatred. She had even counted on Patrick's desire to give him a slow death to provide her time to free him. But seeing David so badly beaten left her shaken.

He was obviously too weak to leave his cell without help. Yet she could not bear to leave him chained and wholly unable to defend himself.

David gave a sudden howl of pain that tore at her heart like a jagged blade. She told herself to keep her wits about her and to focus on her task. There was no room for error. Her timing had to be just right. She waited until the moment after Patrick said one last thing to David and began to turn toward her and the door.

She swung her arm and tossed the lock pick through the bars. She prayed she had thrown it far enough for David to reach and that he would find it.

After locking the dungeon door, Patrick pressed her against the opposite wall. Leaning into her, he examined her face in the torchlight with his hard gray eyes.

"What, no tears?" he asked.

"Nay, but I don't like seeing any man treated that way," she said in a cool, disapproving tone.

Patrick's lips curved in a slight smile. Apparently she had passed his damned test. He tucked her hand in his arm and walked with her, showing the same thin veneer of courtesy he had shown earlier, as if nothing unusual had occurred.

David's heart-wrenching bellows echoed off the walls as Patrick led her back through the undercroft. She prayed to God and all the saints that David would survive until the rescue tonight.

But she could not open the tunnel door with Patrick as her constant companion. Would he never leave her side? For the first time, she truly feared she would fail and that David would die in that pit of misery.

She had never felt so alone.

As they passed the kitchen, she caught sight of a familiar face. The cook had returned to the castle with the other Blackadders. Though his expression was as sour as usual, in the brief moment that their eyes met, he gave her a slight nod. He was only a cook when she needed an army.

But she had one friend in the castle.

***

David bellowed in frustration. His wife, the woman he loved, was in Patrick Blackadder's hands, and he could do nothing to protect her. Though it was useless, he tried to jerk free of his chains until his wrists were raw and bleeding.

At least his rage had cleared his head. *Why did Alison come to the castle?* No matter what Patrick wanted him to believe, David did not doubt her. Alison must believe she could save his life. He wished to God she had not put herself in danger for him. But she must be part of a plan to rescue him. After the risk she took, he would be ready.

After a time, he heard footsteps and hoped it was Hume warriors. Instead, it was Walter, come to take another turn at him.

***

"I've a favor to ask," Alison said, looking up at Patrick from under her lashes as they re-entered the hall. "I lost a ring my father gave me in the laird's chamber. Would ye mind if I look for it?"

"I'll send a servant," he said.

"I'd rather look myself." She lowered her voice. "'Tis quite valuable."

She fought to maintain her innocent expression as he eyed her suspiciously. If he did not believe this excuse for her going into the laird's chamber, he surely would not believe a second one. When Patrick's expression suddenly changed, she worried still more.

"Ye don't need an excuse to get me upstairs," he said. "We've both waited far too long."

God preserve me. Did he truly believe she wanted him? His arrogance knew no bounds.

She could not offend him before he took her upstairs. She must get into the laird's chamber, and this was likely to be her only chance. Her heart pounded as they entered the stairwell that led to the bedchambers.

She prayed she would not have to let Patrick have his way with her, but she would do what she must to save David. Through the cloth of her gown, she touched the dirk strapped to her leg.

One way or another, she intended to succeed in her task.

Panic sang in her veins when Patrick started to pass the door to the laird's chamber. Apparently he meant to take her straight to the first bedchamber with a bed, which was the one she had shared with David. That would be too hard to bear.

"I do want to look for that ring," Alison said, tugging gently at his arm. When he turned to look at her, she tilted her head and forced a smile. "Please?"

She must be better at covering her loathing than she thought, for he turned back and opened the door to the laird's chamber for her. She crossed the room and stood with her back to the wall where the bed had been.

"All the other Blackadder men were furious when ye burned the bed," Patrick said, his eyes fixed on her as he slowly closed the distance between them. "But I knew ye hated to have him touch ye almost as much I hated it."

"The ring fell between the head of the bed and the wall, where I couldn't get to it," she said, her voice coming out high-pitched.

"Ye needed a younger man to satisfy ye," he said, and took a step closer. "Ye needed me."

"I should have looked for the ring as soon as I had the bed removed," she said, frantically looking at the floor, as if she expected the ring to magically appear. "But then there was the siege and…and…everything, and I forgot to look for it."

He was almost touching her, so she dropped to the floor.

"It's down here somewhere, I know it."

She swept her right hand across the floor while surreptitiously running the fingertips of her left hand along the bottom of the wall, searching for a seam that would reveal the piece that unlocked the secret door.

She touched the wall lightly for fear she might actually cause the door to open with Patrick watching. The girls said the door was hidden behind the tapestry, but what if it opened with a loud sound or a rush of air from the tunnel that caused the tapestry to move?

She felt no sign of the moving piece, but it had to be here.

"Forget the ring," Patrick said, and lifted her up. "I'll have a new one made for ye."

She was trapped between him and the wall. "But—"

"I said, forget the ring." Patrick gripped her shoulders and pushed her backward until she felt the cold, hard stone behind the tapestry. "I've waited ten long years to have ye."

"We must be patient," she said. "There's no marriage contract yet." She did not point out that she was still married to another man, lest he decide to remedy that at once.

"I won't wait another hour."

"Ye don't want to cross my brother," she said quickly. "I expect he'll soon be ruling the country in his stepson's name."

"Your brother is more pragmatic than you claim to be," he said. "He'll accept a done deed and agree on the terms later."

She gagged as the smell of leeks on his breath and the rank odor of his unwashed skin filled her nose. When she turned her head, he took it as an invitation to kiss her neck.

She swallowed back her disgust and used his distraction as an opportunity to tap her heel against the base of the wall. When Patrick grasped her breast, she pushed his hand away and squirmed to the side, where she tapped her heel against the wall again. He was so absorbed in slobbering on her that he did not seem to be aware that she was scooting along the wall, inch by inch, as she tried to find the stone that opened the tunnel door.

"I've wanted ye for so long," he said.

Ach, no, his hand was under his tunic now, working the tie to his breeks. She had to do something.

"Not like this," she said. "Please, Patrick, not like this."

"Just like this," he said. "I imagined it a thousand times."

When she tried to fight him, he held her wrists against the wall on either side of her head.

"My brother expects ye to treat me with respect," she said. "We'll be wed in due course, and ye must wait until then."

"Ten years is long enough to wait," he said.

He pulled open his loosened breeks, revealing his erect member. God help her now.

She had suffered degradation for ten years to satisfy the vanity of a cruel and contemptible man. She told herself she could suffer one more time to save the life of a good man, the man she loved and wanted to spend the rest of her life with.

But when it came to it, Patrick reminded her too much of her former husband. The rage she had suppressed all those years when she could not escape burst inside her.

"Ye want me too," he said, pulling up the skirts of her gown. "I know ye do."

"I don't!" she said, and kneed him in the groin.

Everything seemed to happen at once then. Patrick was shouting a string of curses in her ear. She brought her foot down to catch her balance, and the wall gave way behind her heel. A moment later, the tapestry beneath her outstretched hand felt as if it had nothing behind it, and a gush of cold air hit her feet.

She had opened the door to the tunnel.

If Patrick realized it and discovered the tunnel, all was lost. The Hume warriors would be killed one by one as they came through the tunnel, she would never escape Patrick, and David would die a slow and agonizing death in the dungeon.

She must get Patrick out of this room. While he was still doubled over, she ran for the door, knowing he would chase her. But he caught her before she reached it. His hard gray eyes were seething with a violent fury as he slammed her against the wall.

"It's because of him, isn't it?" he shouted, shaking her. "He's ruined ye for me!"

She feared he was going to kill her.

"Nay." Belatedly, she remembered the dagger strapped to her leg and tried desperately to reach it. "I only want ye to wait for the marriage contract."

"Ye wanted me before. All those years, ye wanted *me*," he said, his eyes wild. "'Tis Wedderburn ye want now."

"Wedderburn forced me to wed him," she said, struggling to pull her skirt far enough up the side of her leg to reach her blade. "I had no choice."

"He's chained in a cell," he said through bared teeth, "and you're still loyal to him!"

"I swear it's true," she said, and plunged her dagger into his side. "I am still loyal to him."

CHAPTER 49

Patrick clutched his side. With a shocked expression, he looked down at the blood seeping through his fingers, then up at her and the dirk that was still in her hand.

Alison had never tried to kill a man before, and she clearly had not succeeded. With a roar, Patrick launched himself at her. She fell backward under the force of the impact, and they crashed into a side table and the wall. Stunned and bruised, she scrambled to her feet.

Patrick lay unmoving on the floor. He had a gash on his head and her dagger in his belly. On instinct, she must have brought her blade in front of her when he charged into her. Good God, had she killed him after all? Fearing he would leap from the floor and attack her again, she prodded him with her toe. He still did not move.

How long before one of his men came to look for their laird and found him dead? She could not wait for the Hume warriors to arrive and help her. She and David must escape through the tunnel now.

As she started to leave, her gaze fell on the pouch tied to Patrick belt. She needed his key to the dungeon in case the picklock did not work on it. She knelt beside the body. Gagging when the dead man's blood got on her fingers, she removed the key from the pouch. She wiped her hand on her skirts, then stared down at the blood-smeared silk gown.

In these clothes, she would be easily recognized when she crossed the short span of the hall between the Tower stairs and the stairs to the undercroft. After closing the door on Patrick's corpse, she raced up to the Tower Room, shed her sister's fine gown and elaborate headdress, and changed into a gown and plain head covering of Flora's.

She was taking too long! Any moment, Patrick's body could be discovered.

When she reached the bottom of the Tower stairs, Alison held her breath and peeked into the hall. The room was bustling with activity, which should make a female servant passing through less noticeable. Ducking her head, she scurried across.

Just before she reached the stairs to the undercroft, someone stepped in front of her. She looked up into the face of a Blackadder warrior she recognized. He was one of the young men David had nearly executed and whose life she had begged him to spare.

She saw the surprise in his eyes as he recognized her too. They stared at each other for one heart-stopping moment.

"A favor returned," he said beneath the noise of the hall. Then he turned and walked away.

Once she was out of sight down the steps to the undercroft, she leaned against the wall, her heart thundering in her chest. If the young warrior had given her away, she and David would both be dead soon.

They needed to escape quickly. As she hurried through the undercroft past the kitchens and storerooms, she prayed David had been able to remove his manacles with the picklock. She did not have a key to those.

When she reached the dungeon, she took the torch from the wall and peered through the gloom on the other side of the iron grate. David was collapsed on the floor against the back wall, and the chains were still on his wrists. Her heart sank as she realized he had been beaten again.

"David!" she called in a whisper as she shoved the key into the door's lock.

Panic rose in her throat when he did not answer.

How would she ever get him up the stairs? Even if she could, a man that severely injured would surely be noticed when they passed through the hall.

Time was passing. The lock was stiff, and she could not turn the key.

"David," she called again as she struggled to open it.

Again, he did not answer. *Nay, they cannot have killed him. They cannot.*

She tried to turn the key in one direction, then the other, again and again.

Her screams echoed off the walls as she was suddenly lifted off her feet and thrown against the iron grate. She fell to her hands and knees, and her ears rang from her head banging against the iron bars.

When her attacker hauled her to her feet, she saw it was Patrick, risen from the dead. He had murder in his eyes, and he slapped her with such force that she tasted blood in her mouth.

"David, help me!" she called as Patrick drew his arm back to hit her again.

The blow made stars dance across her vision. David remained

ominously silent.

"You've killed him, haven't you?" she wailed, and blindly pounded her fists against Patrick's chest. "You've killed him! You've killed him!"

"He's not dead," Patrick said. "Wedderburn! Wake up. I want ye to watch this."

Holding her with one hand by her hair, he picked up a bucket of water from behind them and flung the water into the cell. A groan came from the back of the cell.

David is still alive.

The iron bars cut into her back as Patrick again pressed her against the dungeon's door.

"I'm going to fook your wife now," Patrick called over her shoulder.

Alison bit and kicked at him as he tugged up her skirts. When she clawed his face, he slammed her against the iron bars, banging her head again.

He pressed his forearm against her windpipe, choking her, while he unfastened his breeks with his free hand.

"David! On the floor!" she managed to squeak out. "It's on the floor!"

She could not breathe. She scratched at Patrick's hands, trying to get air.

Then the sounds around her faded, and she fell into darkness.

***

David heard Alison calling him, as if from a great distance. Slowly, her voice pulled him to the surface. He fought to clear his head and wiped the blood from his eyes. When he saw Patrick holding her against the door, anguish tore through his battered body.

On the floor! Something he needed was on the floor. Walter had broken his arm, the same one with the damaged hand, but he felt the rough stone around him with his other hand, desperately searching for whatever it was. On the other side of the iron grate just a few feet away but outside of his reach, his enemy was choking and raping his wife. *Jesu*, where was the damned thing?

His fingers touched a thin piece of metal. He knew at once what it was. A lock pick.

Damn it! Finding the keyhole was like threading a needle in the dark. Sweat dripped into his good eye. He could hear Alison gasping for breath as he worked the thin metal shaft into the lock.

Click.

He could not work the pick with his damaged hand for the second manacle, so he held it in his teeth. Alison had gone silent. Time was running out. He had to free himself *now*.

Click.

David no longer felt his pain. He crossed the cell in three long strides, reached through the bar, and grabbed Patrick by the throat with his good hand. Startled, Patrick released Alison. She slumped to the ground, coughing.

David squeezed Patrick's throat, wanting to snap his neck in two. Patrick clawed at his hand, and David squeezed tighter. When Patrick reached for the dirk at his belt, David was quicker. He released Patrick's throat, grabbed the dirk, and plunged the blade into Patrick's heart.

Relief swept through him when he saw that Alison was on her feet. He rested his forehead against the cold iron grate, exhausted from the effort of subduing Patrick. Loss of blood from his injuries had made him weak.

"David." Alison reached through the bars of the grate and held his battered face between her hands. Tears streamed down her face. "What have they done to ye, my love?"

"Nothing I won't recover from if we can open this door and escape."

"I brought the key," she said, pointing at it in the lock, "but I can't make it work."

Using his good hand, he reached through the grate and grasped the key. The lock was old and rusty. Gritting his teeth, he forced the key to turn with scraping click. He was free.

David opened the door—and fell into Alison's arms. At least he managed to catch hold of the door as his knees gave way so he did not land on her with all of his weight. Still, she staggered backward as she attempted to ease his fall to the floor.

When she embraced him, he winced. Every inch of his body hurt, but it did not matter. Alison was here.

"Ach, ye feel good, lass," he said, holding her against him with his good arm.

He assumed his men had somehow gotten into the castle, but he was confused as to why Alison was here.

"What is the plan for our escape?" he asked.

His heart nearly failed him when she told him she had come to the castle alone to open a secret tunnel door for his men. Once she was out of danger, he would tell his wife what he thought of what she'd done. But now he needed to reach that tunnel and get her out of here.

"Our men will be coming through the tunnel soon." Alison's face was pinched with worry as she attempted to wipe some of the blood from the gashes on his face. "We'll have to wait here for them."

"We're not waiting. We must be gone before someone finds us—or him," David said with a nod toward Patrick's body.

"But ye can't even stand, let alone climb two flights of stairs," she said.

"I just needed to catch my breath." Gritting his teeth, he held onto the door and pulled himself up. "Let's go."

She put her hands on her hips and looked him up and down. "You'll never make it through the hall looking like that without being stopped."

David glanced at his bloodied shirt and his hand, which was purple and three times its normal size.

"Aye, we need a diversion," he said. "But we needed one anyway to ensure the safety of our men coming through the tunnel."

At the sound of footsteps coming toward them, David shoved Alison behind him. Blood pounded in his veins, but he relaxed when a thin man with a weak build emerged from the shadows. Even in his current state, David could take him easily.

"'Tis the cook," Alison said from behind him. "He's a friend. We can trust him."

The first time she told David to trust the cook, he had kicked the man out of the castle with the rest of the Blackadder servants. But he was a wiser man now.

"Can ye start a fire in the kitchens?" David asked the cook. "A big one?"

***

Alison coughed on the billowing smoke filling the undercroft as she peeked out from behind the door of the storeroom to watch the servants flee the kitchens. The cook was the last to run out. He paused to glance up the stairs after the others, then he waved for her and David to come out.

"Don't worry that I'm burning the castle down," he said. "The fire is more smoke than flame."

"'Tis a perfect diversion," David said. "My thanks to ye."

"Watch how I clear the hall," the cook said, his eyes shining as if he was actually enjoying himself. He turned and ran up the stairs shouting, "Fire! Run for your lives!"

Alison looked at David. *God help me, how will I ever get him out?*

He was so battered and bloody it was a wonder he could stand. If he collapsed, she could not carry him alone. She wiped more blood from the gashes on his face. His swollen eye looked so painful she did not dare touch it.

"Ready?" David said.

"I'll go alone and bring the others back for ye."

"I just watched a man try to rape and murder ye," he said. "I'll not let ye out of my sight until you're safe."

Ach, he was a stubborn man. There was no use talking to him, so she took his arm. As they started up the stairs, he swayed and had to catch himself with a hand on the stone wall. Alison swallowed back her fear and kept moving.

The hall was in chaos with men and women shouting and running in every direction. Though she thought it should be glaringly obvious to anyone who looked that David was the captured Hume laird, no one seemed to pay them any attention.

She strained under David's weight as he suddenly leaned against her.

"Sorry, lass," he said and straightened almost at once.

"We're almost there," she said.

She glanced behind them and saw that he was leaving a trail of blood. She was desperate to get him out of the hall and upstairs where she could see to his wounds.

Relief coursed through her when they finally reached the arched doorway to the tower stairs. Looking behind her, she caught sight of Walter. The tall, black-haired warrior was pushing people out of his way to reach the door that led outside.

"He's the one who did this to my hand," David said, staring after Walter. "I'd kill him now, but Brian needs his blood on his sword more than I do."

Seeing Walter seemed to give David another burst of strength, and Alison had to run up the stairs to keep up with him. When they opened the laird's chamber door, several Hume warriors were already in the room, and they drew their dirks before they realized who it was.

"Verra glad to see you're alive, Laird, though I've seen ye looking better," Brian said with a wide grin. He handed David his whisky flask. "Better have some of this to give ye strength."

"Ach, you're a good man." David tilted his head back and took a long drink, then wiped his mouth on his sleeve. "That's what I needed."

Alison stayed close to David as the room rapidly filled with Hume warriors who were still coming through the tunnel. Finding their laird there to greet them seemed to put them in high spirits.

David took another drink of whisky. As he handed it back to Brian, he said, "Walter is here."

Brian's expression turned to granite, and he started for the door.

"We go together," David said, stopping him.

"But Walter is mine," Brian said.

David nodded. Then he gave the signal, and the Hume warriors headed out. When David started to go with them, Alison clung to his arm. Had he lost his senses?

"Ye can't go," she said. "You're too badly injured."

"Ach, I've fought in worse shape, lass," he said. "Wait here. This won't take long."

He strode down the stairs with his men, leaving Alison to stare at the drops of his blood on the stone steps.

CHAPTER 50

"Ye rode alone into the castle knowing ye could be killed and almost certainly raped," David said between his teeth. The more he thought about it, the more furious he became.

"Aye, it was a bold plan." Alison smiled at him as she dabbed a healing ointment on his injured hand. "But we Humes are known for that."

Calling herself a Hume softened his anger for a moment, as his clever wife had known it would.

"Ach, this hand is bad," she said. "Does it pain ye something terrible?"

"Hell no," he said, though it throbbed like the very devil.

"My plan did succeed," she said. "We both survived, and we have Blackadder Castle back."

The Blackadders were already in disarray due to the fire when David and the men who had come through the tunnel caught them by surprise inside the hall. In a matter of moments, the Humes had taken control of the keep. The rest of the castle did not take much longer. More Hume warriors, who had been hiding in the trees by the stream, poured in through the gate, which the Blackadder guards had opened to let their people escape the fire.

Walter fought to the death, knowing there would be no mercy for him, and he died by Brian's sword. Most of the Blackadders, however, saw how it would end and laid down their weapons.

"I'm glad ye released most of the Blackadders," Alison said, as she wrapped a long linen strip around his hand. "With the deaths of their wicked lairds, they're no longer a threat."

She had persuaded him to release them, of course. But he had ferreted out the men who attacked the village, and they were no longer walking this earth but burning in everlasting hell. He could not remember much after that until he woke up starving a couple of hours ago.

"Must I wear this?" he asked, as Alison tied a goddamn sling around his arm.

"You're trying my patience, love," she said. "You'll sit there and do as I tell ye after worrying me so. Ye fell like a stone when it was all over. Three days I waited for ye to wake, ye wretched man."

Worrying her? Alison was not going to divert him from what she'd done. The image of Patrick choking her while he hiked up her skirts filled his mind's eye again, and he pulled her onto his lap with his good arm.

"How could ye endanger yourself like that?" he asked, his voice rough with emotion.

"How could I not?" she said. "What would your brothers, the girls, Isabella, and I do without ye? You're the center of our family, the one who binds us together. Beatrix and Margaret knew that. Why do ye think they ventured out on their own to bring ye home?"

David had never expected to find himself encircled by love and family. And it was all because of Alison. She had given him everything he had longed for and never believed he deserved.

"Without you, I'd be like Patrick Blackadder, a man with nothing to live for but hate and vengeance." He tucked a stray strand of her midnight hair behind her ear. "Ye saved me, Allie."

"Ach, you were never like that vicious and self-serving man," she said. "Everything ye did was to protect others. Love was always the reason, even if you didn't know it."

She always saw the best in him. He would strive every day to become the man she believed he was.

"There is something I did that I would like to change," he said.

She tilted her head. "What's that?"

David had struggled with what was best to do. He needed to consider the future of his brothers as well as his stepdaughters.

"I'll destroy Beatrix and Margaret's marriage contracts with my brothers, if that's what the lasses wish," he said. "When they're of an age to marry, I'll let each lass decide."

His gift to his brothers would be to have wives who came willingly to their marriage.

"Thank you," Alison said, touching her fingertips to his cheek. "When the time comes, I hope that they chose wisely, for I would like nothing better than to know my daughters had fierce Hume men to love and protect them all of their days."

"Ye know I love ye dearly, lass," David said. "But now you're going to have to pay for scaring the Beast of Wedderburn witless."

Alison smiled against his lips as he gave her a fierce Hume kiss.

***

With a sigh of regret, Alison broke the kiss and pressed her hand against David's chest. "You're in no shape to do what you're suggesting."

"Ye can see for yourself," he said, "I'm up for the task."

She rolled her eyes and laughed. He laughed with her, but then his expression grew serious again.

"After nearly losing ye," he said, cupping her cheek with his big hand, "I need this, lass."

Alison understood because she needed him desperately too. As they made love slowly, murmuring endearments to each other, she ran her hands gently over his battered body, every inch precious to her. It made her want to weep to see his cuts and bruises, but her husband was strong and would heal.

Afterward she drifted off to sleep to the comforting sound of his steady heartbeat against her ear. She awoke from a dream to the sun shining through the window. Spring had come at last to Blackadder Castle.

"I have good news to tell ye." She took David's hand and placed it on her stomach. "We're having a babe."

"Beatrix and Margaret are like my own daughters, and I would have been content if we'd had no more," he said, his eyes soft and warm. "But a babe. Ach, this is a great blessing. Ye couldn't make me happier."

"You'll be a wonderful father," she said, "which is fortunate since we'll be having so many."

"And ye know this?" The corners of his mouth quirked up in a smile.

"Aye. The old woman who my mother saw when she found the magical stone appeared in a dream just now before I woke," she said. "She told me we'll have six children together."

"Six!" He looked stunned for a moment, then he laughed and kissed her forehead. "I suppose every one of them will be as strong-willed and troublesome as my wife."

"Aye," she said, smiling up at David. "We're going to have a joyous life."

Alison rubbed her thumb over the black stone that was safely back in her pendant and reflected on how very lucky she had been since she found it.

EPILOGUE

Three years later…

"This babe needs to come soon." Alison put her hand on the small of her aching back. "It was kind of ye to come for the birth, Sybil. I hope ye don't have to wait long, for both our sakes."

"I'm happy to get away from Court," Sybil said. "The tension between our clan and the Hamiltons is simmering to a boil. And the queen has sided with the Hamiltons."

"Is it true she wants to divorce Archie?" Alison asked.

"Archie's spies informed him that she wrote to her brother King Henry hinting she wants a divorce," Sybil said. "Henry replied with a lecture on morality, if ye can believe it, and he's thrown his support behind Archie. Of course, that makes the entire pro-French faction adamantly against us."

"Ye should stay here where David can protect ye until this trouble is resolved," Alison said.

"I'm in no danger," Sybil said, waving her hand. "I have friends on both sides. Besides, I expect Archie will prevail in the end."

Alison was not so sure.

"Beatrix is turning twelve," Sybil said as Alison's daughters and Will entered the hall from the tower stairs with Jasper on their heels. "That lad is going to be one handsome man. Has she decided whether she'll have him for her husband?"

"David won't let her marry for years, so there's no hurry," Alison said. "But that's Will you're looking at, not Robbie."

Will was nearly as tall as Robbie and David now. Alison had heard the men remark on his strength and skill with a sword, but Will was still a kind-hearted lad who seemed to be lost in his own world at times.

Alison watched as Isabella and Rob emerged from the stairwell and cast surreptitious glances her way. David had been disappearing for hours at a time and being very mysterious about it. The entire family was party to his secret and did their best to divert her attention. While she trusted her husband absolutely, her curiosity was getting the better of her.

"Have they told ye what the surprise is?" she asked Sybil.

"What surprise?" Sybil gave her a blank look, but her sister was exceptionally good at keeping secrets.

David came down the stairs carrying their son, who was both the joy of the household and as troublesome as predicted, and handed him to Leana. Taking on the role of nursemaid had helped Leana heal, and she and Brian were to be wed soon. Flora and Garret were happily settled in a small cottage that David had given them.

"May I take my wife from ye?" David asked, smiling at Sybil.

He helped Alison to her feet with his good hand. Though he never admitted it, she knew the hand Walter had damaged still pained him at times.

"I've something I want to show ye upstairs," he said as he led her across the hall.

"To relieve my backache," Alison said, "you'll need to do more than show it to me."

A softness came into his eyes. "Ye know I'd like nothing better than to make love to ye, if it's not too close to the baby coming, but that's not what I meant."

As they climbed the stairs Alison's thoughts returned to her conversation with her sister.

"Do ye think this dispute with the Hamiltons will break out in fighting?" she asked.

"I do," David said. "Tensions are high. Any spark will set it off."

"I'm worried about my sisters getting caught in it—especially Sybil," she said. "And she says that Archie is counting on you to bring a large force to Edinburgh when the time comes."

"'Tis worth considering," David said. "If he prevails, your sisters will all be safe, and Archie will be in a position to restore the title to the Hume lands to me, which will save our children trouble down the road."

"I agree, but I don't like it."

"There are troubled times ahead, to be sure." David stopped on the stairs and turned to face her. "But we'll find our way through them together."

Her shoulders relaxed, and she smiled up at him. "Aye, we will."

Instead of continuing up the stairs, he turned and opened the door to the old Laird's chamber.

"'Tis three years late," he said, "but this is my wedding gift to you."

An enormous new bed dominated the room.

"Oh, David!" she said. "'Tis beautiful."

He must have paid a fortune for it. The bed was made of a rich dark wood that held a hint of red, like the color of a roan horse, and there were intricate carvings along the head and footboards. Alison stepped closer and ran her hand over the pattern on the foot of the bed.

"These look a bit like the pigs and horses ye carved for Beatrix and Margaret..." She turned to look at David. "You made this?"

"Aye. I cut the boards from the table at Hume Castle when I was staying there before ye came for me." He gave a dry laugh. "Surprising I didn't cut my leg off as drunk as I was."

She was touched that even when David believed she wanted her freedom instead of him he had enough hope in his heart to undertake making this exquisite gift for her.

"Isabella made the bed curtains," he said, pointing at the dark blue velvet.

Alison walked around the bed, tracing the carvings with her fingertips. She could feel the love he had put into every one of them.

"No lass has ever had such a wonderful wedding gift," she said.

"Ye like it then?"

"Oh, aye," she said, tears burning the back of her eyes.

"Ye should get off your feet, love," David said, giving her a worried look. Then he lifted her up onto the bed and sat beside her.

When she turned and saw the first letters of their names linked together in the center of the headboard, her throat felt tight. She thought of the countless times they would make love in this bed and the children she'd give birth to in it.

She loved him so much. His eyes drew dark as she ran her hands slowly up his chest.

"Shall we find out if this bed is comfortable?" she asked, waggling her eyebrows.

"Are ye sure it's safe?" David asked, looking down at her swollen belly.

Alison caught him off guard and pushed him back on the bed.

"I'm a bold and dangerous Hume lass," she said, leaning over him. "But I promise I'll try to be gentle with ye, *if* that's how ye like it."

David's eyes twinkled as he recognized the words he had once said to her. "Are ye having a bit of fun with me, lass?

"Not yet, but I intend to." She poked his chest. "And ye will enjoy it."

"I will, for certain," he said, a slow smile spreading across his handsome face.

Her heart squeezed as she looked down at the man she loved.

"You're mine, David Hume," she said.

"That I am, lass," he said as he drew her down for a kiss. "Now and always."

THE END

HISTORICAL NOTE

I first came across Archibald Douglas when I was doing research for THE GUARDIAN (THE RETURN OF THE HIGHLANDERS). I was intrigued by this handsome, young chieftain's brazen power play in starting an affair with Scotland's dowager queen, Margaret Tudor, so soon after the death of her husband, James IV. The affair led to lucrative appointments for his Douglas kin, and his eventual marriage to the queen put the Douglas chieftain in a position to vie for control of the young heir to the throne—and the country. For years, Archibald's power rose and fell dramatically. He and his closest male relatives were forced to flee the country more than once to save their necks.

This series was born when I began to wonder what happened to the women of the Douglas family who were left behind when the men escaped. While information on Archie's sisters is sparse, I found enough to suggest they were in serious danger at times. In fact, one sister was eventually burned at the stake in Edinburgh Castle by Archibald's angry step-son James V.

Being a romance writer, I naturally wanted to give the Douglas lasses happy endings with men who would stand by them in tough times.

With this first book in THE DOUGLAS LEGACY series, I've written a fictional story inspired by the real marriage between Archibald's sister Alison and David Hume of Wedderburn. As is often the case with Scottish history going back five hundred years, history and legend are intertwined. I write fiction and take as much latitude as I need to make a good story. That said, the real David Hume did capture Blackadder Castle, did force the widow Alison to marry him, and did contract her two heiress daughters to marry his younger brothers. As best I can tell, he and Alison had six children together, and I found no mention of his having illegitimate children. From these two facts, I wanted to believe this forced marriage led to true love.

A hero has to be heroic, and I confess that some of the things David Hume was alleged to have done created a challenge in that regard. By all accounts, David's father and uncle were lured into Edinburgh to negotiate their dispute with Regent Albany, executed for treason, and had their heads displayed on the Tolbooth. Clearly, David had reason to be angry.

Since David appears to have killed off every Blackadder male who might have been able to challenge Beatrix and Margaret's inheritance rights, I had to make the Blackadders villainous and deserving of their fate. My apologies if they were in fact good and honorable men. I also made David's brothers younger than they actually were so as not to offend myself and my readers. Alison's daughters were likely confined to the castle until they came of age (twelve!), when they were married to David's brothers, who were probably in their 20's. That age difference would have been unremarkable at the time, and the marriages appear to have been lasting.

The character of Lord D'Orsey is very loosely inspired by Albany's close friend, Lord Antoine D'Arcy, who was a much-admired man in his time. There was already bad blood between D'Arcy and the Humes when they had a confrontation regarding the siege at Langton Castle. David or his brothers ended up killing D'Arcy and displaying his head on the market cross at Duns. Hair from his head is rumored to have been kept in a chest by the Humes until the 1800's.

In future books in the series, you'll probably hear more about the mysterious deaths of the beautiful Drummond sisters, Alison's aunts on her mother's side. They may well have succumbed to mere food poisoning, but why were the three sisters the only ones who died?

The next book in the series, CLAIMED BY A HIGHLANDER, takes place when Archibald Douglas is forced into exile for the first time. I invented Sybil Douglas, the heroine, from whole cloth, but I was inspired to create her handsome Highlander hero in part by a remarkable MacKenzie chieftain who lived in this time period.

An excerpt from CLAIMED BY A HIGHLANDER, book 2 in THE DOUGLAS LEGACY, by Margaret Mallory

PROLOGUE

Edinburgh, Scotland
December 1513

Rory MacKenzie wiped the icy rain from his face and limped into yet another tavern. His injured leg was throbbing, his belly was empty, and he had no money, but these were not the worst of his problems.

He waited for his eyes to adjust to the murky light, then swept his gaze over the occupants. Damn. No one but a serving woman and some old men who had the settled look of regular customers. Hunching over to avoid banging his head on the blackened wooden beams of the low ceiling, he crossed the room. Out of habit, he chose an empty bench where he could sit with his back to the wall and watch the door. He gritted his teeth against a hot blade of pain that shot through his leg as he eased himself onto the bench, then took a couple of slow, deep breaths.

"Good evening to ye," he said, speaking in Scots to the old men, who were local merchants, judging by their soft bellies and Lowlander clothes. "I'm a MacKenzie, and I'm hoping to find some of my clansmen in the city."

"Haven't seen any lately," one of the men said around the pipe clenched between his teeth, and the others shook their heads.

Rory doubted these men could tell a MacKenzie from another Highlander, but he had already looked all over the city with no luck. He knew most of the taverns where his clansmen were likely to gather from the year he had been forced to study at the university.

What in the hell was he going to do? He had walked for days just to get as far as Edinburgh. He needed to get home to Kintail to protect his brother.

"Looks as if you've had a rough time of it, lad," the man with the pipe said.

"The English took me captive after Flodden," Rory said, his thoughts skittering back to the disastrous battle. The English had kept the highborn prisoners for ransom and killed the rest. "I escaped a few days ago."

Rory had known better than to wait for his uncle to pay for his release.

"Escaped?" One of the old men said and gave a low whistle. "Tell us your tale, and I'll buy ye a cup of ale."

Rory had the full attention of everyone in the tavern now, including the serving maid, a woman of impressive size with strands of greasy hair falling out of her filthy head covering.

"Add a bowl of stew," he said with a grin, "and I'll give ye a story that will curl your hair."

"Just looking at him is making my hair curl," the serving woman said, then she gave him a broad wink and a nudge when she brought his stew and ale.

Rory did not bother embellishing his tale, as would be expected at home. These old merchants had never fought themselves, so they were wide-eyed at the bare truth. They cringed and made faces when he mentioned the number of lashes he received after being caught the first time he tried to escape. A whipping was a small matter, but the damned English had taken his horse and all his weapons—his claymore, axe, and several dirks.

"I need a horse and a blade to go home," he said, presenting his problem to the old men. The journey would take too long on foot, and only a fool would travel in the Highlands without a weapon, and preferably several.

"Ye can't buy those with a tale or your good looks," one of the old men said, and the others guffawed.

Rory had considered stealing a horse, but the city was on edge in the wake of Flodden, fearing an attack by the English, and armed men were everywhere. He could not take the risk of getting caught and failing to get home.

"I'm good at cards." He had done little else while held hostage. "Do ye know of a game where I'd have a chance of winning that kind of money?"

"Enough to buy a horse and a sword?" a bald-headed man with red cheeks asked in a high voice.

Everyone laughed, except for the man with the pipe, who said, "Mattie, aren't those fancy-dressed nobles having one of their games in your back room tonight?"

"Hush!" She swatted the man with a filthy rag. "They give me good money to guarantee them privacy and clean lasses, and they don't like to mix with us lowly folk."

"I'm a Highland chieftain's son, so I'm as good as any of these Lowland nobles." Better, in fact. When the woman still hesitated, Rory spread his arms out and gave her his best smile. "Come, Mattie, help a lad out."

"What woman could say nay to that pretty face?" she asked the others, then turned back to him. "All right, ye young devil."

Pretty face? Ach. Now he just needed something to start the game with. "If one of ye will lend me a silver coin, I'll return it doubled."

When his request was met by another round of guffaws, desperation clawed at his gut. He never should have left his brother Gavin this long. When he answered the king's call to fight, Rory had not anticipated being held prisoner for two months after the battle.

He reminded himself that his half-brother was sixteen and should be able to take care of himself. Although Rory was six months younger than Gavin, he'd always felt older. Gavin was too goodhearted. He didn't see people for what they were, but as he wanted them to be. That was dangerous for any man, but especially for one who would soon take on the duties of clan chieftain.

Rory was reconsidering stealing a horse when the serving maid plopped down next to him with a heavy thump and wrapped an arm as beefy as a blacksmith's around his neck.

"I'll lend ye a bit of money for the game," she said, her sour breath in his face. With her free hand, she reached inside her bodice, pulled a silver coin from between her ample breasts, and held it up between her thumb and forefinger.

"Isn't that the coin I gave ye, Mattie?" the red-cheeked man said.

"Believe me, lads," she said turning to the others, "I earned it."

"Ye won't regret this," Rory said over the men's laughter. But when he tried to take the coin, she held it just out of his reach.

"Promise, on your mother's grave, that if ye can't repay me in coin," – Mattie paused and grinned at him, showing her brown and broken teeth— "you'll repay me in a manner of my choosing."

Rory's stomach clutched. In addition to her many unappealing attributes, Mattie probably was not "clean" of the pox, like the lasses she provided the men in the backroom. But he could not shake the feeling that his brother was in trouble, so he had no choice.

"On my mother's grave." He jumped when Mattie reached behind him and squeezed his arse with her ham-sized hand. He closed his eyes and thanked God that none of his clansmen were here to see it.

Ignoring the throbbing in his injured leg, he got up and followed Mattie behind a curtain into a dark corridor. At the far end, candlelight spilled through a partially closed door.

"Have a care, Handsome, these are powerful men," Mattie whispered as they paused outside the door. Then she poked his chest. "You'll be no use to me dead."

Though her smell was overpowering, Rory leaned closer to see the men inside. There were five, all young and well-dressed, sitting around a table with cards and small piles of coins.

"Who are they?" he asked in a whisper.

"That one is the new Douglas chieftain, and the one next to him is his brother," she said, pointing a thick finger at two black-haired men, neither of which looked much over twenty. "Their father was killed with the king at Flodden, and their grandfather, old Bell the Cat, died last week, making young Archibald here the Earl."

Rory had never met Archibald Douglas, but he had once caught a glimpse of the beautiful Douglas sisters riding through Edinburgh. He smiled to himself, remembering a giggling young lass with flashing blue eyes and hair as black as a moonless night.

"They say this young Douglas chieftain is 'comforting' our grieving queen," Mattie said, drawing Rory's attention back to the present. "I believe the other men at the table are Boyds and Drummonds, close kin of the Douglases."

Archibald Douglas must have heard her speak this time, for he shifted his gaze to the doorway and called out, "Who've ye brought us, Mattie?"

Rory stepped into the room with no premonition of how this night would change his fate.

CHAPTER 1

March 1522

Sybil set her sketch aside and covered her face with her freezing hands. She wished someone would come and spirit her far away, out of the queen's reach. She was furious with her brothers. After sending reassurances for months and then ordering her to wait for them here, her brothers and uncle had escaped to France, leaving the rest of the family to the queen's mercy. As if that spiteful woman had any.

A shadow fell over her. *How did James find me out here?* She had not left the warmth of the hall and the safety of her uncle's castle to sit under this tree on the frozen ground because she wanted company. Particularly his.

"I thought ye left, James," she said, still keeping her hands over her eyes. "I told ye I won't do it, so go."

When she did not hear James walk away, Sybil was tempted to kick him. Exasperated, she dropped her hands—and sucked in her breath.

A huge Highland warrior stood over her. Her heart thumped wildly as she dragged her gaze from his giant sword, the tip of which rested mere inches from her foot, to the dirks and axe tucked in his belt, and then to his broad, muscular chest. She had not yet reached his face when he spoke in a deep voice that seemed to make the ground vibrate beneath her.

"My name is MacKenzie. I've come for ye."

Come for her? Sweat prickled under her arms. The queen had found her.

"I've done nothing wrong," she said. "What are the charges against me?"

The Highlander merely grunted and held out his hand. She ignored it and forced herself to raise her gaze to his face. Despite the fierce hazel eyes that were locked on her like a cat who has found his prey, the wholly irrelevant thought that he was quite handsome sprang into her head. He had strong, masculine features, and she knew women at court who would kill to have that shade of auburn hair.

"We must go," he said, jarring her back to the danger she was in.

"Do I not merit a full escort?" she asked, attempting to put on a brave front. No matter how formidable this MacKenzie was, it was odd that the queen would send one man to fetch her.

"'Tis easier to escape notice if we travel alone," he said.

Her jaw dropped. "Escape?"

"Aye," he said. "We must hurry, lass."

"I thought everyone had deserted us." Tears sprang to her eyes. So many had called her friend just a few weeks ago.

"Not everyone," he said, still holding out his hand.

She was tempted to pick up her skirts and run away with this stranger, but she had learned as a young girl not to be so trusting.

"Did James send you?" she asked, narrowing her eyes at the tall Highlander.

"Who the hell is James?"

She waved off the question. "Just tell me who sent you."

"No one sent me," he said, sounding insulted. Then he dropped to one knee, and she received the full benefit of his face up close. He was dangerously handsome.

"Who are you?" she asked, her voice coming out in a whisper.

"Your husband, Rory Alexander MacKenzie," he said. "I've come to claim ye."

This was all a mistake. He had not come for her after all. "A damned shame," she murmured to herself.

"That's foul language for a lady," he snapped. "And whether ye like it or no, we have a marriage contract."

Since couples sometimes did not meet until their wedding, Sybil was not shocked that the Highlander did not know his bride by sight. She was sorely tempted to take advantage of it and not reveal that he had the wrong lass until they were miles away. But when he learned the truth, he'd probably dump her by the side of the road.

"I fear you've made a mistake," she told him.

"Most certainly," he said in a clipped tone. "But I'm obligated all the same. A MacKenzie does not go back on his word."

"That is refreshing in a man," she said. "But what I meant was that I'm not who ye think I am."

***

What in the hell was he doing here? He should have torn the marriage contract to pieces long ago. He had only been, what, fifteen when he signed it? Scottish kings renounced commitments they made in their minority all the time, so why shouldn't he?

Rory's gaze drifted over the lass again. Ach, but she was pretty. From the moment he first spied her sitting under the tree, he had known it was her—and she had taken his breath away. But then she had covered her startlingly lovely face with her hands, and he took in the jeweled fingers, delicate slippers, and rich velvet cloak. The last thing he needed was a Lowland court creature for a wife.

No doubt the Douglas chieftain had regretted making the agreement even more than he had. Many times over the last eight years, Rory had planned to make the long journey to the Douglas lands to advise Archibald that he was willing to set the agreement aside. But somehow the time had never seemed right. He had finally come to settle the matter because he needed to free himself to wed.

And now, he could not. *Damn it.* This threw off all his plans.

If only he had acted sooner. When Rory reached Stirling, he heard the news of the Douglases fall from grace and knew he had lost his chance. He could not desert the lass now that the men of her family had been charged with treason and fled the country.

"Perhaps I can help," she said, interrupting his sour thoughts. "Who is the lass you're looking for?"

It annoyed him that his betrothed found it so difficult to believe he had come for her. Clearly, she thought him unworthy.

"Sybil Douglas," he said, drawing her name out, "granddaughter of Bell the Cat and sister of the present chieftain, Archibald Douglas, who is the queen's husband."

When she stared at him with wide eyes the color of violets, Rory's heart seized in his chest. Their vivid color contrasted with her midnight-black hair, ivory skin, and full, red lips. He never spoke without meaning to, and yet the words tumbled out of his mouth without passing through his head.

"You're even prettier than before."

"I'm certain we've never met," she said in an arch tone.

They had not met, but he had seen her once a long time ago. She was not that young girl anymore. Rory tried and failed to keep his gaze from drifting to her lush breasts and the round curve of her hips. She was a woman who could fill a man's hands. The kind he liked.

"If we were betrothed," she said, "I would have been told."

No doubt he was not the husband she expected. His boots and plaid were muddy from the long journey in the winter rains. Even without the mud, he was nothing like the Lowland courtiers she was accustomed to have fawning over her.

"Here's the marriage contract with your brother's signature." He pulled out the parchment he'd carried inside his shirt all the way from Kintail, thrust it into her hands, and tapped his finger on the sprawling signature at the bottom.

When her eyes began moving from line to line, Rory realized the lass could read and was impressed. Her mouth fell open as her gaze traveled down the page. Ach, every move the lass made was seductive. When she finished reading, she fixed those violet eyes on him again.

"I don't understand," she said. "How did ye get my brother to sign this?"

"We were gambling, and he ran out of coin."

"Gambling?" she said, her voice rising. "My brother gave me away in a card game?"

Rory shrugged. "He didn't expect to lose."

The lass opened her mouth but words seemed to fail her for a time. Finally, she said, "But he never loses."

"He did that time."

"I don't believe you. When did this happen?" she fired at him, then returned her gaze to the parchment. Her eyes flew back to him. "Eight years ago?"

"Aye," Rory said. "'Twas not long after Flodden."

"You signed a contract to marry me," she said, her voice steadily rising in volume and pitch, "and waited *eight years* to claim me?"

"Your brother said ye were too young, and I should wait a bit," he said.

"I've been grown up for some time," she bit out. "In any case, I will not be your wife. This marriage contract is—"

"Look, lass, we can decide later whether we wish to abandon the agreement, so long as we haven't yet consummated the marriage..." As he said the words, his gaze fell to her breasts again, and he lost track of what he meant to say. He gave his head a shake. This was no time to let himself become distracted, but with all the blood rushing to his cock, he couldn't think.

"You're telling me that I'm to put my life in the hands of a complete stranger, a wild Highlander at that," she said, "and we'll sort things out later?"

"The royal guard is coming for ye," he said. "If ye wish to escape, we must leave *now*."

Sybil leapt to her feet. When Rory saw that all the color had drained from her face, he regretted his bluntness. But, finally, she appeared to understand the urgency of her situation, and she made her decision quickly.

"I'll have the servants pack my trunks at once," she said. "How large is your carriage?"

"Carriage? There are no roads where we're going, lass," he said. "And we've no time for ye to fetch your things."

"But...I can't just disappear!" Sybil, who had questioned him so coolly before, looked frantic now. "My little cousin will worry. I must tell her where I'm going."

"You'll tell no one," he said. "Someone in this household sent word to the queen that ye were here."

"That would be my uncle's wife," Sybil said between tight lips, then she took a deep breath. "I'll use my drawing paper to write her a note so my cousin won't fret."

Rory tamped down his impatience while he scanned the hills in the direction of Edinburgh. Sybil came up behind him. By the saints, the first his wife touched him was to use his back as a damned table.

"I have been rescued," she said aloud as her quill moved across his back. "Tell my sisters not to worry. Will send word when I am able. Love always, B."

She folded the parchment and set a rock on top of it at the base of the tree.

"We've tarried too long," Rory said and lifted her onto his horse.

He was going to regret this. He already did. Yet, when he swung up behind Sybil and pulled her tight against him, his heart raced.

And it had nothing to do with the twenty riders who had just crested the hill.

ABOUT THE AUTHOR

Margaret Mallory is the award-winning author of the Scottish historical romance series, THE RETURN OF THE HIGHLANDERS, and the medieval trilogy, ALL THE KING'S MEN. Her books have won numerous honors, including *RT Book Reviews'* Best Scotland-Set Historical Romance Award, a RITA© nomination, the National Readers' Choice Award, and two Maggies. CAPTURED BY A LAIRD is the first book in her new Scottish Historical series, THE DOUGLAS LEGACY.

Margaret abandoned her career as a lawyer to become a romance novelist when she realized she'd rather have thrilling adventures with handsome Highland warriors than write briefs and memos. Margaret lives with her husband in the beautiful Pacific Northwest, which looks a lot like parts of the Scottish Highlands. Now that her children are off on their own adventures, she spends most of her time writing, but she also loves to read, watch movies, hike, and travel.

Readers can find information on all of Margaret's books, as well as photos of Scotland, historical tidbits, and links to follow her on Facebook and Twitter on her website, **www.MargaretMallory.com**. If you'd like to hear when she has new releases, be sure to sign up for Margaret's newsletter on her website.

Made in the USA
San Bernardino, CA
08 January 2015